PRAISE FOR SHIFTER
BOOK 2 OF THE HEALER CHRONICLES

"Shifter (The Healer Chronicles Book 2) is a suspenseful young adult thriller. With strong and memorable characters, non-stop action, and high tension, readers will not want to put the book down and anxiously await the conclusion of this exciting trilogy."

—Literary Titan

"Replete with surprising twists and turns, *Shifter* juxtaposes mystery with growth-inducing insights. The result is a fantasy/supernatural story that is every bit as powerful as *Spinner*, but which stands alone with a strong attraction for those new to these events and characters. Libraries strong in young adult fantasy and coming-of-age stories will find the blend of supernatural and emotional growth represented here to be astute and compelling."

—Midwest Book Reviews

"The pacing of this novel is cleverly arranged so that there's always a surprise around the corner and a mystery you'll keep wondering about if you put the book down. I also really enjoyed the diverse representation of differently-abled characters who approach problems in unique but relatable ways. Shifter is a fresh take on YA horror that will surprise and delight anyone who reads it."

—Readers' Favorite

"This was a fast-paced young adult story about genetic manipulation and what some people will do to further their own agenda. There are surprises around every corner leaving the reader to wonder who is friend and who is foe. Alex has only his family and friends who he can trust, or can he? I will be waiting impatiently for the next book in *The Healer Chronicles.*"

—Fallen Angel Reviews

THE FINAL BATTLE BEGINS

THE HEALER CHRONICLES 3

SPOILER

MICHAEL J. BOWLER

CHAPTER ONE

YOU SUMMONED ME, TEACHER?

IT HAD BEEN THREE DAYS since his brother, Andy, tried to kill him, and Alex shuddered every time he replayed the incident in his mind. In addition, it seemed like everyone had descended on the Air Force base where he currently lived, all for the purpose of tracking down and killing his twin before Andy could…what? He wasn't completely sure, though that general guy, Lewis, seemed to think his brother had already caused large-scale riots in several cities since he joined up with the Kalandrian cult.

Alex had sat in on more meetings with adults than ever before in his life and, frustrated, he'd finally wheeled himself out of the hangar that housed Operation Kalandrian. Crossing the tarmac beneath a warm October sun, he trundled up the makeshift wheelchair ramp the base commander, Colonel Walker, had installed at the home he shared with his wife. Thankfully, the house was empty. Rolling down the long, carpeted hall to his bedroom, he entered and closed the door, then sat beside his bed so he could think.

He glanced down at the brand-new wheelchair Mr. Shaw'd had flown in for him yesterday. It replaced his old one, which had been blown to pieces when one of Ms. G's soldiers destroyed the ghost town where Andy tried to kill him. Alex missed his old chair despite the fact he'd been outgrowing it anyway. It had been a prized possession and great for doing stunts—especially landing flips at the skate park. This new one was a bright, shiny blue and moved well, from what he could tell so far. And knowing Mr. Shaw, it probably cost a lot more than his old one. Even with this generous gift, the man had told him yesterday, "I've ordered you a custom chair, Alex, top of the line and almost indestructible, with extra bells and whistles. Given all that's happened to you of late, it could come in handy." He'd offered a wry smile and Alex, already overwhelmed by the gift of this new one, smiled back.

"Thanks, Mr. Shaw, but what about this one? It seems perfect."

"That'll be your backup chair."

Alex had thanked him again, and then Shaw excused himself to continue setting up the hangar where he'd be working.

As Alex sat rubbing his fingers along the pristine surface of his wheel handles, he considered all that had happened to him since being brought to this base less than two weeks earlier. He still didn't understand everything, but what he did know—and what hurt the most—was that his only sibling, his identical twin, the brother he'd only just been reunited with, had turned on him like a rabid dog.

Alex still refused to believe his twin intended to *really* kill him because his innate connection to Andy encouraged him to think it wasn't so, but Andy *had* stolen his healing power, which made Alex feel…what did he feel? Useless? That wasn't quite the right word. Worthless came closer, but the emptiness inside his soul went deeper. He felt like he'd lost the essence of who he was as a person—maybe his only reason to live. On second thought, maybe Andy *had* killed him after all.

Andy already belongs to me.

Those were Ms. G's words in that dream he had last week. Were they true? Had he completely misread the affection he'd felt from his twin? He didn't want to believe it, but… He desperately needed to find Andy and talk with him alone, without Ms. G present. He was certain Andy would not be able to hide the truth from him.

But you don't have your power no more.

That was the big problem. Without his power, maybe their psychic bond no longer existed. It was all so maddening! Especially since Lewis, the hard-ass general from the Joint Chiefs, announced at their first meeting a few days back that Andy would be shot on sight. They already knew Ms. G couldn't be killed, but they figured taking Andy out of the picture would solve many of their problems.

Alex understood the reasons for that decision. He hated it, of course, yet it made a kind of sense. But had Andy fully turned against him? Maybe Alex wanted it to not be true, but since he no longer felt a link to his twin, he couldn't be sure. His only hope was that although Andy could've killed him back in that ghost town, he chose not to. Yes, that was the image he would cling to until he knew for sure.

He didn't know how long he'd been sitting in that room, staring at Andy's unslept-in bed and brooding about what the future held, when there came a knock on the door. It cracked open and he heard Colonel Walker's voice. "May I come in, Alex?"

Alex turned his wheelchair to face the door. He'd known someone would come looking for him. Better the colonel than anyone else. "Yes."

The door swung open, and Colonel Walker sat just outside in his own wheelchair, a regular medical chair, which he needed on account of having been shot by Ms. G's followers. His wife, Amanda, stood behind him, smiling at Alex in that motherly way he'd come to love. She pushed the chair into the room so the colonel could be face-to-face with him.

"I'll be in the kitchen when you two finish," Amanda said. "Anything I can get for you, Alex?"

She looked pretty in a flowered dress with her curly hair framing her open face, but tired too, probably from all the drama that'd been going on the past week.

"No thanks," he replied. "Not hungry."

She seemed to understand at once and placed a comforting hand on his shoulder. "If you change your mind, let me know." She paused a moment. "I agree with you that the jury is still out on Andy."

He pulled a face, never having heard that expression.

"It means we still don't know for sure that he's turned against us," she explained, her voice soft and soothing. "The affection I felt from that boy when he was helping me cook and clean was very real. There's hope, in my opinion." Then, with another warm smile, she stepped from the room and closed the door.

Alex gazed at Colonel Walker. The man looked older than when they'd first met, but that could've been his imagination. There may have been a bit more gray in the close-cropped hair he still had along the sides and back of his head, and the worry lines around his sharp brown eyes seemed deeper. But he looked healthier than he had the day before, with more color in his complexion.

"I told Amanda I could walk over here, but she insisted on the chair," the colonel said with a shrug. "I'm pretty independent, as you've probably noticed."

"Does it make you feel weak, Colonel, the wheelchair?"

Colonel Walker looked surprised by the question but didn't hesitate in his answer. "Before I met you, it would have. But you're the strongest person I know, and I mean here." He tapped his chest. The large white bandage was visible beneath his open blue Air Force jacket. "You've never let that chair stop you from doing whatever you wanted, and neither will I." He offered a crooked smile. "I just wish I could control mine as well as you do yours."

That made Alex smile. "It takes practice."

An unspoken moment of camaraderie passed between them. Alex had liked this man from the moment they'd met and considered him a friend.

"I understand why you got frustrated and left the meeting. All those adults pressing you with questions, laying out plans, plotting how best to…"

Now he trailed off, but Alex knew what he'd intended to say. "To kill my brother?"

Colonel Walker nodded, his craggy face filled with deep sadness. "I know how much you love him, Alex, and I thought I saw love from him toward you. Maybe you and Amanda are right about him, but we can't take any chances. I'm sorry."

No, I did feel it, Alex thought, but didn't say that. Could Andy be that good of an actor to fool even him?

"So, what's happening now?"

"We don't think Ms. G, as you know her, got out of the country, which means Andy is still here too. Every road and airport have been under surveillance. Private planes have been checked, as well. Shaw is coordinating with General Lewis on using technology to locate them, devices such as traffic cameras that are installed all around the country. Father Pat's friend from the Vatican arrives today, that Cardinal Leone. Says he has some ideas where the group might be holed up, and he needs to talk with you in person."

"What's the Vatican, and why does this guy wanna see me?"

"The Vatican is the headquarters of the Catholic Church, the capital, you might say," the colonel explained with the kind of patience Alex had seldom seen from teachers back home. "He wants to speak with you because of what happened at that old church when those…whatever they were possessed you."

Alex's eyebrows flew up in surprise.

"Father Pat and Shaw shared with me what happened back there, so we'd have a fuller picture of what we're dealing with."

Alex relaxed. It made sense to know everything if they were going to defeat Ms. G. Just the thought of her made him tremble with hatred, especially after turning his brother against him. He'd never forgive her for that!

The colonel studied him a long moment. "Still no return of your power? Can you sense my health status as I speak to you?"

Alex focused on the man before him, feeling deep within his soul for…anything. Despair welled up in him once more and he shook his head, looking down at his knees, feeling hollow.

"It's all right, Alex," the colonel assured him in a voice that pretended everything was fine.

"No, it's not!" He looked up into the colonel's compassionate brown eyes. "That was all I could do, Colonel. If I can't heal no one, I'm… worthless."

Colonel Walker's face flashed anger at him for the first time. "Didn't you hear what I said about that wheelchair, Alex? You're a born leader, whether you like it or not. Those other kids need you. William needs you. Sure, he can flip over a jeep, but inside he's a regular thirteen-year-old boy who looks up to you more than anyone he's ever met. That's who you are, Alex."

Alex choked up with emotion and couldn't respond. He saw in his mind's eye his friends from school rallying around him when he'd first joined their special ed class. They didn't know about his power back then. And William? What had he said, something about Alex having a kind face, and that's why he wanted to meet him? William hadn't known what Alex could do either, not at first.

"Thank you, Colonel," he mumbled, feeling stupid for being sorry for himself. His friends needed him, and he needed them. "Where are the other kids?"

"Having lunch in the DFAC."

"I think I'll head over there."

"They'll be happy to see you."

Alex nodded and wheeled easily around the colonel's much bulkier chair, feeling the man's eyes on him the whole time. Stopping at the door, he spun around and pointed at the other wheelchair.

"If you need tips on doing some stunts, I'm your man."

Colonel Walker laughed.

Grinning, Alex wheeled himself from the room.

***

Andy strode down the long corridor from his chamber to the control center. The group's new headquarters was enormous, well-hidden from the world, and impregnable. His long white hair was tied into a pony-tail, and he wore new jeans with a tight, long-sleeved pullover shirt. The rough-hewn walls of this corridor muffled the sounds of his footsteps, as did the asphalt flooring beneath his sneakered feet.

As he entered the massive control room, he found Teacher, Dr. Avila, and Jäger—the artificial man the doctor had created—conversing before a bank of monitors that surrounded them on three sides, monitors display-ing views from all over the world. Andy paused to observe two children in a country called Istanbul playing outside with a small dog; his gaze drifted to a group of people partying in Paris, and then to what looked like young men engaging in a brawl in the streets of Chicago.

Since arriving at the headquarters three days before, he'd often stood observing the world, mostly witnessing the human tendency toward self-ishness and destructive behavior. Teacher waved him to her with delicate fingers. He strode forward and bowed.

"You summoned me, Teacher?"

"Yes, Healer," she replied, her voice silky smooth, but laced with menace. "Mr. Jäger is feeling unwell, and Dr. Avila can find no apparent cause. Scan him with your power and tell me what is wrong."

Andy fixed his gaze on the muscular man who stood seven feet tall and had thick upper arms. Jäger looked pale, not as robust as he had when they'd escaped the ghost town and come to this place.

"Speak to me, Mr. Jäger," he said. "Tell me how you feel."

Jäger stared down at him from beneath heavily lidded eyes that burned less brightly than when he'd been brought to life. "I feel weak, somehow, slightly off, like if good health was a straight line, I feel crooked. But nothing specific that I can pinpoint."

"I can't determine exactly what's wrong with you, Mr. Jäger," Andy said after a moment of silence, "but it feels almost like you are…disappearing."

The big man scrunched up his face in confusion and eyed Avila for support.

"Come now, Healer, surely you can be more precise than that," Teacher coaxed. "Or is this power as imprecise as your shifting ability?"

Andy flinched, but otherwise did not react to her comment.

Dr. Avila cleared his throat, and Teacher allowed him to speak. "Andy, I have found nothing physically wrong with him except that his body seems…weaker. Can you define what you mean by 'disappearing?'"

"I can only tell you what I sense. It's like Mr. Jäger is slowly disappearing and one day will be gone completely." He fixed his glittering blue eyes on Teacher. "As for my shifting ability, I may have missed your intended targets, but the result was what you sought. Demonstrations turned into riots that resulted in extreme chaos at all three locations." He paused, then met her gaze straight on. "Perhaps you are targeting the wrong people."

Her eyebrows rose and her face took on a look of amusement. "Do tell. Who does the mighty Andy think I should target?"

"Your goal is to foment violence and insurrection by targeting the person who is being protested against, say the president, but isn't it better to target the organizers of these events? If those people suddenly die without warning, as happened in the three cities we focused on so far, the mob will explode, destroying, burning, attacking police, killing, even. Isn't that what you ultimately want, the complete breakdown of order and civilization?"

Her amused look vanished. She gazed at him with a new understanding on her face, as though, somehow, he'd come much farther in his thinking than she'd thought possible.

"I confess, Healer, that I like the way you think, and I'm inclined to try things your way. For the time being." She studied him, but he remained impassive. "You have come far since the days of your childhood.

But never allow arrogance to cloud your thinking. You cannot outsmart me. You're powerful, but I am eternal."

"Yes, Teacher," he replied, his voice even, his face set in stone. "Will that be all?"

She nodded. "I'll summon you tonight."

He bowed and turned to leave. As though remembering something, he turned back. "Teacher, I have a question."

"What is it?"

"May I explore our new headquarters?" His voice reeked of innocent curiosity. "It's impressive, and I'd like to know my way around."

She studied him a long moment with piercing scrutiny. "I don't see why not. There are guards everywhere, after all."

He offered a sweet smile. "You sound like you don't trust me, Teacher. Even after I killed my brother for you?"

Her long eyelashes didn't move as she stared, for she seldom blinked when making eye contact. "Whether I trust you or not is irrelevant. You belong to me. Never forget that."

"Yes, Teacher." He bowed once more and exited the control room.

She turned to Jäger, who stood beside her watching the boy retreat. "Your opinion, Kurt?"

"My sense is the boy is loyal to you."

"Thank you. Your observations in this arena are important to me." She eyed Avila. "What do you think, Doctor? Can you make any use of Andy's health evaluation?"

Avila studied Jäger for a long moment. "It's too vague to be of much use, my lady, but I'll do more tests and let you know the results."

"Perhaps he sustained internal injuries from that boy who bested him."

"If so," Avila replied, "I've found no evidence."

Jäger's face clouded over with resentment at her comment. "His prodigious strength simply caught me by surprise, my lady. Should I face him again, I will snap that boy in two."

She reached up and patted one brawny shoulder. "That's the Kurt Jäger I know and love. And I suspect you'll have that chance. Maybe sooner than you expect."

CHAPTER TWO

I'D DIE FOR HIM

ROY WATCHED POWERFULLY STRONG, SIXTEEN-YEAR-OLD Java, struggle fruitlessly to bring down the smaller, even more muscular arm of thirteen-year-old William, also known as Weapon because he was some kind of super kid created by the government. Roy still didn't fully understand William's origins, but he did know the kid was almost indestructible and stronger than any man on this base. He'd been created with the DNA of animals and cockroaches mixed in, though Roy didn't understand how DNA worked. Knowing that the kid could talk to cockroaches and scorpions kind of creeped him out, though.

William sat calmly, his face devoid of expression as it so often was. His elbow planted firmly against the polished metal table inside the dining facility, he exerted not the slightest bit of effort, while Java's face was scrunched into a look of agony, sweat dribbling down his cheeks.

"Give it up, Java," Izzy goaded, clapping excitedly. "You'll never beat super boy."

Roy smiled. Izzy was the best looking of them—except for Alex, of course—possessing what Roy had heard described as smoldering good looks because of his brown skin, thick wavy black hair, and brooding eyes.

"He's right, Java," Roy added. "You got nothin' against him."

Java's biceps muscles looked like they would burst from beneath his dark skin, while William's always seemed to bulge, such that Roy couldn't see much difference in them now. Blond, with hair the exact same color as Alex's and tied back into a short ponytail, William might be the key to helping Alex cope over the loss of his twin. He'd become something of a little brother to Alex in the time since they'd come to this base, and Alex truly cared for the younger boy.

"Shit!" Java finally let go in frustration, his hand looking like all the blood had drained from it during the bout. He shook it and winced in pain. But then he grinned. "Thanks, William. Best arm workout I had since I come here."

William smiled. "You're welcome, Java."

Applause attracted Roy's attention and he looked over the tables toward the entrance. Alex sat in his wheelchair, smiling.

"Alex!" Roy's heart soared into hyperdrive, as it always did whenever he saw the boy he loved.

Alex wheeled himself over and stopped beside William, clapping the boy on the back. "Good job, Little Brother. Showing this fool who's boss." He gave Java a shove, and the African American boy pretended to be offended.

"Just cause you're the only one of these fools who can beat me, Alex, don't gotta make fun."

"Sure, I do," Alex replied, eyeing William with a smirk. "This kid can kick my ass too, remember?"

Java broke into a grin. "Oh, yeah."

Even silent Jorge smiled for the first time since Carlos had been killed by Ms. G's men. Whenever Roy thought of that cold-blooded murder, it filled him with rage. Jorge was "on the spectrum," or something like that, and never talked much. But he could remember everything he heard, like a tape recorder, so they had to be careful what they said around him.

Roy caught Alex's eye. "You okay?"

"I guess. Thanks for worrying."

"Can't help doing that." Roy offered a smile, which Alex returned.

"So, what's for lunch around this place?" Alex asked, checking out the trays of partially eaten food on the table. "I'm starved."

Izzy had a chicken leg in his mouth and offered a thumbs up as he attacked it with gusto. Java held up the crumble cake he was working on.

"Desserts are great." He shoved it into his mouth and washed it down with a swig of milk.

Alex smiled at their antics, and Roy's heart pounded with relief at seeing him coming out of the funk he'd fallen into after what Andy did in that old ghost town. For the past three days, Alex had barely engaged with them at all, and Roy had missed his best friend so much he'd suffered stomach cramps.

"I liked the chicken," he offered with a shrug of his shoulders. "And the fancy potatoes."

"Sounds good."

William jumped up. "I'll get your food, Big Brother. You visit with your friends."

He dashed off and didn't notice Alex's smile drop like a rock. But Roy did. And he knew why.

"Sup, Alex?" Izzy asked, clueless, as always.

"Don't worry, Alex," Roy said, leaning down closer so he could lower his voice. "I'll tell him not to call you that." He turned in the direction of the food service area, but then Alex grabbed his arm.

"Don't do that."

Roy turned back to face him, confused. William calling Alex "Big Brother" reminded him too much of Andy, who called him the same thing. "Why not?"

Alex paused while Roy awaited his answer. "William *needs* me to be his big brother, and I gotta get used to…well, to the idea that…that Andy is…gone. Probably for good. Hurting William ain't gonna change that."

Roy nodded, overwhelmed with love for this boy who always put the needs of others over his own. He squeezed Alex's shoulder and offered him a smile.

"Hey, guys!"

Roy spun around and found himself face to face with Allison, Mr. Shaw's perky daughter. She liked Alex and he liked her. Roy had to force himself not to dislike her, even though he knew his feelings were unfair. She was pretty, especially with the long-haired brown wig she'd been wearing around the base, covering the bald head she'd been left with after cancer treatment. He glanced at Alex and saw him staring in that way he'd seen him look at Tami back at school, before all this craziness started.

"Hi, Allison," Alex mumbled, his cheeks turning red.

"Hey, pretty lady," Izzy piped up, leaping from his seat and offering her the one next to it. "Wanna sit here?"

She studied Alex a moment, maybe to see if he'd object. When he said nothing, she shrugged. "Sure, Izzy," then sauntered around Roy to ease herself into the empty chair.

Izzy planted himself in his own and slid a crumb cake her way. "Try this, it's awesome."

"Thanks." She tossed him a smile that Roy was sure was intended to make Alex jealous.

Alex was staring at her from his side of the table, like he couldn't stop if he wanted to. Roy began to feel ill as he sat back down in his own chair.

"I never told you, well, the hair looks good," Alex said, offering a smile.

"I already told her that, Alex," Izzy blurted, like Alex should somehow have known this.

Allison smiled. "Thanks, Alex. And you too, Izzy." She fixed her bright brown eyes on Alex in a way that Roy hated. "So, you okay, Alex? You kinda bolted from that last meeting and I…well, I was worried."

Alex's blush grew deeper, and he glanced down at his lap. "I'm good, sort of." Then he looked up and tried for a grin that just missed the mark. "I'm gonna teach Colonel Walker some wheelchair stunts."

Izzy stopped midchew, crumb cake stuck to his lower lip. "No shit?"

Java shook his head and shoved Izzy, knocking the piece of crumb cake from his hand to tumble onto the floor at his feet. "Course the colonel ain't gonna be doing that shit, Izzy." Then, as though just realizing Alex might be telling the truth, snapped his head around. "Is he?"

Alex laughed at Java's horrified expression and that got a smile from Roy. "I offered. Up to him."

Just then, William returned with a tray laden with chicken drumsticks, some cooked spinach, and those fancy potatoes Roy couldn't identify. He set the tray before Alex and retook the seat next to him.

"Thanks, William." Alex offered William a beautiful smile that clearly pleased him. "You're the best little brother a guy could ask for." Then he noticed William's muscular forearms resting on the table and added, "The buffest, too."

Java lifted his weakened arm and laughed. "Sure, as hell."

That got a rare laugh from William.

All this talk of little brothers reminded Roy of something. "Where's my little brother, William?"

"Francis is undergoing some tests with Dr. Shepherd," William explained. "She's trying to fix me so I can grow older, and Francis so he can control the change himself, instead of the moon."

Roy nodded. Francis was twelve—a kid, like William, created in the lab from mixed up DNA. Except Francis turned into a werewolf during full moons and hated himself for it. The kid had sort of adopted Roy as his big brother because…Roy wasn't sure why since he didn't think much of himself and couldn't understand why anyone else would either.

No one said anything for a few moments, though the sight of Alex and Allison staring at each other made Roy uncomfortable.

"There's uh, more meetings this afternoon, Alex," Roy said, hoping to distract his friend's attention. "You gonna go? I think Father Pat has some friend coming that wants to meet you."

Alex broke eye contact with Allison and turned to Roy. "Yeah, uh, the colonel told me. I'll be there."

Java stood and stretched, somehow turning it into a flex, maybe to impress Allison, but he tended to do that often, so who knew? "Come on guys, time for a workout before the meeting," he urged them. "The colonel might need us for somethin', so I don't wanna be late."

Izzy groaned and pushed his tray away, glancing at Allison while throwing a thumb back at Java. "Muscle Man, here, is trying to kill us in that weight room."

She laughed, and Roy had to admit, it was a pretty laugh, light and airy. Alex seemed to like it too because he couldn't stop looking her way.

Jorge stood and placed a hand on Izzy's shoulder. "Let's go, Izzy."

Surprised, Izzy tossed him such a funny look that Allison laughed again. Reluctantly, he stood and faced the somber Jorge, who missed Carlos with a vengeance. Jorge was Latino with short black hair and soft features.

"You lift the heavy stuff, Jorge, and I'll watch."

His comment drew a tiny smile from Jorge and the two of them joined Java.

"You coming, William?" Java looked excited. "I wanna see what you can lift."

William stood. "I need to report to Colonel Walker. Maybe later."

Java looked disappointed. "How 'bout you, Roy?" He had both hands on his hips, like a drill sergeant ready to crack the whip.

Roy glanced at Alex. "But Alex still gots to eat his food. I can keep him company."

"I'll keep him company, Roy," Allison said from behind him, and Roy turned to see her staring, not at him, but at Alex, who stared right back.

"It's okay, Roy," Alex said, making brief eye contact with him. "You go with the guys. I'll catch up when I finish my food."

"You sure?" Roy didn't want to leave. He felt the attraction between the boy he loved and this girl who might just steal him away.

Alex nodded.

Feeling as though he was losing the best part of himself, Roy ambled slowly over to where the others had gathered near the exit. Java clapped him on the back so hard he stumbled, and then they were outside the dining facility in the harsh, blinding sunlight.

***

Dane longed to get out of his wheelchair and hit the weights in this amazing fitness place. He'd accompanied his dad, who wanted to work out, because he was itching for something to do. Too many meetings and too much yakking was getting to them both. He hadn't been surprised when Alex wheeled himself out of the hangar this morning. Kid was probably bored to death and tired of everyone talking about him like he was a broken piece of equipment.

Dane glanced down at the massive bandage wrapped around his torso and grimaced with frustration. Sure, he'd had some big-ass piece of rebar shoved through his chest, but the docs had taken care of it, and he was already feeling a hundred percent better. But physical exertion, he'd been told, was "out of the question" until his internal organs fully healed. Still, he wanted to keep his dad company, even if he couldn't do anything himself. These past few days, he'd gotten the chance to really know his father, making him wish he'd grown up with him and Roy, rather than his clueless mother.

Not one to get hung up on the past, he shrugged off the gloomy memories and focused on the here and now. His dad was looking solid on the weight machines, and Dane would occasionally call out some tips he'd learned from working out at other gyms. This place kicked major ass, with just about every piece of equipment one could want. He had to bite back the urge to clamber out of his chair and try some of them.

"Dane, what're you doing here?"

He turned the wheelchair to find Roy and some of his friends striding in through the double glass doors. No Alex, though. He wondered about that.

"Just watching Dad hit the weights and wishing I could too. *You* gonna work out? *My* little brother?"

Roy shrugged. "Java likes to train us."

Java grinned and flexed.

Dane nodded approvingly. "With guns like that, he's a good choice. Least till I'm outta this chair. Then you're all mine." He grinned, hoping to lure a smile out of Roy, but it was as though Roy hadn't even been listening. "Java, man, get the others started. Gotta talk to my bro here."

"You got it, Dane. C'mon, guys." He grabbed Izzy and Jorge by the arms and practically dragged them into the midst of the machines.

Dane studied Roy, who stood fiddling with one of those snakebite piercings he had on each side of his mouth, looking like he'd lost his best friend. "Sup, Roy?"

"Nothin'."

"I know we only just got to know each other, but you can tell me anything, man. That's what big brothers are for."

Roy's head drooped and he looked like he might cry.

"It's somethin' 'bout, Alex, right?"

Roy looked at him directly now. "I think…I think he might be, you know, falling for that…girl."

Dane paused a moment. What…? Oh, yeah. "Shaw's kid, you mean."

Roy nodded again, biting his lip.

"Come here, Roy. Squat down so's I don't gotta keep lookin' up."

Roy stepped closer and dropped to a squat, gripping the arms of Dane's wheelchair to keep his balance.

"It's gonna happen, Little Brother. Maybe this girl, or maybe some other. Alex can't be what you want."

Roy nodded again. "I know. But it just…hurts."

Dane cocked his head and studied the look of despair on Roy's face. "You love him that much, huh?"

"I'd die for him."

Dane felt the passion in those four words and sighed. "I envy you, Roy. I never felt like that about any of the women I been with. I hope I do someday."

"Maybe you don't want to."

"Come here." Dane opened his arms and Roy leaned closer, allowing Dane to encircle him in a gentle embrace. He patted Roy on the back and held him the way a big brother should. He thought he heard Roy sniffle a few times, but no words were spoken.

Roy released him and leaned back, his eyes red, his cheeks damp. "Thanks for, well, everything."

Dane nodded, struggling for something to say to cheer his brother up. "You know, one of these days you're gonna be all hot for some guy and he'll be totally into you, too."

Roy blushed. "Yeah, right."

"It's gonna happen, bro, and that guy better treat you right or I'm gonna kick his ass big time."

Roy's eyes bulged with horror, but when Dane grinned, he laughed. "I love you, Dane."

"Back at you, Little Bro." Dane felt a bit too much emotion for his taste and worried he might start crying, so he added, "Now get out there and show Pop what you can do."

Roy stood and gazed down at him in amazement, as though he couldn't believe what had happened between them. Considering all their years apart, Dane couldn't either.

"When you get better, Dane, we can work out together."

Dane smiled. "Can't wait."

Roy trotted off to where Java and the others were showing Nathan a few tricks with the dumbbells. Wistful, Dane sat in the stiff, uncomfortable wheelchair and reveled in watching his family enjoy just being together.

CHAPTER THREE

SHE'LL COME AFTER ALEX AGAIN

B Y THE TIME ALEX MADE it back to the War Hangar—as Java had named the building—it was almost time for the meeting to start. He'd completely lost track of time talking with Allison and feeling…normal for the first time in forever. He'd been able to put everything else out of his mind—including Andy. It had occurred to him, as he raced his new wheelchair across the vast tarmac toward the hangar, that he'd gotten what he'd once asked Mr. Shaw for: he was finally a regular kid who couldn't spin anyone. He had no more power than Allison or any other teenager.

And yet when he pictured Dane so badly hurt and Colonel Walker in his wheelchair recovering from a gunshot wound, he came to realize that maybe being "normal" wasn't so great after all. If he still had his spinning power, both men would be completely healed.

The side door to the hangar hung open to admit those whom the colonel and General Lewis trusted enough to keep in the loop. William stepped out just as Alex skidded to a stop. This new chair was faster than his old one and had nearly gotten away from him.

"They start yet, William?"

"No." He surveyed the new wheelchair. "How's your new ride?"

Alex did a double take. "New ride? Where'd you get that?"

William looked embarrassed. "That's what Izzy called it. Did I say something wrong?"

"No, it just sounded funny coming from you. And it's great." He saw others approaching and figured they only had a minute or so, and there was something he'd been wanting to say. "Uh, I never, you know, said thanks for saving my life and everything, after Andy…, well, you know. So, thanks."

William shrugged. "Hey, that's what buffer little brothers are for, right?"

Alex cocked his head and studied the impassive face. "Was that s'posed to be a joke?"

William nodded, and then offered a hopeful grin. "Was it funny?"

Alex laughed. "Yeah, it was. C'mon, Little Brother, let's get in there."

The inside of the hangar, which Alex figured was large enough to house one of the planes out on the tarmac, was teeming with personnel. More than Colonel Walker wanted, he knew, but the general had brought in many of his own people from Washington. They were stern looking older men in fancy uniforms with bars on their shoulders who moved from the computer stations to the phone bank and then back to the computer stations. He had no idea what any of them were doing, but the one thing he did know was that they hadn't found Andy or Ms. G.

"Alex!"

He spun around to find Father Pat, wearing his usual black outfit and white collar, head still bandaged, limping his way toward him. Alongside the priest came a rotund little man with bright eyes and a cheerful face. The man's close-cropped gray hair spread out from beneath a small red skullcap, and he wore a flowing black, dress-like getup with a cape over the shoulders and a thick red sash around his waist. The fancy cross dangling from a chain around his neck told Alex this must be Father Pat's friend, the guy who'd come to help them fight Ms. G.

William leaned down to his ear. "Do you need me to stay with you?"

"It's okay," Alex replied, giving him an affectionate pat on one shoulder. "I'm good."

William scrunched his face in confusion. "Of course, you're good."

"That's just something we say. It means I'll be fine."

William nodded and wandered off into the crowd, probably looking for the colonel. Alex scanned the many faces but did not see the base commander. He did spot Dr. Shepherd chatting with Martin, who also sported a large bandage around his head from the underground explosion that had killed two of Shaw's men. Martin was smiling, and so was the doctor. He wasn't used to seeing either of them smile and decided they must like each other.

Father Pat and the other man stopped before Alex, the priest slightly out of breath, the round man with wonder in his wide eyes.

"Alex, this is Cardinal Leone, from the Vatican. He just arrived."

The little man stuck out a pudgy hand and smiled. "Buonasera, young sir. It is indeed a pleasure to meet you."

Alex shook his hand and found himself liking the man at once. He had a Sana Claus kind of vibe about him. "Nice to meet you too. What does bona-what you said mean?"

"Ah. That's Italian for 'good afternoon.' It's our traditional greeting."

The man's accent and upbeat tone relaxed Alex, and he smiled despite the seriousness of their present situation.

"The cardinal would like to talk with you, Alex, before he addresses the meeting," Father Pat explained. "Is that all right?"

"Sure."

"Let's go over to the Vatican station," the priest continued, indicating a corner of the hangar set up with computers and desks.

Alex wheeled after the two men, still glancing around for any sign of Colonel Walker. Voices drifted everywhere, the loudest being General Lewis, a big blustery man with grey-speckled brown hair dressed in a blue uniform adorned with medals and stripes. The colonel had explained that he was the Air Force member of the Joint Chiefs of Staff and wielded a lot of power in that position. Alex watched the general giving orders to Mr. Davalos, who was dressed in his usual business suit and tie. He again marveled at the change in Davalos, who had become such a different person that Alex liked him now. Mr. Davalos was responsible for creating the super soldier, Jäger, whom Alex and Andy had brought to life. But he also created Francis and the other creatures who'd help save Alex. Davalos seemed to have the ear of the general, but Alex knew he was fully loyal to Colonel Walker, which was all he cared about.

Father Pat ushered the cardinal toward a plush office chair behind a mobile computer desk and slid over a plastic chair for himself. Once both men were seated, the cardinal gazed across the desk at Alex in a way that made him uncomfortable—not because it was a bad look, but because the other person thought he was something special. He'd never felt special before, and he for sure didn't now.

"Forgive my rudeness in staring at you," the cardinal said in his soft, accented voice. "It's just that I never expected to meet the Healer in person. It is one of many prophecies the Church has followed over the millennia, though not one of the more popular ones, except with eccentrics like me."

Alex didn't understand half of what Cardinal Leone said, but it didn't matter anyway. "I ain't the healer no more. Didn't Father Pat tell you?"

The man looked surprised, but undeterred. "Yes, he told me about your brother. Andy is, how shall I say this, an outlier in the prophecy, but God has been known to throw surprises at us on more than one occasion. Nevertheless, despite what your brother did, he will never be the Healer. That is you, and you alone."

Alex gazed into the man's open, round face and detected no guile, not even an attempt to make him feel better. But it didn't make sense. He had no power anymore. Andy had taken it from him. He was about to say this when he heard, "The Cardinal is right, Alex. You are still the Healer."

Alex looked in the direction of the voice and saw Colonel Walker, in his wheelchair, being pushed toward them by an old man with wrinkled brown skin and long gray hair tied back into a ponytail that traveled all the way down his back. He was dressed in a mix of colorful clothes with lots of beads and a few feathers dangling from the fringes on his sleeves. It was this man who had spoken, and as they drew closer, Alex felt certain he'd seen him before, somewhere....

Then it hit him! "Uncle?"

Father Pat gasped in shock and the old man smiled as he rolled the colonel to a stop and stepped around the wheelchair.

"How do know me, Alex?"

Alex nodded. "I seen you before, in dreams I got from Andy's mind. We didn't understand it, but we sometimes saw things inside each other. He called you Uncle. Are you my uncle?"

"By blood, no," the man replied, his voice smooth despite his apparent age, which could've been a hundred, for all Alex knew. "It's traditional in some Native cultures for young people to address a male elder as 'Uncle,' so I instructed Andy to do so."

"Alex," Colonel Walker said, interrupting the moment. "This is Samuel Montour, of the Onondaga tribe, a friend of the cardinal, here. He just got in from New York."

The old man shook hands with the cardinal, who beamed with pleasure.

"Always good to see you, my friend," Cardinal Leone exclaimed, but then he frowned. "We knew this dark time would come, did we not?"

Mr. Montour nodded. "Though we be lone voices crying out in the wilderness."

The cardinal chuckled. "Well said."

Alex looked around at all these adults and wished he had William or Roy for company, mostly because he had no clue what was going on. "I'm confused."

"I'm sorry, Alex," the colonel apologized. "Let's everyone sit, and we'll explain."

Father Pat stood to slide another desk chair closer for Mr. Montour, who sat down with ease, which surprised Alex. This guy didn't talk or move like an old man.

"How come you never came to my dreams like you done with Andy?"

Mr. Montour glanced at Colonel Walker, as though for permission to speak.

"Seems like as good a place as any to begin," said the base commander. "But the meeting starts soon, so we have to move fast."

Mr. Montour nodded and faced Alex. The wrinkles and gray hair screamed "ancient," but the brown eyes were young—bright and filled with vigor. Those eyes held Alex in their thrall until the man blinked and broke the connection.

"I'm sure you already know, Alex, that twins were not part of the prophecy. Your mother hid you so well that her tribal family only knew of Andy's birth. Because of that tribal connection, I was able to reach out to him in dreams and quickly understood that Andy needed my help. I did not know where he was but knew his thoughts and what he was being taught. I did my best to instill positive ideas and feelings into him, but he still…"

He trailed off, but Alex already knew the rest.

"Tried to kill me."

Mr. Montour exchanged a look with Cardinal Leone, who nodded for him to continue.

"I overheard you telling the cardinal that you are no longer the Healer. This is untrue. Our prophecy speaks of a great peacemaker *and* a great destroyer. You will always be the great peacemaker. You are the Healer, not because you were given power from the heavens. You are the Healer because you are you, a caring and compassionate human being. That is why the full powers of the Healer are only available to you."

Alex listened in stunned surprise. "But Andy stole my power."

"He only thought he did because he wanted it so badly. Ambition is a dangerous trait when left unchecked. Alas, I have been unable to access his mind of late. He may have learned how to block me, but I intend to keep trying."

Alex attempted to digest all this startling information. "So, you're saying…I'm still the…"

Mr. Montour and the cardinal nodded.

"Then how come I can't spin people no more?"

"You can, Alex," the cardinal assured him. "God would never let someone take from you what is yours. It is most likely your *belief* that you can no longer spin, as you call it, that blocks your power."

Alex thought about that a moment while the others fell silent, leaving only the ambient room noise to fill his ears. "So, Andy can't spin like I could?"

Mr. Montour offered a shrug. "That is undetermined because his shifting power, as he calls it, is an unknown to us. It's possible he shifted some of your power into himself, but his ability to heal will be limited and not long lasting."

Colonel Walker cleared his throat to get everyone's attention. "If I hear you correctly, Mr. Montour, Andy does not possess all of Alex's power?"

"Again, Colonel, that's unclear. He may mirror it for a time, but he can never possess it."

The colonel glanced at Alex before facing the two men. "So, what happens when that woman finds out Andy isn't the real deal?"

"Oh, God," Father Pat exclaimed, almost lurching upright in his chair. "She'll come after Alex again."

"My thoughts exactly," the colonel agreed. "She can easily determine that Alex didn't die in the attack on that ghost town, and she'll come for him." He eyed Mr. Montour and Cardinal Leone. "Do you gentlemen concur?"

The two men exchanged a long look before Leone said, "Yes, we suspect so. That's partially why we have come."

"What's the other reason?" Colonel Walker gazed at Leone with intensity.

"If that woman succeeds in opening the gate she told Alex about, and thousands of those trapped entities are unleashed, you will need the help of an experienced exorcist. I am such a man."

Alex didn't know the word "exorcist." But the colonel obviously did because his mouth dropped open in shock.

A young airman wearing the standard blue uniform approached and saluted the colonel. "The general is ready to begin, sir."

"Thank you, Airman." Colonel Walker returned the salute and the young man retreated, his boots clicking rhythmically against the concrete floor. Facing the other men, the colonel said, "Are you men ready to present your findings and theories?"

"Yes, Colonel," Leone said. "Whether your government listens to us, that is another matter entirely. But this information should only be shared with your most trusted aides."

The colonel nodded. "I understand."

CHAPTER FOUR

ALEX, PLEASE JOIN ME

D ESPITE FEELING MOROSE ABOUT ALEX and Allison, Roy enjoyed his time in the fitness center working out with his dad, with Dane offering moral support from the sidelines. Whatever happened from that point on, if he had his family at his side, Roy knew he could endure anything. Alex never did show up, and his absence—along with the conflicting thoughts as to the reason for it—distracted him on more than one occasion. His dad always managed to bring him back around with just a smile or encouraging word.

By the time the entire group left the fitness center and got back to the War Hangar, the meeting was about to begin. Roy spotted Alex off in one corner with Father Pat, the colonel, and two guys he'd never seen before. He'd started in that direction when William seemed to appear out of nowhere and blocked his path.

"I think they just want to talk with Alex."

Roy nodded, looking over the younger boy's shoulder to observe the exchange.

"Hi, Big Brother," came another young voice at his side, and Roy turned to find Francis gazing up at him with the kind of hero worship Roy wasn't used to. He almost blushed.

"Hi, Francis. How'd it go with Dr. Shepherd?"

Francis shrugged, brushing bushy black hair away from his sparkling hazel eyes. "She's trying. How was the fitness center? Can I work out with you next time?"

Roy noted the eager look on his face, but didn't detect any mockery, given their differences in strength level. He smiled. "Sure. I'll lift the weights and then you can lift me."

Francis looked puzzled, and Roy reached out to tousle his hair. "That's a joke, Little Brother."

Francis broke into a grin. "Oh."

Roy found his attention distracted when Allison entered the hangar. She looked around, spotted him, and waved, but then headed off in the direction of…her father. He'd been sure she would go wherever Alex was, but she didn't even seem to notice his location. Mr. Shaw was in the center of the hangar beside a makeshift stage that had been set up to elevate whoever was speaking higher off the ground. There was a wooden lectern up there with a microphone poking out the top, and for the past few days, whoever wanted to address the entire group had used that.

"Can I sit with you, Roy?"

He looked down at the eager look on Francis's face. "Course you can. We'll sit with my dad and Dane."

The twelve-year-old's smooth, handsome face darkened. "Do you think they like me?"

"They love you, especially since you saved my life." He winked, and the younger boy beamed with relief.

It's funny, Roy thought, *I never wanted a little brother before, but this kid's awesome.*

He threw an arm around Francis's shoulders and led him over to the banks of folding chairs where he found his dad seated beside Dane's wheelchair. They plopped down in two chairs on Dane's other side.

"Hey, Dad," Roy said as he sat. "That was fun, working out with you."

Nathan offered a tired smile. "Been a long time since I worked out that hard. I'll feel it in the morning, especially after that cave-in a few days back."

Dane reached over and ruffled Francis's hair. "How's my other little brother doing?"

"I'm very good, Dane. Thank you by asking."

Dane furrowed his brows in confusion, but Roy said, "He's still learning English."

"Like all of us," Nathan joked, grinning.

"This family's getting bigger every day, Pop," Dane said. "Gonna need a bigger house."

Nathan shrugged. "I'll just build another floor."

Francis looked confused and eyed Nathan, who winked before sitting back in his chair.

A tap on the microphone drew Roy's attention to the lectern. General Lewis stood stiff as a statue, looking badass in his full uniform, while one of his men did the tapping. The colonel had been wheeled onto the stage via a ramp, and Alex sat beside him. In folding chairs next to them sat the two men who'd been talking to Alex earlier. But Father Pat wasn't up there, and Roy didn't spot him anywhere nearby.

He was momentarily distracted as William slipped into the empty chair beside Francis and nodded his way. Roy offered a smile and then turned around to find Java and the others sitting two rows back with Izzy right next to…Allison. She waved again, and he awkwardly returned it before facing forward once more. The general had begun to speak.

"Last night, in Portland, Oregon, twenty demonstrators were killed and another fifty wounded when the apparent leader of that group suddenly dropped dead in the middle of their protest." He said that last word with distaste, practically spitting it into the microphone. "The already unruly crowd turned violent, blaming the death on the police who were present to keep the peace. Rocks and bottles were thrown, and shots were fired from the crowd at officers, several of whom were wounded. The enraged crowd soon turned on each other, and mayhem ensued. The police were vastly outnumbered and could do little until the mob seemed to burn itself out. Now, these anarchist mobs are nothing new in Portland. But the night before, as you know, there was a similar incident in Iowa. Colonel Walker believes—and I concur—that these incidents are the direct result of interference from the woman known as Jeanette Garrett—an alias—and the boy known as Andrew O'Sullivan, twin brother of Alex, who is seated behind me. Thus far, the US government and the military have failed to locate their headquarters. Cardinal Leone, who was sent from the Vatican, believes he knows where they may be holed up." Turning to the black-robed dignitary, he beckoned him to the lectern. "Cardinal?"

As the stout cardinal stood and approached the microphone, General Lewis stepped away from the lectern, then stood beside Colonel Walker's wheelchair. A large movie screen hung suspended from the ceiling behind the stage and on it appeared a computer desktop image. There were folders neatly lined up around the edges and the center was dominated by a blue shield with the letters IHS in front of two keys and what looked like a hat in the background.

The cardinal, shorter than the general, grabbed the microphone and bent it downward toward his mouth. He had a cheerful face that Roy liked, but the downturn of his mouth indicated the seriousness of the situation.

"Buonasera, ladies and gentlemen," he began, his voice heavily accented in such a way that made even his greeting sound important. "That's good afternoon in Italian, as I already explained to my young friend back here."

He waved a hand toward Alex, who nodded, but didn't respond. The little man gazed back out at the assemblage. There weren't many people present—only the core members of the colonel's and the general's staffs—so he only needed to look forward and not side to side.

"These are dark days, indeed, and will likely become darker before we're able to see light once again. I'm going to share with you some secrets the Vatican has harbored, because the Holy Father knows that sharing is the only way to stop what is coming. You already know that Alex is the fulfillment of the Healer prophecy, and you've seen videos of the experiments done right here on this base—miracles this boy performed on his own and in concert with his twin brother. I will not bore you with repeating those details."

Using a clicker, he switched the image on the screen behind him to display a series of paintings showing angels fighting. Roy wasn't religious, but he knew what angels looked like and had always wondered if they were real.

"I can only speak to the theology I know and profess. I accept that other religious traditions have their own narratives and explanations regarding God, angels, and demons. There are no doubt some among you who are agnostic or atheist. I mean no disrespect to anyone's beliefs. We at the Vatican don't pretend to know specifics about Heaven, but it was learned from ancient, unpublished scrolls that there is a separate dimension which may or may not be the Hell spoken of in the Bible."

Now the audience erupted in protestations, especially the scientists and doctors seated together. Dr. Shepherd looked stunned and gazed up at the cardinal in amazement. Once the agitation died down, Cardinal Leone continued. He pressed his clicker again and a map of the world appeared, with seven large red dots blinking in different locations. Roy sucked at geography, so the only place he really knew was the United States, which had one blinking dot on it.

"Over the millennia, the Church has identified seven hot spots, as we call them, seven areas where there is a seepage, if you will, from that other dimension into ours. According to the scrolls we have at the Vatican, this alternate dimension exists to house those entities we call demons so they cannot corrupt humans more than humans have already corrupted themselves. But over time, breaches have occurred at seven locations on the planet, each coinciding with particularly evil behavior from human beings."

He clicked again, and the map zoomed in to one of the red dots. The dot became a satellite photo showing a desolate-looking place of sand and scrub with old buildings built right into hillsides. "This is the Valley of Josaphat. It is east of the old city of Jerusalem and was once known as Gehenna. It was the site of the first breach detected by the fledgling Church. At one time, children were regularly sacrificed to a god called Morlock, which made this spot especially evil."

He paused to catch his breath before clicking a painting of a guy with a beard—Jesus, Roy figured—and what looked like a lot of pigs.

"Some strange incidents are recorded in the Gospels. You may recall the story of Jesus casting out demons from a man and sending them into a herd of swine, which promptly rushed into the sea and drowned. This occurred near the Sea of Galilee and taught us much, namely that these entities we call demons can only successfully possess humans, not animals. We believe it's because they must have a consciousness to control and animals are too driven by instinct, rather than conscious thought. We also know Gehenna was referenced as a place where evil people will burn and gnash their teeth. The Church has attempted to plug this hole, if you will, through spiritual means, but it has never been entirely successful. This has been true of all seven areas of concern."

Colonel Walker was studying the map and pointed at one of the dots. "Is that dot in Russia?"

"Yes, Colonel, not far from the site of the Bolshevik Revolution in 1917. Those of you well versed in geography will notice that some of these breaches exist where some of the most destructive movements in human history have occurred, movements that seriously destabilized mass populations of people and resulted in a tremendous loss of life. Russia, China, and Germany, to name just three. There is also one in Africa, South America, and right here in the United States."

More murmuring and hands in the air from scientists in the audience, but the cardinal held up a hand. "I'll take questions shortly. Now, because of political realities in those countries, we have little current information on the breaches in Russia and China, but the others have, as far as we know, not expanded over time, and there has been minimal seepage. By seepage, I mean, of course, supernatural entities slipping through into our world. I know many of you will always be skeptical, based on your own scientific or religious beliefs, but as one who has performed exorcisms myself, I can attest to their very real and very dangerous existence." He turned around and waved to Alex. "Alex, please join me."

Roy watched—heart hammering with fear over this information he didn't fully understand—as the boy he loved rolled forward and stopped at the cardinal's side.

"Yes, sir?"

"I know it's a painful memory, but please, if you will, share the story of your own possession so they will truly understand the threat we face."

Alex immediately sought Roy in the audience. Their eyes met and Roy felt whole once more.

"Uh, I need Roy to help because I really don't know what I did when, you know, they took me over."

The cardinal studied the audience. "Roy? Can you come up and help? I'm sorry, but I don't know your face."

Roy felt himself go pale with fear, but a small, strong hand gripped his shoulder. He glanced over at Francis, who smiled and nodded. Somehow, that young boy urging him on gave Roy the strength to rise on shaky legs and lurch his way to the stage. He made eye contact with Alex as he ascended the three steps and held that contact until he stood beside his best friend. Only with Alex's help could he get through addressing a group of people, even a small one like this.

Cardinal Leone removed the mic from its holder and handed it to Alex. Together, he and Roy shared their story about the medallion Alex found that turned out to be a gate that let demons into our world, about the possession of their friend Cuong, about attacks on them by what seemed like possessed cats, and about Alex's own possession and eventual release through the special power his friends shared. Alex described the feeling of being taken over, how he felt his very essence disappear and how he didn't even know his own name. They were asked lots of questions and answered them as best they could. Roy found that sharing the story side by side with Alex wasn't as hard as he'd imagined it would be, and when they finished, Roy asked if he could stay up on the stage with his best friend.

"Of course, Roy," replied Colonel Walker, who indicated an empty chair for him to sit.

Patting Alex on the back, Roy handed the cardinal the mic and crossed the stage to sit where he could view the large screen.

The cardinal said, "Thank you, Alex and Roy, for your sharing your suffering with us. My prayers are with your friends who died during this course of events." He looked out at the attentive audience.

"From what Alex and Roy just shared, it would appear that this woman can control animals and use them as weapons, but as I said, we don't believe these entities unto themselves can exist long within an animal host." He glanced down at Alex. "I suspect the woman only made you think that cat spoke to you, since cats have no vocal cords, but we've no way of knowing the full extent of her powers."

He paused and considered his words as he scanned the attentive audience. "The Healer is the only person on earth who can fully open a gate and allow the dimensions to overlap, which would be catastrophic for our already unstable world. Thankfully, in Alex we have a Healer who would never willingly allow that to happen. However, temporarily at least, his brother Andy may possess that power, which makes it imperative that we locate him and stop this imminent disaster. Since General Lewis has assured me that the woman and the boy could not have fled these shores for one of the other gates, it's my belief they are here, quite nearby, in fact."

He clicked his device and the image zoomed in again, this time highlighting a mountain range in the desert with a glowing sunset behind it.

General Lewis looked surprised. "That's in Arizona."

"Yes, General, a place called Superstition Mountain, a three-thousand-foot-high monolith that dominates this mountain range. It has a storied history going all the way back to the Apache who once inhabited that land. Rumors of a gold mine inspired interest from the Spanish conquistadores in 1540 all the way up to a prospector named Walt Gassler in1984 who was found dead at the site, gold ore in his backpack, cause of death unknown. Many bodies over the years were found with bullet holes in them, leading myself and other experts, including my Native American colleague Samuel Montour, here—" he indicated the old man with the long gray hair sitting very close to Roy— "to conclude that the Kalandrian cult, or whatever they may call themselves in the 21st Century, have control of that mountain and whatever lies within it. Officially, General, your federal government owns that land, as you may well know."

The general kept his emotions in check, so it wasn't clear whether he knew this or not. Roy studied his face now that they were so close for the first time. The severe close-cropped hairstyle, sallow cheeks, and stern mouth were off-putting.

"My suggestion to you, General Lewis, is to search that mountain from top to bottom. No gold mine has ever been found, but if the cult is there and if they have support, as I suspect, from supernatural entities slipping through the breach, they will have no trouble masking their presence, even from your satellite searches." He turned to Mr. Montour. "That's all I have. Samuel, do you wish to add anything before we're deluged with questions?"

The old man stood and stepped up to the podium. The cardinal moved back a couple of steps to make room. Mr. Montour's weathered face was etched with a serious expression as he leaned into the mic.

"I am Samuel Montour of the Onondaga tribe in New York. There is a prophecy shared in various forms by some Native American peoples which foretells the coming of the Healer and indicates that he could become the Great Peacemaker or the Great Destroyer. Until now, we interpreted that to mean the Healer would make a choice. Now that we know there are twins, the meaning is clear. Alex is, and forever will be, the Great Peacemaker. His entire life is proof of that. His brother Andy, on the other hand, has all the makings of the Great Destroyer, but even that is not one hundred percent certain."

He paused and glanced at Alex before continuing. "When he was a child growing up within the cult, Andy was tortured and brainwashed. I know because I was able to reach out to him in his dreams. It is a skill my people possess. I planted ideas of hope in his heart and soul to counter the nihilistic teachings of the group. Those positive ideas may yet still exist. As a human being, he always has a choice to do right or wrong. That's all I have to say."

He stepped away from the podium and glanced at the cardinal, who nodded in solidarity. General Lewis strode briskly to the microphone and asked, "Any questions?"

The hangar erupted with chatter and Roy managed to catch Alex's eye. His best friend offered the chin raise, and Roy smiled.

CHAPTER FIVE

ANDY'S TRYING TO OPEN IT!

WEARING A SKIN-TIGHT BLACK OUTFIT, she stood in the control center gazing at the multitude of monitors, scanning the various locations with a studied gaze. Several followers sat in straight-backed chairs managing the console, making certain the surveillance system was fully functional and up to date. The Wi-Fi signal was strong, which seemed to surprise some of her technicians given their current location, but the equipment she'd had installed was the best in the world.

Jäger lumbered into the room, looking pale and favoring his right leg. "Have you chosen a target for tonight, my lady?" His eyes briefly roamed the curves of her shapely figure, but quickly returned to her face.

She offered a seductive smile, reaching up to lightly brush her fingers against his cheeks. "You like when I do this, don't you, Kurt?"

He quickly closed his mouth and stood at attention. "Of course, my lady. You are the most beautiful of women."

"Thank you." She lowered her arm and faced the rows of monitors once again.

"If I'm not being impertinent, my lady, why have you not told the boy his brother still lives?"

"Alex is still alive?"

They both spun around to find Andy standing in the entrance, staring at them in surprise.

"Come to me, Andy," she cooed, waggling a finger in her direction.

He strode forward and stood before her, taller now, and fuller around the shoulders than even a few months past. "Is he, Teacher?"

She gazed with intensity at his impassive face. "Yes. You did not suck him dry, as you thought, and my man was not able to destroy him when he blew up the town. No doubt that meddlesome freak-boy saved their lives."

"William?"

"If that is his name, then yes." She continued staring, but he did not break eye contact. As she had with Jäger, she lightly tickled his cheek with her delicate fingers. "What do you feel when I do this?"

He did not react in any way but eyed her curiously. "Nothing, Teacher. What should I feel?"

She smiled in a seductive manner. "Well, you are a fifteen-year-old boy."

He merely held her gaze but displayed no obvious emotion. She removed her hand.

"Perhaps you'll be happy to know that Roy still lives, as well."

He flinched but held the impassive expression on his face. "Why should I care about him?"

She nodded, continuing to stare, as though willing him to react in some way, but he remained rigid as a statue. "Perhaps it's for the best. I may have a use for them both before all of this is over."

His cheeks looked slightly red, but the overhead florescent lighting may have been the culprit. "Yes, Teacher." He broke eye contact and glanced at the monitors. "Have you chosen my target for tonight?"

She glanced up at Jäger, but his expression had not changed, and then she moved closer to the console which controlled her eyes on the world. "I have a different test in mind, in preparation for the big night." She pointed to one monitor and the boy strode closer to look.

On the screen, a young man and woman sat at an outside table of a restaurant eating and laughing, clearly very happy to be together. The restaurant had a large colorful awning, brightly lit windows, and heating units interspersed between several round tables through which danced waiters wearing black pants with red shirts and carrying trays.

"I want you to shift everything that is good in that woman into yourself and purge it, the way the Healer does. Then I want you to shift some of your anger into her. I know you have anger, Andy. Lots of it. Can you do that?"

Andy stood straighter, his chest puffed out. "I can do anything." He gazed with fierce intensity at the couple on screen, focusing on the smiling, cheerful woman. "All that is good in you—your kindness, your love, your joy, your conscience, all of it will come into me. You are no longer generous or considerate or polite. You have nothing within you but the hate and anger and selfishness I feel inside me."

The woman stopped laughing the moment he began speaking. The man leaned in and said something, but the sound on that monitor was muted. The woman lost her smile and placed a hand to her head as though she had a headache. She pushed the man away.

"Your best qualities, all that make you a nice person, are no longer yours. All you have left is the anger and hate I send you!" His voice rose to a fever pitch and his entire body spasmed, like he'd been shot through with adrenalin. His face twisted with concentration, beads of sweat breaking out on his forehead. He looked like a great internal struggle was raging inside of him and he fought to regain control. After several long moments, he relaxed and straightened to his full height. His face was flushed, but his eyes glittered with triumph.

"It is done, Teacher."

She smiled, almost looking relieved. "Now, let us observe the result."

Once more, they faced the monitor on which the woman and the man were now engaged in a heated argument. He kept reaching for her hand, but she yanked it from him every time, finally slapping him hard across the face. Enraged, the man slapped her back, and that's when she grabbed a steak knife from the table beside her plate. Leaping to her feet, she plunged the knife into the man's neck before he could even react.

The camera shot zoomed out as the man at the console manipulated a few buttons. Restaurant patrons were up and screaming, scrambling from their tables to escape the crazed woman. A male waiter rushed forward to assist the bleeding man, who tumbled from his chair onto the floor. As the waiter drew nearer to her, the woman plunged the knife into his chest and pushed him back before leaping over a small fence surrounding the tables and staggering off down the street.

Andy stared at the scene without emotion and then faced his teacher. "Are you happy, Teacher?"

She grinned with glee. "Delighted. I'm glad all your bragging wasn't for naught. Can you do that with a mass number of people? Thousands or even millions? Do you have that much anger and hate within you?"

His face, as always, displayed nothing that might give away his thoughts or feelings, but once again, he puffed out his chest. "I can do anything. And you know about the anger and hate because you put it there."

She smiled, not at all offended. "I like the bravado. For your sake, I hope it translates into action."

"Will that be all for tonight, Teacher?"

She studied him a moment, as though hoping his stoic façade might crack, and then waved her hand toward the exit. "Yes. I'll call when I need you."

He bowed and strode from the room.

"Jäger."

The big man lumbered across the room to her side. "Yes, my lady?"

"Your assessment of that exercise?"

The man's handsome but unexpressive face seemed to consider her words for a moment. "An unmitigated success, my lady. The boy remains fully loyal to you. He did not even flinch at the havoc he caused, just as our own Hitler youth had been so well trained during the war."

"But he did flinch when I mentioned the queer boy," she said, gazing across the room at the door through which Andy had exited. "It's possible he has feelings for dear, lovesick Roy. We could use that to our advantage in the unlikely event his loyalty wavers."

"Yes, my lady. When will he open the gate?"

She looked up at him. "Do you doubt he can accomplish that?"

He tilted his head, the closest he seemed to get to changing his facial expression. "It occurred to me that perhaps he could not take enough power out of his brother to bring about the opening. I look at myself and, while I have the memories of Jäger, I do not have all his characteristics. They did not transfer. Perhaps the same is true for the boy."

She lost her smirk and suddenly did not look so confident. "You make a very good point, Kurt. Perhaps I need to test the boy first, have him bring some of my brethren through the gate before the big night. Yes, that's what we'll do. Thank you, Kurt. You are indispensable."

"When will you make the attempt?"

"Soon."

***

Alex was glad to be back in his room at Colonel Walker's house with just Roy and William for company. That meeting earlier, with everyone's reactions to what Cardinal Leone and Mr. Montour had told them, became a chaotic free-for-all of questions and answers. It had left his head spinning. Near as he could tell, the only decision made by those "experts" was to initiate an extensive search of that mountain in Arizona. He could've told them that much.

The colonel had assigned William full-time duty guarding Alex based on the possibility that, should Andy fail to open the gate, Ms. G and her followers would try again to kidnap him. Alex didn't mind having William around; he'd come to think of the younger boy as his beloved little brother, although a little brother who could pick him up, chair and all, and throw him through a window.

Amanda had invited the cardinal, Mr. Montour, and Dr. Shepherd to dinner, and, with all the boys present, it had been a loud, but mostly enjoyable experience. The adults seemed to sense the kids needed a break from all the "world is going to end soon" talk, so Cardinal Leone and Mr. Montour shared fun stories of their upbringing in Italy and New York that kept everyone enthralled.

Once dinner ended and the boys helped with the dishes, Alex needed some thinking time and had excused himself. Roy and William followed in his wake. The adults—except for Colonel Walker and Dr. Shepherd—joined the other boys in the living room to play board games.

Mr. Shaw, Martin, and Allison were being housed in Sergeant Stern's home, and General Lewis had taken over another officer's quarters. The cardinal and Mr. Montour had quarters of their own. More meetings were scheduled for the next day and soldiers would be monitoring news feeds all night long, looking for outbreaks of violence or chaos anywhere in the world.

William was used to life on this base and seemed to take everything in stride, not allowing very much to bother him. Roy had said it all made his head swim, and honestly, Alex felt the same way. Closing the door to his room felt like he was shutting it all out for a short while.

***

Colonel Walker sat at the kitchen table with Dr. Shepherd. He'd invited her to dinner because both he and Amanda hadn't spent any time with her of late and she was a significant member of the team. The meal had been raucous, as always, with Alex and his friends at the table, though the addition of William didn't add much to the noise level because he hadn't yet learned how to be a typical kid.

Once dinner and dishes were done, Amanda had taken all the kids into the living room for movies or board games. None of them wanted to challenge her at poker anymore, since she'd cleaned their clocks the week before, but there were other games available to engage them. This left Walker and Shepherd alone to discuss Francis and, more importantly, William, both of whom had been on his mind a lot in the past few weeks.

"I'm making more progress with Francis, frankly," she said after giving him a brief recap of her tests on both boys. "Since I was in on the ground floor of his, well, design," she blushed, looking embarrassed, "I'm confident I can make changes that will allow him to control his own transformations. That way, if he doesn't want to be…Wolfboy, he doesn't have to. I know the Pentagon won't like losing control of the transformation, but, oh well."

The colonel nodded, thoughtful. Yes, she was doing these tests on her own time, at his request, and he supposed they could both be in trouble with the higher-ups but, as William had shown such a propensity for doing of late, they were making a choice—a good one, in his opinion.

"What about William? Do you think he'll always be thirteen?"

Her lovely face collapsed with guilt, and she drew in a long breath, considering her answer. "As you know, Bryan, my father did all the initial genetic programming on him. By the time I took over the Weapon project, that sequence had already been fully encoded, so I focused on other aspects. I'm not…" She trailed off, looking exhausted, the dark circles under her eyes more pronounced. She needed more sleep. "I'm not sure anything can be done because it's part of his DNA sequence. We might just have to wait and see how nature handles it. The same is true for Francis, by the way. He's been out of the tank for almost two years but still looks twelve to me."

He nodded, feeling more weight on his shoulders than ever with the recent turn of events, especially with all these kids to protect. "He does to me too."

She reached across the table and took his hand, squeezing it gently. "I'm sorry I don't have better news."

"I'm sorry our parents ever started that project." He made eye contact with her. "That's a problem with people, I suppose, especially scientists. They think just because they *can* do something, they should. I'm not even religious, with all due respect to our visitors in the living room, but I've come to realize no one should play God when it comes to human life."

She squeezed his hand again, her face burning with shame. "I agree. Those boys are…"

When she trailed off, he finished for her. "Good boys, boys who are every bit as human as Alex and his friends. They deserve better."

"Yes, they do. I'll keep trying."

"Thank you, Liz."

She released his hand, and they sat beneath a heavy silence for several long moments. Then she offered a tiny smile.

"On the plus side, William is sounding more like a regular teenager every day. He's even cracking jokes."

Walker raised his eyebrows in surprise. "I haven't heard that yet, but I have heard him using slang. Let's just hope he doesn't adopt the typical adolescent mood swings."

She chuckled and then took on a faraway expression that intrigued him.

"Thinking about a certain Martin Briceño, perhaps?"

Startled, her cheeks bloomed red, and she clasped her hands together on the tabletop, wringing them in a way he knew meant she was anxious.

"He's a good man, Liz, from where I'm sitting. It's time you moved on and found some happiness for yourself."

She nodded, but said nothing, clearly at a loss for how to respond.

Amanda swept into the kitchen at that moment and noted the looks passing between them. She grinned. "Talking about Martin, I suspect."

Liz looked up from her hands as Amanda slid into the next chair over, looking radiantly beautiful. Of course, she could be wearing a sackcloth and Walker would still find her the most beautiful woman in the world.

"Does everyone know how I feel about Martin?"

Amanda cocked her head, eyes twinkling. "Probably. And what's wrong with that? He's a very handsome man."

"Yes, and I'm…me. Frumpy scientist type."

Amanda frowned. "You are so not. And what you are seems to suit him just fine, based on how he looks at you."

Walker cleared his throat, drawing the attention of both ladies. "I think I'll supervise the kids and let you ladies sort this out."

Amanda blew him a kiss. He stood carefully and ambled from the kitchen, thankful to be using a cane instead of the dreaded wheelchair.

***

Alex sat in silence in the middle of the bedroom, staring out the window at nothing in particular.

"You okay, Alex?" Roy was seated on the bottom bunk and gazing at him with furrowed brows. "You got all quiet during dinner."

Alex nodded. "Just so much going on."

Roy nodded, biting his lip. "Do you think it was Andy who made that lady go all crazy and stab those people?"

Alex had been thinking of little else since he'd been shown the gruesome footage captured by someone's cell phone. "I remember Ms. G saying something about spinning the good out of people and putting in bad. I think she wanted me to do that, but maybe Andy can too."

"But those guys, the cardinal and your uncle, they said you're still the Healer, that Andy can't never be."

"Yeah, but they also said Andy might've took some of my power, so he could've done it."

"You love your brother, don't you?" William sat across the room on what used to be Andy's bed, head cocked, blue eyes filled with curiosity, awaiting an answer to his question.

Alex wheeled over to the younger boy.

"Yeah, I do. But you know what, William? I love you, too. I feel like, well it's weird, but like you're really my brother too." He felt his cheeks burn red and he looked down, not sure why that burst of emotion had poured out right then.

He felt a soft hand on his leg and looked up into William's eyes.

"You don't know how important that is to me, Alex," William said, his voice breathy, like he was having trouble speaking. "Thank you."

Alex smiled, feeling the deep intensity of the other boy's emotions.

Roy rose from the bed and crossed the room in two strides, sitting on the bed beside William. "What's gonna happen to you after all this is over?"

The smile faded and the light seemed to dim in William's eyes. "I belong to the government."

"But that's so wrong," Roy protested, his expression filling up with pain. "You're a person, just like us. Right, Alex?"

"Yes."

"They made me, so they own me."

"Nobody should own kids," Roy protested, eyeing Alex for moral support.

"You're right, Roy," Alex replied, his heart deeply troubled. "But I haven't felt free since I was four. Once I got into foster care, it was like William said, the government owned me too."

Roy's face fell even more, and he gently took Alex's hand, giving it a squeeze before letting go.

William offered up a smile tinged with sadness. "General Lewis was pleased with my rescue of Alex, but mostly because I saved that Pave Hawk helicopter from crashing. Those things cost millions of dollars. At least now he might give me bigger missions."

"I wish you could come live with me," Alex said without thinking, wanting to help this boy who'd already done more for him than he could ever repay.

William's eyes bulged with gratitude. "I would love nothing more." His face fell. "But it will never happen."

Alex recoiled, like someone slapped him.

Concerned, both boys leaned closer.

"What?" Roy asked.

Alex froze, struggling to understand what he was feeling. "I'm not sure. I think...I think it's...Andy!"

"Is he near?" William was on his feet and at the window in a flash, scanning the base beyond.

"No, he's not here," Alex mumbled, his voice trailing off as he dug deep into himself to understand what was going on.

William returned to his side and squatted down beside his wheelchair. "What's happening, Big Brother?"

Alex chewed on his lower lip. "He's doing something…something… big, I think. But it's not working and…he's getting mad." He paused and waited. Then he shuddered with fear. "I feel…evil. Something horrible, like them things that took over Cuong! Andy…he, I think he's trying to let one of them out of…the gate! That gate the cardinal been talking about! Andy's trying to open it!"

William leaped to his feet. "I'll inform the Colonel." He dashed from the room.

CHAPTER SIX

YOU ACT LIKE YOU WANT THEM TO TAKE YOU

ANDY STOOD BEFORE THE CAVE wall, with Teacher by his side. One of her followers stood at attention next to the slim crack in the rock face. This man was one of the airmen from the base, but now, should the boy succeed, he will host whichever of her fellows emerged from the rift.

Andy had both hands against the cool rock, one on either side of the crack. This was no ordinary crack and could not be opened by explosives or other man-made means. This was a gate to the world of the banished who, should Andy succeed, would be banished no longer.

He trembled, and energy radiated about him, encircling his hands and then his upper body before enveloping him completely.

He spoke only one word. "Open."

***

Roy scooted closer, almost falling off the bed. "Did he do it?"

Alex shook his head from side to side, not completely clear on what he was seeing. "I'm not sure…"

Movement caught Roy's eye and he turned back to the door. Colonel Walker walked into the room, supported by William, followed closely by Cardinal Leone and the rail-thin Mr. Montour. They surrounded Alex and Roy.

"What's happening, Alex?" Mr. Montour squatted down and took Alex's trembling hand. His face went blank, his eyes glassy.

"Can you see, Uncle?" Alex's voice sounded slow and deliberate, like he was under a spell.

"Yes," replied the old man, his own voice robotic. "Andy has his hands on the wall of a cave…he's angry, frustrated. Movement around him. At least one of the entities has emerged from the rift, but…" He trailed off.

***

She grinned with pleasure as darkness spilled from the crack to mingle with the light that emanated from Andy. Something slipped through that darkness, at first shapeless, with traces of features that resembled eyes. It floated in the air above the radiating boy but made no move to enter him. She stepped closer and pointed to the young airman, who stood gazing in horror at the hovering entity. Without hesitation, the creature vanished inside the airman, causing him to flail about as he lost control of his body.

But then something unexpected happened. The creature retreated from the airman in a flash of energy, leaving the young man gasping for breath. It struggled in the air for just a moment before being sucked back into the darkness of the other world.

Panting, Andy could no longer maintain his power and released the wall, dropping into an exhausted heap onto the cave floor. Sweat coated his face, and anger filled his sharp blue eyes.

***

"What, my friend?" The cardinal leaned into the old man and placed a hand on his shoulder.

There was a long moment of silence during which Alex was aware of being both inside and outside of himself at the same time. "He didn't do it, did he?"

Mr. Montour squinted with concentration. "No. He doesn't have sufficient power. Let go now, Alex, before he senses you."

Alex closed his eyes and pushed the image away. When he opened them, all he saw was Roy and the others gazing at him with concern etched on their faces.

"You okay, Alex?" Roy grabbed his hand. "Shit, your hand feels like ice!"

Alex nodded, offering his friend a tiny smile of reassurance. "I'm good." He turned to Mr. Montour, who stood next to the cardinal. "What does it mean, Uncle?"

"It means," the cardinal replied with a sigh, "that Andy is incapable of opening the gate. She will need—"

"Me," Alex finished for him.

"Yes," Mr. Montour said.

"This could be to our advantage," Colonel Walker said, rubbing his chin in thought.

The cardinal eyed him. "How so?"

The colonel looked straight at William. "Do you remember, William, in Los Angeles, when we disguised Gabriel as you to trick the police?"

"Of course." Then the young boy's face lit up. "You mean to disguise me as Alex, so they take me to their hideout?"

"What I was thinking, yes."

"And the tracker in my foot will lead you right to them."

Alex looked from one to the other. "I'm confused. And what's in your foot?"

"Remember, Alex, I told you about Los Angeles?" William studied him and Alex nodded. "Afterward, the Pentagon put a tracking device inside my foot so they would always know where I am."

Alex scowled. He did remember William telling him that, and it disgusted him. "But Ms. G ain't ever gonna think you're me. She seen you before."

"After the underground incident," the colonel said, "I doubt she would return here herself. She'd likely send Jäger, Davalos's creation."

"But he knows me too," William insisted. "Especially since I kicked his ass twice."

Colonel Walker's eyebrows shot up, and even Roy looked surprised.

William seemed to understand at once, and his face drooped with remorse. "My apologies, sir. That just slipped out."

The colonel smiled. "I think you're spending too much time with these boys." He indicated Alex and Roy. When William opened his mouth to argue, the colonel went on, "But it's all good, as they say. The more you talk like a modern teenager, the more effective an agent you become."

"Yes, sir." William looked relieved.

"It won't work," Alex said, shaking his head. "Ms. G'll know right away it ain't me, even from far away."

The colonel nodded. "I'm sure you're right. It was a desperate idea, at best."

Alex's face lit up like a beacon because he just had a crazy thought. "You could put one of them tracker things in me, like William gots, in case they get me. I don't feel nothing in my feet anyways, so it wouldn't hurt. Then you could know where they take me."

"You act like you want them to take you," Roy said, his face a mask of fear.

"Course, I don't. But if they do…" Alex shrugged.

The adults exchanged thoughtful looks, as though seriously considering the possibility.

"I'm sure they'll scan you for tracking devices, Alex," said the colonel, "and who knows what they might do to your foot when they find what we planted."

"What if," William said, eyeing the colonel, "you attach a second tracker to the underside of the same foot. Then, when they scan him, they'll remove his shoe and find that device. Once they take it off his skin, they might think he's clean."

"They might, young William," Cardinal Leone said. "But what if they find the other one? If they gain control of Alex before help arrives, we have lost."

"I'll never help them!" Alex felt hatred well up within him for Ms. G and all that she'd done.

"They might have ways to force you," said the cardinal.

Colonel Walker considered all the possibilities. "How much time do you estimate we have?"

The other two men eyed each other, and there was a long pause that Alex didn't like. They clearly had some information they hadn't yet shared.

"We suspect the gate will be opened tomorrow night at midnight," the cardinal said, his tone grave.

The colonel's eyebrows shot up in surprise. "Why then?"

"It's the feast of Samhain, a night known throughout human history for supernatural and demonic activity," Mr. Montour answered.

"Also called Halloween," the cardinal finished.

"The hell?" Roy made eye contact with Alex, but Alex didn't understand what they were talking about either.

"So, the ghosts and goblins aspect is based on tradition?" The colonel studied both men, awaiting an answer.

Mr. Montour nodded at Cardinal Leone. "This is more your area of expertise, Alessandro."

The cardinal seemed to collect his thoughts before responding. "Samhain is an ancient Celtic festival that originated in what we now call Ireland, and it spilled over into Scotland. It marked the end of their year when light segued into darkness. The Celts believed that the walls between the worlds were at their thinnest, allowing evil spirits and demons to pass through. That's why they wore frightening garb and masks, in the hopes they would not be molested by such creatures."

"But it's just a fun night to dress up and stuff," Roy said, perplexed.

"Now, in America, yes," the cardinal agreed, "but I'm referring to thousands of years in the past." He faced Alex directly. "Your last name is Maracle, correct?"

"Yeah, so?"

The cardinal turned to Mr. Montour. "A tribal name, yes?"

The old man nodded.

"But Andy's last name is O'Sullivan," the cardinal went on, sounding like he was just working this detail out in his mind.

"That's cause my parents had my aunt and uncle adopt me," Alex explained. "I seen it in the video my mom left for me. She wanted to protect me."

"That means your birth name is O'Sullivan, which is Irish or perhaps Scottish in origin. It's not important, just another curious detail that connects the Healer to the bigger picture, I think."

"Oh." Alex realized once again that this whole Healer thing was like a puzzle with many pieces.

"Alex, you said Ms. G hinted that something demonic accounted for her remaining young for so long. I suspect she may be inhabited by an ancient creature that has lived in our world since those dark early days of Samhain, or perhaps even before then, taking possession of different people throughout the ages and using them to achieve its evil ends."

Alex thought he understood. "You mean she's possessed like I was?"

"It would seem likely. We know nothing of her background, but clearly, at a young age, she gave herself over to this creature."

Mr. Montour regarded the cardinal with furrowed brows. "Do you believe this entity may yet be driven from her body?"

"No way of knowing."

"If what you say is true," Colonel Walker said, "we have one day."

The cardinal nodded.

Everyone focused on Alex, and he felt that bug-under-the-microscope sensation again. "We should put in that tracker tomorrow, just in case." Alex studied their serious faces and felt resolve fill him. "I ain't afraid no more, and I might be able to…"

"To what, Alex?" The colonel locked eyes with him. "What are you thinking?"

There was a long moment of heavy silence, during which Alex debated whether to say what was in his heart.

Then William said, "You wish to save your brother, don't you?"

Roy gasped, his expression one of pure horror.

Alex nodded, eyeing William a moment before facing the adults. "I know you think he's bad now, but I feel like…I don't know. I need to see for myself."

Colonel Walker exchanged significant looks with Cardinal Leone and Mr. Montour, but none of them spoke for a time. Finally, the cardinal nodded, and the colonel fixed his gaze on Alex.

"All right, Alex, it's best to be safe. I promise the device will be removed immediately after this is all over."

Alex nodded. He didn't smile because he wasn't happy. But he did feel that everything would soon come to a head, and he wanted to help make things happen instead of just reacting all the time. "William's got my back, right, Little Brother?"

"Always."

***

"You are pathetic!" Teacher spat, her voice riddled with disgust.

Andy, still panting from his effort to open the gate, lay on the floor of the cave, damp with sweat, tired, and unable to rise.

"Get him up!"

Jäger strode forward and reached down. Grabbing Andy by his shirt, he yanked him up and dangled him in the air. Ripping sounds filled the air as the shirt began to tear under the strain. Before the weakened boy tore free completely, Jäger lowered him to the floor in front of the woman, holding him upright with one massive hand.

"Typical teenage boy," Teacher taunted. "All braggadocio and no action. I should've known not to trust you. You'll never be able to open the gate!"

The spluttering Andy raised his head. The rips in his shirt revealed a pale, undefined torso, and his face exhibited pure humiliation. "I did… my…best, Teacher!" he gasped, sucking in air in loud gulps. "I thought… I thought I took all his power."

"Well, you didn't!"

"Give me another chance! I did everything else you wanted!"

She circled around him, eyeing his weakened body with distaste. "Even though we raised you to be tough and unbendable, you're feeble. Fortunately, my airman in the chopper failed to kill your much stronger brother. My people on the base will make certain he's brought to me, and then we'll see if you can prove useful."

She nodded at Jäger, and the big man shoved Andy away. The boy stumbled and nearly collapsed, but his features locked into a fierce look of resolve, and he forced himself to remain upright.

"Get out."

Staggering, Andy shuffled his way out of the chamber.

***

Allison had noticed right away that Sergeant Stern's house was much like the colonel's but with only a single story, and it wasn't as large. Stern explained to her that officers did not share quarters with enlisted men on base and were provided "prefab homes," as he called them.

"Made with spit and duct tape," the sergeant had joked over dinner.

His refrigerator, she'd discovered, was almost empty except for some beer and beef sticks. He explained that he always ate in the DFAC since he wasn't married and had never spent time learning to cook. He'd brought food from the dining facility home for them, and Allison enjoyed the salad, meatloaf, and baked potatoes they ate together in his dining room. His table clearly wasn't used much, based on the layer of dust she'd wiped off prior to helping serve the food.

She'd eaten in silence while the men talked, especially Martin and Stern, sharing stories of military life. The sergeant seemed pleased to have them in his home, and she decided he probably got lonely most of the time with no one to talk to. Her dad seemed lost in thought as he absently chewed on forkfuls of meatloaf and washed them down with a glass of wine, which had come from the commissary.

During a lull in the conversation, Allison found her mind drifting to Alex and their time together that afternoon, which prompted her to ask Stern, "Sergeant, do you think there are more spies on this base—you know, who work for that woman?"

Stern seemed surprised by the question. "I'd like to think everyone on this base is trustworthy."

Allison knew that wasn't a real answer.

"What prompted the question, Allison?" Her dad studied her across the table, obviously curious.

She shrugged. "Alex and I were talking about it today."

"Well, I'm sure if the sergeant suspected anyone, he's already reported that information to Colonel Walker."

Stern offered her a tight smile. "And even if I did suspect someone, young lady, I'd not be at liberty to share such information with a civilian."

"Well said, Sergeant." Martin lifted his glass of wine to the other man and took a swig.

Allison nodded but continued to wonder about what the adults were not saying.

After dinner, she helped clear and wash the dishes, with Martin at her side in the kitchen while her dad and the sergeant retired to the living room to talk business. Since Stern had overseen the base surveillance system that her dad had installed, they had some common ground.

"So," Martin began as he dried the plate she handed him, "how are you and Alex getting along?"

She glanced over and noticed his smirk, trying not to blush. "Very well, thank you very much, Mr. Nosey."

He set the dry plate on the linoleum counter and reached for the next one. "I'm just checking on my girl. Can't have any boys messing with her, can I?"

She chuckled. "Alex would never mess with me." She paused a moment. "It's funny, I think I shared everything about my life, including, you know, losing Mom." She noted his sympathetic expression but plowed forward to not get emotional again. "But he didn't say much about himself at all. He talked about Roy the whole time, about how amazing he was and the best friend ever, and he couldn't imagine not having Roy in his life."

She rinsed off the plate in her hand and handed it over, not meeting his gaze because she knew her voice had taken on a petulant tone she didn't like.

"Are you jealous of Roy?"

She jerked her head around, too fast, she knew, and blurted, "Of course not, Martin. They're best friends. It's just…"

He tugged the dripping plate from her hand because she hadn't released it yet. "Just what?"

She turned back to face the soapy water in the sink. "It might just be me, but I have the feeling Alex will never love any girl as much as he does Roy. I know that sounds weird, but it's true."

He set the dried plate atop the others. "It might be true, honey. I had a best friend in high school. Jeff Morley. We joined the service together. Boot camp, basic training, the whole nine yards. We did everything together, even chased after the same girls."

She faced him now, fascinated. He'd never told her any of this before. In fact, she knew little of his life prior to his working for her dad.

"I suspect some of our fellow soldiers thought we were gay or at least bi, but that wasn't it at all. We had just clicked so perfectly in high school, thought alike, even, that, at least for me, I never thought I'd meet anyone I'd be as close to, even any woman. That happens sometimes, Allison, and those kinds of soul mates, if you will, aren't always male and female and don't always involve romance."

She considered his words and heard the twinge of pain underneath them. "What happened to him?"

Martin looked away now, out the window above the sink, out at the darkened base beyond. "He was killed by an IED in Iraq."

She gasped. "What's an IED?"

"Improvised explosive device."

She felt sadness fill her and reached out to place a comforting hand on his broad shoulder. "I'm sorry, Martin. I shouldn't have made you remember."

He tossed out a sad smile. "I never forget. My point is, Alex can love both Roy and you, but love takes time. Don't be in such a hurry."

"I'm not, Martin," she insisted, maybe more strongly than she'd intended. "You know Dad taught me the difference between attraction and love. I only just met Alex, after all."

He nodded, smirking again, which drew a return smirk from her.

"So, what's up with you and that lady doctor?"

Now it was his turn to look surprised. "I don't know what you mean." He grabbed for the dish in her hand and began rubbing it dry.

She reached into the soapy water for the casserole dish that had held the potatoes and smiled. "I saw you flirting with her before the meeting this afternoon."

He looked ready to deny it, but then just grinned. "Was it working?"

She laughed and handed him the dripping casserole dish. "She's totally into you. A girl can tell these things."

He took the dish with a chuckle. "Well, we'll see what develops. She's an impressive woman."

"You better invite me to the wedding."

He laughed. "I thought you weren't in a hurry."

"I'm not, for me," she replied with ease. "But it's way time you got married."

His eyebrows shot up. "Thank you, Dr. Phil."

She shook her head. "Seriously, Martin? Dr. Phil is so ten minutes ago."

They shared a laugh and finished the dishes in silence.

Later that night, something happened that troubled her. Her dad and Martin had gone into their room to work. In conjunction with the Pentagon, they were using satellite data to triangulate on any signals that might be coming from inside Superstition Mountain, but so far, the search had been, as Martin put it, "Like Superman searching for something in a lead-lined building."

She'd been in her own room, which was sparsely decorated and only had the most basic furniture—bed, dresser, bedside table with a lamp atop it, and a small, empty closet. Happily, she'd been given the room closest to the bathroom, which could give her some semblance of privacy. Feeling the need for something to drink, she padded down the hall toward the kitchen in her bare feet, intent on snagging a diet Sprite, when she heard voices coming from Stern's bedroom.

His door was closed, and the speech was muffled, like he was trying to keep his voice down. She knew she shouldn't listen, but for some reason, she decided to stop and press her ear to the door. She didn't hear the other voice, which meant the sergeant was on the phone or computer, and most of what he was saying was unclear.

Feeling like a snoop for even stopping, she hurried on into the kitchen and grabbed her Sprite from the fridge. She supposed growing up with her dad, especially with all that had happened the past few weeks, she'd become suspicious of every little thing, even a guy probably talking to the colonel or the general. Taking a big swig of the lemon-lime soda, she slipped back into her room and resumed gaming on her tablet.

CHAPTER SEVEN

YOU HAVE A PLAN OF YOUR OWN

THE FOLLOWING MORNING, AFTER ALLISON showered, she dressed in clothes her father had ordered along with Alex's new wheelchair. Even though it was almost the end of October, it was still quite warm throughout the day, so she chose light sweatpants and a short-sleeve shirt. After adjusting her wig, she left her room in search of her dad.

Stopping in front of his closed bedroom door, she raised her hand to knock but stopped when she heard Martin's voice.

"Are you sure you want to do this, Russell?"

"Yes. There's no one I trust more than you, Martin. Alex also has Nathan, and he's a good man too."

What are they talking about? she wondered, pressing her ear up against the cool wood to hear more clearly.

"We have the entire U.S. military for protection," Martin replied. "There's no reason to believe anything will happen to you."

"You know me, Martin," her dad said, his voice sounding sober. "I like to plan ahead. I was going to do this anyway once we returned home. Make sure that document is in my inbox today."

"I will."

She couldn't contain her curiosity any longer and knocked on the door.

"Come in," her dad called out.

She pushed open the door and entered the room. Like hers, it was sparsely furnished, but had two beds instead of one. Obviously, Sergeant Stern never had many visitors.

"You'll take care of that right away, Martin?"

"Consider it done." Martin swept past her with a smile and left the room.

"How's it going, Dad?" She stepped closer to the dresser, which housed his laptop computer, open and displaying a topographical map of what looked like a mountain range. "Any luck?"

"No, unfortunately." He gave her a quick once over. "All the new clothes fit?"

She smiled. "Perfectly. Thanks."

"What are your plans today, before the afternoon meeting?"

She shrugged. She hadn't thought about it. There wasn't much to do on this base, and most of it was off-limits to her. "I wanna hang out with Alex, if I can."

He nodded. "He's under constant guard now."

"I know, but hopefully we can talk some more."

He looked ready to turn back to his computer but paused to study her face intently. "You really like him, don't you?"

She felt color rise to her cheeks and was glad it was only him and not Alex she was with. "Yeah."

He offered a smile. "He's a great kid. I hope he can have a regular life one of these days."

"Me too."

"Oh, the sergeant left food in the refrigerator for us before reporting to the command center. Help yourself."

"What about you?"

"I already grabbed something. I'll be heading over to the hangar."

She leaned down and engulfed him in a hug. "I love you, Dad. Try not to work so hard."

He shrugged. "No choice, sweetheart. I'll see you later."

She nodded and walked to the door. Turning before stepping through, she saw he was focused once more on the computer screen.

As she stepped out into the hall and headed for the kitchen, she again wondered what her dad and Martin were talking about before she'd knocked.

***

Alex couldn't help exchanging a look of amazement with Roy when William stepped out of the bathroom wearing only a towel around his waist.

His young baby face was at odds with the chiseled musculature of his upper body. Neither of them had ever seen him shirtless before, and now they just stared for a long incredulous moment.

William furrowed his brows and looked down at the towel. "Did I do something wrong?"

"No, you're just buff as hell," Roy said with a shake of his head.

"We just never seen you with no shirt before," Alex explained. "Now I feel fat."

"Me too," echoed Roy, "and I'm skinny."

William smiled, obviously appreciative of the compliment. "Thank you." He stepped over to the drawer where he'd placed his clothes after bringing some over from his regular room on the base.

He and Roy turned away to give William his privacy. Alex was hungry, but Colonel Walker's orders were that William accompany him everywhere, even within his own house, so they waited until the younger boy crossed the room and stood before them dressed in a short-sleeved Air Force shirt and short pants, along with his usual Converse sneakers.

"We can go to breakfast now," he announced.

"You guys eat without me," Roy said as they filed from the room. "I'm gonna help my dad with Dane. He's stronger than he's been, but I wanna help him anyway I can."

"Okay," Alex replied as they passed through the entryway. "I'll tell Amanda."

They did the fist bump, which William eyed with curiosity, and then Roy slipped out the front door.

***

Father Pat sat across the table from Cardinal Leone and Samuel Montour in the dining facility. He was so worried about Alex and what was to come, he had little appetite. His companions, on the other hand, seemed to be enjoying the hearty breakfast. Especially Leone, who had no difficulty devouring every speck on his plate.

"You should eat more, Patrick," Leone bellowed after taking a swig of wine, which he insisted was traditional at every Italian meal. "As long as we protect Alex, the gate cannot be opened."

Father Pat studied the man's round face and sparkling eyes. "If they fail to open it on Samhain, do they have to wait another year to try again?"

The cardinal set down his fork. "That we do not know. Ancient texts specify the day we call Samhain, but do not indicate if that is the only possible window. At this point, I'm more concerned with what Andy can and might do."

"What do you mean, Alessandro?" Montour leaned in closer, awaiting an answer.

The cardinal frowned, no longer cheerful. "We know the boy can destroy goodness in people, possibly even insert negative thoughts and emotions. We saw that last night. And he appears able to kill from a distance, just as he'd done in concert with Alex before his betrayal. Who might be targeted next? And how many people at a time can he strip of their goodness? Either scenario could be catastrophic, even without the gate."

Montour nodded, eying Father Pat a moment before replying. "I understand the president has been advised to remain off television for the time being."

"Yes," Leone replied, pushing his plate aside. "The Pope, as well. But other world leaders could be targeted, yet we cannot fully warn them without giving away too much information. General Lewis wants as few people in the loop as possible."

"You don't agree?" Father Pat wrung his hands, thinking of Alex and how much danger he was in.

"Oh, but I do," Leone replied with great emphasis. "This Kalandrian group has members everywhere in the world. But it is concerning what they might do next, especially if they cannot recapture Alex."

Father Pat felt a smidgen of relief. "William will protect Alex."

"That young boy?" Leone looked perplexed. "How?"

Father Pat squirmed, hating to keep vital information from these men. "It's classified, Your Excellency."

Rather than look offended, the man nodded. "Ah, well, probably for the best. I already know more secrets than I'd like to."

Montour smiled, and the three men rose from the table to bus their trays.

***

Colonel Walker sat in the War Hangar with General Lewis, Sergeant Stern, and several of Lewis's top aides. A computer screen rested before them, displaying various images—from various angles—of Superstition Mountain.

"Our satellite scans reveal nothing inside that mountain, gentlemen," the general said, sounding testy from lack of sleep.

"Have we scanned the other six locations Leone mentioned?" Walker asked, studying the computer screen.

"Affirmative, Colonel. Even those in Russia and China give no indication of habitation."

"They may have a way to block our scans," the colonel postulated. "Maybe even reflect them back at us."

"Exactly our consensus," Lewis agreed, looking annoyed enough to break something. "Any ideas, gentlemen?"

"Why not surround the mountain with troops?" Sergeant Stern studied all their faces as he spoke. "If nothing else, whoever's inside can't escape."

"Problem is, if they are inside," Walker said, gazing at the computer screen, "they'll know we're onto them."

"With all due respect, General," Stern went on, his voice confident and strong, "they might already know. The boy could've told them he sensed Alex's presence in his mind."

Walker leaned forward in his chair. "We don't know that for sure, Sergeant. Alex has felt no further connection to his brother." He had on the tip of his tongue his idea of planting a tracking device in Alex's foot as a failsafe. But something niggled at the back of his mind, like maybe there were too many at this meeting to broach the possibility. He'd corner the general later and tell him in private.

Lewis considered the input. "Very well, Sergeant. Tonight, under cover of darkness, I'll send in troops to surround the mountain. Are we in agreement, gentlemen?"

All his subordinates nodded. Walker wasn't convinced, but he nodded anyway.

***

Dane hated weakness and needing any help to get dressed was the height of weakness. On the other hand, he felt much stronger and could easily stand on his own. Plus, having his dad and Roy assist him brought back feelings of childhood, of security and safety he'd long forgotten. He felt closer to them than ever before.

As Roy and Nathan stood at each side, Dane held out his sweatpants and stepped into them, and then slid his feet into a pair of sneakers. As Roy gripped him by one arm, Dane said, "Strong grip you got there, Little Brother. All that weightlifting is paying off."

Roy grinned, clearly pleased with the compliment. "Even with a hole through your chest, Dane, you're still stronger than me."

"You'll get there. You're only seventeen."

Roy nodded, and then Nathan assisted him in lowering Dane back into his wheelchair. Because there wasn't enough room in Colonel Walker's house, Dane and Nathan had been put up in one of the other officer's quarters. General Lewis had sent many of the base personnel to another location so he could bring in his own people, so Dane and Nathan shared this home with Lewis's right-hand man, a guy named Ryker. He always left early to report for duty, which left the house all to them.

Not wanting to eat the food in the fridge, Nathan pushed Dane's chair out the front door and, with Roy's help, eased it down the two short steps to the tarmac. At this point, Dane insisted on using his cane to walk to the DFAC, so Roy darted back inside and returned with it. Standing on his own two feet, despite the cane, made Dane feel a thousand times better. Nathan and Roy stayed close at hand, but Dane knew he wouldn't need them. He felt no light-headedness or imbalance, and his legs were strong. He tossed Roy a grin and lifted the cane into the air, showing off his good balance. Roy laughed.

***

Allison knew Alex and the other boys would eat breakfast with Amanda and then either hang around the house or go to the fitness center while the adults tried to figure out their next move. She really wanted to spend more time with Alex, but not necessarily the others. Yeah, Izzy was cute, and Java seriously built, but they were too distracting. She'd seen Roy heading toward the dining facility with his dad and brother and figured this might be the best time to be with Alex.

After ascending the steps to the front door of Colonel Walker's house, she pressed the lighted button and heard the bell echo from within the house. Then she waited, wiping her sweating palms on her sweats. The door opened and Amanda broke into a huge smile that lit up her face.

"Allison! So nice to see you. Come in."

Allison returned the smile and stepped into the house. Amanda led her into the kitchen, where the boys were laughing and goofing around while washing dishes.

"Isn't it great?" Amanda pointed at the activity. "My own dish washing company."

Allison laughed, but her eyes found Alex at once, a stack of dishes on his lap, handing them one by one to Jorge, who handed them to Java, who was doing the washing. Izzy, Francis, and William had dish towels in their hands, drying and stacking. Izzy saw Allison first and offered up one of those endearingly goofy grins he never seemed to run out of.

"Hello there, pretty lady," he said, elbowing Java and almost causing him to drop a plate.

Java glowered, but then nodded at Allison. "Hey, Allison."

She smiled, but her gaze remained fixed on Alex, who turned and froze. Their eyes met, and his cheeks bloomed red.

"Hey." He seemed to forget his job and Jorge had to take the next plate from him.

"Hey," she replied, suddenly unable to offer any of the brilliant witticisms she'd thought of on the way over. Yeah, he was one beautiful boy. "Need more help?"

Amanda laughed. "Let's let the boys do the work, Allison, while we sit and relax. Can I get you something?"

Allison reluctantly pulled her gaze from Alex and shook her head. "No, thanks, Amanda." She sat in the proffered chair, and Amanda sat beside her. They made small talk while the boys raucously completed their task and Allison was astonished no plates were shattered during all the good-natured shoving.

When the dishwashing was complete, the boys decided to watch some TV before heading out to the fitness center. She marveled at their ability to tune out all the doom and gloom going on around them.

Amanda excused herself to work on the laundry, so Allison walked out of the kitchen beside Alex, who hadn't said much to her yet.

"Come watch a flick with us, Allison," Izzy said, looking hopeful.

"Um, maybe later, Izzy," she replied with a smile. "I want to talk with Alex first."

Izzy pulled a face that almost made her laugh. "Whadda ya want with this fool?" He ruffled Alex's moppy hair, pushing it over those gorgeous blue eyes she loved. "Sure, he's cute and all that, but I'm cuter."

Alex flicked his hair out of his eyes and gave Izzy a shove. "Fool."

Izzy laughed and sauntered off into the living room. William stayed put, hovering behind Alex's wheelchair like a guard dog.

Allison regarded Alex, who shyly looked back at her. "You, uh, you wanna take a walk?" Her face immediately crumbled, and she felt her cheeks burn. "I'm sorry, I didn't mean walk, you know, for you to walk, I meant…" She trailed off, caught off-guard by the amused look on his soft, handsome features.

"It's okay, Allison. I don't get bothered by stuff like that. How 'bout I roll, and you walk?"

She sagged, relaxing, and nodded. He waved her toward the front door, and she crossed the entry hall to pull it open. Alex wheeled past her and onto the porch, William on his heels like a shadow. He rolled down the ramp, and William leaped down beside him.

Allison closed the door and dropped down off the porch, eyeing William, unsure what to say.

Alex obviously noticed because he said, "William's gotta stay with me. Colonel's orders."

She looked from him to William and back. "Okay."

Alex pointed across the tarmac at the rows of jets and helicopters. "Let's go that way. Lots of cool stuff to see."

"Sure."

He pushed his way forward, and she flanked him, with William bringing up the rear. She'd hoped to be alone with Alex, but under the circumstances, she'd take any time she could get. As they crossed the tarmac in silence, she studied his profile, the wavy blond hair, the pert nose and hairless cheeks. She thought, not for the first time, that he could be a model with such good looks. But that wasn't what drew her to him.

He was decent and kind and sweet. How many of her friends described their boyfriends that way? Only one that she could think of.

Boyfriend? You're getting way ahead of yourself here, girl!

"So, what do you think will happen tonight?"

He didn't look at her but focused on the jets just ahead as he slowed his chair. "Dunno. What's your dad think?" He stopped and looked up at her, squinting against the bright morning sun.

She stopped too, noticing that William halted a few feet back, watching them closely, like he feared she would abduct Alex. "He doesn't tell me anything. I know he still can't see inside that mountain, even with all the satellites he owns."

Alex nodded. "Same for the military. The colonel told me."

"I'm afraid for you, Alex," she blurted, not having intended to go there. But it was true. He was the one in the most danger, not her or her dad.

He shrugged, blinking a couple of times against the light. His long white-blond lashes seemed to absorb the sun and glow from within. "William won't let nothin' happen to me."

She squatted down so he wouldn't go blind looking up at the sun. Biting her lip, she considered how best to say what she wanted without it sounding like some dorky CW TV show.

"I really like you, Alex," she began, hesitant to go on. But his expectant face and iridescent eyes impelled her to continue. "A lot's gonna happen soon, from what I overhear, and I, well, I want to...I want..." She never finished her thought because impulse took over and she leaned in to kiss him on the lips.

His eyes widened with shock, but then he relaxed and kissed her back.

Allison never imagined a kiss could feel so good. She'd seen all the couples on TV and in the movies kissing up a storm but watching them didn't even come close to the real deal. She pulled away with great reluctance and hoped he wasn't offended. The delighted smile creeping across his face, coupled with his reddening cheeks, told her he was not.

She leaned away, but stayed in the squat position, despite cramping in her quads. "I'm sorry."

"No, it was nice. More than nice." He still smiled, but she saw something in his eyes now, something like a memory.

"Are you thinking of another kiss someone gave you?" She wasn't sure where that idea had come from, but the deeper blush to his cheeks assured her that she was right.

He broke eye contact and looked down. "Was that, you know, your first kiss?"

She understood he didn't want to answer her question. Now she felt her cheeks redden. "Yeah. I spent middle school and part of high school in and out of hospitals, so no romance for me. Thanks to you, I have a second chance at everything."

His face clouded over, and he turned away, rolling a few feet from her. She rose and strode to him, concerned.

"What did I say?"

He sighed, and his voice sounded breathy, like he was afraid to say what he wanted to say. "I just wondered if maybe, well, that's why you like me, because I made you better."

"No," she blurted more quickly than she'd intended. "Why would you say that?"

Still not meeting her eye, he said, "I seen how you look at Izzy. He says it himself; he's hot and girls like how he looks, even he if drives 'em crazy. I mean, I never been a regular kid, with this chair and my spinning and all."

He trailed off and she didn't respond right away. She had sort-of flirted with Izzy a few times, and he *was* hot. But she and Alex had more in common, didn't they? They liked the same bands and…what else? She couldn't think of anything else right then. Could she be attracted to him because he saved her life? She'd seen that scenario on lots of doctor shows, and it wasn't real love. She didn't remember what it was called, but maybe…maybe she was acting out that storyline with Alex?

She glanced at William, feeling kind of weird with the younger boy watching them, and then moved around in front of Alex. "I'm not sure what I feel, except I know I like you and wanna hang out with you." She offered her best petulant look and placed both hands on her hips. "Now, you promised to show me these planes and you're not gonna break your promise, are you?"

His eyes bulged with shock, but when she laughed, he joined in.

"C'mon," he said, glancing back at William. "William can even show you the helicopter he flew when he rescued me and Roy."

She looked back at William, who nodded, and feeling much more relaxed than she had all morning, she strolled among the planes and helicopters with the two boys and enjoyed every minute.

***

Colonel Walker had considered calling for Sergeant Stern to walk with him from the house to the hangar, but something prevented him, some trifling bit of caution tickling the back of his mind. Stern had attached himself rather closely to General Lewis since the senior officer had arrived on base, and Colonel Walker wasn't a hundred percent certain he trusted Lewis. He hated distrusting Pentagon officials, but this situation was so fluid, and the possibility for infiltration so ripe, he thought it better to err on the side of paranoia.

His instincts told him to trust Leone and Montour, so he added them, in his mind, to his inner circle. Mark Davalos was still in his corner, despite being at the beck and call of Lewis, and Walker knew that Mark would report any suspicious behavior. That left Shaw. He was an outsider, yes, and could easily be a cult member, and yet his actions on behalf of Alex seemed to be proof of his fidelity. It was Shaw he sought out now, which was why he'd asked Java to walk with him across the base to the War Hangar, having promised the base surgeon he wouldn't go long distances on his own.

The warm sun did little to dispel the sense of doom he felt in the pit of his stomach. How many people would die before this was over? Could this boy walking with him be one of those casualties?

"So, Java," he said as they passed airmen going about their duty. "Have you given more thought to joining the Air Force?"

Java's deep voice filled the air beside him. "I'd love it, Colonel. Just don't know about them tests and stuff."

"Like I said, son, those aren't everything. I've seen you in action, in an attack situation, and you handled yourself better than many grown men. Keeping a cool head and making smart choices in the field are more important qualities than scoring high on a test."

Java stopped and Walker turned to see the boy looking stunned, clearly fighting back his emotions.

"Are you all right?"

Java nodded. "Nobody never said stuff like that to me, Colonel. You make me believe I could do anything."

Walker offered a tight smile. "You can, and if you're interested, I'll give you my full recommendation. How does that sound?"

Java looked ready to explode with joy. "That be the awesomest thing anyone ever done for me!"

Walker laughed. "Consider it done. Now let's get going."

"Yes, sir!" Java saluted—very respectably, too—and Walker returned it.

He sent Java back to the house to keep the others busy and looked around the hangar for Shaw, who'd outfitted his own corner with computers and electronic gadgets designed for surveillance, many of which the military had purchased and were also using. Walking with greater assurance, Walker saluted several officers before arriving at Shaw's high-tech area. Martin sat at one computer station and Shaw at another. Both were studying topographical satellite images of Superstition Mountain.

"Morning, Colonel," Shaw said, without even glancing away from his computer screen. "Nothing so far at our end. You?"

"Nothing. The general plans to surround the mountain with troops tonight after dark."

Shaw pulled back from his scrutiny of the onscreen map and squinted at him. "Is that wise, to alert the enemy that way?"

"That's what I said, but Lewis overruled me."

When Walker said nothing more, Shaw leaned in closer. "You have a plan of your own."

Walker glanced around for any eavesdroppers.

"Martin will stand watch," Shaw said, glancing over at Martin, who immediately stood up from his station and planted himself where he would know if anyone was trying to listen.

Walker lowered his voice. "It was Alex's idea, actually." He explained about the tracking device that could be implanted in Alex's foot in case he should be captured. "We know they need him by midnight tonight to complete their ritual, if Leone and Montour are correct. That means they'll try to grab him today."

Shaw's face darkened during Walker's recitation. "I don't like it. If we can keep him out of their hands until November first, they can't do anything."

"I agree, Mr. Shaw," Walker replied soberly. "I would never deliberately allow Alex to be captured, but on the slight chance they pull it off, being able to track him is vital. The thing is, I don't want Lewis to know. If worse comes to worse, I want you doing the tracking."

"Why me?"

"You care for Alex," Walker replied. "You'll do anything to protect him. I'm not one-hundred-percent sure about all my people."

"Including Lewis?"

Walker shrugged. "He trusts people I don't know. I know you, and I trust you. Simple as that."

Shaw studied him a long moment. "I'm happy Alex has you in his corner, Colonel. You've got a deal."

"Good. Dr. Shepherd will insert the implant this morning, which will give us plenty of time to test it out. Select a frequency the military doesn't use."

"Consider it done."

CHAPTER EIGHT

YOU HAVE RECAPTURED ALEX?

ALEX GLANCED AT THE GIANT water tanks with the thick, nasty-looking fluid inside and shuddered. William had brought him to the old Weapon lab so Dr. Shepherd could put the device into his foot. Colonel Walker had stayed in the hangar with General Lewis so as not to arouse suspicion. It was just the three of them in the dim, unsettling lab that had birthed the boy Alex called "Little Brother."

Dr. Shepherd wore a mask, but it was pulled down now, and she wore rubber gloves. She'd rolled over a small table on wheels that had sharp cutting tools and big syringes on it. Alex sat watching her movements, more anxious about his surroundings than the actual procedure.

"Do you feel anything in your feet, Alex?" William asked, his young face innocent with curiosity.

"I might feel a prick, but that's all."

Dr. Shepherd held up what looked like a huge Q-Tip, damp with a strong-smelling liquid. "I'm going to numb the bottom of your foot anyway, Alex, just in case. Spina bifida, even an unusual variation like yours, doesn't necessarily result in complete loss of feeling."

He nodded, reaching down to slip one sneaker off his foot, followed by the ankle sock. William took both and set them on the floor. The doctor knelt and lifted Alex's foot off the footrest, holding it out straight. He knew she was doing that, even without looking, so he decided the stuff she was putting on might be a good idea. She swabbed the underside of his foot, on the heel. He felt something cold, but the sensation was minor.

She set the swab down on the table and reached for the syringe Alex had spotted. The needle looked thicker than the ones she used before to take his blood, but he didn't expect to feel much on the bottom of his foot.

"Now, the implant is about the size of a grain of uncooked rice," she explained, holding up the syringe.

Alex leaned down and squinted at the needle. Just behind it, encased in the thin plastic tube, was a tiny gray object that did look like rice.

"You might still feel a pinch when I inject it, but the injection site won't be visible to anyone without a magnifying glass. Are you ready?"

Alex glanced at William beside him.

"It didn't hurt me, Big Brother," William said, "but I have very tough skin."

Alex faced the doctor. "I'm ready."

She lifted his foot once again and lined up the syringe, but not pointed straight in like a shot would be aimed. She had the needle touching the skin of his foot at an angle, almost flat against his heel. She plunged it home. Alex felt a slight pinch, but it wasn't painful. She depressed the plunger and then extracted the needle.

"There. All done."

A tiny droplet of blood bloomed from the site of the injection. She placed the needle on the table and grabbed some cotton and something that looked like a fat white pencil without an eraser.

"This is a styptic pencil," she explained. "It will stop the bleeding." She wiped the blood away with the cotton and then touched the spot with the pencil. The bleeding stopped at once.

"Wow," Alex said, surprised. "It worked."

She offered a pleasant smile. "Yes, it's perfect for small cuts. For the big ones, I recommend William here."

William grinned, but Alex didn't get the joke.

"William saved Colonel Walker's life by stopping his bleeding," she explained.

Now understanding, Alex clapped William on one rock-solid shoulder. "That's my Little Brother for you."

Dr. Shepherd stood and observed the two boys. She looked happier than Alex had yet seen her.

"You boys are good for each other. I'm especially happy for you, William."

He looked pleased. "Thank you, Dr. Shepherd."

She reached for another rice-sized tracker from the table and held it up. "Now, I'll tape this to the bottom of your foot, Alex, with flesh-colored tape, and this is the one that will be activated today. The one inside your foot will only be activated if they succeed in capturing you and removing the outside tracker."

"I understand."

She squatted down again and lifted his foot, this time pressing the rice-sized device against the underside of his heel and then covering it with a tiny piece of tape that looked a lot like his skin color. After that, she slipped his sock and shoe back on and replaced his foot on the foot-rest. Regaining her feet, she smiled down at them.

"Okay, William. You have your orders."

***

Colonel Walker noted General Lewis in consultation with Davalos, which was part of the plan to make certain no one discovered what they'd done to Alex. He consulted his phone. There was a text from Liz: "Done."

He nodded at Shaw, who went to work on his keyboard, activating the two trackers inside and outside of Alex's foot to make sure they were functional. Two red dots suddenly appeared on Shaw's computer screen, which now displayed a map of the base.

"Both functional," he said, studying the screen. "They just left the lab building and are headed in the direction of the fitness center. I'm turning off the implant and will track the external device only."

"Good." Walker glanced at Martin, still standing guard over their section of the hangar. He spotted Leone, Father Pat, and Montour walking in their direction. "Here come the others," he said to Shaw. "Let's fill them in before they talk to Lewis."

"I'll leave that to you, Colonel." Shaw resumed his study of the screen. "Subjects have arrived at the fitness center. Looks like we have some time before William tries to hide Alex."

"Buonasera, Colonel Walker, Mr. Shaw," Leone said brightly. "And to you, as well, Martin."

"Good morning, Cardinal," Walker replied. "And you, Mr. Montour."

Shaw nodded his greetings and invited the two men to sit with them. The cardinal wore his traditional garments with the ornate crucifix dangling from his neck, while Montour wore jeans and a colorful long sleeve shirt.

Leone immediately eyed Shaw's computer screen and the flashing red dot. "So, it is done."

"Yes," Colonel Walker responded, feeling great concern for the boy behind that blinking dot. "Let's hope we don't need it."

"I pray that is so, Colonel."

"So, what's next?" Montour regarded him soberly, hands folded together in his lap.

Walker exchanged a significant look with Shaw before explaining that General Lewis and his staff knew nothing about the implant and the reasons they'd chosen not to tell him.

"Sounds like a good choice to me," Montour responded when Walker had finished. "The fewer people who know, the better. Where's Alex now?"

"Fitness center," Shaw replied. "No doubt with his friends."

"That is good," Leone added. "His friends will help take his mind off the current situation."

Montour leaned forward and rested his elbows on his knees. "Were there any major incidents last night?"

"More of the same," replied Walker. "Riots and chaos, several deaths within the fighting."

"But no obvious assassinations?"

Walker faced Leone's expectant expression. "No. Do you think something's happened to Andy or his power?"

"Andy has always been the variable, Colonel. There's no way to know."

Montour said, "He might have become powerless."

Father Pat, silent thus far, added, "If that's true, then Alex is in imminent danger.

***

She stopped outside the smaller cave that constituted Andy's "room."

Sparsely furnished with a cot and a few changes of clothes, it was what all her people had in this underground fortress.

She pushed her way through the dangling sheet that served as a door and found him sitting on the cot, back straight, long hair trailing wildly down his back and shoulders, staring straight ahead.

"Are you still angry with me, Teacher?" He looked over at her, his deep blue eyes offering nothing as to his thoughts.

Clad in another skin-tight black shirt and pants, she slunk into the room and stroked his frazzled hair. "No. You redeemed yourself later by instigating those riots. Besides, your dear brother will be here by midnight and everything will go as planned."

His eyes flickered a moment at the mention of his brother, but his face didn't move a muscle. "You have recaptured Alex?"

"Soon. Roy too."

A muscle in his jaw twitched, but he said nothing more.

"Rest, Andy. Save your strength for tonight."

She released his hair and turned to leave. Spotting a hairbrush on the rocky floor with his clothes, she snatched it up and tossed it to him. He fumbled to catch it, but the brush bounced out of his slim fingers.

"Brush your hair, Andy. You must look your best when we welcome my brethren into this world." She tossed off a cryptic smile and slipped through the dangling sheet without another word.

***

Roy, Dane, and Nathan enjoyed a fun breakfast in the DFAC, just the three of them yucking it up and telling stories of their childhoods. Roy learned things about Dane and his dad he'd never known. For example, his dad had started learning construction when he was eleven years old because his father let him work summers with a contractor friend of his. It was all under the table stuff, but things were different when Nathan was a boy and adults weren't so paranoid about everything their kids did. Nathan could even go out with his friends on summer days or weekends and hang out all day without his parents freaking out. No kids had mobile phones, so they'd had almost complete freedom.

Dane looked envious at these descriptions and told how protective his mother had been, always telling Dane this activity or that person was "to be avoided." He'd had to sneak out of the house in middle and high school just to hang out with his friends, and she never let him have anyone over.

Roy listened to these stories with a kind of contentment he hadn't felt in the longest time, maybe because the three of them had really become a close-knit family these past few weeks, despite all the danger and drama surrounding them. He missed his mom and so wished she could be there. His mom had tried hard to include Dane in family celebrations, but Dane's mother rebuffed her overtures every time, acting as though Nathan and "that woman" would somehow damage her child just by being around him.

Long after they finished eating, the three of them sat in the dining facility talking and laughing. Roy didn't even mind when Dane asked him when he first knew he was gay. He felt so relaxed now around his older brother that he shared the story he'd told Alex, about that choirboy named Patrick he'd seen in a music video and how he felt so drawn to him whenever he watched it. He also shared that Patrick had been, in his mind, the most beautiful boy he'd ever seen until he met Alex.

Dane listened to every word and didn't pull a disgusted face or make any rude comment like Roy had heard other family members sometimes hurled at their gay kids. When he finished, Dane just smiled. "Thanks for telling me, Little Brother. Like I said before, some hot guy is gonna fall for you sooner than you think."

Roy blushed and looked down at his empty plate. "Thanks, Dane."

After bussing their trays, they had decided to head over to the fitness center to check on the other boys and work out. Dane was still ordered off anything strenuous, but he figured, "Ten pounders can't hurt, can they?"

Nathan eyed him with concern as they crossed the tarmac. "Best start with fives, son."

Dane made such a sound of disgust that Roy laughed.

Inside the air-conditioned center, Roy felt the sweat under his arms begin to cool down as he noted with amusement that Java was already acting like he'd joined the military, drilling Izzy and Jorge on the weight machines. The strange part was, both boys looked like they were enjoying it. Roy had never seen Izzy work so hard, and Jorge was more into the lifting than he'd been since Carlos was killed.

Other than the boys, the place was empty. Roy suspected both the colonel and the general had every man and woman on active-duty status now. He led Dane in between workout machines and stopped where Java was spotting Izzy on the bench press.

"Come on, Izzy, one more!"

Java had his hands under the bar while Izzy struggled to push it all the way up.

"You got this, Izzy," Dane urged. "Lock it out."

Sweating and grunting, Izzy somehow forced the bar all the way up and set it down into the rack with a *clang*. Grinning from ear to ear, he sat up and accepted the exuberant high-five from Java, and another from Jorge, who'd been watching. Java and Izzy wore plain white tank tops and, of course, Java looked buff as hell. Truth be told, Roy could stare at that boy's muscles all day every day. But what shocked him was how ripped Izzy was looking. Never athletic, Izzy had always looked soft in the arms, but now there was real definition, even a bulging vein in the biceps.

"Hey, Roy," Java said, waving him over. "You're just in time." He pointed at the bench.

Roy eyed the weight. On each side was one big plate and one small one. The big plates bore the number forty-five and the smaller ones the number ten. He knew the two tens equaled twenty because he was pretty good with money, and since each forty-five was close to fifty, he figured there was almost a hundred-twenty pounds of weight, not counting the bar.

"I can't do that much, Java." He hated admitting it in front of Dane.

"Sure, you can, Roy," Java urged him, grinning like he knew something no one else did. "I seen you do this much on the machine. You be stronger than you think, bro."

"You got this, Roy," Izzy echoed Java, breathing heavily from his exertion, but looking very pleased with himself.

Roy glanced at Jorge, who reached into his pocket and slipped out a piece of paper, which he handed over. Roy took the paper and gazed a long moment at the bright red V. For victory. That's what Jorge always said, only this time his smile of encouragement said it for him. Could Roy achieve victory on this bench press?

Yes! He'd make it so.

Feeling a renewed sense of purpose, and not even thinking about Alex or whether Izzy would laugh should he fail, Roy sat on the end of the bench. Dane, now seated on an empty bench, caught his eye and winked, which was all the encouragement he needed. Lying back on the bench, Roy reached up and gripped the bar, spacing out his hands the way Java and the colonel had taught him, making sure he was the same distance from the middle on both sides. Java stood behind the bench, arms outstretched, muscles flexing.

"Need a lift off?"

"No. I got this."

Java grinned.

Roy focused on that bar almost as hard as he'd focused on Alex when they brought him out of the coma last week. He heard nothing but the hum of the air conditioning, and the cool air wafting over his face felt invigorating. He gripped the bar, but not too hard, and lifted it off the rack with more ease than he'd have imagined. He lowered the weight, breathing in through his nose, controlling the bar despite the shaking of his arms, and touched his chest so gently that bar might as well have been a feather. Then he pushed, expelling his breath as the bar rose higher and his arms shook like he was in a major earthquake.

"You got it, Roy!" Dane's voice sounded so excited, so proud.

You got it!

That thought pounded through his brain as his arms locked out and he dropped the bar onto the rack, relief, and extreme exhilaration flooding through him. He knew he was grinning like a fool, but he was so proud of himself.

"Yes!" Dane shouted, and the exuberance was echoed by Java, Izzy, Jorge, and Nathan, all of whom clapped Roy on the back and praised him. Java even grabbed one of his arms and raised it into the air.

"The winner is Roy!"

Roy laughed, filled with a sense of triumph. Sure, it was just a bar with weight, but it was something he'd never thought he could do. Other boys, yes, boys with muscles like Java, but not tall, skinny Roy with the broomstick arms. But as Izzy grabbed one of his arms and flexed it for him, Roy realized with a start that it wasn't a broomstick anymore. Somehow, he'd gotten bigger, his arms fuller. Yes, even his chest, he saw as he looked down at it, heaving in and out from his exertion.

I really am growing up.

His dad and Dane praised him so much Roy thought he'd faint from the attention, but Dane quickly resumed his usual challenging tone and said, "Just you wait till I'm better, Roy. No way my little brother is gonna get stronger than me."

Roy grinned and accepted the high five Dane threw up. That's when a clearing throat drew everyone's attention to the area behind Dane and Nathan. Allison stood there, smiling and clapping.

"Very impressive, Roy."

For some reason, her compliment made him blush, and he wasn't even annoyed to see her.

"You gonna work out with us, girl?" Izzy grinned her way and pointed to the bench press.

She laughed. "Not that much weight, but yeah, why not?"

"Hell, yeah," Java exclaimed as he began pulling the heavy weights off the bar. "Name your weight."

She examined the plates around her. "How much is the bar?"

"Forty-five," Java replied, clearly proud to demonstrate expertise in something.

She scrunched up her face. "I'll try a ten on each side."

"You got it," Izzy replied, and began setting up the weight.

She stepped closer and stopped next to Roy. She had wireless earbuds in her ears, and the right pocket of her sweatpants bulged with an obvious phone.

Unsure what to say, Roy asked, "What're you listening to?"

Grinning, she removed the right bud and placed it in his ear. The lyrics of his favorite song blasted into his head. Now he grinned.

"You like Hawthorne Heights?"

She nodded. "My favorite. Alex told me you loved them too."

The mention of Alex from her should've made him frown, but the words to "Put Me Back Together" wouldn't let him feel bad. "Where is Alex?"

"Had an appointment with Dr. Shepherd."

He nodded. Alex had mentioned that earlier. He reached up to remove the bud, but she stopped him.

"Hang on to it. We can both listen while I impress these boys."

He laughed. "Thanks, Allison."

"Are you gonna talk all day or lift?" That was Java, standing behind the bar, now loaded with a ten on each side.

She laughed and sat down on the bench, tossing Roy a wink before lying down and grabbing the bar. He chilled listening to his song while she knocked out ten reps like they were nothing, leaving Izzy gaping like a big fish.

***

Alex squinted against the blinding sunlight as he and William crossed the tarmac toward the fitness center. William seemed to have no trouble at all with the sun.

"Them's good contact lenses you got, William. I'm going blind here."

"Yes, the contacts darken in bright sunlight. How is your foot? Do you feel anything?"

"Not really. I'm sure it's working cause Mr. Shaw is amazing with tech stuff."

"We'll hang out with your friends for a while before trying to hide you from their search."

Alex grinned as they arrived at the double glass doors and the expectantly cool interior. "Sounds like fun." He grinned. "I can't wait to see what you can lift."

William smiled and pulled open the door. A movement caught Alex's eye and he glanced down to see a large, repellant cockroach skitter inside.

"Oh, gross," he said, pointing it out to William, but also recalling the experiments he and Andy had been a part of, when they'd shifted Death from a roach to that man in the bank.

William eyed him a moment and then focused on the roach. "Don't worry. I'll make it go outside." He stared at the roach, which stopped skittering and turned to face him, just like the others had done in the lab. William said nothing, just held open the door and concentrated. Like a soldier obeying orders, the roach twitched its feelers and skittered out the door. William offered a hopeful smile as he closed the door, cutting off the warm air.

"I forgot you could do stuff like that," Alex said, a bit creeped out, but also impressed.

"Does it make you think less of me, Alex, that I'm connected to them?"

Alex considered a moment and realized it didn't. "No. It's just another thing that makes you awesome."

William grinned with relief.

They were in a kind of lobby with more double doors just ahead, behind which the multitude of workout machines awaited them.

As they headed for the glass doors, William asked, "What were you and Allison doing earlier, Big Brother? You know, when you pressed your lips together?"

Alex, ahead of William, spun around to find the youngster eyeing him with curiosity. Trying not to blush like a middle schooler, Alex replied, "It's called a kiss. When two people really like each other, they, well, they kiss like that."

William looked confused. "I like you a lot, Alex. I might even love you. Dr. Shepherd tells me she thinks I can feel love. But I don't think about kissing you like that."

Alex squirmed in his chair. Here we go again. "It's mostly with boys and girls, but not all the time, and it's just, I don't know, a *kind* of love, I guess. I don't know how to explain it. I bet Dr. Shepherd or the colonel could explain it much better than me."

He nodded. "I'll ask them. Shall we go in?"

He pointed at the glass doors and Alex nodded. William darted ahead and pulled one open, allowing Alex to enter first. It was even cooler in the weight room. Alex felt the air tickling his neck and cheeks and it felt wonderful. William didn't seem to notice, and Alex realized that temperature changes had no effect on the boy, causing him once more to wonder how hard it must be for William—so similar, yet so different, from every other kid on earth.

Alex stopped dead upon seeing Allison on the bench press, repping the bar and a couple of small plates on each side with all the boys cheering her on, including Roy.

"Is something wrong, Alex?"

Alex glanced up at William, gazing at him with those wide blue eyes. "No. It's cool to see 'em having so much fun."

He wheeled between the leg machines, William at his heels, and stopped in the open area where all the benches were laid out side by side.

Java looked up from his spotting duties and grinned. "Hey, Alex, check out this girl. She's a beast."

Allison fumbled slightly with the bar, as though startled by something, and then she set it into the rack before sitting up and gazing straight at Alex. The boys clapped, and Alex spotted Roy trying to get his attention, but he found he could not look away from her.

She grinned. "You better watch it, Alex, cause I'm gonna be stronger than you."

Her comment released him, and he laughed. "No way." Then he met Roy's gaze and noticed the earbud he wore. He pointed to his own ear.

Roy grinned. "Hawthorne Heights," and indicated Allison, who pointed to her own ear.

Alex noticed Dane sitting to one side, while Nathan, Jorge, and Izzy stood behind the bench awaiting their turns.

"Wanna jump on, Alex?" Izzy looked pumped up with pride. "I'm catchin' up to you." He flexed, which caused Jorge to laugh.

Alex felt a kind of happiness he'd almost forgotten. These were his friends. His family. It felt amazing to have fun with them once more. No, it felt...perfect. He grinned and glanced at William beside him. "Hell yeah, I'll jump in. But first, we gotta all be embarrassed by my little bro, here. How about it, William? How many plates you want on that bar?"

William eyed him and then glanced at the bench where Allison still sat observing them. "How many plates are there?"

Java's mouth dropped open, while Alex and Roy laughed out loud.

"He ain't bragging neither," Roy told the others. "Load 'em up."

Alex winked at William, who didn't quite get the joke, but Java and Izzy went to work loading up both sides of the bar with forty-five-pound plates. Since these plates were thin, the boys managed to get five onto each side, but there was no room for a clamp to hold them in place.

William strode forward and observed the weight-filled bar with dispassion.

"Got no room for a clamp, bro," Java said, eyeing the bar with furrowed brows. "They might fall off."

William met his gaze. "No, it'll be fine. I have an excellent sense of balance."

Alex stared at the overloaded bar in amazement. "How much you got on there?"

Java shrugged. "Beats me."

Alex glanced at the others.

Izzy looked like he was trying to count in his head, but then gave up. "I can't count that high."

Jorge grinned and repeated, "I can't count that high."

Izzy gave him a good-natured shove.

Dane and Nathan exchanged a look, and Nathan shrugged. "I need a calculator for that much."

Allison looked around from where she stood, shaking her head in amusement. "It's four ninety-five, you guys."

Izzy pulled a face that made Alex laugh. "You can count that high?"

She rolled her eyes and looked at Alex, but he just shrugged. He couldn't go that high either without a calculator. He wheeled closer to William. "That's a lotta weight, little bro. Sure you can handle it?"

William cocked his head, looking puzzled. "Was that a joke, Big Brother?"

Alex just shook his head in amazement. "No. I just don't want you getting hurt."

William offered up a beautiful smile. "Thanks for worrying, but I'll be fine."

He strode to the bench and sat down while everyone seemed to hold their breath in anticipation. The only sound was the bench pad squeaking as William lay back and raised his hands to grasp the bar. Beneath such a prodigious amount of weight, he looked so small.

"I ain't even gonna offer a liftoff," Java commented, his eyes bulging, which garnered a chuckle from Izzy.

Without a moment's hesitation, William lifted the bar off the rack and held it above him, perfectly balanced, like it weighed nothing. But the bar began bending slightly in the middle, so he lowered it to his chest, paused a moment, and then pressed it back up in a strong, controlled movement that didn't come close to dislodging even one plate, and then eased it back onto the rack.

He sat up and smiled at Alex, not the slightest bit winded. Everyone just stared for a long moment in utter admiration, and then Alex began clapping. The others joined in, surrounding William, clapping him on the back, asking him to flex so they could feel the hardness of his arm muscles.

The young boy looked over the moon with happiness at being so accepted by other kids, and Alex was full of love for all of them. This was a moment they might never get again, so he savored every second.

CHAPTER NINE

LET HIM GO!

SHAW STOOD TO STRETCH, AND the simplicity of the action filled Colonel Walker with envy. Yes, he'd been able to get rid of the wheelchair, but the base surgeon, and more importantly, Amanda, forbade him walking around on his own without escort and, of course, no exercise was permitted as yet, even stretching.

"They must be having a good time at the fitness center," Martin commented, gazing at the red dot that hadn't budged for the past thirty minutes.

"Allison texted me she was over there," Shaw commented, slipping out his phone and examining his messages. "But nothing since then. I could call, but I need to stretch my legs. I'll stroll over and check on the kids."

"Shall I go instead?" Francis sat up from his chair, where he'd been sitting since Dr. Shepherd brought him back from the lab. "Roy is over there. I haven't seen him all day."

Shepherd said, "Francis is probably bored after all my tests."

Walker noted the boy's eager expression, the thick black hair haphazardly swept across his forehead, those wide hazel eyes so filled with wonder. Had he, himself, been like that as a boy? As with William, he swore that Francis would have the best childhood possible.

Shaw looked like he was considering the idea, but there was a look in his eyes that troubled Walker. "Something wrong, Shaw?"

"No." He turned to face the eager boy. "Thanks for the offer, Francis, but I really do need to walk. Not young anymore like you." He winked, which drew out an engaging smile from the boy. "I'll tell Roy to come over here when he's finished."

"Thank you, Mr. Shaw," Francis said with a courtly bow.

The cardinal stood, as well, and Montour followed suit. "Samuel, shall we get a bite in the DFAC while we're waiting? The meeting doesn't begin until three."

Montour eyed Walker. "Do you mind, Colonel? We can bring you something."

"Please, help yourself to whatever is there. And coffee for me would be great. Martin?"

Martin pulled his gaze from the monitor. "Coffee for me too. I have a feeling we're in for a long day."

"Will do," replied Montour, and the two men ambled across the hangar toward the exit.

Walker looked around for General Lewis but didn't see him anywhere. "Did you see the general leave, Martin?"

Martin shook his head, then stood and scanned with greater intensity the width and breadth of the hangar. "He's not here. He'll have to be back to conduct the meeting, though. Have the troop movements begun?" He retook his swivel chair.

"Yes, though I'm still not convinced it's the best course of action. Trucks are leaving the base now because it will take over three hours to arrive at the mountain. Edwards in California has also been sending some troops."

"What about Davalos? I haven't seen him around."

"That's because he's readying his own troops to move out."

"You mean those creatures?"

'Yes. They might come in handy if things go south. According to the cardinal, the demonic invaders won't go after animals."

Martin eyed him with one raised brow. "Do you believe all that stuff, Colonel, about another dimension and supernatural entities that can possess human beings?"

Walker considered a long moment before answering. "I believe Alex and Shaw. They saw those things in action. There's also the woman who hasn't aged. And, after all the unnatural experiments conducted on this base, I've learned that there's a lot more out there than most people think."

Martin nodded. "When do *we* leave?"

Walker consulted his watch. "Sixteen hundred. We're going by chopper, so we arrive before the last of the troops."

"And the general?"

"Same mode, different chopper. He likes to have autonomy, and he still resents my handling of that Weapon incident a few years back. He doesn't fully understand what the cardinal has in mind, and of course, everything depends on what happens with Alex."

Martin frowned, pulling that scar above his left eye tight against his skin. "They haven't made their move yet."

Now it was Walker's turn to frown. "I know. That's what troubles me most. They have only eight hours till midnight."

"All's quiet on the perimeter?"

Walker held up his cell phone. "I've been checking the camera feeds every three minutes in rotation. The only activity is the troop transport trucks leaving the base. By my calculations, there should be seven more before the front gate is locked and sealed once more."

Martin looked thoughtful. "My best guess would be they would attack during the troop movement."

"My thought exactly. But so far, the desert out there is empty."

***

Roy had to admit that he'd had a great time working out with his family and Alex, and yes, even Allison. Somehow, her sharing his favorite song—their favorite song—had cemented a kind of kinship with her that dampened his feelings of jealousy. As he worked out and enjoyed watching William best them all at every exercise, he came to understand an important truth—he can never have everything the way he wants and, even if Alex should fall in love with Allison, it would never destroy their friendship unless he—Roy—was the one to do that. Jealousy was an ugly emotion, one worth fighting off at every turn.

William—the only one among them not sweating like a pig—leaned into Alex and whispered something into his ear. Alex nodded and said to Roy, "William and I are gonna go hide on the base, just to see if the colonel can find us. Wanna come?"

Roy furrowed his brows in confusion. It sounded like a weird idea, but hey, it was more time with Alex so, of course, he said, "Sure." He caught Allison looking their way and added, "Can Allison come too?"

Alex looked surprised but pleased. "Course." He waved the girl over and told her the plan.

She glanced at Roy as though for a more complete explanation, but he just shrugged.

They told the others they'd see them later at the meeting and left the cool confines of the fitness center. Roy couldn't believe how hot it was so late in October, but then he recalled some Halloweens in Hawthorne where it was in the eighties, so he just did his best to ignore the pounding sunlight and dry, stifling air.

He noticed the large trucks moving along the tarmac in the direction of the front gate. Soldiers in what looked like battle fatigues were lined up in rows near where the trucks were parked. He squinted against the sunlight and observed one row of soldiers climb into the back of a truck and then close the flap, hiding them from view. The truck then advanced toward the front gate.

"What's going on over there?"

The others stopped to look. It was William who answered his question. "Soldiers heading for that mountain in Arizona."

A chill enveloped Roy, despite the heat, and he eyed Alex with concern. Tonight, at midnight, was the time Ms. G wanted Alex to open that gate-thing. Did that mean Ms. G would try to kidnap him before then? He supposed it must.

Allison placed a hand on Alex's shoulder. "The colonel and my dad will protect you."

Alex nodded, but Roy saw the worry in his gorgeous eyes.

"William!"

Roy looked over William's shoulder to see a man in uniform striding toward them. He knew the guy worked for Colonel Walker but couldn't recall his name.

"Sergeant Stern," William said, clearly surprised by the man's approach. The boy saluted the sergeant as he stopped and eyed the group with an expressionless face.

"Colonel Walker requires your immediate assistance in the hangar."

William scrunched up his face in bewilderment. "My orders are to remain with Alex at all times, sir."

"You have new orders," Stern intoned crisply, without emotion. "I've been sent to guard Alex."

William hesitated, glancing at Alex with obvious uncertainty.

"Go see what the colonel wants," Alex said, offering up a smile. "I'll be fine."

William took another moment to consider the matter before nodding. "I shall return." He saluted Stern before sprinting off across the tarmac.

The sergeant stared at Roy in a way that made him squirm. Roy exchanged a look with Allison, who appeared just as mystified.

Alex was also confused. "Are we going someplace, Sergeant, or you just gonna hang with us?"

Stern glanced over their heads at the trucks and the loading of soldiers. As though making a spur-of-the-moment decision, he ordered, "Come with me. I must speak with the men before they leave."

He indicated that they move in the direction of the activity. Alex wheeled himself forward. Roy caught Allison's eye, and it was clear she felt uncomfortable too. But they flanked Alex, and the sergeant brought up the rear.

***

Shaw strode across the warm tarmac, grateful he'd eschewed his usual coat and tie for a light shirt and slacks. He hadn't told the others, but he'd felt a pressing need to see Allison, as though she might be in danger. On the surface, such an idea was absurd. But with the strange goings on of late, he felt compelled to make certain all was well.

As he walked, he considered the conversation he'd had with his attorney earlier that morning. Had he made the right decision? He'd always been a man to trust his instincts, which had never steered him wrong. And his instincts told him to think long term, especially with the immediate future so uncertain.

Yes, his decision was a sound one, and he could always make changes down the line, if need be.

He spotted the troop transport vehicles lined up near the front gate, each loading a group of airmen before heading out into the desert. He would accompany Colonel Walker on his chopper at four o'clock, along with the rest of the team.

Squinting against the scorching sunlight, he suddenly stopped as another group caught his eye. It was Alex in his wheelchair, but who was with him? He continued forward and finally made out Roy and Allison. Where were they going? And who was… It was Sergeant Stern. What was he doing with Alex and where was William, who'd been assigned to guard him? And why were they heading for one of the transport vehicles?

Something didn't pass the smell test and he quickened his pace to intercept them. Stern led the group in between two of the transport vehicles and Shaw lost sight of them. He broke into a jog, fear clutching at his pounding heart. Something wasn't right here!

Airmen stood in lines awaiting their turn to clamber up into the vehicles. They eyed Shaw as he ran past but made no move to stop him. He passed the final truck in the convoy and spotted the kids behind the transport vehicle just ahead. Stern faced them. While several airmen surrounded them, Stern pulled a gun and pointed it at Allison.

Shaw broke into a run. He skidded to a halt as Stern whirled around, gun at the ready.

Panting from his run, Shaw gasped, "What's going on here, Sergeant?"

Stern eyed him a moment. "Isn't it obvious, Shaw? I'm taking these kids with me."

"The hell you are!" Shaw made a move toward him, but Stern aimed the gun at his chest, and that forced him to stop.

"What do we do, Sergeant?" That came from one of the young airmen, eyeing Shaw with uncertainty.

Stern looked pissed. "Throw him in the truck with the others. Now."

Two men grabbed Shaw by the arms and dragged him toward the open back of the truck. Shaw struggled, his eyes finding those of a terrified Allison, now gripped from behind by another airman.

"Let him go!" shouted Alex, reaching for the men holding on to Shaw.

"Stop!" exclaimed Stern, pointing the gun at Allison. "If you all don't shut up, I will put a bullet in her head. My orders are only to bring the two boys. Now get into the truck quietly, or she dies!"

"Okay, okay," Alex said, holding up his hands. "Don't hurt her, please."

He allowed two of the men to lift his wheelchair and roll him into the truck. Shaw watched helplessly as Roy shrugged off the two men who reached for him and then clambered into the truck on his own. Shaw made eye contact with Allison, who gazed at him with fear.

"It's okay, honey," he said, glancing around for any source of help. They were well-shielded between the trucks, however, and any number of these men might be loyal to that woman. "I'll protect you."

She nodded and Stern shoved her toward the open truck. Roy noticed that she let something drop from her hand as she stumbled, but she made sure it fell away from them so the men wouldn't spot it. Roy only just realized it was her earbud before she slapped away the hands of the man who tried to lift her and climbed up and into the truck.

Shaw wanted to tell Stern he wouldn't get away with this but didn't want to sound melodramatic or give away the idea that they would be tracked. Rebuffing the men at either side of him, he climbed into the truck. Two of the men followed, and then Stern climbed up to join them. One man dropped the flap into place and Shaw felt the truck begin to move, taking its place in the queue.

Ignoring the gun Stern had pointed in his direction, Shaw focused on the kids. They looked unharmed, and not as fearful as he would've expected, especially Alex and Roy. He suspected they'd been through so much already that they wouldn't easily panic. That was good. And, thanks to his training, Allison also had a level head on her shoulders. She would need it.

***

Colonel Walker sat beside Martin while Leone and Montour stood behind them observing. Walker frowned. Why was William taking Alex toward the front gate where the troops were moving out?

He was so focused on that moving red dot that he flinched when he heard, "You sent for me, Colonel?"

He twisted his head around in surprise to find William standing before him, a quizzical look on his young face. "William, what are you doing here?"

The boy's face fell into uncertainty. "Sergeant Stern said you wanted to see me."

Walker felt the color drain from his face as he exchanged a knowing look with Martin. Stern!

"What's happening, Colonel?" Leone leaned in, his accented words laced with worry.

"They have Alex."

Montour gasped as Walker fixed his gaze on the screen. The blinking red dot was outside the base now and heading out across the desert.

Martin sat back and their eyes met. "They got the jump on us."

Walker nodded. "Call Shaw. Get him back here. We need to depart now."

Martin snatched up a cell phone from the computer desk and pressed a single digit. He held the phone to his ear and waited.

***

Alex eyed the gun in Stern's unwavering hand and wondered, for a split second, if he could disarm the man. No, he knew at once. He was no William and trying anything stupid would get someone killed. He glanced from Roy, who sulked, to Allison, who stared at the other two soldiers as though preparing to jump them.

A sudden ringing filled the truck, loud enough to be heard over the rumbling of the tires against the rough desert floor. He turned to Mr. Shaw, and so did Stern. Gun aimed squarely at the man's head, Stern said, "Take out the phone, but make no attempt to answer."

The ringing continued as Mr. Shaw slipped one hand into his pants pocket and pulled out a Shawtech phone, sleek and shiny and lit up with the incoming call. He held it up. The ringing and flashing ceased, but only for a moment. Then they resumed, as though the person called right back. Alex finally saw the face of the phone more clearly and a name was lit up. It began with an M, so he figured it had to be Martin.

"Throw it out of the truck," Stern commanded with a wave of the gun toward the flapping cloth curtain.

Keeping his eyes on the gun, Mr. Shaw reached through the flap and tossed his phone.

"Good," Stern looked at Allison and Roy. "Either of you have a phone?"

Allison looked tempted to say no, but her father shook his head. With slow deliberation, she pulled a Shawtech phone from her pocket and handed it to Stern, who took it with his free hand and tossed it through the flap. Then he glowered at Roy. "Yours too, kid."

"I don't got a phone no more." He practically spat out the words and Alex tried to make eye contact, to calm his best friend.

"You have an earbud, so you must have a phone."

Roy took out the earbud, obviously having forgotten it was there. "It's hers," he said, handing it to Allison.

Stern stared at him long and hard, then nodded at one of the other two soldiers. "Search him. The cripple too."

The man moved closer to Roy and grabbed him around the waist, roughly patting his pants around the pockets. Roy's face twisted with such fury that Alex was stunned. His friend didn't look the least bit afraid. Then the man reached for Alex, who felt so tempted to spit on him that he had to bite his lip to keep from doing it. The soldier slapped his legs around the pocket area and turned to Stern.

"They're both clean."

The man scooted over to rest up against the back wall of the cab while Stern nodded. "No more interruptions. Enjoy the ride."

He sat back against the side of the truck, gun still aimed at Mr. Shaw. With the three men in the truck with them, there was no way to fight back. Not yet anyway. Looks like he'd gotten what he wanted—he'd be seeing Andy very soon. Unfortunately, he'd also see Ms. G. The thought made him shiver.

***

"No answer," Martin said, lowering his phone to the desk with a frown.

"I'm sorry, Colonel," William said, his soft voice laced with guilt. "I shouldn't have trusted Sergeant Stern."

Walker placed a hand on his shoulder. "I trusted him, son, so why shouldn't you?"

"Shall I track them?"

Walker shook his head. "We know where they're headed. You'll come with us."

Just then, Java, Israel, and Jorge bounded across the hangar toward them. Bringing up the rear was Nathan walking beside Dane.

"Colonel," Java said, slightly out of breath, as though he'd run across the base. "I found this where them trucks was leaving." He held out what looked like an earbud for listening to music.

The colonel eyed it with raised eyebrows. "So?"

"It's Allison's," Java went on. "She had it in the gym."

"And Roy had the other one," Israel added, looking afraid.

"What does it mean, Colonel?" Nathan stood beside Dane, indicating the earbud. "We looked for her, but she's nowhere around."

Walker turned to Martin, who'd gone white in the face. "I'll call her cell." He grabbed his phone and punched another number, putting the phone on speaker mode. Ringing filled the air around them. It rang and rang. But then a girl's voice said, "It's Allison. Leave a wicked message and you'll get a wicked reply." A beep followed and Martin ended the call.

"They took her," he announced.

"I think you're right," Walker replied, worrying that this campaign was rapidly unraveling. "Shaw must've spotted them with Stern, and they took him as well." He paused a moment to think. "William, find General Lewis. Inform him what happened and let him know we're heading to Arizona now."

"Yes, sir." The boy saluted and took off at a run.

"Java, you take Izzy, Jorge, and Francis to the DFAC and tell Cardinal Leone and Mr. Montour that we're leaving. Grab something to eat because I don't know when you'll get another chance."

Java saluted, as well. "Yes, sir. C'mon, guys." They ran in the same direction as William.

Walker faced Dr. Shepherd. "Why not go with them, Liz? We'll meet at the chopper in twenty."

She nodded and followed the boys.

Walker eyed Martin, the only one left. "You still up to date on military hardware, Martin?"

"Pretty much, sir."

"Good."

***

William asked every airman and soldier he could find where the general had gone, but Lewis was not anywhere within the hangar, so he exited into the afternoon sun and scanned the base around him. The transport vehicles had all departed, and the front gate in the distance was closed. There was activity around several of the helicopters, which he knew were being prepared for the journey to Arizona. But there was no sign of the general.

He decided to ask the helicopter pilots preparing the birds for liftoff. Trotting up to the first chopper, he nearly collided with an airman carrying a large box who had emerged from behind the helicopter.

William stopped and ducked to one side. "I'm sorry, sir."

The airman ignored him and strode purposely toward the War Hangar. William paused and watched him. There was something odd…a ticking sound? Was that what he'd heard as the man brushed past him? Deciding he might have heard equipment aboard the chopper, he turned and trotted up to the open bay door. Two airmen in tactical gear were arranging some equipment for the journey.

"Excuse me, Airmen," William began, looking in at them.

The men stopped stacking wooden boxes and eyed him. "Yeah, kid?"

"Have you seen General Lewis? Colonel Walker is looking for him."

"I haven't," answered the one who'd addressed him. "You seen him, Pauly?" The other man shrugged and shook his head. "Maybe he left on the earlier chopper."

That news surprised William. Why didn't the colonel know about this? "When did it leave?"

The airman checked his wristwatch. "Bout twenty minutes ago, I'd say."

"Thank you." William offered a salute before backing away from the massive helicopter, his mind awhirl with conflicting thoughts. Why would the general leave without informing the colonel? He suddenly remembered the ticking sound and knew what it reminded him of.

A bomb!

He took off like a jackrabbit for the War Hangar just as a massive explosion sent ripples across the tarmac and debris rained down on him like dirty snow.

CHAPTER TEN

ARE YOU HURT?

ANDY STOOD IN THE CENTER of the circular control room staring at the multiple monitors but seeming to focus on none of them. Teacher strolled among her followers manning the various stations, observing each detail with precision. Jäger sat off to one side. He looked paler than usual, slightly slumped in his chair, as though a growing weakness crept slowly throughout his body.

Andy said, "He is coming."

She turned from the console and faced him, eyebrows raised. "Who is coming, dear Andy?"

"Big Brother."

She allowed herself a curious expression, as though wondering how he knew this information. "Yes. He will be here in a few hours. Does that please you?"

"No." The voice and face remained without inflection or expression.

She sidled closer to him, tickling his neck with her delicate fingers before she swept around behind and whispered into his ear, "Roy is coming too."

He didn't so much as blink. "So?"

She brushed up against him as she circled back around and made eye contact. "That doesn't interest you?"

He held her gaze. "Should it?"

She smiled. "I thought perhaps it might."

"It doesn't."

Still locking her eyes to his, she said, "So you don't care if we torture him?"

Still, he didn't blink or break eye contact. "Do what you want with him. And Big Brother. I don't care."

She finally released his eyes, though he continued to stare straight ahead. "That's my boy." She patted him on one shoulder and resumed her examination of some data coming through the system.

He narrowed his eyes ever so slightly but said nothing.

***

Allison sat against the side wall of the bumpy truck as it pounded through the desert at high speed. She made frequent eye contact with her dad, Alex, and Roy, but refused to even glance at the soldiers who'd kidnapped them. She should've been more afraid because she and her dad were clearly not supposed to be in that truck—only Alex and Roy. Why? That question nagged at her consciousness, but she couldn't come up with an answer.

She knew they wanted Alex to open some gate to another dimension that might, or might not, be Hell. But why Roy? And why were she and her dad still alive? Stern could've shot them both and dumped their bodies into the desert like he had their phones. She made eye contact with Alex and tried to smile but blushed instead, the memory of their kiss resurfacing.

Could Stern know about that? Might they want her—and Roy, for that matter—as leverage to force Alex to do their bidding? She shivered despite the hot, stifling atmosphere of the covered truck. She knew her dad had to be planning something, or maybe already knew of a plan hatched by Colonel Walker for just such an eventuality as this one. Yes, she'd put her hopes on Colonel Walker. If anyone could save them, it was him.

***

The explosive shockwave didn't slow William down in the slightest as he pelted through pieces of furniture and computer components raining down on the tarmac.

That bomb must've been huge, he thought, as he neared the War Hangar. The front wall was buckled outward, but the side facing him was obliterated. Massive sections of corrugated metal lay strewn about the tarmac and debris was everywhere. Half of the podium lay on its side, while pieces of the wooden platform surrounded it, along with computer monitors and broken office chairs.

The door was off its hinges and hung askew, making entry and exit impossible. William gripped the knob and tore the door from his hinges, tossing it aside and leaping inside, instantly searching the corner where he'd left the colonel. Miraculously, this entire side of the hangar had remained largely intact, with the brunt of the damage at the far wall, the one now scattered about the tarmac outside.

He saw no movement and leaped over fallen tables and chairs, arriving at the colonel's station in seconds.

A moan caught his ear. It came from beneath a large section of paneling from the destroyed stage. It looked heavy, but he tossed it to one side with ease, gasping in surprise. Martin lay atop the colonel, shielding him from harm. The back of his shirt was torn from the shattered wood striking him, but he looked uninjured.

"Martin, let me help you." He reached down to the man, who pushed himself off Colonel Walker, coughing and gagging from the swirling dust.

"I'm good, kid." He coughed. "Help the colonel."

He pushed himself to his knees so William could reach down to the colonel. He rolled his commander over, happy to see Colonel Walker's eyes open and blinking. He looked stunned, but unhurt. William detected no bleeding. He pressed his head against the colonel's chest and heard an accelerated but healthy heartbeat.

"He's just stunned," William said. "Can you help me get him into a chair? I can lift him by myself, but I don't want to reopen his wound."

Martin nodded, rising to his feet and leaning on an undamaged chair for a moment to steady himself. William pushed his arm under the colonel, who was stirring now, and eased him to a sitting position. Then Martin grasped him under the other arm and the two of them eased him up and into the chair.

William moved around in front, facing Colonel Walker, who gazed at him in confusion. "William?"

"Yes, sir. Are you hurt?"

The colonel seemed to come back to himself quickly and shook his head. Pushing himself to a more upright position, he glanced around at the destruction. "A bomb."

"Yes, sir," William replied, feeling deep remorse. "I'm sorry I didn't get here in time to stop it."

Martin gave a slight exhalation. "Francis."

The colonel's eyes widened with fear. "Do you see him?"

Martin looked around while William faced the colonel. "What about Francis?"

"He was here." The colonel coughed again. "Heard the bomb and grabbed it."

"Oh, no!"

William stood to his full height beside Martin, both scanning the rubble. The bodies of numerous airmen lay sprawled about the wreckage, but there was no sign of the young boy. William didn't know how to feel panic, but the sensations running through him at that moment might be close. He loved Francis. Yes, he could use that word now. Alex had helped him understand it better. He knew Francis was strong and difficult to kill, but was he strong enough to withstand a bomb of this size at close range?

"You take care of the colonel, Martin. I'll find Francis."

Without awaiting a response, William bounded over a fallen computer desk and, through a series of hops, leaps, and jumps, made his way through the debris and mangled bodies toward the spot where the wall had blown out, most likely the detonation point.

By this time, airmen from outside began pouring into the destroyed hangar and William heard Colonel Walker barking out orders. But his focus was the blackened floor and twisted metal of the damaged wall. Still no sign of Francis. Where could he be?

He heard a moan. Looking around, he focused his hearing. Outside, the twisted remains of the wall shifted slightly. William leaped over the busted remnants of the door and sprinted across the hot tarmac. Just as he reached the massive section of corrugated metal, it flipped up into the air and flew over his head, crashing to the ground with a loud *thunk*.

Francis, bleeding about the hands and face, sat up and shook the dust and debris from his shaggy hair. Relieved, William hurried forward and knelt beside his genetic brother.

"You okay, Francis?"

The younger boy finished shaking his head like a wet dog and flashed a thumbs up. "I guess werewolves are tough too." He offered a little grin as William reached out to pull him to his feet.

"How did you end up out here?" William indicated the damaged hangar twenty feet away.

Francis felt his bleeding face and then stared a moment at the blood on his hand. "I never seen my bloods before."

William examined him with a careful eye. "Just a few scratches. You're lucky."

"I was standing next to the colonel when I heard ticking behind us. I saw the box and was trying to get it outside through that door back there." He pointed at the busted and splintered door William had jumped over. "The box hit the door and I dropped it. So, I jumped outside, and that's when it blowed up. The wall broke loose and took me with it." He shrugged.

William smiled. "Thank you, Little Brother, for saving the Colonel."

The dirty boy beamed. Throwing an arm around Francis's shoulders, William led him back into the hangar.

***

Teacher stared at Andy, who hung his head in shame. He had been attempting for the past thirty minutes to shift all the good feelings from a group of people in Washington, D.C. and insert bad ones, but had failed.

"I don't understand, Teacher," he said in his monotone voice. "I was able to do it two nights ago."

Rather than berate him or express anger, she wore an expression of puzzlement on her face. "Yes, you did. It's as if the power you stole from your brother has disappeared." She drummed her fingers on the console. "Come, Andy."

She led the way out of the control center and into an adjacent series of caverns. The lighting was dimmer, but Andy's eyes had long since adjusted. He tromped after her until she stopped at a hollow covered with a sheet. Pushing aside the sheet, she stepped inside, and he entered behind her.

Jäger lay on his cot—almost dwarfing the bed with his prodigious size—snoring loudly. Dr. Avila sat in a folding chair with a laptop across his knees, examining information on the screen.

"Well, doctor? Do you have a diagnosis?"

Avila looked up at her. There were dark circles under his eyes, and his face looked slack with fatigue. His rumpled lab coat bore witness to his lack of rest. "I have a theory, my lady."

"Before you share your thoughts, our so-called Healer will scan him again." She eyed Andy, who stood beside her with a disinterested look on his face, before leaning down to grasp one of Jäger's massive shoulders and shaking it. His eyes opened, and he smiled when he saw her. Then he looked around at the small area that was his sleeping quarters and the smile dropped.

He sat up with such abruptness he nearly smashed his head against the jagged ceiling. "My lady, I apologize for sleeping. I don't know what's come over me of late."

She offered a conciliatory smile. "It's quite all right, Kurt. I want you well rested for tonight." She waved at Andy, who stepped closer and stared at them both without expression. "Andy, can you sense Kurt's health status?"

The boy furrowed his brow in concentration. He stared and stared and…let out an exasperated breath. "No, Teacher, I can't."

Rather than look angry, she again looked curious, her face lit up with the prospect of a mystery to solve. "Fascinating. First, you told me Kurt seemed to be disappearing. Do you remember that?"

"Of course, Teacher."

"Now the healing powers that you took from your brother have disappeared."

She paused to think.

"What does it mean, my lady?" Jäger looked worried, his toy soldier face attempting an expression of concern, but not quite succeeding.

"My instincts tell me that this transfer process, in all cases, might be temporary."

Andy eyed her with confusion. "What do you mean?"

"Perhaps some aspects of people are not transferable, like the Healer qualities, or…"

"A soul?" Jäger added.

She eyed the doctor. "Have you come to a similar conclusion?"

He cast a nervous glance at the forbidding figure of Jäger. "His body appears to be breaking down, almost as though it were…dead."

"How is that possible?" Jäger looked more confused than angry. "I'm clearly alive."

"Yes," Avila went on, "but your body doesn't seem to know it's supposed to be alive. It's like you said, my lady, it's very possible the soul transfer didn't take, much like a patient rejecting a liver transplant. That's why he's never gained control over small muscles such as those in the face."

She stared at him, clearly debating her options.

"I'm…going to die?" Jäger looked stunned.

"How much time does he have left?" she asked.

Avila glanced at his computer screen. "Based on my latest tests, the body will likely be uninhabitable within eight hours, maybe less."

She glanced at her watch. "Eight hours would be one am."

He nodded, looking fearful, as though she might strike him.

She faced the big man, who sagged with disappointment. "That should be enough time. Alex will refuse to cooperate at midnight. That's where you come in, Kurt, doing what you so enjoy."

An evil smile graced Jäger's lips. "Torture?"

"Yes."

He nodded. "I'll go out with a bang, my lady."

She smiled. "I've no doubt."

Andy shivered.

***

Colonel Walker left Sergeant Lucas, another of his base officers, in charge of the explosion cleanup, as well as the base, in preparation for his departure for Arizona. With Alex already on the move and General Lewis apparently on route too, he felt a sense of urgency to arrive at that mountain sooner rather than later. He knew that bomb had been meant for him, having been left so close to his position. But he'd had a target on his back more than once in his career and it hadn't deterred him yet. This time would be no different.

He stood between two of the modified Pave Hawks—now armed with missile launchers—that would make the trip. Amanda had an arm firmly looped around one of his as he faced those who would accompany him. He'd selected two of his best pilots for each chopper, airmen he hoped would prove more trustworthy than Stern. It felt like a punch to the gut when he considered the betrayal by his long-time aide, someone he'd considered a friend. These pilots had served under him for several years, and he believed them to be loyal.

Colonel Walker felt good about the team he'd gathered. Martin had a military background, while Cardinal Leone, Father Pat, and Samuel Montour had unique expertise on the business of the "Gate." Elizabeth Shepherd would provide medical support, and though he wished it weren't so, her skills would undoubtedly be needed. Java, Israel, Jorge, and Dane, as a group, wielded a special power that could help Alex, should he need it. William and Francis—human weapons—could do more to save the world than anyone except Alex. As for Nathan, Walker couldn't force a man to abandon his sons. Then there was his beloved Amanda, who under no circumstances would let him go without her.

He'd gotten authorization for most of the civilians—especially the teens—to be included, since their presence could make or break the operation. He'd not yet been given approval for Amanda and Nathan, despite her up-to-date first-aid expertise, and suspected it might not come. As a failsafe on being able to include them, he'd purposely avoided any incoming communication on the matter, and soon it would be too late. In any case, all the civilians would remain at base camp, which might prove safer than remaining on the base. Walker still didn't know who was trustworthy beyond this small, unorthodox company, which was another reason he wanted Amanda with him.

It touched him deeply that all of them stood so calmly, so ready for a night that could easily result in someone's death. Even Israel looked focused and unafraid.

He'd assigned Francis to the second chopper that would carry Martin, Nathan, and the kids, while William would accompany him and the other adults in his Pave Hawk. He knew he needed to say something, but speechifying was never his forte.

"Sergeant Stern has no doubt alerted the woman and her people that we will arrive in the area by chopper. We have no intel on what kind of weaponry they might have installed within that mountain. Therefore, we will approach at a high altitude and scan the area with every satellite we can muster. We've already set up base camp as close to the target as seemed prudent, based on our scans and intel from the Edwards troops already on site. Any questions?"

Israel raised a hand.

"Yes, Israel?"

The boy looked embarrassed, indicating the helicopters. "These things got bathrooms?"

Walker almost smiled but fought it back. "No, son, they don't. If you need to go, go now."

Israel nodded and stepped back next to Java, who shook his head in amazement.

"I was just wondering," Israel whispered to Java. "Just in case."

Martin glanced around. "Is Davalos coming with us?"

"No," Walker replied with a quick glance at William. "He's already on route." Martin nodded, and Walker added, "Keep me up to date on that tracker." He didn't want to be explicit because he didn't want everyone to know about Alex at this point.

"Will do, Colonel."

"Alright, everyone, let's board."

***

Alex's chair shifted constantly under the bumpy terrain, despite his brakes being locked. The interior of the truck was hot and stuffy, and no one spoke. Stern kept his gun out and ready, as did the other two soldiers, but Alex was too smart to try anything in such close quarters, and he knew his friends were too.

He wasn't afraid for himself. Ms. G would never hurt him now, not when she needed him to open that gate. But the others? Who knew what she might do to them if he refused to help her? And if he did help her? Father Pat, the cardinal, and Uncle had said he'd be helping to destroy humanity. Just like in the prophecy. It wouldn't be Andy after all, but him that was the Great Destroyer. He couldn't let that happen. But how could he strop it and keep his friends alive?

He considered the real possibility that he might die that night. Or become possessed by those things that would come through the gate.

Such thoughts didn't scare him as much as they should have, but they did make him study the two people before him—Roy and Allison. He'd kissed them both and liked it. Roy loved him unconditionally. He knew that. He felt it; he'd seen it in action. Roy would die for him.

And Allison? She liked him and he liked her, but they barely knew each other. Maybe that's why kissing her didn't have the intensity of Roy's kiss, because Roy's was born of love, while hers was more about attraction. He wondered if they might fall in love if they had more time together. Growing up, he'd been such a loner he'd never really imagined having a girlfriend, and until Roy professed his love, had never considered having a boyfriend either. It was all much more complicated than it seemed on TV.

Roy caught him staring and raised his eyebrows as an unspoken question. Alex just smiled, knowing Roy would somehow get the message. And he did, it seemed, when he smiled back. Yes, they had a bond Alex would likely never have with any girl, or anyone else except maybe Andy, though his bond with his twin was born of nature, rather than love.

He had no idea how long they'd been traveling, but he figured at some point they would stop for a bathroom break. He recalled Colonel Walker saying it would take three or four hours to drive to that mountain. How soon after they arrived would he see Andy? Would his brother be wearing that evil smirk he'd displayed in the old ghost town when he'd tried to steal the Healer power? Alex shuddered just recalling the twisted lips, the smug self-assurance, the smarmy tone of voice his brother had employed.

Please, Andy, please don't abandon me!

***

Colonel Walker sat in the chopper with Amanda on one side and William on the other, looking like a typical American family unit. Across from them sat Leone, Father Pat, Montour, and Shepherd. No one spoke because everything had been said already and Walker didn't want any idle chatter in case the Pave Hawk was bugged. The thundering rotor noise would likely drown out any spoken words, but listening devices were too sophisticated these days to take a chance. He'd had both choppers carefully searched, but there were many places to hide something tiny, and if most of its components were silicon, the metal detectors wouldn't pick it up anyway.

No, the old-fashioned way was best. Once they arrived at base camp, he would update them on the plan, including Davalos's part in the mission. The irony of Stern turning traitor and Davalos staying fiercely loyal was not lost on him, but then anything involving human beings was never simple or clear cut. He was still troubled over Andy's rejection of Alex, wondering again how he could have so misread that boy.

He glanced down at William, who had his eyes glued to the cockpit behind Father Pat. Always alert and ready for action, William would pick up on treachery long before any of the rest of them did and would deal with it instantly. He eyed the boy's long hair, tied into its usual ponytail, and suddenly wondered why Liz hadn't been cutting it of late.

He felt a squeeze to his hand and turned to find Amanda gazing at him with a mixture of love and fear. He offered her a reassuring smile but refrained from hugging or kissing her in front of the others. He was in command. He needed to look strong and in control, and, frankly, he felt strong. He'd healed up quite nicely from his wound, and climbing up into the helicopter had been easy, even though he'd been grateful for William's strong hand assisting him up and inside.

There were so many unknowns, so many aspects of this night that could go terribly wrong. The holy men were prepared to, as they put it, "exorcise the mountain, if need be." He didn't understand that part and left it up to them. But keeping his people safe, especially the kids in the other chopper, and rescuing Alex and the other hostages, were his top priorities. There were no guarantees in war. He wished he knew which of the troops that would be with him that night were loyal, but he didn't. He believed the hand-picked pilots taking them to the base camp were on his side, but could he be certain? No.

He maintained a stoic expression, but inside, turmoil raged. He glanced at his watch. Another ninety minutes, give or take. The sun had set, and the darkened desert below revealed nothing of what might be happening. He'd heard nothing from Martin, so Alex must still be on route with no complications.

He squeezed Amanda's hand. That small gesture brought him great comfort.

✳✳✳

Java knew this whole mess was dangerous, but he couldn't help feeling a certain amount of elation flying in a real Air Force helicopter! He soaked in every detail of the interior and asked Martin, who seemed to know quite a bit, what everything was used for. There were parachutes, of course, which he already knew about, but there was also a grappling hook attached to a long coil of rope, which brought back memories of the one Roy had welded together so they could climb up to Ms. G's second story balcony. There were hand-held flare guns and weapons he and the others were forbidden to touch, let alone examine.

Izzy, Jorge, and Francis, also fascinated by the equipment—and the ride—sat across from him and Martin, while Dane and Roy's dad sat on Martin's left.

"You ain't worried about falling out, Izzy?" Java grinned at his best friend, seated so close to the opening.

Izzy shrugged and tugged on his safety belt. "I'm good. This is fun."

Francis, sitting in the seat closest to the open bay door leaned over to look down into the darkness below. "I wonder what it would feel like to jump out."

"I don't recommend it, kid," Martin said with a grimace. "Long way down."

Francis leaned back in. "I meant with one of these chute things," he replied, pointing at a folded parachute backpack hanging above his head.

"Oh," Martin said, sounding relieved. "In that case, it feels fantastic."

Java grinned, imaging himself dropping like a rock and then pulling that ripcord before drifting the rest of the way to earth. It looked so incredible on TV, but he wondered if he'd freeze up trying it for real.

He leaned forward and eyed Dane and Nathan, huddled close together. Both looked stressed out, and Java knew why.

"Roy's gonna be okay, Mr. Phillips," he blurted, not quite sure why. "Alex too."

The middle-aged man-made eye contact. "Thanks, Java. I hope you're right. I can't lose either of 'em. It'd kill me."

Java frowned, his heart suddenly pounding at the thought of losing either of his friends. It was possible, wasn't it? Ms. G might not need them alive after she got what she wanted.

Dane shifted position. "They better not touch my little brother," he vowed, "or I'll rip 'em apart with my bare hands."

"We got his back, Dane," Izzy said, his voice strong and firm. "Don't matter to us that he be gay and all."

Nathan's eyebrows rose in surprise. "He told you?"

Izzy shook his head. "No, it was that bitch, Ms. G. She be thinking we'd ditch him if we knew. That bitch don't know nothin' about real friendship."

For the first time, Nathan smiled. "No, she doesn't. I'm so grateful you all got my son's back."

"I never had loyal friends like you guys," Dane put in. "Roy's lucky. Alex too."

Java grinned and sat back, basking in the camaraderie they all felt for each other. Like Alex always said, they really were a family. Impulsively, he scooted over near the cockpit and stared wide-eyed at the massive T-shaped control console.

The two pilots sat in their chairs, staring out through the windshield at a dark, empty desert landscape. The pilot on the left used a joystick to turn the massive helicopter as needed, but mostly they just floated on air, it seemed, under the loud *whup whup whup* of the rotors.

The pilot on the right turned his head and noted Java. "'Sup, kid?"

Java couldn't take his eyes off the gazillion buttons and switches. "There be so many buttons and stuff. How long it take you guys to learn to fly this?"

The pilot chuckled from behind his motorcycle-style helmet. "Took me about two months. How 'bout you, Daron?"

The other pilot glanced over. "About the same, I think. Half of these buttons we never use unless the chopper's in trouble. She practically flies herself."

Java's heart swelled with excitement as he pictured himself in that cockpit, wearing the helmet and flying this bird.

"You wanna fly one of these someday?"

Java lit up like a beacon. "Oh, hell, yeah!"

"You sound like me at your age," the man said. "I joined up right outta high school."

Java saw through the face shield that the pilot was young, probably early twenties at most.

The man gazed out of his helmet shield at Java for a long moment, suddenly losing his smile and looking…Java wasn't sure. Sad, maybe? Or guilty?

"I seen the missiles, or whatever they be, mounted on the front," Java went on, his deep voice loud to compete with the rotor noise. "How do they fire?"

The pilot exchanged a significant look with the other pilot, as though asking permission. The pilot on the left nodded.

The first pilot eyed Java. "What's your name, kid?"

"Java."

The man nodded. "Good name. I'm Randy, and he's Daron." He pointed through the windshield. "See the colonel's chopper up ahead?"

Java nodded. It was dark outside, but the chopper was visible by its lights.

"If that was our target, I'd first flip these switches." He reached over to a small green screen and flipped two switches underneath it. The screen lit up like an old-school video game, displaying a moving circle with spokes converging in the center. The glowing outline of a helicopter drifted in and out of the circle.

"How does it know you got a chopper in sight?" Java leaned forward as much as he could for a better view.

"Satellite imagery creates the outline of our target," Randy replied. "Once the target is locked, we fire."

Java watched, mesmerized, as the chopper image moved around in the circle, but never quite hit dead center. He saw the real chopper through the windshield off in the distance ahead, but he had no sense of how far back they were. He returned his gaze to the small green monitor just as the outline of the helicopter landed at the point each spoke touched the center.

Then, to Java's horror, Randy pressed the red button.

CHAPTER ELEVEN

WE'LL SEE ABOUT THAT

COLONEL WALKER DIDN'T NEED A satellite map to know they were over Arizona. Despite the sun having set, he recognized some mesas and other landmarks by their outlines. So far, so good. William hadn't taken his eyes off the two pilots, but there had been not even the slightest hint of treachery on their part. Montour had his gaze fixed on the darkened landscape below. There wasn't much to be seen, though, as the moon was waning.

Cardinal Leone's head lolled back against the interior padding, drifting in and out of a doze, while Shepherd kept staring at the back of William's head, as though struggling to figure out how to resolve his inability to age. And, of course, Amanda sat at the colonel's side, cradling his hand in hers.

A warning alarm began beeping.

"Colonel, we have incoming!"

Walker whirled around to face Airman Peters. "From where?"

"The other chopper, sir," she replied, her tone tense but professional. "Executing evasive maneuvers."

Peters and her copilot swung the copter sharply to one side and pointed her nose toward the sky, accelerating up and away from the incoming missile, at the same time releasing a bright flare intended to confuse the missile.

Amanda gasped and released Walker's hand as he made eye contact with William. "Weapon."

As Liz, Leone, and Montour became aware of the impending peril, William leaped to his feet and slipped a noose around both ankles. The noose was attached to a thick rope. Before anyone could react, he leapt from the open side of the copter and vanished from view.

***

"Martin!" Java screamed as loud as he could, despite Martin being only a few feet away. The big man had no sooner stuck his head into the cockpit beside Java when Randy pulled out a handgun and aimed it at them both.

"I'll shoot the kid if you try anything," he said, the muzzle of the gun pointed squarely at Java's head.

"The hell are you doing?" Martin was livid, the veins in his forehead pulsing as he glowered at the two pilots.

"Carrying out the lady's wishes," Daron explained as he turned the chopper to follow the colonel's now wildly zig-zagging helicopter.

Izzy, Jorge, and Nathan had gathered behind Java and must've spotted the gun because Izzy exclaimed, "Oh, shit!"

Java ignored him, focused on the missile streaking through the night sky straight at the colonel's copter. It glowed from the rear and was easy to follow. Plus, there were bright lights dropping from the helicopter that lit up the night sky. Java spotted something fall—no, jump—from the other helicopter. He squinted into the night and gasped. It was William! He had both arms pressed against his sides and dove like a bird straight for the incoming missile.

"The hell?" Daron leaned toward the windshield in surprise. Randy did the same, and Java was tempted to make a grab for the gun, but Martin nudged his arm and shook his head. The weapon was still aimed right at them, and any bullet fired in such close quarters would kill someone.

Java stared wide-eyed through the windshield just as William landed on top of the missile and wrapped both arms around its girth. Java's heart pounded with disbelief as the young boy swung the missile off its course and pointed it down toward the ground. He released his grip on the streaking projectile and it continued its new course away from Colonel Walker's helicopter. At that point, William's entire body jerked to a stop, and he seemed to float in midair before Java realized he had a rope tied to his ankles that kept him tethered to the colonel's chopper. Astonished, he watched as someone aboard the other Pave Hawk began reeling the boy back in. That's when Java heard the animal growl behind him, and all hell broke loose.

***

Father Pat, stunned by what had just occurred, worked the winch that had begun hauling William back up into the helicopter after his heroic deflecting of the missile. The priest would never have believed such a thing was possible, but this kid, artificially created in a laboratory, was truly superhuman. But he was also kind and generous, the human traits he sought to foster in everyone. How was such a thing possible?

An explosion below lit up the night sky in glowing orange and the chopper shook from the concussion.

"You still have him, Father?" Colonel Walker pushed his way to Father Pat's side and stuck his head out the opening. He sighed with relief to see William, who'd righted himself and now grasped the rope with both hands while the end remained wrapped around his ankles. The boy's ponytail had come undone and his blond hair whipped around his face and head with wild abandon.

"He can handle the winch, Bryan," Amanda said, her voice no-nonsense and firm, as she joined her husband and glanced without fear at the dangling boy.

The colonel made no move to assist, but Father Pat didn't need any help. The winch operated itself. He'd merely need to help the boy into the copter when he was close enough, if this particular boy needed any help, of course, which he doubted.

"Airman Peters, any radio contact with the other chopper?" Colonel Walker had turned away to face the cockpit, shouting above the heavy rotor noise.

"Negative, sir," came Peters' voice from behind the wall separating the cabin from the cockpit. "There seems to be a struggle going on over there. The Hawk is becoming unstable."

Father Pat caught the look of trepidation on the colonel's weathered face and felt fear clutching at his soul. The other kids were over there.

Please, God, let them be safe!

***

"Holy shit, it's a werewolf!"

Izzy's terrified exclamation was all Java heard before something small leaped over his head, using his shoulders as a springboard as it tore into Randy and sent his gun flying.

Martin reached out and snatched the gun from the air even as Daron made a lunge for it, releasing the throttle and sending the helicopter into a dive.

Java grabbed on to the seat to keep from being thrown forward and watched in open-mouthed horror as the…yes, it looked like a real werewolf, clawed at Randy's face and then flung open the door to the airman's right. The door flew open, and warm air poured into the cockpit with a loud whooshing sound, but Randy remained belted into his seat. Within seconds, the werewolf had ripped through the restraining straps with long, razor-sharp teeth and shoved Randy hard out the open door. With a scream of anguish, the young airman tumbled out into space and vanished from Java's line of sight, his scream fading quickly in the driving wind.

Martin, to Java's surprise, gazed at the werewolf as though he'd known it would show up. "Wolfboy, don't kill this one," he said, indicating the obviously terrified Daron, who'd righted the helicopter after its sudden dive. "I need him to fly the Hawk."

Java was stunned to see the furious werewolf stop in the action of grabbing for the cowering Daron. It pulled back its clawed, hairy hands and sat in Randy's now empty seat, calm and panting like a dog. Java finally realized it wore clothes that looked familiar, but before he could say anything more, the creature writhed and twisted in obvious pain.

"Martin, what's goin' on?" His voice came out raspy with fear.

"Just watch," Martin replied, the gun in his hand now aimed squarely at Daron. "You, fly this bird and don't try anything or Wolfboy'll tear you to pieces!"

Face twisted with horror, Daron kept a tight hold on the throttle, leveling it out as Java stared in open-mouthed disbelief at the creature twisting with pain in the co-pilot's chair.

"He's changing back!" Izzy's voice rang out over the rotor noise, but Java was too mesmerized to ask what his friend meant.

Then, to his utter astonishment, the creature's thick black fur sunk into the skin and the claws vanished, leaving small fingers in their place. Within moments, sitting in that seat where seconds earlier had been a werewolf straight out of the movies was…Francis!

"Holy shit," he mumbled, and then he heard Izzy behind him repeat the same expression of disbelief, only his was louder.

"Thank you, Francis," Martin said calmly as the young boy sat up straight in the seat and rapidly pulled himself together.

All the wolf hair was gone, along with the sharp fangs and nails. Java couldn't believe it.

Martin caught his eye and offered a reassuring smile. "He's a special kid, like William, but I'll explain later. Francis, I need that seat."

The boy, looking like his usual self now, stood up. "Yes, Martin." He crawled over the back of the leather seat and squeezed in beside Java, who found himself flinching away in fear as Martin, gun still trained on Daron, plopped into the empty seat.

"Call the other chopper," Martin ordered, the gun aimed at Daron's chest. "Is this a dedicated channel?"

The frightened pilot nodded.

"Good. Let me do the talking." He reached for the headset in front of his seat and placed it over his ears while Daron flipped some switches on the massive dashboard.

As Martin began making his report to Colonel Walker, Java found himself staring at Francis. The boy looked small and innocent, like he always did, shaggy black hair partially covering his hazel eyes.

He felt a hand grip his shoulder like a vise and turned to find Izzy gazing at him with wide, terrified eyes. "Java, what is that thing?"

"Relax, Israel," Nathan said as he inched closer to study the boy with wonder. "He just saved our lives." He faced Francis with a look of gratitude on his ruddy face. "Thank you, son."

Java faced the younger boy, who looked hurt by what Izzy had said, but happy about Nathan's affirmation.

"I am not just Francis," the boy said quietly, eyeing them all. "I am Wolfboy, and I will protect you."

***

Father Pat sat beside William, who'd clambered back up into the cabin with ease and untied the rope around his ankles, eyeing the men staring at him in awe, all except the colonel who'd stuck his head into the cockpit to communicate with Martin in the other chopper.

William had jumped from a moving helicopter, grabbed on to a speeding missile, redirected the missile into the ground where it exploded without harming anyone, and then crawled back into the copter, looking as calm as though he'd just finished playing a game of Go Fish. Alex had assured Father Pat that he'd felt the same soul in William as he had in every other person he'd healed. That information had filled the priest with confusion as to the very nature of creation. This boy before him was a child of God just as Alex was, but he was so much more than every other human in the world that it was almost too much to comprehend.

Dr. Shepherd seemed unfazed by what William had just accomplished, but she offered to examine him for injuries.

That only brought out an amused smile. "You know I'm not hurt, Dr. Shepherd."

She returned the smile in an easy kind of way, indicating the long-standing relationship they had forged. "I know. You never cease to amaze me."

That generated a broad, almost angelic smile from William, who was quite a striking child, Father Pat observed, never having studied the boy's features before this moment. If William weren't some kind of super boy, he could easily be on television. But what a waste that would be when this boy was so very much more than the sum of his looks.

The colonel pulled back into the cabin and faced them all.

"Well, Colonel?" Leone was leaning forward, thick arms planted across his knees.

"Martin has everything under control over there." He studied William with a look Father Pat had so often seen at his parish—the look of a parent who's proud of his son. "William, I don't know what we'd do without you."

It might have been the inconsistent lighting within the moving helicopter, but Father Pat was almost certain he noticed red blooming on the boy's cheeks.

"You're welcome, sir."

The colonel faced Dr. Shepherd and offered a small smile. "Looks like you were successful with Francis, Liz. That adrenaline spike idea worked. He morphed into Wolfboy long enough to disarm Airman Malone and throw him out of the chopper."

Her smile vanished. "Oh, no."

The colonel didn't look upset. "His control was excellent, Martin said, and he morphed back into Francis the moment the situation was under control. We're all grateful for your hard work with him."

She nodded but glanced over at William and held the boy's gaze a long moment. "I haven't given up on you, William."

"Thank you." William offered nothing more than that, but Father Pat heard something in those two words, an underlying sense of urgency he didn't understand.

Cardinal Leone cleared his throat. "Are we safe now, Colonel, do you think?"

The colonel wore an expression Father Pat suspected he hated—uncertainty. "I think for the moment, yes. Our radar will detect any weaponry on the ground that might attempt to target either chopper, so we should arrive safely to base camp." He glanced at his heavy-looking wristwatch. "We'll be landing in an hour." He studied Father Pat and the other two men. "Are you prepared for the exorcism portion of our attack?"

Leone and Montour exchanged looks with Father Pat, who nodded.

"Father Pat has been given dispensation by the Vatican to assist me in what I predict could be a mass exorcism, if the gate should successfully open."

Samuel fixed his sharp brown eyes on the colonel. "I am primarily here as someone who might be able to connect with Andy, should the opportunity arise. I will attempt such communication when the time feels right."

The colonel nodded and faced his wife. She didn't look as frightened as Father Pat felt, but he supposed she had faced other difficult threats over the years as the wife of a military man.

"I do wish Alex had been able to fully heal you, Bryan," she said quietly.

"I'll be fine," he assured her. "You know it takes more than a bullet to bring me down."

She chuckled.

***

Allison had dozed off, resting against her dad's solid and comforting form, and when she awoke, she had no idea how long she'd been out. Both Roy and Alex gazed at her, but each wore a different expression on his face, making Allison wonder what they were thinking. She sat up and stretched, noting Sergeant Stern still pointing his gun steadfastly in their direction. She glared at him and then eyed her father, who looked calm and collected—odd given the circumstances.

He gave her hand a slight squeeze and studied Stern as though contemplating a business deal. "How long have you been planning to betray the colonel?"

Stern, seemingly lost in thought, focused on the question a moment before answering. He shifted his body position, but not enough for any of them to make a grab for the gun. "I never had any intention of betraying Colonel Walker. I have deep admiration for the man. It just so happened that the Healer"—he glanced a split-second at the silent Alex— "ended up at Groom Lake. My loyalty to our lady goes back to my teen years, so she's more important than anyone."

Shaw wore the poker face he always adopted when hustling a deal. "And the extensive background checks to be stationed at Groom Lake didn't uncover this other, more important allegiance?"

"Freedom of religion is guaranteed by the Constitution, Mr. Shaw," Stern replied with a shrug. "They never even asked."

Shaw nodded. "No, I suppose they wouldn't." He paused, shifting his weight to a more comfortable sitting position. "And you really think this plan to destabilize the world is a good one? You seem much too smart for that, Sergeant."

"This planet is doomed, Mr. Shaw, unless we act now. Look at the damage extreme political ideology has done just in the past few years. While it's true the Healer can bring out the best qualities of human nature, he's only one person, and there are many more humans who choose self-centeredness over altruism. Tonight, we'll push that majority over the edge, and they will wipe out the so-called 'kind' humans. After that, we remake the world under our control, with the lady as absolute ruler."

Allison flinched with disgust at the man's words, but her dad didn't even react. He said, "Hitler, Stalin, Mao, Castro, the ayatollahs of Iran, Vladimir Putin. I've heard it all. Take over the world. Establish a supreme, one-world order. Has it worked yet?"

Stern shifted with discomfort. "No, but they didn't have the lady."

"Oh, but they did," Shaw replied, sounding rather smug. "I did some research. Seems she was an advisor to most of these dictators, for all the good it did her or them. The problem with your plan, just like theirs, is that far too many people like making their own choices. I admit, many are sheep and follow the crowd or the media or irrational government mandates. But there are enough who will always resist, and I don't believe you can eliminate them in one fell swoop, as you intend."

Stern smiled, and Allison shivered because his expression was smugness mixed with nastiness. "We'll see, Mr. Shaw, once the gate is opened."

Shaw frowned then, as though he'd forgotten that detail. Allison still didn't quite believe all that stuff about demons and a different dimension, but she could tell Stern did, and that scared her.

"You forget something, Sergeant," Alex said from his corner of the truck.

"And what is that?"

"I'm the only one who can open that gate," Alex replied, his voice deep and resolute. "And I ain't going to."

Stern lost his smirk, his pinched face clouding over with the first hint of concern. He tried to stare Alex down, but Alex gazed across at him with such intensity even Allison had to look away.

Stern broke eye contact, fixing the gun steadily on Allison. "We'll see about that."

***

Andy stood at the cave entrance staring out at the darkness that didn't fully obscure the influx of US soldiers into the surrounding desert. She watched him from a short distance away, but he made not the slightest movement.

"I know you're there, Teacher," he said quietly, without turning his head.

Smiling at his intuitiveness, she approached and stood beside him, studying the troop movements below.

"How is it we can see out, but they cannot see in?" He still did not look at her.

She reached up and touched what looked like empty air. "This is the supernatural version of a two-way mirror. Only those loyal to our cause may see it or enter. For hundreds of years, it has prevented enemies and greedy gold-seekers from finding these caverns. The gate has been protected, as was ordained by those who came before me."

"I see." He said nothing more. Just stared out into the dark night for another long moment. "How will my brother get past these soldiers?"

"I have it all arranged," she replied with her usual confidence. "Are you ready?"

"Of course, Teacher," he replied without hesitation. Finally, he turned to face her, his expression impassive, his blue eyes opaque. "When you have no more use for my brother, may I be the one to kill him?"

Her slim eyebrows rose in surprise. "What is the reason behind your request?"

"I'm tired of being second to him in everything. Before he dies, I will once more suck him dry of power, only this time I will finish the job."

She raised her long, slender fingers and seductively caressed his cheek, but he did not react. His intense blue eyes only held the question he'd asked.

"Yes, Andy, you may kill your brother. And if there is anything left of Roy after Kurt is finished, you may kill him, as well. Will that please you?"

"Yes, Teacher, very much.

Had his mouth twitched when she'd mentioned Roy? Possibly, but it no longer mattered. At midnight, they will have all outlived their usefulness and will be sacrificed. Andy didn't know it yet, but once his tasks were completed, he would be the final offering to her master.

CHAPTER TWELVE

FOR VICTORY

Passing around the Superstition Mountain range at what Colonel Walker hoped was a safe altitude, he understood why it was such a popular hiking location. Despite the darkness, he could make out standing stones in rows that looked like a monolith graveyard, with the mountain range a short distance behind. The highest peak rose to a point, as though leading the way to Heaven itself, while the rest of the range had a fortress-like quality to it, resembling the battlements of an ancient castle built right into the mountains—a citadel, almost. The rocks seemed to glow red in the darkness, and natural trails that meandered around the range to the top looked like quiescent rattlesnakes. Shrubs and small trees dotted the landscape around the range, but it was giant three-armed cacti that dominated the vegetation, reaching for the sky in supplication.

The Pentagon had closed the park days ago, so no tourists had come anywhere near, but he spotted troop lanterns scattered about the terrain on both sides of the mountain range as his helicopter swung around to reconnoiter the area. The troop transport vehicles were all parked a distance away at the base camp, and he saw the large trucks Davalos had brought with him that were the size of moving vans. Tents and folding tables had been set up throughout the base camp, and he spotted General Lewis at once, lit by one of the arc lamps. Lewis stood beside a large table with several men surrounding him.

Once his Pave Hawk landed, Walker met at once with the general, while Airman Peters showed the civilians where they should wait. William clearly wanted to stay by his side, but Walker gave him a nod to assure him he would be safe. He found it interesting that William didn't trust

Lewis, but better to be alert to all possibilities than be caught up short as he'd been with Stern.

He walked between tents with as much confidence as he could muster, despite the residual tightness in his upper chest and a slight shortness of breath, stopping at the command table where Lewis stood with four soldiers. Before them was spread a topographical map of the area and several tablets displaying live satellite images of the base and the mountain range.

"General." He saluted.

"Colonel." Lewis returned the salute, turning to his men. "You have your orders. Dismissed."

The four of them saluted and moved off among the tents.

"I see Sergeant Stern relayed my departure to you," Lewis began in his typically gruff voice. He was shorter than Colonel Walker, but broad-shouldered and intimidating with a rough, swarthy complexion and beady brown eyes that could stare down even the most hardcore enemy.

Walker grimaced. "No, sir, he did not. Stern is an enemy agent, loyal to the woman and her cult."

The general's thick, graying eyebrows shot up in surprise, but he maintained a stoic attitude. "Give me your full report, Colonel."

Walker filled him in on Stern kidnapping Alex and the others, trying to blow him up in the hangar, and the attack by the turncoat pilots from the second chopper. Lewis listened intently but did not ask any questions until Walker finished his report.

Lewis looked genuinely shocked by the colonel's news. "I trusted that man."

"So did I. For over five years."

The general nodded. "You say he's on his way in a transport vehicle?"

"Yes, sir."

Lewis paused, as though unable or unwilling to say something more. He cleared his throat. "The Pentagon has ordered me to turn over command of this operation to you, Colonel Walker, given your intimate knowledge of the key players and your experience in dealing with them. I will act in a field capacity managing the troops surrounding the mountain."

Walker was stunned but forced himself not to display any emotion.

He waited for the general to continue, listening to the sounds of troop movements preparing for battle.

"There is one caveat," the general continued, making direct eye contact with Walker. "If this operation goes south and it appears the other side might do what they've threatened, I will order an airstrike on the mountain and destroy it."

Walker knew better than to argue. "Yes, sir, I understand. Let's hope it won't come to that."

"You have a plan, I presume?"

"Yes, sir, I do, but much of it is speculative as we don't know exactly what the other side has planned."

"Let me hear the particulars."

Walker thought of William and his ability to sense who to trust and who not to, so he provided a broader outline of his plan—minus key points he would later share with his core team—out of an abundance of caution.

The general listened with his usual attentiveness and seemed satisfied with Walker's proposals. "It's your show, Colonel, as I already told you. I'm the backup guy this round. But bear in mind, I will not hesitate to launch the attack. I'm going out to examine my troop positions. Good luck." He raised his hand and snapped off a crisp salute, which Walker promptly returned.

"Thank you, General."

He watched as the thick man strutted away toward the mountains and then took charge at once, establishing camp perimeters, protocols, and surveillance teams that would alert him the moment any transport vehicle veered off course. Of course, Martin was still monitoring the tracker in Alex's foot, so they'd know exactly where Stern stopped and the precise spot he and the others entered the mountain. Finding that entrance was key to the success of the operation.

He radioed Davalos and then, feeling fatigued from all the standing, he sat at a makeshift folding table with a topographical map of the area spread out before him. After several minutes, he glanced up as Davalos approached with Airman Peters.

"Here she is, Colonel." Davalos, dressed in camo gear, looked weary after his long trek across the desert towing his unorthodox team of combatants. But then, this was his chance to prove his theories correct, that his "soldiers" were more effective in battle than enlisted men and women.

"Thank you, Mark. Could you gather up our core team while I brief Peters?"

"Yes, sir." Davalos hurried off between makeshift tents and folding tables.

"How may I assist you, Colonel?"

Walker studied Peters, who stood at attention, her camos in perfect order, her blonde hair tied up and off her face. She was attractive, and many of the young men on base had shown their obvious interest. But she'd rebuffed them all, to the best of his knowledge, preferring not to mix business with pleasure. And she was up for any assignment, exactly what he needed.

"At ease, Airman."

She relaxed only a bit, her blue eyes focused on him, awaiting her orders.

"You've been at the base for six years, rising up the ranks steadily and efficiently. You've successfully completed several major rescue operations in the mountains. The other airmen respect your no-nonsense approach to task completion. You're fit and strong. I've witnessed that in the fitness center on multiple occasions." He paused to gauge her reaction. She looked nonplussed, as always.

"Yes, sir."

"Your opinion of Sergeant Stern?"

She flinched, offering a slight grimace of disgust. "He is a traitor. Sir."

He nodded, certain he'd chosen wisely. "His defection has left a hole in my staff, and I'd like you to fill it."

She finally reacted, her mouth dropping open in shocked surprise. Just as quickly, she regained her aplomb. "I'm not a staff sergeant, sir," she replied, her voice even and assured.

He waved that away. "You're a senior airman at the top of your game, Peters. After this is over, assuming we all survive, you can complete Airmen Leadership School for your promotion. Right now, I need someone I can trust who will follow my orders to the letter. Are you that person?"

She didn't hesitate. "Yes, sir, I am."

"Good. Sit here with me and go over these coordinates. We must know every inch of this topography before the operation begins."

He glanced up at the sky. The waning moon hung high in the night sky, surrounded by millions of twinkling lights. She pulled up a chair and sat beside him. He held up a large tablet for her to study.

"Live satellite feed of this entire area," he explained as she squinted to examine the image on screen. "We don't yet know where they will take Alex, but we need to be able to move in any direction at a moment's notice."

She looked up and studied his face. "The general is positioning the troops at this time."

"Yes."

"Permission to speak freely, sir?"

"Of course. That's why you're my second in command."

"Based on the general's rhetoric back at the base, I'd be concerned that he might act before it's certain you have failed."

He nodded. "I agree, which is why we must succeed."

Hearing a commotion behind him, one loud male voice exclaiming that he was "starving," Walker turned on his chair to welcome Davalos and the rest of the team, including the always energic Israel, whose voice had so punctuated the warm desert air. He couldn't help but smile.

***

Alex's stomach rumbled again. He'd only been given a few drinks of water from an old canteen since leaving the base and nothing to eat. He didn't know how long the truck had been traveling, but it had been hours, for sure. Allison had drifted off to sleep again, her head firmly lodged against her father's chest, his arm securely wrapped around her shoulders.

He felt Roy staring at him and glanced over. His best friend looked exhausted and hungry, but there remained that fire in his brown eyes that wouldn't be quenched. Like himself, Roy seemed to have had enough with the kidnappings and threats. Between the two of them, he knew, they would put a major dent in Ms. G's evil plans.

Somehow.

The truck suddenly veered to the left and the ride became even bumpier. Shaw stared at Stern with an unreadable expression. "Sounds like we're approaching the destination."

Stern looked surprised, but his wan face refused to give away anything of his thoughts. "What makes you think that?"

"I studied the terrain around this area. We're approaching a mountain."

Stern's eyes widened with admiration. "That's correct. We'll be going the rest of the way on foot."

As though to emphasize his words, the truck reduced its speed and rolled to a bumpy halt, nearly knocking Roy right into Alex's chair.

Allison woke with a start and looked around. "What happened?"

"We have arrived," Stern replied, the gun still raised and ready to fire. He stood and twisted his upper body to get out the kinks. "Before departing the vehicle…" He waved a hand at one of the other airmen.

The airman holstered his gun and picked up a handheld device from the floor that looked like a metal detector. He turned the device on and waved it around and over every inch of Alex's body.

"What are you doing?" Shaw's voice was sharp, like a protective parent.

Stern smirked. "Checking for a tracking device, obviously."

Alex held his breath, waiting. In moments, the wand beeped and glowed red as it passed over his foot.

The airman faced Stern.

"Remove his shoe and sock," the sergeant intoned, as though playing a child's game that had such an easy solution.

The airman reached for Alex's foot, but Alex brushed it away. "I can do it myself." He slipped off his sneaker and bent forward to slide off the sock.

The airman lifted his foot and examined it with a small flashlight. "Found it, Sergeant, not so cleverly hidden under flesh-colored tape."

Stern clucked and eyed Shaw. "So obvious, Mr. Shaw." He faced the airman. "Remove it and leave it here in the truck. The rest of you, it's time to start walking." He aimed the gun at Shaw. "You may exit the vehicle first, Mr. Shaw."

Alex glared at the airman, who pulled off the taped tracking device and stuck it to the back wall of the truck. He only hoped the device inside his foot would lead Colonel Walker to his location.

Shaw exchanged a reassuring look with Allison before rising stiffly to his feet. Allison glanced with fear at Alex, but he could offer her no reassurance. His mind was on the impending meeting with Ms. G.

And Andy.

***

Colonel Walker sat beside Peters on one side of the tactical table, as he'd dubbed it. The surrounding area glowed with bright LED lights on three-legged stands interspersed throughout the camp. On the other side of the table, his team of civilians sat in small pods. Java held court over Israel and Jorge, while Martin had been assigned to oversee Nathan and Dane, who would take orders from him. Cardinal Leone oversaw the exorcist squad that included Father Pat and Samuel Montour. Amanda and Elizabeth were teamed up to provide medical support should there be injuries. Walker had medical personnel on site, and they'd been placed under Elizabeth's direct supervision. Davalos oversaw his hybrid creatures, which he'd prepped for an invasion of the mountain or a battle in the desert should that woman send out troops of her own. The two genetically engineered boys, William and Francis, were the final team, dressed in black from head to toe, unaffected by the warm temperature, and standing beside William's motorcycle.

This wasn't the ideal core team he would've chosen, but with no certainty as to the loyalty of any service man or woman present—other than Peters—Walker would take no more chances. He'd almost been assassinated twice in the same day by his own troops. He did not want the third time to be the charm.

He glanced at the red V Jorge had handed him on a rumpled scrap of paper, and then studied his "troops." He believed their plan, discussed and tweaked by the others, had a strong chance of success. The unknowns of what lay within that mountain behind him could easily unravel what would soon be set in motion, but he had faith in Alex and Roy, who'd pledged to do their part prior to their kidnapping. And Shaw? He knew the basics of their plans and would, Walker believed, do his best to disrupt enemy electronics from within. He glanced at his wristwatch.

"It's now 2100 hours. Any questions?"

Naturally, Israel thrust his arm into the air like he'd won a gold medal.

"Yes, Israel?"

The boy lowered his arm and thrust a thumb at Java. "Do I really gotta take orders from this fool?"

Java squinted his eyes and glowered.

Walker bit back a smile. "In the absence of any adults from this group, yes."

Israel glared right back at Java, like they were about to exchange blows. Then Israel cackled and shoved the bigger boy. "Just messin' with you, fool."

Java shook his head and made eye contact with the colonel as if to say, "I really gotta work with him?"

"Java," Walker said, his tone deadly serious, "remember your orders out there. No unnecessary chances, whatever happens. You job is to save lives, not take them."

Java stood and thrust out his chest. He pressed his straightened hand against his forehead. "Yes, sir!"

Walker returned the salute and Java reseated himself.

"Colonel, I have them!"

Walker swiveled his head around to Peters, who gazed intently at one of the tablet screens. Outlines of trucks heading into base camp filled the screen, but one truck had veered off toward the base of the mountain.

Peters looked up and made eye contact. "They're exiting the vehicle, sir."

Walker pointed at William and Francis. "Go."

Without hesitation, William leaped onto the motorcycle and Francis hopped onto the back of the seat. He'd no sooner wrapped his arms around William than the older boy gunned the engine and the motorcycle took off through the camp, kicking up sand and dust and turning the heads of troops still setting up stations.

Walker studied the screen, pointing to an unmoving red dot. "They found the tracking device and removed it. Peters, activate the second tracker."

She tapped some keys on the laptop, and a second red dot appeared, blinking as it moved away from the first one.

"Between the tracker, William, and Francis, we'll know where they enter that mountain." Walker turned to the others. They all looked sober, fearful, and determined. Even Jorge—the quiet kid who'd lost his best friend in the attack in the underground tunnels at the base—even he was ready for whatever the future may hold.

Walker held up the red V high enough for all to see. "For victory."

CHAPTER THIRTEEN

NO ONE SUMMONS ME

WILLIAM'S KEEN NIGHT VISION EASILY spotted the parked truck at the base of the peak. The passengers had already debarked, but Alex's wheelchair was easy to spot as it rolled along the rocky terrain. He stopped the cycle and waited.

William made out the tall, lanky figure of Roy, the broad-shouldered Shaw, and the long-haired Allison, and two figures he did not know, likely other traitorous airmen. Sergeant Stern brought up the rear, pointing a handgun at them, urging them forward. Despite the distance, William heard the exchange.

Alex stared at the sheer wall of rock before him and sneered. "We're supposed to go up that rock? Yeah, right."

Stern chuckled and waved the gun again. "Not up, through." Alex stared at him a long moment, but Stern only barked, "Move. Or my men will carry you."

That seemed to strike Alex's pride and he angrily pushed himself toward the rock face, the others silently following.

William and Francis hurried forward on foot to get a better view. As far as William could make out, there was nothing resembling an entrance, not even a crack in the mountainside. He and Francis skittered forward as close as they dared, darting behind tall extrusions of rock before hunkering down behind a large boulder thirty yards away from Alex and the others.

William stared in stunned amazement as the solid wall of rock seemed to shimmer, and then an opening appeared. Standing within an enormous cavern, backlit like a monster, was Andy.

***

Alex gasped when the wall shimmered and vanished, but his mouth fell open when he saw who was standing inside a gigantic cave.

"Andy!"

Andy looked neither pleased nor unhappy to see him. "Hello, Big Brother." His monotone voice gave away nothing.

Roy surged forward to Alex's side, clenching and unclenching his fists. "You better hope I don't get my hands around your neck, Andy!"

Andy didn't react.

"Chill, Roy," Alex said, his tone calmer than he'd have imagined.

"He almost killed you, Alex!"

Roy was livid, as mad as Alex had ever seen him.

"But he didn't."

Roy stared at him like he was crazy.

From behind them, Alex heard Stern snap, "Inside. All of you."

Without hesitation, Alex wheeled himself forward. As he passed through the shimmering barrier, he felt a chill ripple through him. Then he was on the other side and the sensation vanished. Roy followed and then the others. Once everyone stood within the high-ceilinged cavern, the shimmering barrier vanished and once more became a solid rock wall.

***

William pelted up the rocky slope, Francis keeping pace at his side. He stopped before the rock wall and reached out with both hands. Solid. He felt around for any indication of the shimmering barrier he'd seen. Nothing. He and Francis exchanged a mystified look.

"How you think they got inside, William?"

William furrowed his brow in thought. The entrance had been there moments ago, at this very spot. Therefore, there must be a way to trigger the change and allow people inside. Unfortunately, he couldn't imagine what it was since no one on the outside had done anything.

Wait a minute! Maybe it must be opened from inside! That would explain why Andy was there to greet them.

William unclipped his walkie-talkie and radioed Colonel Walker.

***

Walker was in the process of dispersing his team when William's call came through. He listened, not surprised at the news. "Whatever that barrier is, it cut off the signal from Alex's tracker, probably the second it closed."

"What are your orders, sir?" came William's voice over the walkie.

"Study the area, Weapon, search for any possible way into that mountain. I'll be in touch."

"I take it they found the entrance?" Martin gazed at him like the soldier he once was, with the conviction that he already knew the answer.

"Yes, but it doesn't make sense." He explained to them all how the rock face shimmered into clarity and allowed the group to pass through before resuming its former hardness, cutting off Alex's tracker. Everyone listened in amazement, except for Cardinal Leone. The rotund man nodded his head and took on a faraway expression.

"You know something, Cardinal?" Walker eyed him with hope.

The short man shook his head, making his cheeks wobble beneath the arc lights overhead. "But it makes a sort of perverse sense. That mountain houses one of the largest gates on the planet and that woman clearly has supernatural powers. My best guess is she's hidden the cave entrance all these years with an otherworldly façade, one that to us is quite real and impenetrable."

Dane slowly stood to his full height, still using the cane for support. "So how do we get inside?"

Leone faced Walker again. "What was William's assessment of how they entered?"

"He thinks, because Andy was right there in the cavern, that the entrance can only be opened by someone within."

"And I suspect," the cardinal went on, stroking his gray beard stubble with one chubby finger, "that whoever is inside must invite newcomers in or else they cannot enter."

Israel piped up with excitement. "Like vampires, right? They gotta be invited into your house."

Java glared at him, but Leone did not appear the least bit annoyed by the interruption. "Precisely, Israel."

"But no one in there will let us in," Nathan put in, "'cept maybe Roy or Alex if they got the chance."

Walker exchanged a look with Davalos, who calmly stood by awaiting his orders. "We're going to stick to our plan. I'll take my group up to that entrance. Some men will bring explosives. We know the cave entrance is there, just hidden."

"I wouldn't place much hope in your explosives versus her power, Colonel," Leone intoned gravely.

"Maybe not, but I need to try. You head up to your vantage point. Radio when you need the chopper."

"Yes, Colonel," Leone said, glancing at Montour beside him.

Walker faced Elizabeth and Amanda. "You remain here at base camp and prepare for casualties. We don't know what will go down, so be prepared for anything."

Elizabeth nodded, but a terrified Amanda grabbed Walker and pulled him into a passionate kiss. Embarrassed, he pulled back and glanced sheepishly at the others. Leone was beaming and the others looked touched, rather than self-conscious.

Clearing his throat, the colonel said, "Martin, you, Dane, and Nathan have your assignment. Find out what you can, but observe only, and please, don't get caught." He saluted.

The three men returned the salute and set off away from base camp toward the troop positions surrounding the mountain. As Martin passed Elizabeth, he stopped and hesitated a moment before turning and pulling her into a kiss every bit as passionate as Amanda had given to Walker. She was gasping when he released her.

"Stay safe," he told the flabbergasted doctor before trotting after the others into the darkness.

She met Walker's gaze and blushed, but he nodded his approval. Then he faced Leone. "Can any of you three drive a jeep?"

Leone and Father Pat exchanged a look that clearly indicated they could not.

Montour stepped forward. "I can, Colonel. No problem."

"Very well. Good luck to you."

They nodded agreement and wandered off to their tent to retrieve their tools of the exorcism trade.

He turned to Davalos. "Your team ready, Mark?"

The tall man nodded. He looked quite unlike the smug, pompous bureaucrat he'd been less than two weeks ago, always decked out in a suit and tie. Now he wore military fatigues and hadn't even bothered to style his hair, which sat on his head looking like a nesting animal.

"They know not to kill anyone, just disarm and disable," Davalos said, his voice firm with resolve.

"Good. We don't know what will happen to these men surrounding the mountain. If that woman manages to gain control of them, we don't want them killed. I confess, Mark, that I never had much faith in your project. I thought it crazy and your creatures unpredictable."

"And now?"

"I've seen that they can be managed. And given that they aren't human, they can't be controlled by her or her entities."

Davalos momentarily sported the smugness of old. "I confess, Colonel, I never expected them to be used for this purpose. I always envisioned them for riot control and perhaps leading a ground invasion on foreign soil." The smug look faded. "I've come to like these creatures, something I never thought possible. William was right. They're like pets, almost, and fiercely loyal to those who care for them."

"Just remember not to deploy them unless a battle breaks out," Walker reiterated. "Even then, make sure they know whom to disarm."

"Of course. Shall I get them into position?"

"Yes."

Davalos turned to walk away.

"And Mark?"

Davalos turned back to face him.

"Take care of yourself."

"I will, Colonel. Best success on your end." He strode off into the darkness.

Walker studied his tactical team. Peters was locked and loaded, as the saying went, ready for anything, so he looked over the three boys before him. They had been boys when he'd first met them, but somewhere along the way, they'd inched much closer to being men. Even Israel's motor mouth seemed to have run out of gas. Java was still the most solid, but Walker felt in his gut that the others would not crumble under pressure either.

"I don't want any unnecessary heroics from you boys," he announced, his tone as serious as he could muster. "If you can save lives, do it, but take no risky chances. If I'm in any way incapacitated, Peters is in command, and you will take orders from her. Are we clear?"

All three shouted, "Yes, sir!"

The gravity of their situation precluded a smile, but he felt one behind his stoic expression. "Airman Peters, bring the jeep around."

"Yes, sir." With a sharp salute, she trotted off into the darkness.

Walker felt the boys staring at him in the dark and knew what each of them was thinking. "We'll do everything possible to save your friends. You have my word."

***

Amanda helped Liz sort out supplies on several long foldout tables outside the large medical tent. Liz seemed distracted and dropped a package of wrapped bandages, scattering them around the desert floor. Amanda squatted down to help her collect them.

"It's about time you found some personal happiness, Liz," she said quietly, startling the other woman into dropping the bandages she'd just picked up. "It's been a long time since Victor."

Liz's cheeks colored red, but she smiled. "I like Martin a lot."

Amanda chuckled. "That's obvious." Liz joined in the laughter. "Martin's a good man. I hope it works out."

"Thanks, Amanda." She hesitated a long moment. "I practically grew up with Bryan, as you know, and, I guess, despite him being more like an older brother, I idolized him as a girl. What you and he have together… well, that's what I've always hoped for. The Weapon project…it took away so much of my humanity. I see that now. I wonder if I've recovered enough of it to make Martin, or any man, happy."

Amanda reached out and pulled her into a hug. "The answer to that is yes. How you've changed toward William is proof enough."

"Thank you. Your friendship means the world to me."

They separated, and Liz swiped a tear from one eye, recovering her professional aplomb.

"We'd better get these supplies ready," Amanda said, rising and replacing the rolled bandages into their boxes.

Liz stood beside her, depositing another batch. "I hope we don't need them."

Amanda's face clouded over as she pictured Bryan, or those boys injured or…No! This was a different kind of battle, but he was tough and protective of his troops. They would survive!

***

Roy seethed with anger at the casual way Andy led them through the winding, dimly lit rock tunnels, passing several caverns of various sizes and heights. He wanted nothing more than to strangle the little bitch for what he did to Alex, feeling more like Java than himself. Few things angered him to the point of violence. Hurting Alex was one of them.

What enraged him the most was how calm Alex was at seeing Andy again, like he didn't care that the other boy had almost killed him. He loved how Alex could always find the best in everyone, but he felt in his gut that Andy was rotten to the core and Alex was fooling himself by thinking his brother might come back around.

He heard machinery, like maybe a generator or more than one generator, which made sense inside a mountain like this. But the caverns he passed were furnished like rooms at his home, like people lived here all the time, though the beds were camping cots rather than real beds.

Andy stopped at one of these and pulled back a sheet partially covering the entrance. "This is my room. We are to wait here."

Stern's gruff voice startled Roy as it echoed around him. "Inside, all of you."

Flashing Andy the meanest look he could muster, Roy followed Alex inside the small chamber. Shaw and Allison followed. The two soldiers entered, guns still drawn, and stood in front of the opening. Stern ignored them as he addressed the soldiers. "I'm reporting in to the lady. Guard them."

"Yes, sir," the two men said simultaneously, like they were zombies.

Stern vanished from view and Roy finally took in his surroundings. There was a cot and some clothes folded up on top of a small trunk. Next to the trunk was a table with a large clear pitcher of water, with five empty glasses around it.

Andy indicated the water. "You must be thirsty. Help yourself to water."

Mr. Shaw stepped forward. "Where's the woman?"

Andy gazed at him, stoic despite Shaw's aggressive tone. "Teacher will summon us when she is ready."

Mr. Shaw scowled. "No one summons me."

"We are all summoned here, Mr. Shaw."

Mr. Shaw looked angry.

"Don't worry about it, Dad." Allison leaned in closely and Roy barely heard her add, "We should focus on how to escape."

Mr. Shaw nodded and reached for the pitcher of water. Pouring two glasses, he handed one to Allison, who gulped it with gusto. He handed the other glass to Alex, who took it, but didn't drink. Shaw poured two more and Roy greedily swallowed his entire glass in one gulp. Alex just stared at Andy, who stared right back. Roy wondered if something was passing between them.

"Do you hate me this much, Andy?" Alex's question generated no reaction from Andy.

"I feel no hatred toward you, Big Brother." Andy indicated the several chairs, adding to Roy and the others, "You might as well sit. It might be some time until we are summoned." With that, he turned his back and walked to his cot, sitting and staring at the solid rock wall of the cavern.

Roy wanted to slap him, but one look at Alex's disappointed face curbed his anger. He pulled a folding chair next to his best friend and sat. He heard Mr. Shaw and Allison sitting on creaky plastic chairs, but he focused on Alex. Whatever happened, they were together.

***

Colonel Walker exited his jeep a bit stiffly. His chest still felt tight where he'd been shot, and, for the first time in recent memory, he felt old as he trudged up the mountain alongside Peters and the two boys. The moonlight provided some illumination, but no arc lights had been set up this close to the entrance, so his and Peters' flashlight beams scanned the ground ahead to make sure they wouldn't lose their footing. The base of the mountain was sandy and covered in small rocks that could present a slip factor, so he made sure the boys saw exactly where to step.

They arrived minutes later at a wide flattened shelf, where William and Francis stood dutifully waiting. The boys saluted and Walker returned it, eyeing the sheer face of rock rising into the night sky.

"Report?"

William said, "We've felt all along the mountain where the entrance appeared, but it's solid. There's no way in."

"Show me."

William led the way forward to the mountain, which seemed to glow beneath the moonlight, and pointed. The indicated area looked pristine, not even a small crack that might indicate the presence of a cave entrance behind it.

"My best guess, Colonel," William went on, his pale face floating in the dark beside the rock wall, "is that someone on the inside has to open the door."

"The only one who might let us in is Alex," Java said from behind, "or Roy. But we got no way to contact them."

Walker eyed him a moment. "No, we don't." He considered his options for a few moments. "Our best bet is to try and blast our way through. If this rock wall is a façade, we should be able to penetrate it."

"Blast with what?" Francis asked, his dark hair blending into the background.

A light rumbling sound was heard, and everyone turned to look behind. A tactical all-terrain vehicle bounced along the rocky ground on its thick rubber tires and rolled to a stop beside them. Two of Walker's men hopped out and proceeded around back to grab a large box filled with explosives. Walker had no interest in desecrating a monument like Superstition Mountain, but the situation was too grave not to make some attempt to penetrate the rock barrier.

The men set the box on the ground before him and saluted. One of them asked, "Where do you want us to plant the explosives, Colonel?"

Walker led them to the spot indicated by William and pointed. The two men set to work.

***

Martin peered through the binoculars, while Dane and Nathan stood beside him. They were up on a bluff overlooking the troop positions. At the far end of the perimeter sat a lone tent belonging to General Lewis. Martin's orders were to observe Lewis and report any suspicious activity to the colonel.

"See anything strange, Martin?" Dane leaned closer, keeping his voice low and his head out of the moonlight, which spread outward just behind their position.

Martin studied Lewis giving orders to several of his men. Everything appeared to be on the up and up, but with the inability to overhear their conversation, Lewis could be ordering those men to kill Colonel Walker, for all he knew.

He lowered the glasses and faced the other two. "It's too dark to see much and I can't hear what he's saying." He furrowed his brows, considering what course of action to take. His orders were to observe, but not engage. He whipped up the glasses and focused on the tent once more. Lewis and another officer were walking away from the tent, working their way through the troops toward Superstition Mountain.

This was their chance.

He let the binoculars dangle from his neck. "C'mon, let's go."

Nathan asked, "Go where?"

"To search the general's tent."

Dane faced Martin straight on. "You heard the colonel. No engagement."

"The tent's empty," Martin replied, knowing they had to move fast while the window of opportunity remained open. "We'll be in and out before he gets back. Let's go."

Without waiting for a reply, he scuttled down the low embankment, kicking up small clouds of dust. At first, he heard nothing behind him, but then the sound of boots stepping carefully on the sand and rock told him the others were with him.

***

Father Pat sat in the back of the jeep as Mr. Montour navigated his way up the rocky incline to their final position, Leone seated beside him. The big mountain towered above them, but their station lay on a bluff jutting out from the adjoining mountain range. These other mountains were much lower in height than the main peak, but high enough so they would have a good view of the troop movements below. If what Leone feared came true, they must be prepared for a mass exorcism the likes of which had never been seen in human history.

Father Pat had studied the ancient ritual and practiced the portions in Latin, since it had been many years since he'd studied the language in earnest. The last time was back at the seminary, in fact, and that had been almost twenty years ago. Back then, he didn't even believe in the existence of demons, despite Church teachings to the contrary. Now, this very night, he may face off against an invasion of such creatures. He'd told Alex that God would not abandon him, but was he just comforting the boy? Did God take an active role in our world anymore or did he leave everything up to humans to figure out for themselves?

If what Leone said was true, it had been God who'd sequestered these creatures, whether they be the fallen angels of legend or merely dark entities that have always existed. Wasn't it, therefore, God's responsibility to make sure they never escaped? Of course, it wasn't God who planned to unleash them. It was human beings, so Father Pat supposed the responsibility for stopping them lay with other human beings. Human choice was the driver of all good and evil on this planet, after all.

The jeep screeched to a halt and Father Pat lurched forward slightly, thrown from his reverie back into the real world. Darkness surrounded them, so much that he was certain no one below could see them. He threw his long legs over the side and clambered out of the jeep, joining Leone and Montour in gazing down at the troop movements below. Only minimal lights glowed, mainly flashlights, in an attempt to hide the location of the troops from those inside the mountain. Of course, even the colonel didn't know if they were being spied on, but he suspected that the woman and her people had hacked into satellites and were tracking their every movement.

Father Pat eyed Leone's face in the darkness, unable to read the cardinal's expression. "Do you think we have a fighting chance, Cardinal?"

The rotund man turned to face him. "We have teams at every gate around the world, even China and Russia. We have a plan of attack. We have the Healer on our side. Have faith, Father."

Father Pat felt his face redden with embarrassment, grateful for the darkness hiding his shame. Of course, faith was the key. So much had happened these past few weeks to shake his very foundations that he'd forgotten that most fundamental tool—faith.

Leone clapped him on the back and turned to Montour, decked out in colorful regalia replete with dangling beads and feathers. "Come, my friends, we must be ready."

Father Pat followed them back to the Jeep where they began unloading their supplies.

CHAPTER FOURTEEN

THE SUMMONS HAVE COME

THE MOONLIT DARKNESS, PUNCTUATED BY the occasional random flashlight beam, made it tricky for Dane and his dad to follow Martin around the perimeter of the troop deployment to the rear of General Lewis's tent. Nathan stayed close by his side, and the cane helped, but Martin moved quickly. The soldiers in position were all seated on the ground gazing up at the dark mountain peak, illuminated by the waning moon. Dane felt stronger than he had since he'd been hurt, but this was the most walking he'd done since his surgery, and it was beginning to tire him.

Glancing around at the empty desert spreading out before him, he saw twisted shapes of cacti rising from the ground, but no human activity. Martin waved him over to the corner of the tent and squatted down to untie the cord holding the back two corners together. Lifting one flap, he held it aloft so Dane, followed by his dad, could enter. Dane's chest felt tight, but he managed to duck under the flap. Martin entered last, dropping the flap back into place.

A small camping lantern cast low illumination within, but Dane's eyes were already adjusted to the darkness outside, so he had no trouble seeing as he stood beside Martin. There wasn't much to see. A small cot sat off to one side with a tiny foldable table next to it. A lantern sat on this table, and on the bed rested a duffle bag. He figured the general hadn't brought much since this operation should be over in one night. Depending on what happened at midnight, he wasn't sure why the general might need a bed. He didn't think anyone would even have an opportunity to sleep.

He felt his dad pressing in behind him as he leaned into Martin's ear. "What are we looking for?"

Martin swiveled his head halfway around. "Anything that looks odd for a general to have on a battlefield. Looks like that duffle bag is all we've got. Let's check it out."

He crossed the small tent in two strides and reached for the duffle. It was camo-colored with a large American flag and the words *U.S. Air Force* across the middle. Dane eyed his dad as Nathan crept closer. Martin unzipped the bag and dumped its contents onto the neatly made cot. There wasn't much: closed laptop, canteen (full, if the sound it made when Martin shook it was any indication), a few protein bars, a flak jacket, and a small ornate box. Martin picked up the box and examined it. Made of metal, there were symbols carved on the lid that Dane didn't recognize.

"What is that?" Nathan leaned in for a closer look.

"No idea," Martin whispered in reply.

He held up the box and shook it. A small rattling sound came from within, but it was muffled, like there was something soft inside muting the sound. Lowering it, he examined the lock. A key was clearly required to open it.

"If I break it open, he'll know someone is on to him."

Nathan reached into the pocket of his fatigues and slipped out a small, wrapped bundle.

Martin squinted in the dark. "What do you have there?"

"Lock picks," Nathan answered, his voice heavy with worry. "Give me the box and I'll open it."

Martin handed it over and Nathan sat carefully on the cot, box in his lap. Dane grabbed the lantern, held it up over the keyhole, and Nathan went to work. Unrolling the small bundle, he extracted a tiny pick tool and wiggled it around inside the box keyhole. In a matter of seconds, Dane heard a click sound and the box popped open.

Martin took the box from Nathan and lifted the lid. Dane leaned closer and Nathan stood up for a better look. Within was a soft lining that looked like velvet, but the only object inside was a ring. Martin picked it up and held it out. Dane raised the lantern so that its meager light fell directly on the ring. It was gold and quite shiny, large, and heavy looking. A man's ring. The top was flat and embossed with some kind of bird, its wings spread open.

"A bird?" Nathan said what was in Dane's mind. Why would the general lock up a ring like this?

"Any idea what it means?" Dane asked Martin, who studied the ring carefully, as though recalling something.

"I remember this symbol from Cardinal Leone's briefing on that organization, the one holed up inside the mountain. This bird is their symbol."

"Quite right, young man" came a deep, resonant voice to their right.

All three of them spun around and Dane was shocked to find General Lewis, wearing camo fatigues, framed in the tent entry, a gun aimed in their direction.

***

Colonel Walker crouched behind an outcropping of rock fifty feet from the hidden cave entrance, William, and Francis on either side, with Peters crouched low beside Java, Israel, and Jorge. His four explosives experts had planted the dynamite at strategic points around and on the rock face that they predicted would yield the best results. Now those four men huddled on the opposite side of the target area, prepared to detonate on Walker's orders.

Walker called out, "Now!" and then pulled his head down and away from the expected fallout.

A second later, an enormous flash lit up the darkness all around him, accompanied by a tremendous percussive explosion that made the earth tremble. Dust and small bits of rock rained down from the sky, but Walker had covered his head, and so had the boys. After the rock shower ceased, he raised his head and gazed at the side of the mountain. It was too dark to see much; however, a definite indentation was obvious.

But no cavern was visible.

***

Roy was tired of waiting. Shaw had been checking his watch and now reported it was ten-forty-five. Suddenly, Andy stood and faced them.

"The summons have come. Follow me." He strode to the cavern entrance and the two soldiers moved aside. Without another word, he stepped into the tunnel. Roy exchanged a look with Alex, but he looked stoic as he followed his twin. Roy trailed after, and Allison followed him. Shaw came last, the two-armed men bringing up the rear.

Andy led them through several well-lit tunnels that had lights embedded in the rock ceiling. He turned finally and stepped into an enormous cavern that had to be three times Roy's height at the ceiling and bigger in area than the whole downstairs of his house back in Hawthorne.

A long computer console pressed up against the uneven rock walls and stretched more than halfway around the circumference. Above the console, attached to the rock walls, were hundreds of monitors with words attached to the bottom of each, but he didn't recognize any of the words. However, images played out on all of them, live images from what he could see, of people walking the streets of cities, people eating at outdoor restaurants, even teenagers at high schools walking to their classes. And the people wore different kinds of clothes, some of which he'd never seen before, like maybe they weren't American but lived in other countries.

He had little time to consider the meaning of all this equipment because standing right next to a man operating the computer console was Ms. G herself! His blood boiled at the sight of her, flanked by the smirking Dr. Avila and the hulking form of Jäger. He was shoved from behind by Stern and had to move farther into the room, quickly taking up a position at Alex's side, determined to protect his friend. His nostrils and stomach reacted with disgust at a foul odor permeating the chamber. It smelled like a dead squirrel he'd had to pull out from behind a wall in the garage one time. The animal hadn't been dead for long, and the smell had made him nauseous. That's what this room reminded him of.

Alex clearly noticed the smell too, as he glanced around to determine its source. Ms. G either didn't notice or didn't care. She offered that jack-o-lantern grin and placed both hands on her hips like she just saw her dream date approaching.

"At last, Alex, we're together again."

Shaw shouldered his way past Roy and challenged Ms. G. "Forget the phony pleasantries, lady. Let us go now or you will feel my wrath."

She eyed him like a bug she was about to step on. "Stand down, little man. All your wealth and power are meaningless here. If you get in my way, Kurt will crush you." She indicated Jäger, who grinned with eagerness, clenching and unclenching his massive fists.

Roy studied the big man a long moment, struck by how much paler he looked, at how his skin seemed discolored in spots, not like bruises, but just discolored, like maybe he had a disease. And he didn't look healthy. Alex noticed too. Roy could tell by the way his friend studied the man.

Allison waved her hand in front of her face and wrinkled her nose. "He may be big, but he needs a shower."

Jäger grimaced and a low growl rumbled from deep within him.

Roy decided to distract Ms. G too. "He don't look so good no more, not like when William kicked his ass last time."

Jäger lurched forward as though to grab Roy, but Ms. G held out a hand to stop him. Roy was grateful because if the man had gotten much closer, he was sure the stench would've made him faint.

Alex was staring long and hard at Jäger and said, "He's dying."

That announcement surprised Roy, and the others too. But Ms. G didn't deny it. She remained silent and waved her hand at Avila.

"It's true," Avila said to Alex, how voice somber. "This body has rejected Jäger's soul and has been rotting away. He doesn't have much time left."

"How tragic," Shaw commented, his tone laced with sarcasm.

Ms. G eyed him with contempt. "Don't worry, Russell, he has enough life left in him to kill all of you several times over."

Shaw looked like he was about to respond, but then his gaze locked on to the computer operator, who was typing into a keyboard, shifting the images on each monitor to a different scene with different people. Shaw stepped closer to the massive console. The cocking of a gun halted him in midstride, and he glanced back at Stern, who aimed his weapon right at Shaw's head.

Shaw faced Ms. G. "This is all Shawtech electronics."

She chuckled. "Nothing but the best."

He squinted as though studying her face more closely might reveal something. "Who are you, and what is this place?"

Roy watched Ms. G, certain she would say nothing. But she smiled and replied, "We have some time. Why not?"

Roy caught Alex's eye, and his best friend looked deeply troubled, like he knew—or suspected he knew—something the rest of them didn't. Roy turned to Allison, who wore a determined look on her face that mirrored his own. She wouldn't go down without a fight. He was disturbed to see Jäger leering at her like he'd seen guys at school do to pretty girls. The only person who displayed no emotion whatever was Andy. He might as well have been a wax statue as he stood beside the computer console awaiting his orders. Roy noticed that his hair was tied back in a ponytail, and he wore a black jumpsuit, like what Ms. G wore, only hers was tight-fitting and slinky.

Ms. G indicated the multitude of monitors with a sweep of her well-manicured fingers. "My operators here hack into security cameras all over the world. Many cities, as you well know, have cameras on street corners to monitor unsavory activity. Other cameras belong to private businesses and homeowners hoping to protect their premises. Using satellites, we're able to observe people everywhere on the planet."

Shaw folded his arms across his chest and stared her down. "Why?"

"So that Andy can shift the good out of random people and replace it with bad. Simple as that."

"Again, why?"

She offered him a dismissive look. "Don't play dumb, Russell. You don't mind if I call you Russell, do you?" Without awaiting an answer, she went on. "I'm certain that pompous cardinal from the Vatican told you what he suspects are our plans, and he's mostly correct. By removing the good qualities from human beings and enhancing the bad, violence and mayhem will increase ten or even a hundred-fold."

"Isn't there enough violence in the world already?" Allison glared at Ms. G like she wanted to drive a stake through the woman's heart.

Ms. G sauntered closer to Allison and smirked. "Pretty girl. I can see why Alex likes you so much. Now he has a choice between you and Roy."

"Leave her alone!" Shaw lurched forward, but one of the soldiers grabbed him and held him back.

"That all depends on Alex."

She tossed a knowing look at Alex, who seemed to understand it, even if Roy did not. What was she talking about?

Ms. G faced Allison again. "In response to your question, yes, there's quite a lot of violence in the world, often fomented by those who seek to undermine societal structures and values. They have done our work for us these past few decades by spreading nihilism, especially here in America. The Soviets used to call such people 'useful idiots,' and they are. By breaking down established traditions, they've played right into our hands because in their wake, they've left divisiveness and chaos."

Roy didn't understand what she was talking about, but Shaw clearly did, based on the wide-eyed expression he wore.

"You have helped, Russell, you and all the other tech companies, addicting children to phones and tablets and apps and social media and making them so easy to brainwash. It's the perfect storm. Now, tonight, when we open this gate to the other side, all the other gates on earth will also open. My peeps will flood the planet and plunge the world into darkness."

She grinned, her face a mask of gloating pleasure as she studied the horrified expressions on the faces of Shaw and Allison. Roy was still confused, but Alex's disturbed facial expression indicated that he understood some of what she'd said.

"Who are your 'peeps'?" Shaw asked, obviously trying to keep the conversation going. Roy figured he was stalling for time, maybe hoping the colonel or someone could find a way inside.

Ms. G understood what he was doing because she glanced at her fancy wristwatch. "I get that you're trying to distract me, Russell, but it won't work. We're still right on schedule. I have within me one of the oldest, for want of a better word, entities, in existence. The Bible tells its version of how the Creator cast demons into Hell, but all other religious traditions tell similar stories. In Hinduism, we are called asuras. Buddhists give us different names than does Christianity. China calls us guei-shen, and Japan has labeled the most powerful of us the oni, and the tengu are those of us that possess human beings. Some Native Americans call us majii manitou. The bottom line, Russell, is that we have been here since the dawn of creation, locked away in an alternate dimension. Tonight, all that will change, thanks to the Healer."

Now she fixed Alex with a piercing stare that made Roy squirm. To his credit, though, Alex didn't so much as flinch. He glared back at her with pure defiance and Roy felt pride well up within him for his friend's courage.

"I'll never help you," Alex said, his voice quiet but imbued with conviction.

The crooked smile spreading across her face chilled Roy to the bone, especially when she broke eye contact with Alex and fixed her penetrating blue eyes on him. Fortunately, Allison came to his rescue by distracting Ms. G.

"What's wrong with you anyway, lady?" she demanded, her tone strong and challenging. "You one of those kids who grew up poor and wants to get back at the world?"

Shaw snorted. "No, Allison, she was a spoiled rich kid, just like most activists. Remember how the 9/11 hijackers were all from wealthy families?"

She nodded, clearly recalling this information.

"No," Shaw continued. "I suspect this woman wanted for nothing growing up."

Ms. G smirked but looked amused, rather than offended. "I wouldn't talk, Russell."

His face clouded with anger. "I grew up dirt poor. I earned every penny I have through hard work and innovation. What did you do? Get some monster to help you. I bet you also wanted to be young forever. That was part of the deal, wasn't it?"

She shook her head, still smiling. "You do know people, Russell. Alas, however, only for a hundred years, give or take. My youth, that is. But I've enjoyed every second of it. I've gotten to take part in some of the most destructive movements in human history—the rise of the Nazis, Stalin and Mao and international communism, the Cuban Revolution, the Iranian Revolution in the seventies, the rise of international terrorism. To name a few. As the religious among you say, I've been blessed."

Allison shook her head in disgust and eyed her father, but his troubled expression clearly didn't calm her fears. Roy didn't understand a lot of what Ms. G had said, but he did remember the Nazis from history class and knew they were evil.

Ms. G glanced again at the time on her watch and strode over to where Alex sat gazing fiercely up at her. "Soon, Healer, you will help your brother shift the good out of all these people you see on camera."

"And if I don't?"

The smile she offered in response was chilling.

CHAPTER FIFTEEN

I WON'T HELP YOU, ANDY

GENERAL LEWIS PEERED AT THEM in the meager light, but even with his face in shadow, Dane squirmed under the intensity of the man's gaze.

"Colonel Walker sent you, I presume?"

Dane didn't reply and neither did Nathan.

Martin stood tall and straight, making no attempt to hide the box and ring in his hand. In fact, he held up the ring. "How long ago did you sell out your country, General?"

Lewis winced, but otherwise maintained a stoic expression. "What does Walker think I plan to do?"

Martin shrugged. "He didn't say. Our orders were to establish your loyalty, and now we know where it lies."

"You know nothing, Mr. Briceño, except that I have that ring. You may return it to the box and set it down on the cot."

Eyeing the glinting muzzle of the gun, Martin did as he was told.

"I don't suppose if you call the Colonel, he'll come here to me?"

"No, General," Martin replied, his voice much calmer than Dane felt.

"Very well." He tilted his head toward the tent flap behind him. "Airman."

A young airman in camos darted inside the tent and saluted. "Yes, General?"

"Bring me Amanda Walker, the colonel's wife. You'll find her in the medical tent."

The airman saluted again. "Yes, sir." Then he was gone.

Martin eyed the general with contempt. "Why do you want Amanda?"

"The colonel will come when informed that she is my prisoner."

Dane watched Martin, expecting a comeback, but there was nothing. Obviously, Martin had no plan to help them escape. That sucked.

***

Alex felt his insides twisted into knots. Ms. G stared at him with hungry eyes, but he refused to tremble in fear, even though deep down he *was* terrified. But not for himself. What would Ms. G and Jäger do to Roy and the others if he refused to open the gate? He knew she was pure evil and cared about nothing except the fulfillment of her plans. If he helped her, he was condemning the people of earth to death or madness. And even if he did help, what chance was there that she'd set Roy, Allison, and Shaw free? Very slim, he figured.

An explosion shook the mountain, startling Alex, but the cavern was apparently so secure not even a single light flickered. Shaw looked surprised, but Ms. G only smiled.

"They will never find the entrance. It's hidden from all your technology." She faced the soldiers and Sergeant Stern. "Sergeant Stern, leave two men here. Take the others and eliminate whoever you find at the entrance. Then meet up with General Lewis. He'll give you further orders."

Stern looked relieved to be excused. "Yes, ma'am." He waved at two of the soldiers and they followed him out of the chamber.

"Lewis is one of yours?" Shaw gazed at her with contempt.

She smirked, something she excelled at. "One of our best men in the field."

Shaw shook his head in disgust.

"Alex," Ms. G went on, her tone one of annoyance. "Your brother needs your help to shift larger groups of people. He can't do it alone."

Alex folded his arms across his chest. "I won't help him." He caught Allison's eye and she nodded approvingly.

Ms. G clucked her tongue. "That won't bode well for your loved ones here." She indicated the others.

"Teacher," Andy began from behind Alex, "may I speak to my brother?"

"Of course."

Andy waved Alex over to the farthest corner of the cavern, at the very end of the computer console. Alex followed, knowing Ms. G could probably hear whatever they were saying anyway.

"I won't help you, Andy."

Andy squatted down to be face to face with him and spoke in a low voice. "If you don't help me, Jäger will torture your friends." His eyes involuntarily shifted to one side, and Alex glanced over to see that Andy was looking at Roy. "They will suffer terribly, Big Brother. And so will we. Is that what you want, just to spare a bunch of strangers you've never even met?"

Alex was caught off guard by the argument because it made a certain amount of sense. He didn't know any of the people Andy would shift, but he did love the three people held prisoner because of him. Could he allow them to suffer untold pain just to spare strangers from hurting each other?

That quick look Andy had sent toward Roy intrigued Alex. "Why do you care what happens to my friends?"

Did Andy flinch, just a little? Alex wasn't sure because the facial expression remained carved in stone.

"I don't, but I know you do," Andy replied, monotone in full force. "So, Big Brother, what will it be?"

Alex stared at him without speaking because he wasn't sure of his answer.

***

Colonel Walker's demolition team approached the jagged indentation in the mountain face. Without warning, the area began to shimmer, and three figures appeared. Before the men could respond, the figures opened fire, striking three of Walker's men in the chest, but missing the fourth because he ducked down behind the outcropping where he'd hidden during the explosion.

Walker stood, gun out, and aimed. He recognized the man in the lead. It was Stern. "Sergeant Stern!"

Stern whirled and opened fire, but Walker shot first, catching his former aide in the shoulder and spinning him sideways into one of the other soldiers. William and Francis were up and over the embankment in a flash and sprinting toward the men. Stern stumbled away into the dark and Walker lost sight of him, but the others opened fire on the two boys and were met with fists of iron that knocked them both unconscious.

"William," Walker called out, "go after Stern. Bring him to me. Francis, help the wounded men until medics arrive."

William didn't need to be told twice. He sprinted down the mountain in search of Stern, while Francis jogged over to the wounded men, who rolled and pitched on the rocky ground, struggling to contain their bleeding.

Walker and Peters hurried over and provided first aid while the other three boys stared at the cave entrance. Walker looked in that direction. Despite the large, jagged indent in the formerly smooth rock surface, there was no sign of the shimmering entrance that, moments before, had been visible.

***

Davalos squatted on a bluff overlooking the battlefield below. He easily spotted Leone and his crew on an adjoining bluff and, with binoculars, could make out the spot where Colonel Walker had tried to blast a hole into the mountain. When Stern and his men had emerged shooting, Davalos was tempted to send in Kitty and Dog to take them out. But Walker's orders had been explicit—these creatures were only to be deployed if the situation devolved into chaos. That was, after all, one of the prime reasons for their creation—riot control.

He lowered the binoculars after watching William pursue Stern and Peters radio for medics. When he'd been pursuing the Healer all those years, he never imagined it would come down to this. Yes, he'd known that a shadow organization wanted the boy for nefarious purposes, but he'd never bought into those rumors of supernatural activity. And now, here they were, fighting to stop a so-called demonic invasion of earth. He'd never had much use for religion, which is probably why he'd dabbled so much in creating artificial life. His arrogance led him to think he could do whatever he chose. Now his creation was on the loose, and who knew how many people Jäger might have killed already.

At least his instincts in designing the creatures with him now had proven sound. No, they couldn't make choices like William, but then they weren't even part human, so that innate corruptibility that's within every human hadn't tainted them. They snuffled and growled in the darkness, with Scorpio clicking its legs together. In a way, they knew they'd be going into battle the same way a dog knows it's about to go on a walk. And just like a dog, they were excited. He hadn't told the colonel the whole truth, and that troubled him a bit.

He'd programmed the creatures to disarm and disable, that much was true. But he had also implanted in their minds the need to kill the evil being known as Kurt Jäger. He had to undo the terrible mistake he'd made, and this seemed the most equitable way. After tonight, assuming the world survived, he would destroy all the other artificial bodies back in the lab. As far as he was concerned, no one should ever attempt an experiment like that again.

***

Amanda stood beside Liz, gazing past their table of medical supplies at the scattered lights dotting the potential battlefield. Bryan had told her that the Pentagon had no intel as to how many enemy combatants might be holed up inside the mountain. Then there was the "Gate" business Cardinal Leone had shared with them. Neither she nor Bryan were churchgoers, but she supposed she believed in a supreme being. She'd read enough about intelligent design and the meticulous planning that appears to have gone into even the creation of DNA and simple proteins, let alone the rest of the universe. This talk of demons seemed more like something out of Hollywood, not reality. But if the cardinal was even partially right, all the medical supplies in the world would not be enough to save those brave men and women surrounding that mountain.

The eerie silence around them unnerved her. It was like the quiet before the storm. The night sky looked like someone had tossed glitter into the heavens, and the waning moon added its pale glow, but the absence of sound seemed surreal.

Footsteps crunching on the desert floor drew her attention to a soldier striding out of the dark toward her. She exchanged a look with Liz, who shrugged in confusion. The soldier stopped in front of them both and spoke in a crisp, efficient voice.

"Mrs. Walker. General Lewis has sent me to bring you to him."

Her hackles instantly rose. Something wasn't right. She indicated the walkie-talkie on the table beside her. "Why didn't he just call me on this?"

The young man's face remained immobile. "I couldn't say, ma'am. But you are to accompany me."

Her eyebrows rose and her back stiffened. "That sounds like an order, airman."

"Yes, ma'am, it is."

She eyed Liz again in the dark.

Liz shook her head. "Something's not right, Amanda."

"I agree." She turned back to inform the airman she would not be accompanying him and found herself staring down the barrel of his gun.

"Sorry, ma'am, but the general's orders must be obeyed."

Lewis had avoided her the entire time he'd spent on the base, and now he's sent this kid to bring her to him, at gunpoint even. Anger surged through her, and she determined to give him a piece of her mind.

"It's all right, Liz. I'll go. Let Bryan know when you speak with him."

Liz looked concerned, her pretty face scrunched with worry. "Are you sure, Amanda?"

Amanda smiled wryly. "Someday I'll tell you about Lewis and me. Don't worry, I can handle him." She turned back to the soldier. "Lead the way, young man."

He stepped aside and indicated the direction she should walk. She strode forward with confidence. She could handle Lewis. Or so she hoped.

***

William had no difficulty tracking Sergeant Stern. The man had stopped running a few minutes earlier, but his smell and tracks, even on the rocky surface of the mountainside, were easy to follow. William's keen eyes made certain his footing never wavered as he leaped from rock to rock and avoided the sandy spots that held no traction. An outcropping of several large rocks loomed just ahead. He heard Stern's breathing despite the man's best efforts to control it. He also knew Stern was lying in wait, prepared to shoot whoever approached.

He slowed his pace and kept his footfalls silent as a cat. The jutting rocks grew taller as he approached, but he had no fear. Stern could do nothing to harm him. He was tempted to show off by climbing the steep rocks and dropping onto the man from above, but he knew the colonel wanted Stern conscious, so he took the short way around. Darting forward, he rounded the rocks and came face to face with the sergeant.

Startled, Stern raised his weapon and opened fire. The bullets damaged William's camo fatigues but did nothing to him but ricochet off in different directions. Stern's mouth dropped open in stunned disbelief before William snatched the gun from his hand and smashed it against the rocks.

"How?" Stern backed away in horror.

"I have tough skin." William lunged forward and clocked Stern a hard punch to the face, stunning him. The sergeant crumpled into a moaning heap at his booted feet. William reached down to grab the limp form. Throwing him over his shoulders fireman-style, he sprinted back up the mountainside.

***

Dane stood in the same spot, the general pointing his gun at him and his dad. Dane's chest ached. He knew he was pushing himself too hard after such a severe injury but refused to show even a smidgeon of weakness in front of this traitor. His dad stood right beside him, giving him support so he wouldn't lose his balance, and he used the cane for assistance on his other side.

Lewis had said nothing since the soldier left, and neither Dane nor Nathan had attempted to talk with him. What good would that have done? The man was clearly their enemy.

The tent flap opened, and in stepped Colonel Walker's wife, followed by the young airman. The general nodded toward the airman. "Wait outside."

The airman saluted and exited the tent.

Lewis studied the colonel's wife in the shadowy darkness, but she gave him no opportunity to explain his actions. She turned to Dane and Nathan. "Are you two all right?"

"Yes, Amanda," Nathan replied.

"Except *he's* working for that woman," Dane blurted, unable to contain his anger, indicating the general.

Amanda looked shocked. "That's not possible, Dane. Jason Lewis would never betray his country." She turned to face the general. "Would you?"

Lewis winced but said nothing.

Amanda faced Dane and Nathan again. "Since middle school, Jason wanted to serve his country. He joined up after high school and never looked back. Shot up the ranks with tours of duty in the first Gulf War and the Iraq War, two purple hearts and one silver star. The Pentagon job might have broadened his midsection a bit, but it would never dampen the fire in his heart. Whatever you may suspect, I promise you it's not true."

Dane stared at her in disbelief, and even the general looked stunned. And yet, there was something about her voice, an undertone even, that made Dane suspect she was playing a part, rather than acting genuinely shocked.

Nathan asked, "How do you know him so well, Amanda?"

She smiled warmly, as though retrieving fond memories. "He and I were an item, before I met the colonel."

Dane's mouth dropped open. Her and the general back in the day? How crazy was that?

She eyed General Lewis and frowned at the gun. "You going to shoot me, Jason?"

His eyes became the size of boiled eggs. "Of course not, Amanda!" He hesitated and then lowered the weapon to his side. His stiff posture and uncertain facial expression left no doubt that he was conflicted about how to proceed. "You meant what you said just now?"

Her warm smile didn't change. "You know I did."

Lewis opened his mouth to respond, but then closed it. He looked like he had two voices screaming in his head, each telling him to do something different. "But I must get the colonel here. I must. Those are…"

He didn't finish, but Dane was sure he was going to add, "my orders."

"Why, Jason?" She studied him as though sizing him up for a new medal.

He took a long pause, and then raised his walkie-talkie.

***

Colonel Walker observed Dr. Shepherd and the medical team treating his wounded men. Fortunately, none of the bullet wounds were life-threatening. Once she'd assessed the health status of the men, she'd taken him aside.

"Bryan, Lewis has Amanda."

Walker recoiled. "Why?"

"I don't know. He sent an airman to bring her."

Furious, he snatched his walkie-talkie off his belt and was about to radio Lewis when the general called him. He clicked the talk button while Liz looked on with concern. "General Lewis, I understand you have my wife. Why?"

"News travels fast" came the gruff voice out of the speaker. "I need you to come to my tent, Colonel, and that seemed the best way to ensure your cooperation."

Walker fought to control his anxiety, as he'd learned to do on the battlefield. "I have my own part in this operation, General, and it's rather strained here at the moment."

"Change of orders, Colonel," the voice crackled through the speaker. "Knowing that you don't trust me, I felt the presence of your wife would guarantee that you follow this order. Report to me at once. Lewis out."

The speaker crackled and went silent, and Walker fumed. Liz placed a hand on his arm, and he gazed into her sympathetic eyes.

"He won't hurt her, Bryan."

"You don't know that. If he's in league with that woman in there, he's capable of anything."

He gazed long and hard at the mountain. Just as he was about to call over Peters and place her in charge, William climbed up from below, dragging a disheveled Stern by one arm. The sergeant looked angry, but also fearful.

Good, Walker thought. *I can use that.*

He said to Liz, "See to the wounded, Doctor. Francis, with me."

She nodded and returned to where the men had been laid out side by side, their wounds being tended to by several medics.

Walker strode forward with an excited Francis in tow and clapped William on the back. "Good job, William." He glowered at Stern, who refused to meet his fierce gaze. "Sergeant Stern, I trusted you implicitly for five years. How long have you been a traitor?"

Stern looked up, haughtiness illuminating his dirty face. "I'm no traitor, Colonel. My loyalties lie elsewhere."

"I have limited time, Sergeant. Can you get us inside this mountain?"

"I refuse to answer."

Walker noted the man's smug expression and decided to wipe that look off his face. "Francis, tie the sergeant's hands behind his back." He indicated a pack with supplies lying on the rocky ground. Before the dark-haired Francis could move, Java had scurried forward, holding out a small coil of rope.

"Thank you, Java," Walker said, taking the rope from the one boy and handing it to the other. Within seconds, the struggling Stern had his arms behind his back and his wrists trussed up like a steer at a rodeo. William and Francis gazed up at Walker, awaiting their next orders.

"Bring him over here." Walker crossed the bluff to the edge that looked out over the steepest part of the slope. Even in the dark, he saw the fear in Stern's wide eyes as the two boys hauled the man along and forced him to stand at the edge.

"Now, William," Walker went on, his voice the picture of calmness, "lift Stern over your head and throw him down this incline."

Without hesitation, the blond boy grabbed Stern and easily hefted the squirming man up above his head. Francis giggled at the sight.

"Wait, Colonel, you can't do this!" Stern's voice had risen several octaves, and his terror became obvious.

William stood calmly, awaiting the order to toss the traitorous Stern down into the darkness below.

"At this point, Stern, I can do whatever I want," Walker replied smoothly. "We're at war against a powerful enemy. Now, I repeat, can you get us inside the mountain?"

Stern whimpered in terror but did not respond.

Walker said, "Very well. Now, William."

William turned to face the edge of the bluff. Only darkness rose from below.

"No, wait, I'll talk, I'll talk! Please don't let him kill me!"

Walker had seldom heard a man beg, and it seemed so out of character for the Stern he thought he knew. He nodded to William, who lowered the quivering man to the ground and set him on his feet. Stern's legs wobbled and gave way, so both William and Francis had to prop him up to face Walker. Despite the cooling of the night air, Stern had beads of perspiration lining his forehead and upper lip.

"Can you get us into that mountain behind me?"

Stern shook his head. "No, someone inside must invite you in. If I radio the lady and ask to be readmitted, she'll know it's a trick."

"How will she know that?"

"Because I have no further business inside."

Walker considered for a moment. "Describe the interior to me. Where are Alex and the other hostages relative to this entrance?"

Like a kid after downing several sugary drinks, Stern babbled for five minutes about the tunnels and the control room, where the hostages were being held. He didn't know the entire plan, but Alex was supposed to help his brother shift people around the world, and then Alex would open the gate. If he refused, Jäger would torture his friends to death.

Walker listened with growing fear for Roy and the others. He was no closer to breaching the entrance and gaining access than he had been a few hours ago. He glanced at his watch. It had been over ten minutes since the general's call. He had to leave.

"What were your orders, Stern, when you exited the mountain?"

"To, uh, to report to the, uh, general. Sir."

The earlier haughtiness was gone now, replaced by a man whose voice quivered with fear as he spoke. Walker grabbed him by one elbow. "Then that's exactly where you're going." He glanced around. "Airman Peters."

Out of the gloom, the tall woman materialized like a ghost. "Yes, Colonel."

"How are the wounded?"

"Out of danger, sir. The medics are loading them into their transport vehicles and returning to base."

"Good. Stern and I are paying a visit to General Lewis. You're in command, Peters, and I don't just mean here. If anything should happen to me, or you cannot contact me, the operation is yours. Carry it out as planned."

She saluted. "Yes, sir."

William stood before Walker, looking up at him with worry. "Shall Francis and I accompany you, Colonel? You know they will never see us."

"Just you, William. I trust your judgment to handle whatever comes up. But this is an order—if something goes down with the general, you save Amanda first. Is that clear?"

William saluted, his blue eyes glittering beneath the moonlight. "Yes, sir."

Walker reached into his camouflage pants pocket and extracted a small device that looked like an Air Pod. He handed it to William. "Put this in your ear. It will let us communicate as needed."

William took the small white device and slid it into his right ear.

"Francis." Walker gazed down at the eager expression on the dark-skinned boy's face. "Remain here and protect those other boys. Whatever happens, they are your priority."

Francis saluted. "Yes, sir." He trotted back to the others, quickly swallowed up in the darkness.

Setting off down the mountain, Walker pushed Stern along while William skulked in the shadows, just in case the general or his men were watching from below.

CHAPTER SIXTEEN

SAVE YOUR STRENGTH

Ms. G GLANCED AT HER watch again and Alex knew she was becoming agitated, which meant he couldn't stall much longer. In the background, Shaw stood with his hands tied behind his back while a guy dressed all in black—which seemed to be the favorite color among these people—pointed a gun at him and Allison. She hadn't been tied up. Yet. She met Alex's gaze and held it, offering just the tiniest shake of her head. She wanted him to hold out. He studied her pretty face, but there was no hope on it, not even in her light brown eyes. She believed they would all die there, and he felt sure she was correct.

But could he continue to hold out when any moment the big guy would probably start torturing her or Roy, even if the result would be that they'd all die anyway? He couldn't watch his friends—people he loved—be hurt and do nothing about it, could he?

Ms. G glared at him and then snapped her fingers at Jäger. The big man not only smelled putrid, but he looked much weaker than when Alex had helped bring him to life. Jäger leered with delight and fixed his beady eyes on Allison for a long moment.

"If you touch her," Shaw growled, "it'll be the last thing you ever do."

Jäger chuckled. "Big words from a man who is tied up and can't do anything to stop me."

He took an aggressive step toward Shaw, but Allison lunged between them and spat on him. Because he was so tall, her spittle only reached his chest, but his eyes blazed with fury. He reared back a fist to smack her when Roy stepped closer, his fists clenched.

"Leave her alone!"

Jäger glanced at Roy, his eyes gleaming with malice. Before Alex or anyone else could react, he'd swung his fist hard into Roy's midsection. Roy grunted as the air left his body and the sound of cracking ribs was loud and clear. Blood spat out of Roy's mouth, and his eyes bulged with shock. He crumpled to the ground.

"No!" Alex started to wheel himself forward, but Ms. G blocked his path. "Get out of my way, you bitch!" She merely glanced over at Jäger and nodded for him to continue.

The big man reached down and grasped the gagging, choking Roy by his shirt and yanked him upright. Before Alex could call out, the massive fist slammed into Roy's face, snapping his head to one side and sending blood flying so far some of it landed at Alex's feet.

"Stop it!" Allison lunged at Jäger, but he backhanded her, and she stumbled into her father, both barely able to keep their footing.

"Roy!" Alex felt his insides burning with fury and remorse.

Somehow still conscious, Roy looked up from the crumpled heap he'd become at Jäger's feet. His battered face managed a tiny smile. "Stay strong…Alex. Gonna…" He spat out a wad of blood onto the rocky ground. "…kill us anyway…"

Before Alex could respond, Jäger grabbed Roy with such roughness that Alex feared his friend's back might break. Carrying Roy like he was a doll, Jäger slammed him down into a wooden straight-back chair set off to one side. Roy was semiconscious, slumping against the chair like he would slide off any second. Jäger kept one hand on Roy's lolling head to keep him upright and with the other ripped open Roy's shirt, exposing a reddened and bruised torso.

"Leave him alone!" Alex screamed, turning back to Andy for support. He was shocked to see his brother wearing an expression of sympathy on his face, but the moment Andy noticed Alex staring he replaced it with his usual deadpan look.

Roy's grunt of pain caused Alex to spin back around. He caught Allison's look of horror in the corner of his eye as he stared, open-mouthed, while Jäger affixed a second wire to Roy's chest with one of those alligator clips. Before he could call out a protest, Jäger released Roy, whose head slumped over the back of the chair, and picked up an electrical box. He flipped a switch. The crackling sound of electricity filled the air and Roy jerked in the chair, almost flying off and onto the ground. Alex watched his best friend's eyes bulge wide with agony, but it was Roy's tortured scream that would haunt him forever.

Jäger flipped the switch to off and Roy stopped vibrating, his limp body sliding off the chair into a heap on the ground.

Allison muscled her way free from the goon restraining her and dropped to Roy's side, gently touching his face and cradling his head. Tears coursed down her cheeks.

Alex pressed his chair forward with such force that Ms. G had to leap aside. His eyes blinded by tears, he stopped before them and gazed in horror at the best friend he would ever have. Allison met his gaze as she cradled Roy's head and took one of his hands in hers. Despite her grief, she wore a look of intense resolve and once more shook her head.

Alex knew Roy still lived, but just barely. If his injuries weren't healed soon, his best friend would die.

Jäger's shadow fell across them as he approached. "Now, pretty girl, it's your turn."

***

Colonel Walker shoved Stern ahead of him, the man's hands still trussed behind his back. As Walker moved among the soldiers and airmen standing like dark statues in the night, most saluted him; some did not. It didn't matter. He had to deal with Lewis. If the man had indeed turned, William would have to disable him. But how many of the general's men had also turned and would attack? That was the question he pondered as he approached the only tent visible on the desert floor.

Why would Lewis want Amanda? He knew, of course, that they'd had a relationship before he entered the picture and that Lewis had initially been angry when Amanda chose Walker (then a lowly airman) over the older, more politically savvy man. With the colonel and Amanda, the relationship had been perfect from the get-go. They were made for each other, unlike Amanda and Lewis, who, by her accounts, often differed on significant issues. Lewis had been determined to ascend the ranks as fast as possible and she admired his ambition. To a point. It was his willingness to step over anyone to get what he wanted that ultimately soured her on him as a person.

Walker couldn't imagine any circumstance where Lewis might hurt

Amanda, but this mysterious woman leading the Kalandrians seemed capable of controlling just about anyone. He quickened his pace, urging Stern along with not-so-gentle shoves of his fist. The sergeant hadn't said anything about General Lewis, but that matter should be settled any moment now.

Two airmen looked up as he and Stern approached the dark silhouette of the tent.

"Halt, Colonel Walker," one of the men announced.

Walker grabbed Stern and forced him to stop as he eyed the young man.

"I'll inform the general you're here." He saluted and ducked into the tent, letting the flap fall back into place before Walker got more than a glimpse of the interior.

Walker gazed at the other young airman, who stared straight ahead as though a senior officer wasn't even present.

He knew William was hiding somewhere, invisible as always, and would listen in on the exchange with Lewis. If all went well, William was under orders to return to Peters at the cave entrance and continue to search for a way inside.

The first airman exited the tent and faced Walker.

"You may enter now, sir. Sergeant Stern will remain under guard out here." He offered a crisp salute and vacant facial expression.

Colonel Walker didn't want to let Stern out of his sight, but he didn't appear to have much choice. He returned the salute and pushed his way inside.

He found Amanda standing beside Martin, Nathan, and Dane, with General Lewis off to one side holding a small, ornate metal box in one hand. The lantern light cast their faces in ghastly shadows, but Amanda breathed a sigh of relief when he entered and hurried to engulf him in a hug.

"Thank you for coming, Colonel Walker," Lewis began, his tone neutral, his expression guarded.

Walker kept one arm around Amanda. "You didn't give me much choice, General."

"I'll get straight to the point," Lewis went on, as though Walker hadn't spoken at all. "You sent these three civilians to spy on me. Why?"

Walker retained his composure. "You could've asked me that over the walkie-talkie, sir."

"I prefer face to face, Colonel. Well?"

Walker exchanged a glance with Amanda, who offered an encouraging smile.

"I explained to Martin and the others that Jason couldn't possibly betray his country," she said with conviction, "and that there had to be some sort of mistake, them searching his tent."

"No mistake, Colonel," Martin spoke up in a confident voice. "Check out what's in that box he's holding."

Walker raised his eyebrows questioningly as he gazed at the ornate box. "You found something, General?"

Lewis's craggy face shifted its expression, as though he'd expected Walker to be accusatory, rather than inquisitive. "As a matter of fact, I did. One of the men had it. Look for yourself."

He handed the box over and Walker took it. Metal, but lightweight and soundless as he moved it about. Filled with curiosity, he flipped up the latch and opened the lid. Within sat a gold ring on a purple velvet lining. He extracted the ring and held it up so the lantern light illuminated the design.

"You recognize it, of course?"

Walker looked from the bird with its wings spread wide to the imposing figure of Lewis regarding him with an unreadable expression. "Of course, I do. It's the symbol of our enemy, as Cardinal Leone showed us back at the base. You say one of the men had it? Did you question him?"

Lewis bristled but kept his composure. "Naturally. He admitted nothing, but the proof is in your hands. Shall we call in Sergeant Stern? My guess is, he has one exactly like it."

Walker glanced at Martin and offered the tiniest shake of his head. He didn't want anyone speaking and potentially damaging this opportunity to determine where the general's loyalties lay. He studied the ring a moment longer. "By all means, General, but his person has been searched and no such ring was found on him."

Lewis nodded, then called out, "Bring in Sergeant Stern."

Walker took that moment to give Amanda a reassuring hug before one of the young airmen entered with the still-bound Stern at his side.

Walker met his former aide's eyes and was rewarded with a glower of distaste.

"That will be all, airman," Lewis told the young man, who saluted and vanished back through the flap.

Stern gazed up at Lewis almost in awe, but Lewis only scowled at him. "Are you prepared to answer my questions, Sergeant?"

"Yes, sir," Stern replied at once. "I don't believe you'll threaten to throw me off the mountain if I don't." He glared again at Walker, who merely shrugged at Lewis as though he had no idea what Stern was talking about.

Lewis took the ring from Walker and held it up before Stern. "Do you know this symbol?"

Stern smirked. "Yes, sir, I do."

"To whom do you pledge your allegiance, the United States or the group represented by this symbol?"

"I have done both, General, throughout my career. You know—"

Lewis raised a hand to cut him off. "On this operation, which side do you support?"

Stern appeared confused by the general's attitude. "Hers, sir, as you well—"

"That's all I need to know. Airman!"

The young man entered at once and stood at attention.

"Take Sergeant Stern back to base camp and secure him somewhere he cannot get away. Take two other men with you. Under no circumstances allow him to escape."

"Yes, General." The airman saluted crisply and then grabbed Stern by his upper arm.

"But General," Stern began, looking completely thrown off-guard. "I thought—"

"Enough, Sergeant!" Lewis looked livid. "You're a disgrace to that uniform. Get him out of my sight."

The airman roughly pushed the blustering Stern through the flap.

Walker heard one last plea, "But General—" before he was apparently shoved by the airman because after that, there was quiet.

The silence that filled the tent was thick enough to be stifling. Walker decided to wait for General Lewis to make the next move.

Lewis gazed at him intently. "Now, Colonel, do you have any concerns you wish to raise?"

"No, sir." Walker noticed Dane about to speak and gave a slight shake of his head.

"Good. Now, any progress accessing the cave?"

"No, General." Walker explained what they'd done and what Stern had told them about needing to be invited inside.

Lewis frowned and placed both hands behind his back. "That's most unfortunate, Colonel. Most unfortunate. I must contact the Pentagon now to report your news. You may all remain if you wish, since this concerns everyone."

He pulled his laptop off the cot and set it on the small table. Walker watched with sober attention, fearing that news of his failure to breach the mountain might prompt an extreme Pentagon response.

***

Allison cradled Roy's head in her arms, not the least bit repulsed by his blood dripping onto her skin and clothes. She fought to keep her anger in check, knowing that Roy was right in telling Alex not to give in. She saw it on her dad's face when they'd first arrived in this dank cave—that woman had no intention of allowing any of them to live.

But knowing that and gazing at the battered friend in her arms—a boy so sweet she couldn't imagine anyone ever wanting to hurt him—she struggled to control her flowing tears.

Roy's eyelids opened, his long lashes fluttering a few times like butterfly wings, and he gazed up at her, first in confusion, then with a tiny smile gracing his bloody, puffed-out lips. "Thanks, Allison." His voice was breathy, like he didn't have enough air in his lungs. She'd heard at least one rib crack. Could it have punctured one of his lungs?

"Don't talk, Roy," she whispered through her tears. "Save your strength. Alex will spin you."

Roy's crooked little smile blossomed into something almost beatific at hearing Alex's name, and he glanced over at the boy in the wheelchair. Allison followed his gaze and met Alex's wide, watery blue eyes. His expression was more bereft of hope than any she'd ever seen before, even her father's when her mother had died. She wanted to say something, to reassure him that everything would come out all right, but how could she when there did, indeed, seem to be no hope?

Ms. G grunted with disgust. "Jäger, start on the girl. We're running out of time."

The big man looked weaker and sicker than ever. It was obvious now that his body was dying. Purple dominated his exposed skin, probably the result of blood barely circulating within his body. He was still strong, but not as much as when they'd first arrived in this cave. But his evil mind was obviously active enough. He leered down at her, and she stiffened, not knowing what he had in mind. Without warning, he swung a huge fist down and clocked her right in the face. She released Roy and went sprawling to the hard, rocky cave floor, pain shooting through her face and head, her consciousness swimming in and out of reality.

She heard her dad growl, "Leave her alone!" Through blurred vision, she saw him yank free from his captors, and even though his hands remained tied behind his back, he lunged forward like a charging bull and slammed his head into Jäger's midsection. The big man let out an "oof!" of surprise and doubled over, the air knocked from his lungs as he toppled backward into Dr. Avila, sending both men to the ground.

One of Ms. G's goons grabbed for her dad before he could continue the attack, pulling him back and restraining him.

Her dad twisted in fury, but the young man held him fast. He looked down at her, panting from his exertion. "You…all right…Allison?"

She sat up, amazed that her wig was still on her head after such a blow. It took a moment to reorient herself, but she nodded. "Yeah, Dad."

Avila disentangled himself first and assisted the bigger man to his feet. Jäger's face was red with fury, and he staggered toward her dad.

"Dad, look out!"

Shaw spun around, but too late to escape the massive fist slamming into his midsection. With a groan, he slammed the man behind him back against the rock wall before crumpling to the ground next to her, gagging and gasping for air. The man who'd been holding him struck his head against the rocks and fell to the ground, unconscious.

"Dad!" She crawled to her father's side and rolled him over. His handsome face was etched with pain, and he continued gasping. Furious, she spun on Jäger and spat at his feet. "Pick on someone your own size, asshole!"

The big man's grin turned to anger, and he reached down to grab her. "Enough!"

That was Alex. She spun around and gazed at the boy she may or may not be in love with. He practically shook with anger, his beautiful face twisted with rage and hate.

"I'll do what you want," he spat at Ms. G. who grinned. "Just leave them alone!"

"No, Alex," groaned the semiconscious Roy. "You…can't."

Tears filled Alex's deep blue eyes, making them look like small fishbowls. "I can't let them keep hurting you all. You're my family and I love you."

"A wise choice, Alex," Ms. G purred like that cat she used to favor as a companion.

"Get him away from them," Alex ordered, pointing at Jäger.

Nonchalantly, she snapped her fingers at the big man. "Stand down, Kurt."

He looked disappointed but obeyed and stepped behind Avila, who had to support him so he wouldn't topple over. Allison wondered how much longer before he died. Couldn't be soon enough to suit her.

Alex turned to Andy, who looked tense, rigid, as though what was happening bothered him on some level, but Allison could never tell with him because Andy's moods were all over the map. Beneath the artificial lights, with his flowing white hair and delicate features that mirrored Alex's, he looked oddly like images of angels she'd seen, which was weird given all the terrible things he'd done.

He extended his hand, and Alex reluctantly took it. Alex froze, his body stiffening in his chair like he'd been jolted with electricity. She studied him as he stared, wide-eyed at his twin brother. Andy, of course, remained stoic and impassive, but Alex looked…stunned. That's the only way to describe it. Like he suddenly understood something earth-shattering. The moment passed quickly because Andy turned away to face the wall of video screens showing people around the world. Ordinary people doing ordinary activities.

"All goodness in every one of you, come into me," Andy intoned, his deep voice almost echoing throughout the cavern.

For a moment, nothing happened. Then Andy smiled, which shocked Allison so much that she blinked to make sure it was real.

"Goodness to Alex," Andy ordered, and then Alex shuddered. His body relaxed, and the tightness of his features melted away, leaving only the soft, delicate beauty that had attracted Allison from the beginning. Alex stayed this way, calm and serene.

Andy stared at the screens. "Hate and anger, all that have been inside me my whole life, leave me and enter them. Enter all of them. Now!"

Allison pulled her gaze from Alex to focus on the screens behind him. The world had erupted into chaos. Families were attacking one another in parks and playgrounds, even the children. One boy threw a large rock at a man she presumed was his father, hitting him in the face and opening a bloody gash on his forehead, knocking him to the ground.

At an outdoor restaurant, patrons had grabbed sharp knives and began plunging them into anyone within reach. On the streets, rioting and looting had ensued, with people running wild and burning buildings or fighting with the police. Some of the people were randomly attacking each other and even burning cars and storefronts. It reminded her of riots she'd seen on the news, only much worse. Screen after screen displayed violence, murder, wanton destruction, but no kindness. No one tried to help anyone else. She understood that Andy had taken those aspects of human nature away from all the people who'd been on screen, and people who'd not been on screen were likely reacting to the violence against them with more violence. Fire to fight fire. She shivered and glanced at her dad, who stared wide-eyed at the carnage. He didn't look as surprised as she thought he should, but then he'd seen a lot more of the bad side of human nature than she had.

"Excellent work, boys," Ms. G said, her voice humming with joy. She strolled over to the man sitting before the keyboard. "A new set of camera locations."

He typed in some commands and the screens cleared for a moment, only to flicker back to life, displaying all new places, people, and activities.

Ms. G. faced Andy. "Again."

Andy made brief eye contact with Alex, who had apparently spun all the good feelings out of himself because he once again looked stressed and guilty. Allison couldn't tell what passed between them, but she knew they were "talking" somehow. Then Andy faced the screens, repeated the process, and more carnage ensued.

Ms. G. crossed the cavern to where her remaining two soldiers stood at attention near the entrance. "Gather up all our troops within the mountain. Take them outside and engage with the soldiers surrounding us. Focus on wounding them only, no killing. I need those soldiers alive."

"Yes, my lady," one young man intoned, his voice sounding robotic. Then he and the other man left the cavern.

Allison heard their footfalls echo away down the tunnel and gazed at Ms. G. The woman must have sensed her staring because she turned and eyed Allison with a smirk.

"You have something to say, Ms. Shaw?"

Allison shook her head and Ms. G turned back to watch the onscreen annihilation of humanity.

CHAPTER EIGHTEEN

I HAVE MY ORDERS, AMANDA

JAVA WATCHED AS PETERS PACED back and forth, keeping a sharp eye out in all directions for any incoming threat. They hadn't heard anything yet from the colonel, and he knew that worried her, but she seemed to keep her cool no matter what was going down. Francis sat poised on a large rock, his sharp eyes roaming the mountainside for any potential threat. He looked like Batman high up on some building in Gotham City.

The darkness and warm stillness felt heavy as it squeezed in on Java, and he eyed Izzy and Jorge to see how they were handling the wait. He gave Izzy a friendly punch to the shoulder and the chin raise, which the other boy returned. Izzy didn't seem to be afraid, which impressed Java.

Jorge, on the other hand, never seemed to stress over anything. It was always hard to know what he might be thinking. In that way, he was like that little bitch Andy.

If I get my hands on him…

Java felt his heart begin to pound and quickly squelched his anger. He had to maintain control, the way Colonel Walker needed. He studied Jorge a long moment. The other boy stared out at the adjoining mountains, seeing or hearing something Java could not. Then, quiet as a cat, a figure rose out of the dark from below and landed beside Java, startling him.

"William!"

Peters turned and hurried over to the boys. William stood to face her while Java and the others looked on. Francis left his perch and moved to William's side.

"Report, Agent Weapon," Peters said, her tone all business.

"The colonel has established that General Lewis is not a traitor," the boy replied, a soldier giving his report. "At least not yet."

Peters looked relieved, though it was difficult to see her eyes in the dark. "Anything else?"

"The colonel wants us to keep trying to find a way inside. Me and Francis will scout around in case there's an opening one of us can squeeze through or widen if it's too small."

"You want me to come with you?" Java asked, hoping to get in on some of the action. So far, he hadn't done anything.

"Thanks, Java," William replied, "but I think we can get around more quickly on this rocky ground."

He glanced at Francis, and the younger boy nodded.

"Okay." Java tried to hide his disappointment.

Movement caught his eye, and he looked past Peters toward the cave entrance. Shimmering light appeared, and then men became visible. A LOT of men! He wasn't good with numbers, but it looked like two or three football teams of men emerging from the mountain.

"Airman Peters!"

He pointed, and she spun around, gun at the ready.

The first of the men through the opening heard his shout and raised their weapons. With the light behind them, they were eerie silhouettes, but their intention was clear. Peters fired first, striking one man in the chest. He fell into a dark heap and didn't move.

"Get down!" Peters ducked down and fired again, striking a second man in the shoulder. The large group of figures sprinted away from the mouth of the cave into the darkness. All Java saw as he dropped below an outcropping of rock were sparks of light as bullets were fired. *Pop, pop, pop* echoed through the hills.

Francis morphed into Wolfboy faster than he had on the chopper and followed William forward to deflect the bullets, both sprinting into the midst of the men like wild animals. Wolfboy attacked with his claws, while William punched and kicked any who came near. Most of the men scattered in fear, but the shooting continued.

Java glanced up and saw Izzy still standing, mesmerized by the fighting. Jorge was already hunkered down. Java grabbed Izzy's sleeve and tugged. "Down, Izzy!"

Bullets sailed over his head, and he heard Izzy grunt before his best friend toppled onto him like dead weight. "Izzy!"

It was too dark for Java to see the wound, but as he gently pushed Izzy off him and laid him on his back, his hands came away sticky with blood. The coppery smell almost made him gag, and he exchanged a terror-filled look with Jorge, who had crawled closer and stared at Izzy's unmoving form.

"Airman Peters, Izzy's been hit!" Java poked his head over the rocks. The shooting had stopped, and all was dark. The light from inside the cave had vanished, meaning it was closed to them once more.

Peters was suddenly by his side, flashlight in hand, examining Izzy. The blood poured out of the right side of his chest, and he was unconscious. William and Francis—once more a dark-haired boy—crouched on Java's other side.

"We took out some, but most got away," William said, looking at Izzy with concern. "How is he?"

"Not good," Peters replied. "He needs pressure on that wound." She eyed Java. "Keep your hands pressed right here." She indicated the spot where blood had soaked his camo shirt. Grabbing a backpack, she reached in and extracted a thick roll of gauze and some medical tape. "William, Francis, help lift his torso so we can wrap him."

With a gentleness that was the opposite of the ferocity they'd just shown, William and Francis gripped Izzy under each arm and gently lifted him to a half-sitting position.

Peters pulled off an enormous wad of gauze and handed it to Java. "Press this into the wound."

Java took the ball of folded gauze and pressed it up against Izzy's chest. It was instantly soaked with blood, but he held it against his friend with as much force as he thought necessary. Peters expertly wrapped a large, thick bandage around Izzy's upper body, threading it under his armpits and wrapping it around and around, covering the gauze so that Java had to let go. She finally ran out and tugged hard to make the binding as strong and tight as possible. After securing the bandage to itself with a clip, she fished in the backpack and pulled out what looked like a rough blanket, handing it to Java.

"Press this up against him and don't let go." She nodded to William and Francis. The two boys carefully lowered Izzy back onto the ground.

Java took the blanket, his hands trembling. He placed it against Izzy's chest and held it in place.

"We need medics." She stood, wiping the blood onto her camos, and snatched up a walkie-talkie from her supply stash.

As she radioed for help, Java looked up at Jorge and fought to keep his voice steady. "He's gonna make it, Jorge."

Despite the darkness, Java was sure he saw tears in his friend's eyes.

"Take care of him, Java," William said as he stood, his white hands dark with blood, Francis at his side like a shadow. "We must find a way into this mountain."

Java met his gaze. "Thanks, man. I got this."

William nodded, and then he and Francis dashed off into the night.

***

Dane stared at the computer screen in horror. If he didn't know that what he was seeing was real, he'd figure it was another of those crazy-ass Purge movies. Lewis had contacted his bosses over at the Pentagon—the Joint Chiefs, he called them—all of whom sat in small boxes on the computer screen. When the President of the United States joined the chat, Dane knew this was serious.

They all talked about how time was running out, and then Lewis's computer was filled with news feeds from around the world. That was the Purge part. People were going crazy, hurting and killing, robbing and looting, burning, and crashing cars. It was like everything bad they'd ever wanted to do, they were doing!

Once the president and the Joint Chiefs filled the screen again, the colonel was forced to admit that he hadn't managed to penetrate the mountain. "But my team is still on it, Mr. President."

The president looked grave. "We don't have time, Colonel. As you just saw, the world is crashing in on itself. While I don't fully understand about these gates, the Pope has assured me they are quite real. We cannot allow them to open. He, along with your own Cardinal Leone, are agreed that if the gate inside Superstition Mountain fails to open, the others will also remain closed." He glanced at his watch. "There is less than one hour until midnight. If I have not heard that you've taken that woman and her people out, General Lewis, I order you to blow the mountain to kingdom come."

Amanda gagged. "But Mr. President, that'll trap everyone inside. Alex and the others will be killed. They're just kids!"

"Mrs. Walker, you know as well as your husband that in war, the bigger picture must be the priority. We cannot allow whatever it is that woman is harboring to escape the mountain. Collateral damage is to be expected."

Nathan stepped forward, fearless even before the president. "That collateral damage is my seventeen-year-old son and three fifteen-year-olds. And Russell Shaw, a good man who's gone out of his way to help those kids."

The president's face softened a bit. "I'm sorry, sir. I truly am. But those are my orders. At eleven-fifty-five tonight, General Lewis will be up in a Blackhawk with two pilots and will commence bombardment. You have until then to rescue the hostages. Now I have other fires to put out. Good luck, all of you."

The president and the other serious faces vanished from the screen.

Amanda clutched at Lewis's arm. "Jason, please. You can't do this!"

Lewis studied her with a look that might have been sympathy. "I'm sorry, Amanda, but I have my orders. Now if you'll excuse me, I must move my troops farther back from the base of the mountain. Good luck, Colonel."

He saluted, and Colonel Walker returned it. Then the general swept out through the flap, leaving the colonel to deal with Amanda's indignation and that of the others. They would want to know why he hadn't protested. That was easy—the general was right. Stopping the invasion was more important than saving any individual life. He just wasn't at all certain blowing up that mountain would stop anyone except the humans inside. Even that woman might walk out of the rubble unscathed. He needed to contact Cardinal Leone, and they had precious little time.

***

Java's forearms and shoulders ached from holding them in position so long, but he refused to let up on the pressure he was applying to Izzy's wound. His best friend hadn't awakened, but Peters assured him Izzy's breathing was steady. Jorge pantomimed taking over for Java, but he shook his head. *He* would take care of Izzy, no matter what.

He had no idea how much time had passed since William took off and Peters called for medics, but it seemed like forever. Finally, he heard an approaching truck. Its wheels ground to a halt on the rocky ground somewhere out in the dark and then he heard scrambling feet getting closer.

Dr. Shepherd jogged across the rough terrain toward him, followed by two men, with Peters shining her flashlight ahead of them so no one tripped in the dark. Java's pounding heart lurched with relief when she dropped down beside him.

"You can let go now, Java."

Her calm tone was just what he needed. He removed his sticky hands, afraid to touch anything until he'd washed them. He'd long since gotten used to the nasty smell of fresh blood.

Dr. Shepherd used small scissors she took from a big first aid kit to cut the shirt around Izzy's wound. She inspected the bandages and glanced at Java. "You did a good job."

"Uh, that was Airman Peters."

"I see." She began cutting through the sopping bandage, blood staining her pale fingers. "But you kept your head and took care of him. That will make all the difference."

He nodded, feeling pride in himself for not panicking.

Once the bandage was removed, blood trickled out, but didn't flow steadily as before. Java glanced up at Peters, who leaned down to observe the proceedings.

Dr. Shepherd waved over the other two medics. "Remove his shirt, then clean the wound. That bullet must come out here. No time to get him back to base camp."

"Yes, Doctor," one of the young men said, and they both went to work on Izzy.

"He gonna be okay, right, Doc?" Java gazed at her with wide eyes.

Her face looked strained. "I hope so. I must get my surgical kit. It's in the other bag." She stood and hurried away into the dark.

Peters' radio squawked and she snatched it off her belt. "Yes, Colonel?"

Java heard Colonel Walker's voice pound out of the walkie-talkie. "Has William found a way inside yet?"

"Not that I know of, sir. He's searching now."

"You need to get everyone off that mountain. In less than forty minutes, General Lewis is going to launch missiles to bring the mountain down on everyone inside."

"The hell?" Java blurted out his feelings without thinking.

"Who was that?" Walker asked.

"Java," Peters reported.

"Java, listen to me," the colonel said, louder than before. "These orders come from the president himself. We must follow them."

"What if they're wrong, Colonel?" Java hadn't meant to argue, but he couldn't help it. Alex and Roy were inside that mountain. And Allison.

There was a long pause on the colonel's end. "I agree with you, Java, but Lewis doesn't. You must clear out and hope William can breach their security and rescue the hostages."

"Colonel, we have a situation here," Peters said and promptly relayed what had happened.

"Any idea where those men of hers went?"

"No, Colonel. They vanished into the dark, but I heard them descending the mountain."

There was another pause. "Tell Liz to work as fast as she can and then get everyone as far from that mountain as you can."

"Yes, Colonel." She ended the call and replaced the walkie-talkie on her belt. Java met her gaze in the dark. "We still have a little time. Let's take care of your friend."

***

Amanda had returned to base camp with Martin and the others, checking her watch every few seconds, it seemed, and knowing they were almost out of time. Nathan was a broken man, unable to contain his grief over what was about to happen to his boys, and Dane was livid.

She felt she could still persuade the general, but she had to get to that chopper before it lifted off. Not wanting Martin to follow, she excused herself to go to the medical tent.

Once Martin and the others were out of sight, she ran as fast as she could toward the makeshift airfield where the copters were waiting. She stopped and scanned the darkness for any sign of Lewis. She saw movement. Three figures, all heading for the largest Black Hawk. She sprinted in that direction.

By the time she reached the chopper, the pilots were in their seats, and the bird was warming up. She ran to the open cargo doors and craned her neck to see inside. Lewis sat in the seat directly behind the cockpit, looking solemn.

"Jason!"

He looked up, shocked to see her. "Amanda. What are you doing here?"

"I'm here to reason with you. Now help me up."

His face was shadowed, but for a moment, she saw the compassion that had drawn him to her in the first place. "You won't change my mind."

"Are you going to help me, or do I clamber in by myself?"

He sighed. "Still the same stubborn woman." He leaned over and stretched out one meaty hand. She grasped it with both of hers, stepped up onto the foothold, and then, with a hard tug from him, she was up and into the seat beside him.

"There, that's better," she said, eyeing him in the darkened interior. The rotors began spinning faster now and she heard the pilot say. "Lifting off, General."

"Make for the big mountain," Lewis replied, glancing at Amanda. She said nothing, only stared at him. Her intensity made him uncomfortable, just as it always had. Lewis was still intimidated by strong women, she realized, despite his career trajectory.

The chopper rose into the air, the cabin roaring with wind and the noise of the gigantic rotors. She felt her stomach drop, as it always did when she ascended into the air, but the sensation quickly subsided.

"I have my orders, Amanda."

"Orders you know are wrong."

"No, orders that are unpleasant, but under these circumstances, not wrong."

Exasperated, she huffed. "They are immoral, at the very least. Killing those children will accomplish nothing."

"It will stop that gate from opening, and at the moment, that's our prime objective."

"You only met Alex on a video chat, Jason," she insisted. "I know that boy and he will find a way to stop this from happening."

Lewis eyed his watch. "He has twenty minutes."

"Just wait, that's all I'm asking. Wait till after midnight. Let's see what Alex can do."

His lined face looked filled with shadows as he frowned. "And if those things invade?"

"Cardinal Leone and his people have plans in place to fight them."

Lewis said nothing, but Amanda knew he was considering her idea.

"Please, Jason. Do it for me if for no other reason."

He studied her in the dark, and she wondered if she'd pushed too hard. Then he turned to stare out at the dark desert beneath them. The tall mountain loomed ever closer.

***

Father Pat gazed down the mountainside from his perch atop the large bluff that gave him a clear view of the "battlefield" below, though he could not make out individual soldiers without binoculars. He could not see all of the entrance to the big mountain but could make out movement on the bluff surrounding it. He was startled to see multiple figures scuttling down the mountainside toward the soldiers on the desert floor. There was no way to warn them, so he focused on his job.

He eyed Leone as he applied last minute touches to his station. Leone was the trained exorcist, so Father Pat would merely assist him. He'd reviewed the rite and felt as prepared as he could be, but memories of the horrific beings that had inhabited Cuong and then, briefly, Alex sent waves of terror throughout his body. He'd never felt such malevolence as he had from those creatures, and now the possibility of facing hundreds or thousands of them was almost too much to bear.

He'd helped the cardinal set out the flasks of holy water, the copies of the rite each would hold, the large crucifix each would wear. Leone had also brought a piece of equipment with him from Rome that Father Pat had never seen. The cardinal described it as a "kind of Geiger counter for spiritual beings." Supposedly, the device would detect the presence—and any increase in numbers—of supernatural entities that came through the gate. There was an electronic measurement feature and a small satellite-type dish protruding upward in the air. When Leone activated the unit, the dish would spin, searching the area for signs of incursion. It was an ingenious device and made Father Pat wonder what other technological marvels the Vatican had developed for fighting supernatural evil.

He and Leone had donned their vestments at the base camp, and these had also been blessed and sprinkled with holy water. Montour, decked out in tribal regalia sprinkled with colorful beads and lots of feathers, had set up a large pot that he would use along with traditional tribal incantations to drive off evil spirits. Father Pat wandered over and asked what exactly was in the pot, noting that the leaves possessed a yellowish color.

Montour said, "This is a tribal form of tobacco called *o-yen'-kwa*. It is used exclusively in all our religious rites. It's mixed with an herb called *degokimak*."

Father Pat studied the mixture, noting that the ones Montour called an herb resembled bay leaves.

"I will burn this mixture as an offering to the spirits that may or may not emerge from the mountain. In that way, they may leave us alone long enough for you and Alessandro to do your ritual. I will also be attempting to contact Andy, if he has not moved beyond my reach."

The cardinal had also prepared the helicopter prior to leaving base camp. He'd left a large box of consecrated hosts, and Montour a box of his sacred tobacco, and instructed Colonel Walker what needed to be done and when. The colonel had assured him he or Peters would fly that chopper when the need arose.

So now, it was a waiting game. Father Pat studied his watch in the darkness. Eighteen minutes till midnight. Did that mean eighteen minutes till Armageddon or eighteen minutes till humanity scored a painful but blessed second chance? He'd know soon enough.

He heard a crackling noise, and then Colonel Walker's voice came over the walkie-talkie. He hurried to the folding table just as Leone grabbed the unit and opened the talk button.

"Yes, Colonel?"

"Are your teams assembled at the other gates?"

"Yes. We have our best people present. There are also fire trucks on site which will perform the same role as your helicopter."

"Good. Now listen, Cardinal. The president has authorized a missile strike on that mountain at 11:55 if we haven't found a way in by that time."

Father Pat gasped, and the cardinal frowned, glancing at Montour a moment. "How does the president reason such a strike will help? These are supernatural creatures. They can withstand any weaponry."

"Yes, but Alex can't," the colonel's voice went on. "By the president's figuring, if he kills Alex, the gate cannot be opened."

"No!" Father Pat couldn't contain himself.

"Please, Father Pat," Leone said calmly. "Colonel, I admit his reasoning is sound, but I don't wish to sacrifice the Healer or any of the other hostages."

"Me either. Just be ready to do your part. I'll do what I can to prevent that missile attack."

Leone's thick eyebrows rose in surprise. "You would defy your own president?"

"I learned from an artificially created boy that immoral orders must be disobeyed."

"But you will have to face a court-martial, Colonel," Montour said, leaning closer to the walkie-talkie.

"A chance I have to take. Walker out."

The unit crackled into silence, and Leone set it down beside the bottles of holy water. "A brave man, the colonel."

"Very," agreed Montour.

CHAPTER NINETEEN

WE'RE OUT OF TIME

ALLISON STARED IN OPEN-MOUTHED HORROR at the carnage and wanton destruction happening around the world. It seemed the entire planet had gone up in flames ever since Andy had begun shifting goodness out of people and inserting anger and hate. She'd never thought much about the duality of human nature, though she had read *The Strange Case of Dr. Jekyll and Mr. Hyde* for a book report once. She figured that was just a story and that in real life, most people were basically good. That's what she always heard in school—that when people did bad things, it was the fault of society.

But now, watching individuals wreaking havoc and mayhem, she understood that the human soul was much more complicated. Roy moaned and she hurried back to him, leaning down to whisper assurances in his ear that help would be coming. But would it? The only person who could prevent Roy's death was Alex, and Allison was pretty sure the evil bitch who ran this place wouldn't allow it.

She was startled from her thoughts by the woman announcing, "That will be all, Andy. I think we've sufficiently stirred the pot."

Andy released Alex's hand and stepped away from the computer console. Alex sagged in his wheelchair, like all the energy had been drained from him. But it was more than that. He looked like he might vomit any moment, and Allison thought she knew why. Alex understood that it was his power that had caused all the death and devastation, and those were things Alex detested more than anything else. His conscience must be working overtime condemning him for what he'd been forced to do.

Jäger had sat in a wooden chair during the shifting, and his stench had grown so bad Allison thought she might throw up. She glanced over at him. Avila stood beside him, checking his pulse. The doctor wore a grave expression, which hopefully meant that sadistic prick Jäger would die any second.

Allison turned and looked down at Roy, at the bruises, the bright red burn marks on his chest where the electricity had jolted him. In that moment, as he lay there, head lolling side to side in a semiconscious state, she knew she could fall for him too. They had a lot in common and, in many ways, their personalities overlapped more tightly than she and Alex. Alex tended to brood, whereas she could tell Roy was more of an open book when it came to his feelings.

He tried to move, but she placed a gentle hand on his shoulder. "Lie still, Roy."

His half-open eyes fixed on her, and she knew he recognized her. A tiny smile graced his lips, and the snakebite piercings—which she liked—glinted beneath the overhead lights.

Ms. G strode over to Alex and studied him, but addressed Andy. "You didn't drain his power again, did you?"

"No, Teacher," Andy replied in that annoyingly monotone voice Allison hated. "I think he feels guilty about what we did."

Ms. G kept her eyes on Alex. "Snap out of it, Healer. You have more work to do." When Alex didn't respond, merely sat staring, she slapped him across the face. *Crack!* The sound echoed around them.

"Leave him alone, bitch!" Allison couldn't help herself, glancing back at her dad.

Shaw was red-faced with fury, but she could tell he was up to something. He caught her eye and shifted his expression slightly to indicate he didn't want the others to notice him, so she turned back as Alex, red mark blooming on his right cheek, glared at the woman, enraged. She just smiled.

"There, that's better. Now that I have your attention, it's time to get into position. The gate must be opened in ten minutes."

That slap must've reawakened Alex's natural tenacity because he blurted, "Open it yourself!"

Ms. G sighed and rolled her eyes. "They never learn." He turned and snapped her fingers at Jäger.

Allison was glad to see the monster needed help to stand, but once he gained his feet, that G.I. Joe face morphed into a twisted, sadistic grin. He stepped closer to Roy. Allison leaned forward to cover Roy with her body.

"Leave him alone, you sick freak! Why don't you just die already?"

Jäger growled like a wolf and grabbed for her hair. Yanking it hard, he found a long brown wig in his hands, staring at it in confusion.

Allison smirked and stuck out her tongue.

Incensed, the big man tossed the wig aside and leaned down to backhand her across the face. Pain slammed through her, and she flew off to one side, landing at her father's feet.

Her dad shouted, "I'll kill you for that!"

"Stop!" Alex wheeled forward, but Ms. G blocked his path.

Jäger ignored all of them. With one massive hand, he gripped Roy around the throat and lifted him off the ground. Roy gagged and struggled but was too weak to resist. Then Jäger slammed him down hard at Alex's feet.

Allison didn't quite know how, but suddenly her dad was no longer tied up and he lunged at Jäger, swinging out with one fist and clocking the man on one side of his face. Despite the size difference, Jäger staggered. As Shaw moved in for another blow, Jäger swung wildly with one arm and connected with her dad's chest, sending him tumbling back into the rock wall. He struck his head and collapsed, dazed, to the floor.

Allison crawled to him, her face throbbing from the blow she'd taken. "Dad!" She rolled him over and saw that he wasn't out yet, so she gently rubbed his face and hands to keep him awake.

"Stop, stop, stop!" Alex had screamed so loud she felt certain anyone outside the mountain would've heard him.

Allison took that moment to look around. Jäger had collapsed into a heap and Avila was examining him. He looked up at the woman and shook his head. She clucked her tongue and faced Alex.

"Well, Healer?"

Andy squatted down in front of Alex and took his hand. Alex made eye contact with his twin, and, once more, something passed between them, something even Ms. G noticed.

"What are you doing, Andy?"

Andy broke eye contact with Alex and looked up at her. "Helping to convince him."

Alex mumbled, "Okay, I'll do it. Just don't hurt them anymore."

She purred, "Now that wasn't so hard, was it? Follow me."

She crossed the cavern to the rock wall where the computer console ended. Alex wheeled closer, Andy right behind him. She pointed to a thin crack that ran from floor to ceiling. "All you need to do is place your hands on this wall near the crack. Think you can manage that?"

Alex glared at her, but then he did something Allison found odd. He looked back at Andy, and they locked eyes. Again, some silent communication passed between them. He faced the woman again.

"Before I do, I want Roy and Allison over here with me. Shaw too. They're my family."

She looked amused, rather than angry. "You're in no position to bargain, but I'll grant that one concession. The girlfriend and boyfriend only. Not Mr. Shaw. I have plans for him."

She waved over Avila, and he scurried forward, clearly terrified of her. "Drag the boy over behind the wheelchair."

Avila nodded. "Yes, my lady." He hurried to Roy's limp body and reached up under the arms, dragging him over the rough ground more gently than Allison would've expected. Then Ms. G eyed her from across the chamber.

"Well? Your boyfriend wants you with him."

Allison glanced down at her dad and made eye contact. He was fully conscious now but pretended not to be. He gave a slight nod for her to go. Knowing he had some plan in mind, she rose to her feet, wobbling a bit from the blow she'd taken, and then made her away across to crouch behind Alex's wheelchair, right beside the unconscious Roy.

Ms. G consulted her watch. "Six minutes and counting." She sounded excited, like a girl right before her sixteenth birthday bash.

Alex refused to look at her. He merely stared at the rock wall, at the crack not even large enough to allow ants to crawl through.

Ms. G glowed with energy as she stared at the wall. "Almost time, my brethren."

***

Amanda gazed into the cockpit and out through the windshield as the mountain loomed closer and larger. She knew the pilots would swing around the mountain seeking the area that Bryan had already blown up, figuring that cave entrance might be near the main hub where Alex was being held captive. She only had minutes, if not seconds, to convince Jason to call off the attack.

Jason sat beside her, irresolute as a statue, though she knew him well enough to know he hated following this order. He'd never been so macho that he considered civilian casualties acceptable toward winning a battle. But this order had come directly from the president and if he aborted the mission, his career, his pension, perhaps even his freedom might be over.

"Jason, please," she tried again. "He's only a boy and a very special boy."

He turned to face her, his expression grim. "Don't you think I know that, Amanda? I was there when he saved the astronaut. I watched as he saved those people in that bank. The kid is a one-of-a-kind gift to this country. But I have my orders. I'm sorry."

She stared at him, amazed that he'd opened up his feelings so much.

"What Walker suspected was true, Amanda," he said so quietly she had to lean closer to hear. "I did betray my country to that woman. I set up your husband to get blown up on base. I brought the troops here as bait because she told me to."

Amanda knew she should be shocked, but she wasn't. She'd suspected as much back in his tent. "What turned you against her?"

He met her gaze in the dark. "You. What you said about me. I remembered who I used to be before she clouded my mind and my loyalties. I must destroy her, Amanda. I must stop this invasion to make up, in my mind, at least, for betraying my country."

He turned away and gazed out the windshield. Not sure how to respond, Amanda glanced at her wristwatch. Less than two minutes to go.

***

Ms. G continued staring at her watch, but Alex was focused on Roy slumped next to his wheelchair. Roy's health status was weak and growing weaker. He had to spin his best friend if he still could. Maybe Andy would help, but he had to act fast or…

"My lady, incoming chopper," intoned the computer operator, who so far hadn't spoken a word.

"Armed?"

"Yes, my lady."

"You know what to do."

"Yes, my lady."

As Alex watched, the man leaned forward and flipped a series of switches. An explosive, propulsive sound filled the chamber and the mountain seemed to rock, like an earthquake had struck.

Ms. G smiled.

***

Amanda saw a flash directly ahead and flinched.

One of the pilots barked, "Incoming, General. Evading."

Lewis glanced at Amanda with concern. "Hang on, Amanda."

Just in time, she gripped the bench seat with both hands as the copter lurched violently to one side, veering off and away from the mountain. She slammed into Jason, almost landing in his lap. The moment was awkward, but familiar given their long-ago courtship. She heard it then, the missile, as it whizzed past at incredible speed.

"Well, now we know they're armed," Lewis grumbled. He leaned forward into the cockpit. "Any others?"

The two men studied their readouts. Amanda spotted another flash of light in the distance.

The pilots swerved again, but Amanda was ready. This time the chopper lurched upward, and the missile whistled past underneath.

Jason glanced at his watch. "Two minutes to midnight. Can we get off a shot?"

"Negative, General, not at any precise target. If you just want to hit the mountain anywhere, I'll fire."

"We're running out of time, Airman. Take your best shot."

"Yes, sir."

The pilot flipped several switches and opened a small hatch, revealing a red button. He gazed out through the windshield as the other pilot flew the Black Hawk. Amanda knew this was a top-of-the-line aircraft capable of tricky moves and fierce combat, and it had excellent targeting capabilities. She bit her lower lip and stared out the windshield at the looming peak in the distance.

Another flash from the mountain lit up the sky and she cried out, "They fired again!"

The main pilot swung the chopper to the left just as the other one pressed the red button.

She felt the Hawk vibrate as the missile flew from below and headed for the mountain peak. Then she was hanging on for dear life as the chopper swung a wide arc around. It must not have been wide enough because suddenly everything lurched, the rear rotor exploded in a fireball, and the Hawk started spinning out of control.

Lewis grabbed her hand and pulled her in close.

Her heart raced as the spinning grew more intense. She barely had time to glance up at Lewis's stoic expression before she felt herself slam into the ground, and everything went black.

***

With his fingers digging into crevices like a professional rock climber, William crouched against the craggy face of the mountain. He watched as the outgoing missile, which came from above, sheared off a portion of the rear rotor and sent the chopper into a tailspin. The whistling sound reminded him of the incoming missile fired by the Hawk.

"Hang on, Francis!"

The younger boy was dug in beside him, able to hold his own.

The missile slammed into the mountain peak, rumbling the rock face and raining down a shower of boulders onto the boys.

***

The cavern rocked with an explosion. The ground trembled, and Alex feared the entire cave might collapse in on them.

"Do not fear, Healer," Ms. G said, completely unfazed. "We are quite secure here."

Alex glanced at Allison, who looked spooked by the rumbling ground beneath her.

"Chopper is down, my lady," the computer operator intoned like a zombie.

Alex wondered who might have been in that helicopter. If it was William, he knew not to worry. But what if it was Colonel Walker?

"Excellent, Franz." She studied her watch. Alex figured it must have something ticking down the seconds. Her blue eyes alight with power, she looked at him. "Now, Healer."

Feeling like he was made of lead, Alex lifted his arms and opened his hands, pressing them firmly against the warm rock wall. Energy surged through him, even more than when he joined with Andy. His body thrummed and vibrated. His fingers felt hot; the heat soaked into his arms and powered its way throughout his body. His body built up an intense charge, making him feel like he might explode any second.

The crack began to widen.

***

Colonel Walker had tried to reach General Lewis on the radio, but Lewis must've put the chopper on radio silence. He was leading Martin, Dane, and Nathan back up the slope toward the cave entrance, but Dane was tiring from all the exertion, and Nathan had to support him, which slowed their progress. When the first missile shot from the mountain above, Walker led the men to a sheltering outcrop of rock, and everyone crouched down to avoid fallout should the chopper return fire.

When the third missile struck the Hawk, he tried with increasing desperation to raise the pilot, if not the general. He only received static in return. Martin crept closer.

"Anything I can do, Colonel?"

As he watched the chopper spin out of control, Walker shook his head. He glanced up at the incoming missile.

"Down!"

They all crouched beneath the outcropping and covered their faces with their hands. The ground rumbled and shook from the impact, but they were far enough away not to feel any shattered rocks rain down on them.

Poking their heads out like turtles, they stared soberly into the desert as the Black Hawk crashed into a heap of twisted metal that did not, for the moment, burst into flames.

"Go, Martin, help evacuate the wounded," Walker ordered, his tone crisp and clear.

"Yes, sir." Martin leaped up and barreled down the mountainside toward the wreckage in the distance.

Walker grabbed for his binoculars and scanned the area. Soldiers who had scattered to avoid being crushed were now hurrying to the downed copter. Walker lowered the glasses, wondering if Lewis had survived. Then another thought occurred to him. William and Francis! They were on the mountain trying to get inside. He tapped the earpiece in his right ear.

"Walker to Weapon, do you read?"

He waited a full minute, but there was no response.

***

Java heard the missiles but couldn't see them from where he and Jorge sat side by side, watching Dr. Shepherd operate on Izzy to take out the bullet. He didn't know how long she'd been working, but it seemed like forever. When he heard the first missile, he glanced up at Peters, who crouched in a defensive posture eyeing the darkness beyond.

"Missiles," she said. "Someone inside the mountain is firing them."

"At what?"

"Undetermined, at this point. But whatever it is will likely fire back."

Moments later, an explosion sounded overhead, and rocks and dirt showered down from above. Peters leaped to her feet, and so did Java. Debris raced down the mountainside from on high and piled up a few feet from their location. Peters looked up and around, but there was no second hit.

"Dr. Shepherd," she said, spinning around to face the doctor. "How much longer till he can be moved?"

Without even glancing up, she said, "I've extracted the bullet. Suturing now. Have that stretcher ready."

"Yes, doctor." She turned to the two medics who had accompanied Shepherd. "You men ready?"

"Yes."

"Then let's hope there're no more attacks." Peters glanced at her watch. "We're out of time anyway. It's midnight."

***

Allison stared in horror as the crack in the rock wall widened, but not a speck of light emerged. Instead, a thick, oppressive darkness, like a heavy raincloud, was all that became visible. Alex gazed at the ever-widening gap with fear. Andy stood by his side, immobile, watching the opening with wide-eyed interest.

The woman Alex called Ms. G grinned like she'd just won the lottery. Then her features began to change, to shift like a dissolve in a movie. Her face became a mix of the beautiful blonde woman she'd been for so long and something hideous, almost amorphous. A face, yes, but twisted and ugly and cruel. And her blue eyes became dark as coal, squinting and malevolent. Allison nearly cried out in terror.

Then came a sound from deep inside the black void opening before her. Rushing water? No, more like wind. A powerful driving wind, like a tornado or hurricane. It started low, like the beginning of an earthquake, as though far away. Then it increased, growing louder and more overbearing. Still, Allison saw nothing in that vast void. The gap was easily wide enough for two or three people to pass through.

The wind noise increased so much she clamped both hands over her ears. Alex released the wall and did the same, but Andy seemed unfazed. Before she could even wonder why, the cavern was blasted with something escaping the void. It wasn't wind, and it wasn't clouds. It was…creatures! Things! She couldn't even describe them because they, like the thing inside Ms. G, seemed to be shapeless black masses of varying sizes that howled as they poured forth from the void and raced across the cavern into the tunnel beyond. The suction was so strong that she held on to Alex's wheelchair to keep from sliding away.

The cavern became so cold her teeth chattered and she could see her breath. Her body felt numb, not just with cold but with malicious evil, as though the "things" sweeping past her were the incarnation of darkness itself.

Ms. G cackled with delight, her true self now fully visible on her face—ugly and repellant and inhuman.

Allison decided this might be the end after all.

***

The army of men in black clothing Father Pat had seen scrambling down the mountainside poured out onto the battlefield and began firing on the soldiers stationed there. Right after that, he'd watched in horror the missile battle that had taken the huge helicopter out of the sky, and prayed that whoever was aboard had survived. His companions did the same. Montour was the first to sense the ground beneath his feet shifting, like perhaps there had been an earthquake many miles from their location. Soon Leone and Father Pat noticed the same sensation. But it was more like a vibration, like something powering upward from deep within the planet.

Then Leone's demon detector began beeping with uncontrolled frenzy, the dial pinned to the red zone.

"The gate is open," Leone spoke softly and with sober dispassion. "Battle stations, my friends."

The three men scrambled to their assigned stations. Montour added more fuel to his smoking pot of tobacco, and the thick plume twisted upward into the night sky. Father Pat and Cardinal Leone grasped the rite of exorcism in one hand and a vial of holy water in the other. For his part, Father Pat prayed their helicopter would not be late.

Then, to his horror, one side of the mountain peak seemed to explode outward, and the air became black with flying, twisting, blackened creatures the likes of which he'd only seen once before—when Alex had been possessed back in California. The massive wave of evil descended the mountain, heading straight for the soldiers battling it out on the dark desert floor.

***

Colonel Walker was once more leading Nathan, who was still supporting Dane, up the rugged hillside when a roaring wind seemed to pour down on them from the mountain above. He froze in place, and then his blood turned to ice as the mass of entities emerged from the mountain in an enormous black cloud that looked like exhaust fumes.

"Holy shit," Dane muttered, staring as the cloud soared above them toward the soldiers below.

Walker had no idea how many men the enemy had sent to engage his soldiers, but there were more than enough to keep them busy. Based on what Leone had told him earlier, he thought he knew why the creatures were headed toward the men. He grabbed his walkie-talkie.

"Walker to Peters, do you copy? Over."

Her voice crackled out of the speaker. "Peters here, Colonel."

"Status report?"

"We managed to avoid those things that emerged from the mountain and the boy is ready to be moved."

"Get everyone off that mountain and return to base camp. I need you in the air ASAP."

"Yes, Colonel. Peters out."

Nathan leaned closer, his face twisted with fear. "Do you think Roy and Alex are still alive?"

Walker studied him in the dark. "Alex is, or that gate would not be opened. I'm sorry, Nathan, but we can't go any closer. We need to get up to Cardinal Leone. He's the only one who can finish this." He paused, frowning. "And William. I need William even more."

He tapped his earpiece. "Walker to Weapon, respond. Over." He waited, but no sound came through. "Damn!" He eyed the two men. "Can you make it up there, Dane?"

He pointed to the bluff behind them. It was higher than the crag where Java and the others were waiting, but the way up looked easier to traverse.

Dane didn't hesitate. "Yes, sir."

"Good, let's go."

Leading the way, he backtracked to an adjacent path and began his ascent, the other two following more quickly than he'd have thought possible.

***

Davalos had seen enough. When the chopper went down, he'd nearly deployed his team to help with the rescue, but when soldiers surrounded the wreckage searching for survivors, he'd held back. But now, there was pandemonium. Whatever the things were that had emerged from that mountain, they were wreaking havoc on the men below. In the ensuing battles between the general's men and those of the woman, the helicopter crash was forgotten. Now there was chaos, and any survivors would surely die.

He held up his remote-control device and called his team to him. They approached from out of the darkness.

"Time to go into action, my children. Disarm and disable, but don't kill."

His command was rewarded with snuffles, growls, clicks, and a bark.

"Griffin will stay with me."

The massive, winged creature mewled, apparently liking that idea.

Davalos pressed the "send" button and the others started down the steep slope. Bear lumbered along faster than his bulk would suggest, but Dog and Kitty, the two most nimble, leaped from boulder to rock to path with the ease of circus performers. Scorpio skittered down the rocky hill with ease, having been bred for the desert.

Davalos turned to face Griffin. The massive lion face loomed before him, and he stroked the creature's muzzle with love. How he'd ever dismissed these beings as mere experiments he'd never know. They each had their own personality traits, and all of them responded to love and affection.

"Griffin, fly me down to that helicopter wreckage, but keep above those things flying around until we're directly above the chopper."

The huge animal mewled again and licked Davalos's cheek with its thick, rough tongue. Davalos had been warned by Leone to avoid any contact with the supernatural entities lest he become possessed by one, and he intended to heed that warning.

Clambering onto Griffin's back, Davalos gripped the thick mane surrounding its head and said, "Go!"

The creature's gigantic wings flapped and caught air. Davalos was up and out over the slope before he could catch his breath. The sensation of flying was one he'd never become tired of, but now his focus was more serious: rescue any survivors. They soared out away from the mountain range toward the desert floor below.

***

William punched his way out of the pile of rubble that had descended the mountain like an avalanche and dragged him and Francis all the way down to the ground, covering them completely. It only took them seconds to fight their way out of the rocks, but when they emerged into the dark of night, William heard it—an ominous wailing kind of wind coming from the other side of the mountain.

"What do you think it is?" Francis peered at him in the gloom, brushing rock dust out of his bushy black hair.

William listened. In addition to the howling sound, the ground vibrated beneath his booted feet. Dread filled him. The gate. Alex must've failed to stop that woman. His attention was drawn downward as the roaring wind zoomed past the mountain base and headed for the soldiers fighting on the desert floor.

He reached up for his earpiece, but it was gone. "I lost my communicator. I need to get to Cardinal Leone. You change into Wolfboy and head back around to the cave entrance. Make sure Java and the others are okay and do what you can to keep them safe."

"Okay. But why as Wolfboy?"

"Cardinal Leone said those things don't like to possess animals."

"Got it." He focused; his young features scrunched with concentration. He twisted this way and that as he transformed, and within moments, Francis had become the hairy, clawed werewolf. William patted the frightening creature on the back, and Wolfboy bounded off around the mountain's base.

William jogged off in the opposite direction, heading for the adjoining mountain bluff and the exorcists who, he was sure, were battling these monsters even now. He knew his job. He and the colonel had worked it out before leaving the base. As he picked up his pace, finding his footing solid and unwavering, William understood that he might be the world's only hope.

CHAPTER TWENTY

I WILL NOT GO BACK

BY THE TIME MARTIN GOT near the crash site, pandemonium had broken loose all around him. Soldiers from within the mountain were battling those of General Lewis, and now, those monstrous things from the gate Alex had apparently opened were not just swirling overhead and confusing everyone, but were diving into the bodies of living soldiers and taking them over!

Martin had ducked and darted and lain flat on the desert floor to avoid bullets and demons. He'd scooped up a fallen rifle but shooting at the flying creatures did nothing but draw their attention toward him. He remembered clearly what the cardinal had said to them all—do not let any of these things get near you. Looking around, he knew what the man had meant.

Soldiers who were possessed looked like monsters from a zombie movie. Their faces were distorted and twisted, their eyes burning with malevolent hatred. He had to shoot several who took aim at him. He aimed to wound, not kill, but it pained him to attack U.S. soldiers.

Finally, the wreckage loomed up in front of him. The screaming, shooting, and howling of the creatures filled the night air, but he focused on the smoking heap of metal.

Could anyone be alive in there?

He sprinted around toward the cockpit and peered through the dust-covered, partially shattered windshield. The two pilots were slumped over, dead. A long shard of glass had pierced the torso of one, and the other's head was nearly sheared off. He dashed around to the cargo bay and instantly spotted General Lewis, still strapped in, but buried under all the equipment that had broken loose and fallen on top of him. He couldn't tell whether Lewis was breathing or not, but blood trickled from the older man's mouth, which could indicate internal injuries.

Clambering up into the bay, he carefully pushed aside parachutes, heavy boxes of flares, rope, and other equipment. After a few minutes, he'd uncovered enough of Lewis's body to find the man's wrist. Feeling for a pulse, he found none. He gently lowered the hand back to the general's chest and studied this man who'd been at the Pentagon since before Martin had enlisted. Anger welled up in him for the way Lewis had betrayed his country. Despite the slickness of Colonel Walker and his wife in forcing the man to return to the right side, the fact is, Lewis had sold out to that evil woman who sought to destroy this country.

A moan somehow penetrated the screaming and mayhem out in the desert, and Martin leaped from the chopper, searching in the darkness for the source of that moan. He scanned the cacti and shrubbery but didn't—

Wait!

The moan came again.

He spun to his left and headed in that direction. He spotted a dark form lying on the sandy dirt of the desert floor and quickened his pace. At first, he assumed it was a fallen soldier. For the moment, the fighting had moved away from him and closer to the mountain. But as he jogged closer, he saw it was not a soldier at all, but rather…Amanda!

He dropped to his knees to examine her. What the hell was she doing on that chopper? She bled from several puncture wounds and had abrasions on her arms and face. He felt for a pulse. It was there, thank God, but weak. *Very* weak. She needed medical attention and fast!

He knew Liz and several of the medics were up on the mountain helping Israel. But there were more medics back at base camp. He needed some way to transport Amanda. He whipped his head around, scouring the desert for any abandoned vehicles. There were none!

Damn!

Then he heard a ferocious flapping sound above his head, accompanied by a loud growl of triumph. He looked upward just in time to see that gigantic Griffin creature flap its wings again, kicking dust into Martin's eyes and forcing him to squint. Then it executed a perfect landing a few feet from him. Seated atop the griffin was the last person Martin expected to see—Mark Davalos.

Davalos jumped off the creature's back and landed in the sand with ease. "Need help?"

***

Java had jumped back and pulled Jorge down below the outcropping as the cave entrance exploded outward with a gigantic wind made up of those same things that had taken over Cuong and Alex at the abandoned church back in California. Dr. Shepherd and the two medics had also hunkered down beside Izzy, uncertain what was happening, but Peters stood her ground and stared like a statue at the massive cloud of amorphous entities emerging and soaring off into the night.

Almost as fast as the swarm appeared, the wind seemed to die down, and a sense of calm returned to the bluff.

Peters said to the medics, "Get the boy into the truck. I need to get back to base camp. Hurry, before more of those things show up!"

The medics and Dr. Shepherd laid Izzy on a stretcher and hurriedly carried him to the truck, Java and Jorge trailing after them. Izzy had more color in his face, and the doctor had assured him his friend would live, which relieved Java more than he thought it could have. Everyone was climbing into the truck except Peters, who'd wandered back toward the place where the creatures had emerged.

Java froze. He knew about those things. They could get inside you. They could make you kill…

"Airman Peters!" he hissed urgently, jogging away from the truck toward her.

She turned, but in the dark, he couldn't make out her facial expression.

"Don't get too close. Them things can take you over, make you do stuff you don't wanna do. I seen it before."

She glanced once more at the dark, quiet rock face and then started across the sand toward him.

Then Java saw it—a lone "thing" zooming out the entrance and heading straight for Peters.

"Airman, look out!"

She spun around, gun at the ready, but it was too late. The thing descended from the sky like a rocket and vanished inside her. She stiffened, just like Alex had stiffened. Java's heart hammered in his chest, and he glanced back at Jorge, standing beside the truck. For the first time since the night they'd seen Alex taken over, Jorge looked scared.

Dr. Shepherd, leaning out the front seat window, whispered, "She's possessed. We need to get out of here." She started the truck engine.

"How?" Java asked, backing away from Peters and closer to the truck. "She got a gun."

Peters stood straight as a pole, gun at her side. But the face! That's what freaked out Java. Her face had become a mix of her own and a new, twisted, and malformed version of the thing inside her. But the scariest part was her eyes. They glowed blacker than his own skin. Pitch black, in fact. She raised the gun, took aim at him, and fired.

***

Father Pat gazed down at the possessed soldiers fighting each other, his mouth agape. It was chaos in the desert, with screams and gunshots permeating the air every few seconds. But it was no different than what was happening around the world. He stared at Leone's laptop, split into multiple screens displaying the other gates, all of which had clearly opened because the same mayhem was evident outside each of them.

He watched the chaos play out on the various feeds from around the world, as soldiers of varied armies ran helter-skelter to avoid the marauding entities and exorcists fighting those people who had become possessed. He knew they had to close the gate inside Superstition Mountain within the next few minutes or it would be too late for humanity.

Montour stood staring straight ahead, the tobacco smoke swirling about him. He looked like he was in a trance, and Father Pat hoped he succeeded in contacting Andy. He refocused his mind on reciting the rite alongside Leone, calling upon God to intervene on their behalf and free those who'd become the victims of possession.

***

Java refused to close his eyes as the gun fired. He knew this was the end, but he would not be weak anymore. Something dark flew in front of him, and the bullet never touched him. Whatever had taken the bullet for him rolled over on the ground and leaped up to two legs like a man. Only it wasn't a man. It was…Wolfboy!

Java felt weak in the knees. His pledge to be strong faded now that he'd been spared. His breathing came in short gasps as he watched the growling Wolfboy jump at Peters and grab the gun from her hands, tossing it over the bluff. Peters grabbed for the smaller figure, herself a wild animal, and attempted to throttle him. But Wolfboy was too light on his feet. He leaped up and over her head and dropped down behind. He grabbed both arms and held her wrists together in what must've been an iron grip because, despite being possessed by something stronger than humans, she couldn't move.

But Java remembered how strong Cuong and Alex were when they were possessed. He sprinted for the truck calling out, "Gimme some chains!"

One of the medics leaned out the back of the open-bed truck and handed him a coil of heavy chain meant for towing. The links were heavy, but Java didn't even slow down. He darted back to the possessed Peters, still held in place by Wolfboy. He expected the wolf to growl and snarl, but it was Peters uttering the most unearthly sounds of anger and hate he'd ever heard. Not sure how close he should venture to Wolfboy, he held out the chain. The young werewolf held Peters' arms in place with his furry left hand and wrapped the chain tightly around both wrists with his right. He moved with amazing speed and, within seconds, had the chain wrapped around her torso, pinning her arms to her side.

Java stepped closer, but the possessed Peters growled and lunged at him with bared teeth, like she wanted to take a bite out of him. Before he knew it, Dr. Shepherd was by his side, staring in horror at the "thing" that used to be Airman Peters.

"Now what do we do? The colonel expects her in the air five minutes ago."

"Why?" Java studied her shadowy face.

"To help defeat these things."

"Who else could fly one a them birds? You?"

She shook her head. "Oh, hell, no." She paused, then snapped her fingers. Without another word, she grabbed the walkie-talkie off her belt and clicked the talk button. "Shepherd to Martin Briceño, come in."

She waited, and Java waited with her, liking the way she thought. If anyone could fly one of those Hawks, it would be Martin.

The walkie crackled and a voice filtered through the static. "Briceño here, over."

"Your location?" Shepherd asked, her voice sounding funny to Java, like she was nervous talking to Martin. Who could be nervous talking to a guy that cool?

"Base camp, Doctor. Medical tent."

She sucked in a breath of surprise. "Are you hurt?" there was fear in her voice.

"Not me. Amanda."

Shepherd almost dropped the walkie, and Java gasped in shock. Amanda, hurt?

"What happened to her?"

"Helicopter crash. Can you get here ASAP?"

"On my way. Shepherd out." She signed off and turned to Wolfboy. "Can you get her back to base camp?"

The werewolf growled and nodded.

"Good." She grabbed Java by the arm. "C'mon!"

They ran back to the truck and Dr. Shepherd leaped up into the driver's seat, Java riding shotgun. She revved the engine and took off down the mountain.

***

Allison sat on the hard ground, frozen with terror as the noxious, evil wind ceased for a short time and then resumed, filling the chamber with a thick aura of malevolence. Ms. G threw her head back and laughed, her arms outstretched as though to welcome those misshapen monstrosities into the world. Allison heard a groan and glanced across to where her father was stirring. She was glad to know he was all right, but what could even he do against such an onslaught?

Roy, laid out by her feet, stirred, and she reached out to him. His long lashes fluttered open, but his lovely brown eyes were engraved with pain. Then he must've felt the malice all around them because he shivered and tried to speak. "Wha…" His eyes found the widened crack, and she knew he understood everything. He groaned, not in pain but in despair.

The roaring sound was deafening, and yet her ears seemed to have adjusted. She saw anguish on Alex's beautiful face, while Andy wore a look of triumph, but more the kind of triumph when you put something over on someone, which confused her. Wasn't this what he wanted?

"Teacher," Andy called out against the wind.

The woman stared at him, her face distorted, her eyes glowing black as pitch. "Yes, Andy?"

"Remember how I told you I'd never be in a cage again?" His tone was taunting.

Her hideous face merely smiled, which made her look even more disfigured. "A meaningless demand on your part."

Andy grinned. He looked happy. No, elated. "Do you know what a spoiler is?"

Her facial expression shifted into one of puzzlement.

"It means someone who spoils your plans from the inside. Like me. Now, Big Brother!"

He grabbed Alex's hand, and Allison was stunned to see that Alex had been expecting it. Joined as one, the twins began to glow with power. They planted their free hands against the rock wall beside the crack and held them there.

At first, Allison thought nothing would happen. But then, amazingly, the wind stopped. Nothing came out of the void anymore. In fact, nothing moved. Entities preparing for entry were suspended in midair, and so were those inside the cavern.

Ms. G shrieked like a banshee. "No!"

But she was too late, Allison realized. Suddenly, the wind reversed, and the deafening noise went in the opposite direction, back into the void. And with the wind, so went the shapeless things that were trying so hard to escape. They struggled against the suction, but it was no use. Andy and Alex glowed even more brightly as their power swelled.

"How?" Ms. G spluttered, unable to get near the boys because the powerful wind was tugging on her too.

From within the glow, Andy's voice floated out as though on a cloud. "Alex and I can shift anything. Even direction. This was my plan all along, Teacher, and you fell for it."

She screamed again, but the suction only grew stronger. She was knocked to the ground as the massive body of Jäger flew through the air, struck her a glancing blow on the shoulder, and then vanished into the void. Dr. Avila grabbed onto a chair, but it was no use. The pull was too great. He called out to Ms. G.

"My lady, help me!"

He reached for her as the suction pulled him closer to the crack, but she fought for her own existence and ignored him.

Allison gripped Alex's chair and pulled one of Roy's hands over to grab the footrest. For some reason, maybe because they were controlling the suction, neither Alex nor Andy was affected. She shouted at Roy, "Don't let go of the wheelchair!"

He understood because he wrapped both hands around the footrest and gripped hard. Allison looked across at her father. He had hold of a thick stalagmite, which was standing firm.

A scream drew her attention to the crack as Avila sailed through the air, white lab coat flapping like wings, and vanished into the blackness, quickly followed by the computer operator, who vanished with a final anguished cry. With nothing to grab on to, Ms. G skidded across the rocky floor until the yawning crack was upon her.

"No! It can't end this way! I will not go back! Andy, please, I'll give you anything you want!"

Andy's voice sounded deeper, more manlike, as he replied, "The only thing I want you'll never give me—my freedom. Goodbye, Teacher!"

Allison smiled at Ms. G's fear, but the smile faded when the woman leaped across the crack and grabbed the handle of Alex's chair, which stopped the suction tugging her in. She wore a gloating look on her face.

"I've had just about enough of you two!" She reached out with her free hand and grasped Alex's wrist, trying to wrench his hand free of the wall. Alex fought her. Allison saw that. But he was no match for Ms. G's supernatural strength.

Not even thinking of the consequences—only of Alex—she clambered to her feet and worked her way around his wheelchair, holding on with one hand. She reached the grinning woman and pushed her so hard that Ms. G had to release Alex's wrist to keep from tumbling into the void.

"You cannot defeat me, little girl," she said, cackling like a witch. "I have ten times your strength."

"Allison!"

Allison looked over her shoulder at her dad, clinging to the stalagmite, his face a mask of fear.

"Allison, get back!"

"I have to help Alex, Dad!" she called back over the roaring wind. "I love you!"

Before she lost her nerve, she spun around and kicked Ms. G's hand where it gripped the wheelchair handle. The hand fell away, and Allison thought she'd won, expecting to see the woman fly backward into the darkness. She didn't notice until it was too late that Ms. G had used her other hand to grip the wheelchair on Alex's right side, out of her line of sight, so when she leaned forward to push the woman away, Ms. G snaked out her free hand and grabbed Allison's wrist. Before she knew what was happening, the woman tugged her so hard her arm almost wrenched from its socket.

Suddenly, Allison was free. The wind chilled her bald head as she rose into the air and sailed toward the opening. She barely heard the woman laugh, caught a quick glimpse of Alex's glowing blue eyes, and heard, as though from miles away, her father's anguished "Allison!" before she was sucked into the void and darkness consumed her.

CHAPTER TWENTY-ONE

YOU TOOK MY POWER

FATHER PAT WAS BUFFETED BY the winds hammering them from below. His kept his arms raised, but his priestly garments—stole and surplice—blew into his face, distracting him. Leone was faring even worse. He was an older man, and his excess weight clearly reduced his lung power because the heavy wind seemed to be driving the air from his body.

Below, the chaos had subsided as each of the released entities found a host body from among the soldiers and those others loyal to that woman. Now they were massing like a horde of zombies and approaching the base of the mountain, clearly awaiting the appearance of their leader.

But she hadn't appeared yet, which made Father Pat curious—whenever he thought of anything but staying on his feet. Attempting to exorcise so many, especially given the distance, was a daunting, if not impossible task. Still, he and Leone continued chanting the rite while Montour stared at the mountain with such intensity that beads of sweat glinted on his face and forehead. Then he said something startling. "Andy is on our side."

Shocked, Father Pat lost his place a moment and had to pick up the words from Leone's raspy, but loud voice.

"...command you, moreover, to obey me to the letter, I who am a minister of God despite my unworthiness; nor shall you be emboldened to harm in any way these creatures of God, or the bystanders, or any of their possessions."

They splashed holy water into the air from the vials in their hands, but it was too little and too far away to make any of the horde do more than flinch before pressing forward with even more determination. These monsters had been shut away for eons, and now that they were free, they intended to stay that way. They would not give up these men and women they'd possessed without a much stronger attack against them.

What did Montour mean about Andy? He had to maintain his focus but listened in case the older man said anything more. So engrossed was he in both the ritual and listening to Montour, he didn't notice Colonel Walker approach from behind. He was startled but kept his train of thought on the rite. From the corner of his eye, he spotted Nathan trailing behind the colonel, supporting Dane. Walker defied the gusty wind and reached the cardinal's side.

"Cardinal, William should be on approach, and the chopper will be in the air within minutes."

Leone offered a curt nod, his face dripping with sweat, his features twisted with strain. Father Pat didn't know how much longer the cardinal could hold out. His own muscles had weakened, his legs felt like rubber, and his shoulders burned with pain from holding out his arms for so long.

The colonel raised his binoculars and scanned the landing strip below. No helicopters were even lit up. He lowered the glasses and whipped up his walkie-talkie. "Walker to Peters, come in, over."

There was no response but static, barely audible above the howling wind.

"Peters, this is Walker, come in!"

Still no answer.

***

Davalos watched from above the field as his hybrid animals bowled over the possessed soldiers, knocked others to the ground, destroyed the weapons that were turned on them and otherwise created havoc among the orderly march toward the mountain. He smiled at the swift efficiency of his children, who, unlike men, could not be seriously harmed by the bullets fired at them from all sides. And given his ability to control their ferocity, none of the men they took down were killed—merely incapacitated. He did notice that once a soldier was rendered unconscious, the "thing" within rose into the night in search of another host body. That's the primary reason Colonel Walker ordered him to stay far from the battlefield. If one of those things gained control of him, he'd lose control of his army.

The formless beings made their way toward base camp, which could be disastrous for anyone there, especially Martin, Amanda, and the medics working on her. It occurred to him that perhaps this wasn't the best strategy. At least inside the soldiers, those things were contained. He decided to call off the attack and send his troops to base camp as a protective force. He held out his remote and began tapping the colored buttons in the necessary sequence to redirect the hybrids.

***

Java lurched in his seat when Dr. Shepherd hit a small bump as she pulled the truck to a stop in front of some tents. She leaped out, leaving the driver's side door hanging open, and darted around to the back. Java jumped down and hurried to the rear to check on Izzy.

Shepherd was already directing the medics to find an empty tent for Izzy and to put him on an IV. Java watched as his best friend was carried away. Jorge hesitated and then followed Izzy. Java wanted to follow too, but Martin stuck his head out of the biggest tent and looked relieved to see them.

"Liz, she's bad."

The doctor didn't hesitate. She grabbed her medical kit from the truck and followed Martin into the tent. Java ducked in after them. Lanterns provided warm light that illuminated a gurney on wheels beside tables of medical supplies. On the gurney lay a dark form. Amanda. Two young medics were giving her oxygen through a big, clear mask that covered her nose and mouth, and tubes extended from her arms to several upside-down plastic bags hanging from metal stands.

Dr. Shepherd pushed past the medics and leaned over the unmoving Amanda. She lifted each eyelid in turn and then listened to her heartbeat with that thing around her neck. She glanced at the medics.

"Crushed sternum, for sure. What else have you found?"

"Possible liver damage," the shorter man said solemnly. "Check her readings."

Shepherd leaned in toward a beeping machine that had numbers and words scrolling across it that Java didn't understand. The doctor must've, though, because she looked grave. "We need to operate at once. Relieve pressure on her lungs and liver. Prep her."

She turned to face Java and Martin. "Martin, the colonel needs your help flying one of the Hawks."

Martin's mouth dropped open. "I've never flown one of these new birds."

"Peters is compromised. Call Walker, he'll tell you what to do. And keep Java with you. I need to save Amanda." She turned away, but then spun around. "Not a word to the colonel about this."

Martin's face crumpled with shock. "He has a right to know."

"If he knows, he'll think of nothing else and head over here. The entire operation could fail. He needs to be in command."

Martin looked uncertain, his brows furrowing and making that scar over his eye look menacing. "Okay, nothing for now. But you keep me in the loop. If she worsens, I'm telling him."

"Agreed." Her features softened, and she placed a hand on his arm. "I believe in you, Martin. You can do this."

Martin's face relaxed under her touch, and he nodded. "Let's go, Java."

Java followed him out of the tent. Outside, he raised his walkie-talkie and signaled Colonel Walker. Java gazed up at him and saw in his deep-set brown eyes that he hated lying to the colonel, but Java agreed with Dr. Shepherd. The colonel needed a clear head right now.

"Walker here, Martin. What's happening? Over."

Martin, with some input from Java, filled in Colonel Walker on the possession of Peters and the lack of anyone to fly the helicopter.

"What about you, Martin? You had experience in Iraq."

"Not with these big Hawks, Colonel."

"Martin, I've got no one else, and that bird needs to be in the air ten minutes ago. Look, they practically fly themselves. I'll talk you through the take-off and landing. After that, use the throttle."

Martin glanced at Java, who nodded his head and whispered, "You got this, Martin."

Martin's face took on a look of resolve, and he said into the walkie-talkie, "I'm on it, Colonel."

"Take Java with you. There's a job for him too."

"Yes, sir. I'll radio you from the chopper. Out."

Martin eyed Java a moment, then clapped him on the back and they set off running toward the airfield.

***

Alex's scream of anguish mixed with Shaw's as Allison's floating form vanished into the blackness of the void. Tears rolled from his eyes and his entire body shook with rage, especially at the grinning mask of evil that was Ms. G's twisted face. He wanted to grab her around the throat and choke the life out of her. He nearly released his hold on Andy and the wall, but he felt a hard squeeze to his hand that forced him to make eye contact with his twin.

"Don't let go, Alex, or we'll never be free of her!" he hissed, his face blanched white with fear.

Alex forced calm into his breathing but couldn't slow the thundering of his heart.

The thing that was Ms. G purred, only now it sounded like a growl. "You'll never be free of me, Andy."

A cry of agonized rage ripped through the cavern, and Alex turned to see Shaw, red-faced with fury, release his hold on the stalagmite and start running toward Ms. G like a defensive tackle out to destroy the entire opposing team. She laughed and held out her arm as though to swat him away. The suction from the void made Shaw look like he was practically flying.

Ms. G attempted to push him away, but he ducked down under her outstretched arm and slammed his head into her midsection like a raging bull. Her grip on Alex's chair was no match for his speed and much heavier bulk. With a shriek of horror, her hand came loose, his arms wrapped around her torso, and the two of them sailed off into the void. In seconds, only blackness remained.

"Now, Big Brother, close it!"

Andy released his hand and stepped back from the wall. In shock over Shaw's sacrifice on the heels of Allison's loss, Alex wasn't sure what to do.

"Just want it to close, and it will," Andy urged by his side.

Alex thought of nothing else but the crack to be sealed and the suction to stop. Almost at once, the air in the cavern went silent and the suction ceased. As it had opened, the crack eased its way shut until the blackness beyond was but a sliver, and then vanished altogether.

Exhausted, Alex slumped in his chair, even more filled with despair than when he'd lost Juan, Cuong and Tami.

"Allison," he mumbled, tears still dribbling down his cheeks. "Mr. Shaw…." He couldn't believe what had happened, especially in such a few seconds.

"Big Brother."

He looked up to find Andy squatting down and looking right into his eyes. Then he understood what he'd seen in Andy's mind when they joined hands. "You planned this all along. From the beginning. To join Ms. G so you could destroy her."

"It was the only way." Andy's voice, usually without inflection, sounded as though he felt guilty. "I'm…sorry…about…everything."

Alex focused on those deep blue eyes and looked straight into Andy's heart. His brother spoke the truth.

A groan distracted his attention, and he glanced down at the rocky ground beside his chair. A crumpled Roy stirred, releasing his hands from Alex's front wheel, and opening his eyes. Andy bent down to him. When Roy saw the movement, his eyes bugged out, and he tried to scoot away.

"It's okay, Roy," Andy said in the softest tone Alex had ever heard from him. "Alex is going to heal you."

Alex flinched. "But you took my power."

Andy shook his head. "I took some of it, to convince Teacher I was on her side, but I could never become you, Big Brother, just as you can't become me."

Alex said nothing, afraid to try for fear of failing.

"Can you talk, Roy?" Andy asked, offering a hand so Roy could sit up.

Roy nodded but glanced at Alex before taking Andy's hand. Andy helped Roy to a sitting position against the rock wall. Alex studied his best friend and understood at once that his injuries were life threatening.

"Tell me, Roy, tell me all the pain. Hurry."

Roy's voice began slow and weak, but as he continued to describe his pain and anguish, Alex began to sag and grow weak, His breathing became shallow, and he would've fallen from his wheelchair had Andy not caught him.

"Let me help, Big Brother. You get rid of what you took, and I'll take over so you get a rest."

Alex nodded, his face covered with sweat and anguish. He'd seldom felt such searing pain, even from Allison when he spun her cancer away. Andy took his hand, the power surged through him, and his twin shifted the remainder of Roy's injuries into himself. Andy almost let go of his hand as he hunched over and cried out in agony, but Alex was sitting up after purging the suffering he'd already taken from Roy, so he was ready when Andy shifted the last of the injuries into him.

The pain hit him like a truck and nearly took his breath away. He understood Andy's reaction now, and nearly cried at the agony his best friend had endured for him. After several minutes of focusing, he pushed the last of the injuries out of himself and once again sat up straight. When he could focus clearly, he saw Roy's handsome face glowing with gratitude from below where he sat on the ground. Only now, his face was clear and unblemished, his chest was no longer caved in, and the blood remained only on his ripped clothes.

"Thanks, guys," Roy muttered, blushing as he made eye contact with Alex and, for a split second, with Andy.

Strangely, Andy seemed awkward too, almost embarrassed, but Alex suspected it might be guilt hitting him hard.

Then Andy turned away and focused on the computer screens embedded in the cave wall. Alex followed his gaze and watched with renewed horror as people attacked each other, destroyed property, smashed their cars into buildings or into other cars. The world was still going crazy, even though the gates were all closed.

"Why?" He rolled closer to Andy. "We closed the gates!"

Andy faced him, eyes welling with guilt, but features inexpressive as ever. "Because I shifted goodness out of them. We have to shift it back."

"How?"

Andy cocked his head, as though Alex should know. "You, Big Brother. You're the Healer. You have more goodness in you than all these people combined, more than enough to heal the world. I just need to shift it from you to them to offset the anger and hate I put in."

Alex blanched white with shock. But then he remembered what Father Pat had told him about the Healer: "Evil is like a virus that spreads from person to person. The Healer would be able to slow that virus down and bring people closer to their own goodness."

Andy studied him intently. "Father Pat is correct."

Alex flinched. "You read my mind?"

Andy offered what could, for him, pass for a smile. He extended his hand. "This is your moment, Big Brother. This is what you were born to do."

"He's right, Alex," Roy said as he rose to his feet, looking healthy and strong. "If anyone can bring goodness back into the world, man, it's you."

Alex felt the uncommon rush of self-worth flood through him, and, suddenly, he knew they were right. He grasped Andy's warm hand, felt the power rush through every inch of him, and then focused on Andy as his twin sent the Healer's energy out into the world.

***

With the hybrid creatures gone from the battlefield, Colonel Walker watched how the possessed soldiers seemed to act with a hive mentality, lining up in perfect formation and standing before the mountain, as though waiting for something to happen. Walker needed William, and he needed that chopper! Glancing at his watch, he was distracted by movement below. The possessed were stirring. They were agitated, as though something had happened that they didn't like. This was just the chance he needed, if only—

"I'm here, Colonel."

Startled, Walker whirled around to find William standing behind him, attentive and ready for orders. "Don't sneak up on a man like that, Agent Weapon."

"Sorry, sir."

"Are you ready to do your part?"

"Yes, sir."

Walker led him to the foldout table and the open laptop. The screen continued to show live feeds from each of the gates around the world. Those exorcists were not faring well, but all the fire engines were in place, awaiting his order.

"You can control them over the whole planet?"

"Yes, sir. In a sense, I am their alpha."

Walker studied him a moment, but the boy was neither being arrogant nor facetious. "Good. Now I need Martin in the air." He raised the walkie-talkie to his mouth. "Walker to Briceño, come in Martin."

***

Java had followed Martin to one of the big Black Hawk helicopters and clambered in after him. Martin sat in the right pilot's seat and told Java to wait in the back for their orders. As before, Java marveled at the technology, at the sheer muscularity of this bird, which was even more impressive than the Pave Hawk. He hoped, once all this ended, to fly in one just for fun.

If all of this ever ended, of course.

The cockpit radio blasted out, "Walker to Briceño, come in Martin."

Martin slipped on the helmet and engaged the radio. "Briceño here, Colonel. We're in the chopper and ready to take her up."

"Excellent. Can Java hear me?"

Martin turned to face him, and Java called out, "Yes, Colonel, I hear you."

"Listen carefully, son. There's a large box in the cargo bay. It contains a lot of wafers and what will look like leaves to you. Do you see it?"

Java glanced around in the dimly illuminated cabin and spotted a large cardboard box. "Yes, Colonel, I see it."

"Good. Now, outside the chopper, on the right-hand side, you'll find a large valve. This leads to a water storage tank. Unscrew that valve and dump in everything that's in that box. We're very short on time, so you must hurry. Dump it all in and replace the valve cap. Then join Martin in the cockpit."

Java was completely confused, though he did understand the instructions. "But Colonel, why am I—"

"No time for questions, Java. Do you understand my orders?"

"Yes, sir."

"Then carry them out. I'll work with Martin to get the Hawk flight ready."

"Yes, Colonel." Java made brief eye contact with Martin, who tossed him a thumbs up, and then dragged the large box toward the open cargo bay door. It wasn't heavy, just bulky, and he was able to ease it down to the ground on the right side of the bird without much difficulty. He set it in the sand and scurried along the sleek exterior looking for that valve Colonel Walker mentioned. His eyes were well adjusted to the dark by now and he easily spotted it, especially with the word "water" right next to it.

He dragged the box over below the valve and, using both meaty hands, unscrewed the cap and let it dangle from its chain, kind of like the gas cap on his dad's car. Ripping open the box, he found just what the colonel said he'd find—some leaves and a whole lot of small, flat little wafers. No longer caring what they were, he grabbed massive handfuls and shoved them down the opening into the water tank.

***

Colonel Walker proceeded to walk Martin through the steps necessary to launch the Hawk into the air. From the corner of his eye, he observed the exorcists fighting against exhaustion as the wind continued to howl around them like a flock of angry birds. William stood calmly off to one side. His eyes were closed as he concentrated, readying his part in this final assault. Martin asked him a question, and Walker focused on giving him the correct answer.

***

Java had shoved every leaf and every wafer down that tube, and he was sweating hard. Harder than after some of his gym workouts! But the job was done, and hadn't taken long, he was proud to say, so he screwed the cap back into place and kicked the box away from the helicopter. By the time he'd climbed up into the cargo bay and slid into the copilot's seat, Martin was ready to take off. He flipped some switches, and the engine sprang to life. More switches and the rotors began turning.

"Strap in, Java, and put on that helmet."

Java grabbed the seatbelt and clicked it into place, reaching down for the helmet at his feet and slipping it over his head. The fit was comfortable, perfect really, like it was made for him.

"Briceño to Walker, ready to launch."

Java heard the colonel in his own headset as well. "Launch."

Martin flipped a few more switches and the bird rose slowly into the air. It lurched slightly, but Martin held on to the throttle and kept her steady. Then, with a whoosh that left Java's stomach somewhere on the desert floor, the Hawk was up like a shot and soaring out over the desert toward the mountain range.

Java looked down and saw the possessed soldiers. The headlight from the chopper illuminated some of their misshapen faces. Then the colonel's voice spoke into his headset, giving him his instructions.

***

Roy watched in astonishment as Andy shifted Alex's essential goodness to…well, the whole world, it seemed. Alex glowed a yellow-white as his power seemed to grow stronger with each passing second. And he sat up straighter, blue eyes swirling with energy, his face that of an angel straight out of a painting. Roy had to force himself to look away from that perfect, radiant face to see what they were accomplishing on the monitors.

In location after location, people stopped fighting, stopped burning and looting, stopped hurting each other. They all just sort of froze and looked around, as though they had no idea where they were. Upon seeing the devastation around them and the injuries of others, everyone leaped into action helping each other, putting out the fires, cleaning up the destruction. Whatever part of Alex that Andy was shifting into them changed their personalities and their actions. He'd never seen so many people working together in his life.

As Andy switched the monitor views to different groups of countries and cities, he continued the shifting process, and for each new group of places, the result was the same. Alex was transforming the world before his very eyes. Of course, Roy wasn't so dumb that he didn't know these people on screen were only a handful of the world's population, but maybe they could spread their newfound kindness to those who hadn't been touched by Alex. If so, the world might truly become a better place.

As Roy gazed into Alex's luminous face, his breathing nearly stopped, and his heart pounded with wild abandon. Just being in his presence sent a wave of warmth over Roy, accompanied by a deep feeling of content-ment. He closed his eyes and basked in the warm peacefulness that had engulfed him. He knew Alex could never love him the way he loved Alex, but somehow, basking in the glow from his miraculous friend, that didn't matter anymore. Alex was his brother, his best friend, and would love him always. And that would be more than enough for Roy.

So lost was he within the overwhelming harmony that he barely noticed the glow around Alex fading until it was nearly gone, and the warmth had drifted away from his face. When he opened his eyes, Alex looked like he always did, except more energized and grinning with de-light. Andy stood beside him, expressionless, gazing at Roy with a serious intensity.

"We've done all we can for now," Andy announced. "We better get outside and see if we can help."

Alex studied his twin for a long moment. "Thanks, bro. That was…I don't know…beyond amazing."

To Roy's shock, Andy smiled. "It really was."

Andy's smile drew one from Roy, and the three boys left the empty cavern and headed back down the tunnel.

CHAPTER TWENTY-TWO

YOU NEED TO GET TO THE MEDICAL TENT

COLONEL WALKER SCANNED THE AREA below. His heart accelerated at the sight of the Hawk lifting into the air and heading for the desert around the mountain. The possessed men were scattering now, and Walker knew something had to have happened inside the mountain. The surging crowd of possessed, clearly enraged, turned and headed for the bluff where Walker now stood.

"You ready, William?"

"Yes, sir." The boy stood rigid as a totem, arms outstretched, concentrating on the task at hand.

"Look, it's Alex!" shouted Nathan with exuberance.

"And Roy!" Dane chimed in. "Roy, up here, little brother, up here!"

Walker looked down toward the base of the big mountain and spotted three figures moving in the darkness. One was clearly in a wheelchair, the other had long hair waving in the breeze, and the third was tall and lanky. The lanky one turned at Dane's call and waved excitedly.

"Dane! Dad! We're okay!"

Their voices drifted up in the darkness, sounding farther away than they were because the possessed soldiers were snarling and grumbling as they began clambering up the slope toward the bluff.

Walker raised his walkie-talkie. "Walker to Briceño. Come in, Martin."

***

Martin focused on keeping the Hawk level as he swung her around toward the moving mass of possessed soldiers. He heard the colonel in his headset.

"Briceño here, Colonel."

"Martin, douse every one of those men with water the second you get overhead. Java, do you read?"

The boy glanced over at Martin, surprised for a brief second. "Yes, Colonel, loud and clear."

"You're in charge of the water. Make certain to spray everyone below you, except us, of course."

"Yes, sir." Java placed his hand beside the lever that controlled the water sprayer. "On your command."

"Stand by."

Martin caught Java's eye and winked.

***

Alex stared up at the bluff of the adjoining mountain. He spotted the exorcists. They were yelling and chanting in a language he didn't understand. He also saw Nathan and Dane huddled together. But it was William he focused on. His little brother stood near Colonel Walker with his arms outstretched.

Something skittered by Roy's feet, and he jumped in surprise. "Oh, shit!"

Alex looked down and gasped. The ground was covered with roaches! Hundreds, maybe thousands of them, crawling like an army in the direction of the bluff.

"The hell's going on?" Roy's voice reeked of disgust.

Alex was for once grateful his feet were not touching the ground. But he looked up again at William and noticed the entire slope extending up to where the boy stood seemed to be moving, like a lake surface shimmering in the breeze. He didn't know the answer to Roy's question, but he did know who was behind it.

"William," he said and continued to stare at the boy with the outstretched arms.

***

Java watched as Martin gained more confidence with the throttle and copter controls. The takeoff had been a bit bumpy, but he quickly had the

Hawk leveled off and soaring high. Java leaned forward to see outside the cockpit windshield. The possessed soldiers were storming the mountainside where Colonel Wallace and the others were huddled together. The soldiers suddenly became aware of the helicopter closing in on them and turned to look up. Even under the pale moonlight, Java made out the hideously distorted features on everyone. What he hadn't expected was to see all the soldiers raise their guns and start firing.

***

Walker ducked the moment the soldiers below began firing up at them. Some of the possessed targeted the approaching chopper, but the others fired round after round up at them.

"Fall back from the edge of the bluff!"

Father Pat stopped chanting first and rushed to the sagging Leone, grabbing the man's thick arm and dragging him back out of the line of fire. Montour released his concentration and charged after Father Pat.

Walker waved at Nathan and Dane to fall back, leaving only William standing at the edge of the bluff. As though knowing that William was the one to target, the possessed opened fire on him, but those bullets that struck William did not even disrupt his focus for a second.

Walker watched as the helicopter swerved to avoid the gunfire and then swung back around to approach the soldiers from the rear.

***

Martin righted the Hawk after his sharp turn and headed back for the army of the possessed. More bullets flew up at them, but Martin managed to keep out of their range. All he needed to do was get overhead. It didn't matter how high. Once Java released the water, gravity would do the rest.

Checking his coordinates, he angled up and over just a bit to bring the Hawk directly overhead.

"In position, Colonel."

***

Colonel Walker saw the chopper hovering above the possessed soldiers. "Let 'er rip, Java," he said into the walkie-talkie. Then he held up a cell phone to his ear and said, "Start spraying them with water." That call was to a Vatican official who would relay the command to fire engines at all the other gates. He glanced at the computer screen displaying those other gates, and the rampaging possessed people at those locations. The fire trucks began spraying at the same time Java went to work.

Holding his breath, he watched the chopper. Holy water, blessed by Leone, began spilling out from beneath the Hawk. With only a light breeze, the water droplets sailed downward like an air raid of bombs. Mixed in were the bits of tobacco mixture and wafer that Java had dumped into the tank. The first drops struck the possessed, and all hell broke loose.

The soldiers shrieked like wild animals, began writhing and twisting, their guns forgotten. Tendrils of smoke rose from their exposed skin, and one by one, they toppled to the ground, rolling and thrashing about in the desert sand. As more water tumbled from the sky, more of the possessed went down.

That's when Walker saw it—dark, amorphous shapes rising out of the fallen men and into the air above them. The more water that fell, the more of the creatures fled their human hosts, unable to take the combination of ingredients that had been used against them.

Walker eyed William, then glanced down at the ground around the boy's feet. He almost leaped back in disgust. Thousands of roaches had gathered on the bluff. Nathan and Dane were backing away in horror, but Walker knew the insects were no threat to them.

Walker studied the computer screen where the other gates were visible. The possessed people were behaving in the same fashion as those in the desert below—as the water struck them, they collapsed. The demonic beings emerged and flew around, seeking new hosts. Walker returned his gaze to the desert stretched out before him. The dark, shapeless forms had massed together and were moving in his direction.

He eyed the rigid William and said, "Now!"

***

"What's William doing?"

Alex didn't answer Roy because he was fixated on the younger boy atop the bluff, wondering the same thing. William lifted his arms as though to heaven, and Alex half expected lightning bolts to rain down. But what happened was very different. A gigantic brown cloud rose into the air around William until Alex could no longer see him.

He gasped and Roy mumbled, "The hell?"

The massive cloud pulled away from William, who kept his arms raised, and soared past Alex's field of view toward the front of the mountain.

***

Java's mouth hung open as a massive cloud of flying roaches soared past their helicopter, heading for the black, incorporeal mass moving toward the bluff. Some of them broke off and descended on the confused men lying on the desert floor, flying in circles above them. He spotted William still standing there with his arms raised, but now the main cloud of roaches collided with the black mass of entities that had been possessing those men. There were so many roaches that Java could no longer even see the supernatural creatures. It was like they'd been swallowed up by a whale.

Java glanced at Martin, who looked just as stunned, but neither of them spoke. Martin kept the chopper level as they hovered high up and away from the battling demons and roaches.

***

Colonel Walker stared through his binoculars at the mayhem. The swarm of roaches had engulfed the creatures, just as William had intended. These entities, according to Leone, couldn't live long on earth without a human host to inhabit. Since the men were now blocked by the roaches and, since the roaches were the only living creatures within reach, the demons began vanishing inside them.

Yes!

Leone limped over to stand beside him, along with Father Part and Montour. "Your plan is working, Colonel," he said, his voice full of weariness.

"Our plan, Cardinal."

"Look at the other gates," Father Pat exclaimed, pointing to the computer screen.

At all the other locations, roaches had swarmed around the freed creatures, and, just as at their location in Arizona, the entities were entering the only living things they could find—the roaches.

Walker raised his binoculars once again and studied the desert below. All he saw were the fallen men, now stirring and looking about in confusion, and the cloud of roaches hovering overhead. Not a single supernatural creature could be seen. He lowered the glasses, turned to face William, and nodded.

William lowered his arms and then waved them in a sweeping motion. The enormous cloud of roaches flew out into the empty desert beyond the mountain range. Within moments, it was gone, and only the moans of fallen soldiers filled the night.

Montour hooted with joy and the others clapped each other on the back in jubilation.

Walker turned to face William. "Thank you, son. We couldn't have done it without you."

William beamed.

It was over.

They had won.

***

Alex, Andy, and Roy had moved to the very edge of the bluff, where they'd watched the battle between the entities and the roaches. Alex understood what happened because he'd seen William control roaches back on the base. He and Andy explained it to Roy, who stood with his mouth open in shock. The silence that followed the disappearance of the swarm into the desert was both eerie and peaceful. He heard some moans and groans from below, but the soldiers he could make out in the darkness seemed unhurt as they staggered to their feet and tried to get their bearings.

It was over, he thought. Ms. G was dead. Gone forever. Then his heart lurched, remembering that Allison and her dad were gone too. He felt heavy, as though he weighed a thousand pounds. He made eye contact with Roy and knew at once his best friend felt the same loss. But it was Andy he needed.

Turning his chair, he faced his twin straight on. Andy looked back, making no attempt to avoid his eyes. "You was plotting against her the whole time, weren't you? Ever since we met you?"

Andy nodded. "It was the only way, Big Brother. I knew she would never let me go, so the only way to destroy her was for her to think I was on her side. I had to spoil her plans because no one else could have. She would have killed me, too, in the end. She didn't think I knew that, but I did." He paused, shuffled his feet a bit, looking uncomfortable. "I had to do terrible things, to you and Roy and, well, everyone. It was the only way she would believe me. I'm sorry, but I had to do them. I had to be free. And so did you. She would've killed you too."

"I know." And he did. "I saw everything in your mind when you took my hand. I understood it all then."

"So, you was never against us?" Roy stared with suspicion at Andy.

Andy made eye contact with Roy and Alex thought he saw his brother blush, but it was dark, and he might've been mistaken.

"I like you, Roy," Andy admitted, his deep voice a sharp contrast to his shy, almost little boy attitude. "I never wanted to hurt you. Or Alex. Or any of your friends. Only her. To get back at her for the terrible things she did to me. Do you believe me?"

Roy glanced at Alex, who nodded before answering. "Yeah, I guess. But you been a hard guy to like."

Andy said nothing more. Then he turned to Alex. "I'm sorry about Allison and Mr. Shaw, but they saved you. They saved all of us."

Alex nodded, tears welling in his eyes.

They stayed that way for a few moments, with Alex quietly crying and the other two awkwardly avoiding each other's eyes. Alex raised his head and wiped his eyes, determined to regain control.

"C'mon, guys, let's get back to base camp."

***

Father Pat sagged with relief as he gazed down at the desert below. The soldiers were on their feet, overcoming their disorientation and looking reasonably steady after such an ordeal. He couldn't believe the plan had worked so well. When the colonel had told them that William could control roaches, Father Pat had been incredulous. But the boy had come through—and then some. William had sent them into the empty desert and ordered them to stay there. According to Cardinal Leone, the entities within each roach would die without any human hosts to inhabit. Father Pat prayed no humans happened upon any of those roaches in the meantime.

The cardinal was seated in a foldout chair, struggling to catch his breath. The mass exorcism, which had really been more of an attempt to hold the creatures at bay, had taken its toll on the older man. But it had been Leone's idea to add consecrated hosts to the holy water, figuring that their presence might help drive out the creatures. He'd added the sacred Onondaga tobacco because the more holiness in the water, the better. Montour was resting beside Leone.

Father Pat asked him, "Did you make contact with Andy? I heard you say his name."

Montour nodded. "I saw a glimpse of his mind and heart. He was never against us."

Father Pat looked stunned. "You sure?"

Montour nodded. "We'll let him explain when the time is right."

Father Pat accepted that for now and simply allowed the surrounding peacefulness to fill him. He noted the colonel standing beside William, gazing down at the recovering soldiers.

How like father and son they look.

The colonel raised his walkie-talkie. "Walker to Briceño."

After a moment, Martin's voice crackled out of the speaker. "Briceño here. Congratulations, Colonel, on a complete victory. Over."

"You can thank William when you see him," the colonel replied, placing one arm on the boy's shoulder. William looked up at him with a look of hero worship on his young face.

"I'll do that. Shall I land the Hawk now, over?"

"Do you need my help, over?"

"I understand the basic controls now. Plus, I have a first-rate co-pilot, over."

The colonel chuckled. "That you do. See you back at base camp. Walker out."

He clicked off the walkie-talkie, but then it squawked again.

"Walker here."

"Bryan, it's Liz," came over the speaker.

"Yes, Liz, what is it?"

"You need to get to the medical tent."

"What's wrong?"

"Amanda."

***

Shepherd gazed at the peaceful face of her dearest friend, her heart breaking into a million pieces. She'd done everything she could, but the internal damage was too great. Amanda's breathing was shallow and her heart rate slow. There wasn't much time. She hoped Bryan would get there soon.

She should've called him sooner, but what if he'd been too upset to follow through with his plan? They were free now. Francis had run in and told her that the creatures had been defeated by William and a horde of roaches. Her guilt over William's creation was somewhat assuaged after what he'd just done.

She'd sent the other medics out into the field in case there were more injured, so it was just her and Amanda in the main tent. She watched the gentle but weak breathing of her friend, the tiny rise and fall of her chest, not quite processing this moment in her life. Of all the people to die...

Peters stepped in through the flap, professional, but anxious. "I just heard about Mrs. Walker. How is she?"

Shepherd bit her lip and shook her head, forcing back the tears she knew would come.

"Oh, God..." Peters, looking no worse for wear from her own possession, approached slowly and gazed down at the prone form of Amanda Walker. "How did she end up like this?"

"Apparently, she went up in the helicopter with General Lewis, probably to stop him blowing up the mountain. They were shot out of the sky and crashed. Her insides are...crushed." Shepherd stepped forward and took Amanda's hand. It was still warm, but not what it should be. She caressed the palm with gentle compassion.

She and Peters stood together for who knew how long before the flap burst open and Bryan pushed his way through. He was followed by Cardinal Leone, Father Pat, Samuel Montour, and William. The colonel staggered forward, his usually strong features twisted with anguish. Liz and Peters stepped to the side to make room and he took his wife's hand, holding it more gently than Liz had done.

"Amanda…" His voice sounded hoarse, strained, carrying nothing of the timber it usually did. "My love…" He used his other hand to brush his thick fingers lightly across her cheek. She seemed almost to sigh, to relax ever so slightly at his touch, but Liz decided that had to be her imagination.

"We did our best, Bryan," she said, her voice raspy with grief.

Without removing his loving gaze from the face of his wife, he said, "I know you did, Liz. Thank you."

She choked back a sob, knowing she would crack at any moment. The heartrate monitor slowed as the beats became less frequent. It was only a matter of seconds now.

The cardinal stepped closer. "Would you like me to give her the anointing of the sick, Colonel?"

He didn't look up. "We're not Catholic."

"God doesn't mind."

The colonel nodded, and the small, round man placed his hand on Amanda's forehead, made the sign of the cross with his thumb, and said some prayers. "Father Pat, the oil from my bag, please."

The priest fumbled around in a large satchel and extracted a small vial of viscous yellow oil. He handed it to Leone, who dabbed his right thumb with it and again made the sign of the cross on Amanda's forehead. After a final prayer, he stepped out of the way.

The colonel stood rigid, unable to move. He almost looked as though he'd ceased breathing. He kept hold of her hand and gazed at her peaceful face, as though locking the memory in his heart forever.

Shepherd heard the tent flap rustle and craned her neck around to see Alex rolling inside, followed by Roy and Andy. At least they were safe.

That's when the heartbeat monitor flatlined. Liz gasped and looked down at Amanda. She placed on hand atop Colonel Walker's. "Amanda's gone, Bryan."

"No!"

Startled by the outburst, Shepherd looked past the adults and saw that it was Andy who had cried out. He grasped Alex's hand before the other boy knew what was happening. Alex stiffened, and Andy looked straight between the shocked adults at the unmoving form of Amanda.

"Injury and death to me!"

Shepherd felt the air around her ripple with energy, a kind she'd never felt before. Then, to her astonishment, Amanda groaned. Colonel Walker gasped and reached for her hand once again. But the real drama was playing out with the boys.

Andy whispered, "Injuries, to Alex," and then pushed Alex away from him. Alex cried out in pain, doubling over in agony. He croaked, "No, Andy, you gotta shift Death!"

Andy, always pale, suddenly turned pasty gray in the face, and began sagging. Father Pat rushed forward to help.

"Hello, boys, miss me."

Shepherd, so focused on the boys, didn't even notice anyone enter the tent. She looked up and gagged with horror. It was that blonde woman, the one behind all of this!

"Holy mother of God!" Father Pat exclaimed, holding up the crumpling Andy.

"How?" Roy gaped at her, backing away as she stepped inside.

"I slipped back in through one of the other gates before they closed. And now I'll have my revenge on the traitor who betrayed me." She stepped toward Andy. "Not looking so good, are we, Andy?"

Andy murmured something Shepherd couldn't hear.

The woman smirked. "What did you sa—" She stopped in midsentence, frozen in place, her face ashen.

Smirking, Roy stepped boldly forward. "He said, 'death to her.'"

The woman's eyes went wide with fury before she collapsed to the ground and lay unmoving.

Roy reached for Andy. "Andy, are you alright?"

He and Father Pat helped the sagging boy to stand, and Alex reached out to grasp his brother's hand.

"Amanda!"

Shepherd glanced down at her best friend, drawn by the urgency of the colonel's voice. Amanda's eyes were open, and the heart monitor had resumed beeping. Not just beeping, she saw as she scanned the readings, but beating normally. Liz felt as if her heart had stopped. It was just like in the lab. Andy and Alex had shifted death out of Amanda and sent it into that evil woman.

As the colonel helped Amanda sit up on the gurney, his eyes wet with joy, she grinned at him.

"What happened?" Amanda seemed confused, disoriented.

The colonel turned and pointed to Andy. All the adults stared at the boy in awe, so completely stunned by what had taken place in just a few seconds that it was hard to process.

"Andy took death from you into himself," the colonel explained, his voice weak with worry and amazement. "He would've died if that woman hadn't returned."

"Help me stand, Bryan," Amanda said, her voice stronger and more forceful.

He eased her off the table, but there was no sign of weakness.

"Be careful, Amanda," Shepherd said, prepared to help if the other woman should stumble. "You were badly injured."

Amanda got her bearings, standing straight and tall, moving her arms and legs with ease. "Not anymore." She passed between the flabbergasted men and approached the boys.

Andy stood on his own now, without help from Father Pat or Alex, who looked pained, as though he'd been injured. Andy let go of Alex's hand as Amanda stepped up to him. Andy seemed shyer and more uncertain than usual.

"Thank you, Andy," Amanda said. "But I don't understand why you risked your life for me."

Andy looked down at the ground. "Alex remembers our mom, but…I don't." His voice was quiet and almost breathy. "You…well, you're the closest person I have to a mom, and I… I couldn't let you die."

Amanda's face melted with love, and she opened her arms, engulfing Andy in a tender hug. "Thank you, sweetheart. I'm so grateful."

And then Andy did something else Shepherd thought him incapable of—he began to cry. Softly at first, but then his whole body was wracked with sobs as he clutched the woman whose life he'd just restored, holding on for dear life.

Alex and Roy looked stunned by Andy's tears, exchanging an expression of mutual shock.

Colonel Walker reached out to clasp Shepherd's hand and give it a gentle squeeze.

Father Pat, Cardinal Leone, and Montour edged around the boys, and Montour placed a supportive hand on Alex's shoulder. They stared down at the remains of the woman who'd caused worldwide devastation. Shepherd stepped forward with the colonel to get a better look and gasped when she saw the remains. A beautiful young blonde woman had entered the tent, but what lay in the sand at their feet was an ancient, desiccated corpse.

"Her true age," Father Pat murmured, his voice sounding tired, yet relieved.

"So, it's finally over," Montour said, rubbing his chin absently as he gazed down at the remains.

"Perhaps," replied the rotund cardinal in his Italian accent.

Startled, Father Pat stared at the man with wide eyes. "What do you mean, Cardinal?"

Leone pointed to the body. "That's the human host. But what became of the creature inhabiting it?"

That's a very good question, thought Dr. Shepherd.

Perhaps it wasn't over after all.

Everyone stood without speaking. The only sounds were Andy's quiet sobs against Amanda's shoulder.

CHAPTER TWENTY-THREE

DO YOU THINK PEOPLE WILL BELIEVE THAT?

ALEX WAS ECSTATIC TO SEE Java, Izzy, and Jorge, and quickly used his power to fully heal Izzy and Dane of their wounds. Colonel Walker too. There was so much debriefing to do that Colonel Walker had a tent designated the "Debriefing Tent" in which he sat with a recorder and notepad and called everyone in one by one, or in small groups, to report on their actions during the battle.

Of course, everyone wanted to know what had happened inside the mountain, but Walker insisted Alex, Andy, and Roy tell him first so he could decide if some part of their story might have to remain secret. Naturally, everyone had noticed the absence of Allison and Shaw, but Alex couldn't tell that part without breaking down, so Andy relayed the basics of what had happened, though not in his usual monotone voice. He sounded genuinely sad as he described how they had sacrificed themselves to save Alex and help close the gate.

Alex was grateful they didn't all come to express their condolences to him. In fact, they went to Martin, who was more devastated by the news than anyone. The moment he heard the news, Martin choked up and looked like he might break down. Alex wheeled over and threw his arms around the tall man's waist. No words were spoken. They'd been through too much together to need any, and each already knew how the other felt.

When it was his turn to debrief with Colonel Walker, he insisted that Andy and Roy accompany him because they were all in the cavern with Ms. G at the same time. The colonel agreed but requested that Andy answer questions before the others spoke. There was a table set up with a sound recorder on it. Colonel Walker sat behind it, and there were several chairs for visitors to sit. Roy pulled up a seat next to Alex as Andy faced the colonel.

"You may sit, Andy," Colonel Walker said, his voice not the least threatening.

"I'd like to stand, Colonel, if it's all right with you." Andy sounded firm and in control.

"As you wish." He glanced at something he'd written on his notepad while Andy waited for his questions.

The colonel wouldn't blame Andy for everything, would he, wondered Alex? *Maybe even want to put him in jail? That would be crazy!*

"Andy, I'd like you to tell me about growing up with those people, especially as regards the woman you called 'Teacher.'"

Andy launched into his earliest memories, told of the tests and the pain, even about the puppies. Alex had seen much of this in Andy's mind but hearing him describe such a horrific childhood froze his heart in his chest. Roy gasped several times—this information was new to him.

Maybe, thought Alex, *Roy will understand him better now.*

When Andy finished, Colonel Walker looked like he'd lost all the color in his face. He cleared his throat and shuffled some papers. He hadn't even written anything down.

"So, at what point did you decide to betray Teacher?"

"Before Mr. Davalos's men captured me," Andy replied right away. "I had made a deal with her to help capture Alex, and in return, she would never lock me up again. I knew she was lying. I've learned that about adults. They always think kids don't know when they're lying. So, after she let Mr. Davalos's men take me, I carried out her plan, all the time knowing how my own plan was going to end." He paused, tilting his head and thinking for a long moment. "It was hard to keep my true plans hidden from everyone, especially Alex, who can read my thoughts. That's why I avoided him whenever I could. Since Teacher wanted me to bring that man to life using Mr. Jäger's spirit, I went along with Mr. Davalos when he proposed it." He gazed at the silent Colonel Walker, and his voice took on a sense of urgency. "It was the only way to destroy her, Colonel. And even then, she came back anyway." He sighed. "If you feel I need to be punished, I accept it without argument."

Alex was about to defend his brother, but Colonel Walker shook his head. "You will not be punished, Andy. Your childhood was punishment enough. Thank you for sharing your story. It clarifies much."

"You're welcome, Colonel."

Colonel Walker gazed at him as one would look at a dear friend or loved one. "Son, about Amanda. You gave me back my reason for living. If there's anything I can ever do for you, I will make it happen."

Andy glanced down.

Even off to the side, Alex saw his cheeks redden.

"Alex, Roy, come forward please," Colonel Walker said, and the boys complied. "Now let's hear what happened when you were inside the cavern."

Alex began with their kidnapping by Sergeant Stern, and then Roy picked up the story once they'd joined Andy inside the mountain. Between the three of them, they described everything that had happened and what they'd done toward making the people of the world worse before making them better. Alex almost broke when he spoke of Allison's heroics in trying to save him, and then Mr. Shaw's last-ditch effort that sent Ms. G into the void. By the time they were finished, they'd been with the colonel for over an hour.

"Thank you, boys. Not just for telling your story, but for what each of you did singly and together to put an end to this nightmare. Even though we stopped the invasion, people were still killing and destroying all over the world. You and Andy halted that, Alex. It's not something the world can ever know, but you have my undying gratitude."

Now it was Alex who blushed, right alongside Andy. Roy, sitting between them, threw a long arm over each of their shoulders and pulled them in close.

***

Martin had been riddled with guilt for not informing the colonel at once that Amanda was injured, but he'd been overjoyed at seeing her alive and well when he'd returned to base camp with Java. He'd informed Walker about finding her and how Davalos had used that gigantic griffin-creature to transport her to the medical tent. Amanda shared her tale of how she'd come to be in the helicopter with General Lewis in the first place. She also revealed the general's confession that he'd been in league with that woman for some time before coming to his senses, which troubled both Martin and Walker.

After debriefing with the colonel, Martin asked about the mountain cavern that had been the secret base of that group.

"The Pentagon is sending a team today that will catalogue everything and empty the computer memory banks. After that, I expect they'll seal it up."

"Are you going inside to have a look around?"

Walker nodded. "My orders are to secure the site and ascertain that it's safe. I'm bringing Leone, Montour, and Father Pat to examine the gate. Care to tag along?"

Martin nodded, sadness sweeping over him once again. "I'd like to see where Russell and Allison died."

Neither Alex nor Roy wanted to go back into the mountain, and Martin didn't blame them, but Andy volunteered to show the colonel's team around. That boy seemed different, Martin noticed, as they made their way in through the blasted-out cave entrance, now fully visible in the bright morning sunlight. It was a beautiful day, sunny and warm, a stark contrast to the night before.

The caverns were extensive, and Martin marveled at how they'd been made so habitable. Because there were generators for electricity, the space was furnished with refrigerators, heaters, air conditioning units, and microwave ovens. People could've lived inside that mountain indefinitely if they had to. It was a marvel of engineering prowess. The main computer room was as high-tech as what could be found at any major corporation.

"Do you know how they got all this equipment in here, Andy, without the rest of the world knowing about it?" the colonel asked as the group looked around at the computer consoles and myriad monitors embedded in the cavern walls.

"Teacher said they started killing some prospectors long ago and making others disappear so people would be afraid to come here. Then, over the years, at night, they'd sneak in all this stuff. If someone saw them, that person disappeared or was killed, adding to the legend of the mountain."

Andy seemed so willing to help, so much more positive than before. Martin didn't know what had happened to change him, but he'd find out eventually. He became somber when Andy showed them a crack in the rock wall that had been the gate. Martin stared at the tiny crack that ran up and down the wall from top to bottom. It was barely wide enough for his fingernail to fit, and yet somehow, his best friend and niece were behind this wall, vanished into some other dimension. It didn't seem possible, and yet it happened.

As though he understood Martin's grief, Andy placed a hand on his shoulder. "They were both very brave, Martin. They saved us all."

Martin eyed him, studied him, thinking back on the strange boy who'd never seen a television. This boy before him, expressing empathy, feeling sorrow, was not the same boy. "Thanks, Andy, for saying that. Russell always wanted to do something heroic."

Andy nodded, and they watched as Cardinal Leone ran one stubby finger along the crack.

"Looks like it's sealed up tight," Montour said, touching it with his own finger.

"Could it be opened again, Cardinal?" Father Pat asked, gazing at the wall with a sober expression.

The elderly cardinal nodded. "The Healer can always open these gates. Fortunately, we know Alex will never do that." He waved one arm toward the computers and faced Colonel Walker. "Your people will likely uncover many secrets, not to mention collaborators, when you search these hard drives. The Vatican would be appreciative if you shared that information."

"I'll pass along your message, Cardinal," replied the colonel.

The rotund man smiled. "I'm sure the pope has already contacted your president."

The colonel nodded.

Martin stared at the rock wall that had taken his family. "Any chance they could be alive in there, Cardinal?"

The man shook his head. "Seeing as how the supernatural entities don't breathe air, there would be no need for air in that dimension. I'm sorry for your loss."

Martin stood rigid, his last hope dashed. He nodded and walked out of the chamber.

***

Per Colonel Walker's orders, Java was supervising Izzy and Jorge in packing up equipment for the return trip to the base. The colonel had been happy with how well he'd carried out his orders the night before, and that excited Java more than he thought it should. Other than in the weight room, he'd never felt so comfortable in any place as he did with these military guys. He wanted to be one of them so badly, he could taste it.

Once healed by Alex, Izzy found out all the action was over, and he was pissed. Even Jorge laughed at how mad he was, but the colonel reminded him he was lucky to be alive.

"Oh, yeah, I guess so," Izzy had grumbled.

But as they packed up the medical supplies into boxes, Java knew his best friend was still angry.

Dr. Shepherd entered the tent and surveyed their work. "Good job, boys. Colonel Walker says we should be headed back to the base within the hour."

"Better than this dusty old place," Izzy complained as he stuffed a roll of bandages into a plastic bag and added it to the box.

Dr. Shepherd made eye contact with Java and pointed at Izzy.

Java shook his head. "Don't ask."

She nodded. Martin stepped into the tent, spotted Dr. Shepherd, and hurried to her side. Java tried not to look when he hugged and kissed her, but he couldn't help it. In his opinion, they made a good couple.

"How was the mountain?" she asked.

His face clouded over, and he released her. "Very sophisticated. Once I saw the spot where Russell and Allison…well, that's when I waited outside. Leone and Montour wanted to seal the gate even more by placing bits of those wafers into the crack, but I guess they wouldn't fit."

Java looked up from his packing. "What were those wafers anyway?"

Martin faced him, his expression thoughtful, as though remembering something from his childhood. "According to the Catholic Church, it's the body of Jesus Christ."

Java's mouth dropped open. "Yeah? You mean Jesus is inside those things?"

Martin shrugged. "That's what they believe."

"That's different from my church," Java added, shaking his head, and returning to his packing.

***

Nestled beside Amanda on the Hawk, Colonel Walker felt content. He knew he should be exhausted after all that had happened over the past two days and nights they'd spent in the desert cleaning up after the near disaster on Halloween, but it was a brilliant morning, the blue sky almost cloudless, and the desert below peaceful and serene. And he had the love of his life beside him. He squeezed her hand and they exchanged warm smiles.

He'd debriefed everyone and now had a complete picture of what had gone down that night. He gazed across at Alex, his wheelchair locked in place beside Andy and Roy. William sat on Roy's other side. The boys all stared out of the chopper, clearly enjoying the wind whipping their hair around, not the least bothered by the loud noise of the spinning rotors.

He nudged Amanda and leaned in. "If you had told me even two months ago that a bunch of kids, men of the cloth, and the world's pre-eminent tech genius would combine forces to save the world, I'd have said you were crazy."

She chuckled. "But what extraordinary kids they are. I'm living proof of that."

Alex must've overheard because he made eye contact with Walker. "How you gonna explain…well, Mr. Shaw and Allison…" He trailed off, but the colonel got the gist.

"I was discussing that with people at the Pentagon. We can't tell the truth, especially about your part in it. With all the footage of people going crazy, we released a story to the media about a strange, toxic gas that erupted from several sites around the world and drove those people temporarily mad. We'll say that Shaw and his daughter were kidnapped by extremists and held captive in those caverns. They'd hoped to extort money from Shawtech, but the gas had leaked out before they could do that and drove them to blow up the caves, burying everyone alive."

"Do you think people will believe that?" Andy sounded dubious.

"It's our best shot."

"But the caves didn't blow up," Roy put in, his face scrunched with confusion.

Walker glanced at his watch. "They have by now. My men had orders to dynamite them after the Pentagon guys extracted all the information and video footage they could find."

Alex looked surprised. "Video footage?"

Andy said, "She had cameras everywhere."

Alex nodded.

Walker gazed across at them, feeling as much admiration for them as he had for any man. "You're the bravest bunch of kids I've ever met. Your other friends too."

Alex reddened in the face. "Thanks, Colonel."

After that, they sat without speaking, comfortable in each other's presence, until the chopper reached the Air Force base.

***

It was late afternoon by the time everyone had gotten back to the base, and Alex was exhausted. He hadn't slept well the past couple of nights, especially in those tents on the hard ground. Mainly, he'd dreamt of Allison and Mr. Shaw—saw them sucked into that void—and he'd repeatedly awakened in a cold sweat. He looked forward to the soft bed in Colonel Walker's house and a hot shower before that. He felt and smelled nasty.

Amanda's first order upon their return, to all the boys, was to shower and clean up. Then, anyone who wanted to help her prepare dinner was welcome in the kitchen. All the boys were tired, even Java, and slogged to their rooms to comply. Roy, Andy, and William insisted Alex enter the shower first. He didn't object but did wonder as the warm water cascaded through his hair and down his torso how his brothers might be getting along. When he exited the bathroom, hair damp, but feeling like a new person in clean clothes, he found Roy and Andy seated together on Andy's bed, looking quite content, with William sitting cross-legged on the floor at their feet. Roy entered the bathroom next after tossing Andy a small smile, and the twins gazed at each other in silence.

"Do you think Roy's dad still wants to adopt me after all I did?"

Alex recoiled at the question. It shocked him, frankly. He couldn't imagine Nathan not wanting Andy, but after everything that had happened, he didn't know for sure.

"I think so," he admitted, obviously unsure. "I mean, you were on our side the whole time, even though…well, sometimes it looked like you weren't."

Andy nodded. "Where will I go if he doesn't want me?"

That Alex knew the answer to. "With me. We're brothers, Andy, and we stick together no matter what."

Andy smiled, as though that was the answer he'd hoped to hear. And it was a beautiful smile, Alex noticed, innocent and free, no longer shackled to a pretense of being trapped between two opposing forces.

"I'll probably ask you a million questions about everything," Andy warned, and Alex laughed.

"No worries, bro. I can handle it."

Alex studied the silent William a long moment and said, "I'm so happy you're our little brother, William."

"Me too," Andy added with a smile.

William looked very moved and stammered, "That…means…a lot to me. No, it means…everything."

Alex and Andy patted him on the back, and he looked gratified.

Once they were all showered and wearing clean clothes, they headed out to the living room to find Java, Izzy, and Jorge already lounging around. Amanda popped in at that moment and asked, "Anyone want to help with the cooking?"

Andy immediately responded. "Me."

Alex laughed at his eagerness. Roy eyed Alex a moment and then made brief eye contact with Andy. It was like they'd come to an understanding while Alex was showering, and it sure looked like Roy had forgiven Andy.

"I'll help too, Amanda," Roy said with a grin. "I do a lot of the cooking at home."

"We want to help too," said William, trotting over with an eager Francis at his side.

Amanda eyed Alex, her brown eyes twinkling. "And you, young sir?"

Alex grinned. "Well, I rock with microwave ovens."

With a warm motherly smile, she ushered them all into the kitchen, where they enjoyed preparing thick, juicy burgers, fries, heaping bowls of salad, and even some pasta on the side. Alex almost forgot the trauma of the past few days.

Almost.

Dinner was more subdued than previous meals because, Alex figured, everyone was thinking about all that had happened on Halloween night. And they were tired too. Cardinal Leone, Father Pat, and Mr. Montour joined them, and the dining room was full to bursting. Still, even the usually chatty Leone ate quietly and said little.

Colonel Walker thanked Amanda and the boys for the wonderful meal and then excused himself. He'd called a meeting in the living room for everyone once dinner concluded, and he wanted to get ready.

CHAPTER TWENTY-FOUR

SO MUCH FOR MY FREEDOM

COLONEL WALKER SAT IN HIS living room beside Mark Davalos reviewing their presentation to the kids. It was essential they get it right so everyone would tell the same version of the story. Mark once again wore a tailored grey suit with a blue tie; his hair was slicked back and styled, his demeanor every inch the Pentagon spokesman he had become. Walker was glad to have him at his side.

Once everyone trickled in from the kitchen—looking a bit more energetic after having downed a good meal—the kids, including William and Francis, sprawled out on the floor around Alex's wheelchair while the adults took over the couches and chairs. Walker waited until everybody was settled before speaking.

"It's been a tough few weeks," he began, "and I, for one, am happy to be near the end of this matter. First, some general information. Our people from the Pentagon have learned, from computer files, the names of every follower that woman had, and those individuals are being rounded up as we speak. So far, most of them act like Sergeant Stern—muddled and confused over some of their actions. They recall the blonde woman whom they served but can't seem to remember why they served her. We're still questioning all of them. But the bottom line is, we believe Alex and Andy are no longer in danger. Therefore, tomorrow, all you kids are going home."

The boys erupted with a mixture of excitement and, in Java's case, a small groan of disappointment.

"What're we 'sposed to tell our folks?" Israel looked at Walker expectantly.

Walker waved a hand toward Davalos. "That's what Mr. Davalos is going to explain right now. Mark, you have the floor."

Davalos stood and faced the boys. He looked tired, or perhaps distressed was the better word, and Walker thought he knew why.

"As the head of the Healer Project, all that has happened over the past month or so is my responsibility," he began, his voice strong and clear. "I've spent most of the afternoon on the phone with your parents."

The boys reacted with varied levels of surprise.

Java mumbled, "Bet my dad didn't even notice me gone."

"On the contrary, Java," Davalos continued, focusing on the African American boy sitting cross-legged on the carpet, "he sounded extremely relieved to hear you were safe and on your way home. I do believe he was quite worried, as were all the other parents."

"Did you tell 'em the truth about what's been happening?" Israel had sat up and was listening with better than normal intensity.

"No, and that's what we need to focus on now. I gave them a modified version of the truth, different even than what the president is giving the country, and it's important you stick to this version too. We all need to be on the same page."

Andy pulled a confused face. "On the same page?"

"It means we all have the same story," Davalos continued, "so if anyone asks us what happened, we stick to the same version."

"What is this version, Mr. Davalos?" Roy asked.

"Unknown to the media, an invasion force bent on bringing about the end of the world penetrated the borders of the United States. Your teacher was one of them, helping to send their agents around the country from California. You kids knew she was up to something and told Lieutenant Cole, who was one of my special undercover agents. The group kidnapped you and planned to kill you all, but Cole and some of my men intervened and rescued you. Unfortunately, three of your group died, Juan, Cuong, and Tami, along with Cole and some of my men."

Walker noticed Alex wince, and Jorge took on a look of intense sadness.

"My surviving men took you to a secure military location for your protection while we tracked down and captured, or eliminated, the invading forces before they could do more harm. But even then, they managed to attack the base and unleash a toxic gas here in America and around the world that drove people to temporary madness and caused them to kill and destroy. The media have dubbed what happened on Halloween 'Purge Night,' after some fictional movies. We couldn't contact your parents because we feared your teacher might send her agents to hurt or kill them to find you. Now that the invasion has been stopped, you're free to go home."

He stopped and gazed out at the kids for their response. Israel shook his head. "I only got about half of that."

Java glowered and shoved him. "Fool."

"We'll go over it many more times between now and tomorrow when you reunite with your families," Davalos said before turning his gaze on the adults, quietly seated around the room. "The president is putting out a similar version of the tale, obviously not mentioning you kids at all, and suggesting it was a world-wide plot by a doomsday cult intent on bringing about Armageddon."

"Not entirely untrue," Cardinal Leone said, shifting his bulk in the stuffed armchair into which he'd wedged himself.

"Obviously, all supernatural elements have been eliminated. You and the pope will have to decide how or if you want to share that information with anyone other than the higher ups." Davalos faced Alex again. "Yours and Andy's abilities have also been erased from the official account for your protection. This country has many enemies who would stop at nothing to use you to their advantage. I'm guessing you're both all right with not having the public know what you can do?"

The twins nodded simultaneously and then grinned at their synchronicity.

"Now, tomorrow, Colonel Walker and I will accompany you back to Hawthorne, but I will do the talking to the parents, especially those of the children who died. I think that's all I have. Any questions?"

Israel still looked blank-faced, but Jorge, with his ability to memorize everything, seemed clear, as did Java, Roy, and the twins. Davalos stepped back and indicated that Walker continue.

"The media already has this basic story, without any of you being mentioned, and so far, no one has snooped out any connection to your disappearances," Walker explained. "Let's hope it remains that way. However, because we don't know everyone who members of that group might have communicated with while under the woman's influence, the Pentagon, and frankly me too, are concerned that down the line Alex and Andy might once more be targeted."

Alex, who was leaning on one wheel of his chair, sat up straight. "You really think so, Colonel?" He exchanged a worried glance with his brother.

"Yes. The Pentagon has insisted that two bodyguards accompany you back to Hawthorne and stay with you for the foreseeable future."

"Foreseeable?" Andy asked, his pale eyebrows raised quizzically.

"That means an unknown amount of time," Walker responded.

"So much for my freedom," Andy grumbled, pulling an angry face.

"I'm on your side, bro," Alex said. "Really, Colonel, we gotta have a couple of guys in sunglasses following us everywhere, like in the movies?"

Walker couldn't help but smile. "Not exactly. I convinced my superiors that I already had the perfect bodyguards that no one would ever suspect." He glanced past the twins at William and Francis. "William, Francis, that's your new assignment. You'll pose as cousins who lost their parents during the purge and are now living with Alex and Andy. And Nathan too, of course. Will that be a problem, Nathan?"

The twins reacted with excited surprise at Walker's words, as did William and Francis. But Alex turned to find Nathan, seated on a couch beside Dane, looking floored.

"Well, of course, I'd love to have them," he replied, eyeing all the boys sitting together on the floor. "Might need to add another floor to the house." He chuckled.

Martin spoke up for the first time. He'd been sitting beside Liz the entire time on a loveseat across from Nathan. "Don't worry about that, Nathan."

Nathan eyed him quizzically, but Martin said no more, and Nathan just sat back on the couch, awaiting whatever came next.

An impressive man thought Walker. *He seems to take in stride whatever comes.*

Walker noticed that William, while smiling at the news, had grown pensive. He'd have to find out about that later. He glanced at his watch, then motioned to Davalos, who strode toward the large flat screen and tapped some keys on a laptop connected to the TV via cables snaking around the back.

Walker focused on the boys. "Boys, someone is coming on in just a moment, live from Washington D.C., who wants to talk with you." He waved a hand at Davalos, who opened the secure video chat window on the laptop and then turned on the television screen.

At first, nothing happened. The screen looked like one of those Zoom rooms where you wait until the host lets you in. But then the image changed, and a man came into focus, an older man seated at a desk in the Oval Office of the White House.

Walker eyed the boys, wondering if any of them knew this was the President of the United States. Davalos adjusted a webcam on the laptop and fixed it so the group of boys was visible in a small window in the bottom corner of the screen.

"Boys," the president began, "I'm the president of the United States, in case you don't recognize me."

Alex and Roy exchanged startled looks, as did Java and Israel. Andy and Jorge looked perplexed, while William and Francis sat up at attention for their commander-in-chief.

"Boys, this country…no, this whole world, owes you a debt of gratitude we can never repay, especially when you were all brought to this base against your will. I did not authorize your capture, but I am thankful you were there and able to stop this invasion. Alex and Andy, your unique abilities are the only reason the world is, for the most part, at peace today. William and Francis, your part in saving us cannot be diminished. I understand that you, Roy, suffered greatly at the hands of these enemies, and for that you have my sympathy. It makes me happy to see you well once again. The tragic loss of Russell Shaw and his daughter, Allison, will not be forgotten. I'm also grateful to Java, Jorge, and Israel for all you did to help. I know that, without you boys, the world would be covered in darkness right now. I cannot acknowledge your deeds in public, hence this phone call, but I will do my best to recognize you in some other way that will demonstrate my gratitude. For now, you have my thanks and the thanks of the American people."

Alex made eye contact with the Colonel, and Walker knew he was asking if he should speak. Walker nodded.

"Thank you, Mr. President," Alex said, his voice strong, with not the least trace of nervousness. "We're just glad it's over."

"So am I," the president said, grinning.

That seemed to relax all the boys, and they grinned back.

"I do have one request of you, Alex, you and Andy," the president continued.

"What is it, sir?"

"Should a major problem arise in the world that may require your unique abilities, can we count on you both to help us?"

Walker thought his boss was being too oblique, but he watched as Alex and Andy exchanged a look. Andy pointed to Alex, as though the decision was his. Alex faced the president once more.

"As long as Colonel Walker is the one in charge of whatever it is, we'll help."

The president looked surprised, though not as surprised as Walker. "Why Colonel Walker?"

"Because I trust him." Alex glanced at Walker, who felt touched in a special way by this boy's faith in him.

The president smiled. "That can be arranged. Take care, all of you. You're fine Americans, truly the best of us. Good night."

The image was replaced with the seal of the president filling the screen. Now, Walker knew, it was time for Cardinal Leone to address the group. "Cardinal, you're up next."

The little round man hauled himself out of the chair with some difficulty. Father Pat extended a hand to assist him, but Leone waved it away and gained his feet on his own. He waddled forward, reaching into the folds of his cassock, and extracting a small flash drive. He stood before the group, but focused on the boys.

"On behalf of the Catholic Church, the Holy Father in Rome has sent you boys this message. In particular, it's addressed to the Healer and the twin who completes him. It is in Spanish, so I will translate."

He inserted the flash drive into the laptop and opened a video file. Walker had known what the president was going to say, but he had not been told the pope's message. The boys sat staring at the screen with anticipation.

An image appeared on the flatscreen—the Vatican logo that they'd previously seen during their daily briefings prior to the big battle. The logo vanished, and an older Latino man appeared on camera, seated in a large chair. He was clad in white robes, at least as far as what was visible in this head-and-shoulders shot. His white hair was partially covered by a small purple cap like that worn by Leone. The pope smiled into the camera and began speaking in Spanish. Leone repeated his words in English.

"It is my honor to thank you, Healer, and your twin for all you have done for the world. I confess I had never put much faith in that prophecy, but I was wrong. Our Father in Heaven clearly made the right choice in you, Alex, and in you, Andy. You are both a blessing to the faithful and the world at large. I very much look forward to hosting you in a private audience so that I might get to know you both. We will settle on a time that is mutually beneficial. For now, accept my thanks and my blessing for what you have done. I also send my thanks to all your friends and associates who helped defeat this evil incursion." He made the sign of the cross and smiled once more, causing his eyes to almost twinkle before the image returned to the Vatican logo.

"What did he mean by a private audience?" Alex asked.

Leone smiled. "He has invited you to Rome to meet with him."

"Where's Rome?" asked Andy, looking from Leone to Alex and back.

The cardinal chuckled. "A long way from here, in Italy, across the Atlantic Ocean. It's where I came from."

"Wow," Alex muttered.

"Alas, I must return there tomorrow and write up a complete report of this event, so this is where I will bid you all arrivederci."

Israel pulled a face. "Huh?"

Leone laughed. "It means goodbye, Israel. But I do expect to see you all again. We've been through too much together to leave each other behind. For now, I say thank you, thank you, thank you to Alex and Andy, to you Roy and you Java, especially to William for his crucial part in saving the world. All of you pulled together as a team to defeat this insidious enemy, and your heroism will never be forgotten. As the president said, the public may not know of your courage, but the Vatican Archives will forever preserve the story in full detail for future generations. You will never be forgotten."

He stepped forward and extended his hand to Alex, who shook it with a smile. He did the same with each of the other boys, including William and Francis. He paused by those two, gazing at their young, eager faces in wonder.

"Despite how you came to be born, both of you have a divine soul, as we all do. Guard it well."

William's cheeks appeared to redden, but his smile couldn't have been more genuine. "Thank you, sir, we will. Won't we, Francis?"

The dark-haired boy grinned. "We will."

The cardinal laughed and then moved to Father Pat, who stood reverently. "Thank you, Father Pat, for your faith and strength. I've contacted your pastor at St. Joseph's to excuse your absence. I told him it was official Vatican business."

Father Pat grinned. "Thank you, Cardinal, for risking everything to come here."

"It is my job. And yours. Keep up the good work."

Father Pat smiled as Leone moved on to Montour. "Are you ready, Samuel?"

Montour stood and said, "I need to say goodbye to the boys." He stepped around the cardinal and approached Alex and Andy. "I will be leaving tomorrow as well, back to New York."

"Must you go, Uncle?" Andy said, his voice sounding lost. "We haven't had any time to talk, like we used to in my dreams. I didn't even know you were inside my head during the battle."

"And I didn't get any chance to talk to you either," Alex chimed in. "Especially about our mom's family."

Montour placed a hand on each of their shoulders. "We'll have plenty of time for that. If Nathan allows it, I'd like you both to spend time with me next summer—and you'll meet your people too. You'll learn all about your heritage."

"That would be sick," Alex exclaimed.

"Super sick," Andy added, tossing Alex a grin.

Montour scrunched up his face in confusion, but turned to face Nathan, still seated on the couch. "Would that work for you, Nathan?"

"Sure," he replied without hesitation. "I want them to know where they came from."

"Splendid," Montour said with a smile, turning back to the boys. "I'll email Nathan all the details."

Roy cleared his throat and said, "Uh, Mr. Samuel?"

"Yes, Roy?"

"Well, could I go out there with Alex and Andy next summer? It does sound pretty wicked."

Montour smiled at Roy. "Are you three not brothers?"

Roy paused a moment, as though processing the question. "Yeah, we are."

"Then of course you are welcome," Montour said, drawing out of Roy an enormous smile. He fixed his intense brown eyes on Andy. "Andy, I'm pleased that you chose not to be the Great Destroyer. Your people honor you. *Onęh go' hya?*. That means 'goodbye for now.'" He bowed and strode from the room without another word. Leone followed, leaving a long moment of silence in their wake.

Colonel Walker looked over everyone in the room. They had a lot to digest, so he decided to bring the meeting to a close. "Unless there are any questions, we'll adjourn this meeting and you're all free to watch television or just relax. I suspect everyone is still tired. I'll be in the kitchen with Amanda if any of you need me."

He rose, eyed them all for a moment in case of any last-minute questions, and then left the room. He found Amanda in the kitchen cleaning the stove where she and the boys had grilled the burgers.

"How did it go?"

He reached for the scrub pad and took over scrubbing the grease. "Considering it was information overload, I'd say it went well. They're all still pretty wiped out, but the prospect of going home perked them up."

"Colonel?"

Walker turned to find William standing in the kitchen doorway. "Come in, William."

The boy approached, looking oddly pensive, as though unsure of himself—not his typical demeanor. "Something on your mind?"

"It's about me going to live with Alex."

Walker stopped scrubbing and turned to face him, setting the scrubber down on the counter and wiping his hands with a towel. Amanda also stopped cleaning to focus on William.

"I thought you'd love the chance to live with Alex," Walker said, choosing his words carefully since he hadn't seen this mood in the boy before. "You can be a kid for a change, instead of a soldier."

William's face lit up. "Oh, I do want to go." Then his soft features clouded over with doubt. "But, well…"

Walker exchanged a look with his wife. This was unprecedented behavior on the part of William. "You can tell me anything, William. I thought you knew that."

"I do. It's just…you know how I don't have any real mom or dad."

Walker grimaced, feeling that old guilt rising to the surface. "Go on."

William looked down, another unusual action. "Well, I guess I've been, I mean, I know I shouldn't, but I've been sort of thinking of you and Amanda as my mom and dad and…I'm gonna miss you."

Amanda let out a tiny gasp and squeezed the colonel's arm.

William raised his eyes and looked on the verge of tears.

Walker felt a swell of emotion surge through him, and he momentarily couldn't form the proper response. He cleared his throat and met the boy's moist eyes. "William, you're a son any man in his right mind would be proud of, and I'm honored you think of me as your dad."

"And me as your mom," Amanda chimed in, herself brushing away tears. "We love you so much, William."

William's eyes became huge saucers of amazement, and he looked from one to the other.

"It's true," the colonel confirmed. "I couldn't imagine a better son than you."

William threw his arms around them both and cried into the colonel's shirt. They held him until he managed to get his emotions in order, and then he wiped away his tears with the sleeve of his shirt.

"We're not sending you away because we want to get rid of you, William," Walker said, locking down his own runaway feelings before he lost control. "Alex and Andy need protection. And it's not like you won't see us. We'll video chat every week, and Amanda and I will fly out to visit regularly."

William smiled, his worries clearly assuaged. He glanced furtively over one shoulder and, seeing no one else entering the kitchen, leaned in and said in a quiet voice, "I know you're my commanding officer and all, but when I'm off duty and no one's around, can I call you Dad?" He shifted his gaze to Amanda. "And Mom?"

That brought a fresh round of tears from Amanda, and she pulled him into another hug. The colonel leaned down and whispered in his ear, "Nothing would make me happier."

William grinned, an adolescent boy with parents who loved him. Exactly what all children needed, no matter how they came into the world.

CHAPTER TWENTY-FIVE

UNFORTUNATELY, IT'S THE LAW

WHEN ROY FOLLOWED HIS DAD through the front door of their dark, empty house in Hawthorne, he almost had to stop and catch his breath. He'd only been gone a few weeks, but it felt like forever. Alex wheeled himself inside, followed by Andy, William, Francis, and Dane. The colonel had dropped them off and then left with Mr. Davalos to bring the others home.

Nathan switched on a couple of lights—even though it was midafternoon—and the place instantly felt like home. Roy knew it was crazy, but he turned to Alex.

"C'mon, guys, let's check out my room," as though somehow it would've disappeared while he was gone. Alex and the other boys followed Roy down the hall, while the men headed for the kitchen to determine if there was any food to eat.

Roy flung open the door to his room, relieved to see it was exactly as he'd left it. Clothes were tossed on his unmade bed, alongside the PS4 game controllers. At the foot of the bed sat the small monitor he used to play his games, and the Hawthorne Heights posters adorning the walls remained in place.

"Did you think somebody broke in and stole everything?"

Roy spun around at the sound of Alex's deep voice, which broke into his weird train of thought. He laughed. "No. It just feels good to be home."

Alex nodded. "Yeah, it does."

"Whadda ya think of my room, guys?"

Andy looked around at the strewn clothes and some empty candy wrappers. "It's messy." He faced Roy. "I like it."

"On the base," William said, "my quarters had to be ready for inspection at any time. This would be a, what do you guys call it? Oh yeah, an epic fail." He laughed, and the others joined in.

"Compared to that cage I used to live in, this room is perfect," Francis added, his eager face taking in every detail of what freedom looked like to him.

Roy grinned and reached for the four game controllers. "Who wants to play some video games?"

Andy, William, and Francis all looked at the controllers Roy picked up from the bed with raised eyebrows. It was obvious they'd never seen anything like it.

"Don't worry, guys," Alex said, wheeling up to his side. "We'll teach you."

Roy passed out the controllers to the other boys, not taking one for himself. He knew he'd love teaching the newbies how to play, and that's exactly how it went down. Between him and Alex, they were good teachers, and all five of them had a blast. William, of course, picked up how to use the controller with ease and mastered every game.

And so, for the first time in the longest, Roy felt like a regular kid, enjoying life with his newly acquired brothers. It was a feeling he hadn't felt since before Ms. G entered their lives, and he loved it.

***

Dane rifled through the cupboards, looking for dry or canned foods. Nathan checked the freezer, which contained a fair number of frozen dinners. They'd looked into the fridge, but all the fresh fruit and vegetables had rotted, so they threw them out. Laughter and loud talking wafted in from Roy's room down the hall and Dane smiled, happy his little brother was back home.

"Hey, Pop," he said, closing the cupboard above the stove and looking at his father across the kitchen. "I been thinking."

"Yeah, son?"

Dane ambled over and Nathan closed the freezer door. "I know you gots to figure out where all these kids are gonna sleep, and I don't wanna make things worse, but I thought…maybe I could move in and help you. I mean, five kids are a lotta work."

Nathan grinned, his weathered face stretching out his old laugh lines. "I'd love the help, son. But I gotta figure out about where they's gonna sleep before them social workers come snooping around. Mr. Davalos called Alex's caseworker, and she's gonna flip when she sees the other boys."

Dane nodded, suddenly worried that the county would take the boys away from his dad. He sighed, spreading his arms around at the kitchen. "We gotta do some shopping, that's for sure. How about pizza tonight? On me."

Nathan clapped him on the back. "That'll work."

***

Colonel Walker was fascinated by the diplomacy Mark Davalos was able to employ with the boys' families. He displayed true empathy in sharing the story with each family and explained how impressed he was by the way each of the kids had handled the experience. They dropped off Jorge first. He lived in a small home with his single mother and no siblings. His mom was astonished when Jorge pulled her into a hug and said, "Missed you."

Walker mentioned that he'd seen a lot of growth in Jorge, who always managed to remain calm. Jorge's mom, who spoke broken English, was amazed at the changes in her son, and so grateful that he'd been returned to her safe and sound.

Israel's parents spoke perfect English and descended on their son with so much love and affection that the boy was overwhelmed. It became clear to Colonel Walker that Israel's absence had made his parents realize how much they loved him. After Davalos told the story and Israel confirmed it, Walker made it a point to complement their son.

"At first he talked a mile a minute about random subjects," Walker began, smiling at the blushing Israel, "but as time went on, it was almost as though he forgot about his ADHD. He also conquered his fears over these past weeks. You should be very proud of how he handled himself."

Both parents beamed, and it was clear to the colonel that they seldom, if ever, received positive comments about their son from school officials. As with Jorge's mom, they expressed undying gratitude at Israel's safe return.

Java's parents, at first, proved a bit tougher. His dad was skeptical about some of the story Davalos laid out for him, but Java insisted it was all true and his mom told her husband to be grateful they'd gotten him back safely.

Walker knew Java had a strained relationship with his father and now, having met the man, he understood why. Mr. Moore seemed unable, or unwilling, to balance out his intellect with his emotions. He didn't even hug Java, but merely gazed at him and said, "I'm glad you're all right, son."

Walker also understood why Java had glommed on to him as a kind of father figure, because his own seemed so far out of reach. Davalos praised Java on being levelheaded and protective of his friends, which made the boy puff up with pride. But when his father seemed dubious about that account, the colonel felt the need to speak up.

"Mr. Moore, as commander of a large military base, I see the best and sometimes the worst in new recruits. Your son impressed me more than many of those recruits and I believe he'd be a major asset to the United States Air Force, which he has expressed interest in joining."

Mr. Moore looked taken aback that anyone might even consider offering his son a job. "Yes, well, what about the, well, the—" he lowered his voice "—special ed part?"

Java looked down at the floor, his face a mask of humiliation.

"He just needs to finish high school, Mr. Moore," Walker went on, focused on the man's face. He slipped a business card from his uniform pocket and handed it over. "That's my card. Give it to any Air Force recruiter and tell them to call me. I'll make certain Java is given only practical exams that don't require reading or writing. This boy already displays exactly the qualities of bravery and clear-headed thinking that I look for in my men. I'd be honored to have him serve under me."

The reactions couldn't have been more different. Java looked like he might float away with joy, while his father honestly looked as though someone had just shot him. It troubled the colonel how some parents completely missed the reality of who their kids were, much like his own father had done with him. Yes, Mr. Moore and Walker's dad would've likely gotten along quite well.

The man finally unfroze when his smiling wife nudged his arm.

"Why, yes, Colonel, I will certainly do that." He turned to stare at Java, who stood straight and tall, thick muscles pressing the fabric of his shirt to its limit, as though seeing someone brand new. "I never thought…"

"I was good for anything, right, Dad?" Java didn't look angry, just resigned to reality.

To the colonel's surprise, Mr. Moore stepped closer to his son and extended one hand. "I'm proud of you, son."

Java looked stunned, his body stiffening. Then he reached out his own hand and clasped that of his father, shaking it with vigor.

No hug, the colonel noted, but progress had been made and this family would be stronger as a result.

After leaving Java's house, it was time to meet the families of those who died. He didn't envy Davalos this duty and was determined to help in any way. All the parents of the deceased had been notified, so this follow-up visit was a formality out of respect. What the colonel hadn't known until after the attack on the base was that Davalos had sent a team to recover the bodies of the dead from that old church in California and had had them shipped to the base, where they'd been kept under refrigeration in the morgue. One of the purposes of these visits was to determine from the families where to ship those remains.

Once again, Davalos presented himself as empathetic and understanding. Cuong's parents primarily spoke Vietnamese, so an older sibling translated for them. They'd been told the news the day before and it was obvious they, and the other four children, had been crying off and on since.

"We will make whatever arrangements you'd like," Davalos explained, his tone soothing and warm.

Cuong's father, an older man with thinning hair, said something in Vietnamese to Hin, the boy who was translating, and Hin said, "We cannot afford a funeral. What can we do?"

Davalos replied, "All you need to do is decide where you want your son taken. The United States government will cover all costs."

Hin translated, and the older man looked surprised, but he nodded and fell silent. Neither parent asked any follow-up questions, and the meeting ended shortly after that. Hin took the business card Davalos handed him and said they would email the necessary information.

Back in the car, Walker said to Davalos, "You're handling today better than I ever could've. Thank you."

Davalos, who looked older and perhaps a bit wiser, replied, "It's my job, but it's difficult."

They drove to Tami's house and found her mother an emotional wreck. Her eyes were puffy, and her face blotched from continuous crying. Tami's father was stoic, yet looked ready to crack at any moment. He'd asked Davalos many questions on the phone, and added even more in person, mainly why Tami would have been targeted by these criminals in the first place.

"All we know, sir, is that Tami was friends with Alex, one of the boys whose teacher was the ringleader. The teacher must've thought Alex told Tami what he suspected. My men did their best to save all the kidnapped youth, but she died protecting Alex. I'm so sorry."

Tami's dad looked like he might argue but decided against it. Unlike Cuong's family, they provided the name of a mortuary in Hawthorne for the remains to be sent. The colonel felt their pain. It seeped out of them in waves. Tami was their only child, their only hope for a future of extended family and grandchildren. Now they'd lost everything. He thought of William, who he'd come to regard as a son. He'd be devastated if William died, and that boy wasn't even his by blood. He left Tami's house feeling more dejected than he'd felt leaving Cuong's.

Davalos had already spoken to Carlos and Juan's social workers and given them the news. Carlos had often spoken to the boys of a grandma, but his social worker knew nothing of such a person. Carlos's father and older brother were in prison and his mother was dead. There was no next of kin to bury the boy. Likewise, Juan had no family ties, either.

Davalos assured the social workers that the U.S. Government would handle all burial expenses and arrangements for both boys. "Their friends," Davalos had told her, "need the opportunity to say goodbye."

Both ladies agreed and would email the proper paperwork for Davalos to sign.

"That was a magnanimous gesture, Mark," Walker said.

Davalos looked somewhat embarrassed. "It's the least I can do, Colonel. You know how close Jorge was to Carlos, and Alex lived with Juan for many months."

"Yes, I know. Thank you."

By this time, it was late afternoon, but they had one more stop to make—the Hawthorne Police Department. Entering the two-story glass structure, they stopped at the front desk. Davalos flashed his badge, as did Colonel Walker.

"We're looking for a Detective Gordon," Davalos explained.

The female officer behind the desk squinted at the IDs as though they might be fake and then picked up a phone. "Detective Gordon. Two feds here to see you." She paused and hung up. "He'll be right up."

The colonel stepped away from the counter alongside Davalos and waited. Wanted posters were pinned to bulletin boards, along with public service announcements regarding legal support, bail bond agents, and local ombudspersons. After only a few moments, a grizzled, somewhat unkempt middle-aged man pulled open a heavy door leading back into the station and ushered the men through.

They followed him past a series of workstations, most occupied by officers or plainclothes police working on computers or writing up reports. Gordon stopped at a messy desk and shoved an empty donut box into a wastebasket. He ushered them toward the two chairs near his desk and then planted his sizeable girth in the creaky wooden desk chair.

"Now, what can I do for you?" The voice was gruff, the tone suspicious.

"We're here about Detective Cole," replied Davalos.

Gordon sat upright in his chair. "You know where he is?"

Davalos looked grave. "Unfortunately, he's dead. I'm sorry."

Gordon looked momentarily flummoxed at the news, but quickly regained control. "How?"

Davalos explained about Cole being a special undercover federal agent, and even displayed a copy of Cole's federal ID, and shared the same story he had with the kids' families. Cole had suspected something was up and tailed the kidnappers to their hideout. He called in backup, and soldiers soon arrived. In the shootout that followed, Cole was struck by several bullets and died.

Gordon stared at them for a long moment and Walker thought he might go off on them. "All because of that little bitch boy in the wheelchair," he spat, disgust in his voice. "I told Cole that kid was trouble."

Walker's temper rose faster than he'd have thought possible. But Davalos remained calm. "Detective Gordon, the boy you mentioned had nothing to do with Cole's death except that your partner was trying to protect him and the other students who'd been kidnapped. That boy is a victim, and Detective Cole a hero."

He stood up to leave, and Walker rose beside him.

"Funeral arrangements are pending, Detective," Davalos continued. "You'll be given the details when they're finalized. Good day."

He turned, leaving the flabbergasted Gordon with his mouth hanging open. Still angry, Walker strode after Davalos.

As he strapped on his seatbelt, Walker looked over at Davalos. "Seeing the expression on his face when we left was the only fun I've had all day."

Davalos chuckled and entered traffic, heading for the Phillips home.

***

Alex hadn't felt so relaxed since the day before he had the dream about Ms. Ashley. It had only been about a month, but so much had happened he didn't feel like the same kid. He still felt guilty laughing it up with his family when Allison and Mr. Shaw were dead, not to mention the others he'd lost along the way. But he suspected neither Allison nor her dad would want him feeling sad.

The time flew by until finally Nathan knocked on the door and stuck his head inside. The boys, except for Alex, were all sprawled out or sitting atop Roy's double bed taking turns with the game controllers and having a blast.

"The colonel and Mr. Davalos are back," Nathan announced, cracking a smile. "Sounds like everything went pretty well. They wanna talk with you boys, so come on out to the living room."

"Okay, Dad," Roy replied as he took out another enemy combatant.

Alex entered the living room first. Colonel Walker stood by the old brick fireplace—burned black on the inside—while Mr. Davalos stood near the front window with his back to the closed drapes.

Alex parked his chair while the rest of the boys sat cross-legged on the floor or took over the couch. Nathan sat in the single stuffed chair that seemed to be his favorite, while Dane stood behind him looking serious, as always.

"Mark handled everything with grace and class today," Colonel Walker began, indicating Mr. Davalos. "Now the next step is to get you kids in order. You must go back to school soon, but Martin phoned while we were out and told me not to enroll you until he has a chance to come over and explain."

"Do we have to go back?" Roy's look of disgust was so comical, Alex laughed.

Smiling, Walker nodded. "Unfortunately, it's the law. But at least you don't have to go right away."

"Where is Martin anyway?" Alex asked. He'd been wondering why they hadn't heard from their friend yet.

"He has a lot on his plate," Colonel Walker said, "helping sort out everything after Mr.—after losing the head of Shawtech. He said he'd be over soon."

"The bigger issue," Davalos went on, "is Alex's social worker coming here to check his living conditions. I informed her that other kids will be living here besides Roy. She's been told that William is your cousin, Alex, and Francis is Roy's cousin. Both sets of parents were killed during the Purge night. We've created false sets of 'parents'"—He used the air quotes with 'parents'—"so when she back tracks, she'll see that the boys' background is legit. William, your last name is Maracle, like Alex, and Francis, yours is Phillips. That leaves Andy." He focused on Alex's twin. "Your background has been the trickiest to falsify, so we decided to go with some semblance of the truth. You were stolen as a baby and kept locked up most of your life until you finally managed to escape. You don't know why, only that they never let you go to school or let you out. The two kidnappers shot themselves when the FBI tried to arrest them. You didn't even know you had a twin until the authorities tracked down Alex and brought you here. Are you clear on your story?"

"Sure," Andy replied. "But I will get to stay with my brother, won't I?"

"Of course, you will," Mr. Davalos answered firmly. "This is where you belong."

Colonel Walker studied the boys. "So, is everyone clear on what to say if the social worker, or any social worker, asks you questions?"

The boys nodded. William and Francis looked especially pleased, maybe because they finally had last names.

"The final order of business is where you'll all sleep," Mr. Davalos went on. "Social services will not let you sleep on couches or the floor, so tomorrow morning bunk beds will be delivered and installed." He looked over at Nathan, who stood and looked over the boys.

"I'm sorry, Roy," Nathan said, "but you'll have to give up your room for now."

Roy flinched. "Why?"

"Mr. Davalos says social services prefers not to have unrelated kids sleep in the same room, if possible. Since Alex can't get upstairs, he'll have to use your room. Andy and William will also sleep there because they're, well, family."

"But they aren't," Roy insisted. "Least not William."

"We want the social services to think they are, Roy," Nathan continued. "Do you want Alex and Andy moved to a foster home? It might happen if we don't get this right."

Roy made eye contact with Alex and smiled. "Course they can have my room. Just surprised me, is all."

"Good," Mr. Davalos went on. "You and Francis will share bunk beds up in the guest room and Nathan will have his own bedroom." He looked over at Dane, who thus far had said nothing. "Dane, you have your own apartment, correct?"

Dane glanced at Nathan before replying. "Uh, yeah, but I was thinking of moving back here to, you know, help Pop with the boys. Teenagers can be pretty wild." He winked at Roy, who grinned.

"I think that's admirable," the colonel said, "but right now there isn't space for you that would satisfy social services, so it's best you keep your apartment until things here settle down."

Dane eyed his dad. "That work for you, Pop?"

Nathan shrugged. "I love the idea of you living here, but I guess we gotta do it this way for now."

Dane nodded. "Okay."

"Good," Davalos said, looking pleased with how everything was going. "We're bringing in some sleeping bags tonight for you boys to use. Will that be all right?"

Roy grinned. "Sure. Like having a campout."

Alex laughed.

"After sleeping in the desert for a couple of nights, you boys are pros," Colonel Walker added with a smile. "Mr. Davalos and I are staying in a hotel nearby. If you need anything, just call. Otherwise, we'll take off now and see you in the morning."

Nathan strode forward and shook the colonel's hand. "Thank you, Colonel, and you Mr. Davalos." He moved to the other man and shook his hand. "I'd be lost without your help."

"We want this to work as much as you do," Mr. Davalos replied, offering an amiable smile.

Alex once again marveled at how much the man had changed. Like night and day. What was that expression he'd heard? Oh, yeah, maybe an old dog *can* learn new tricks.

CHAPTER TWENTY-SIX

FIRST IMPRESSIONS ARE EVERYTHING

ONCE THE BEDS HAD ARRIVED and the bedrooms made ready for the social worker the next day, Roy was tired from moving all his stuff. It was already after three and everyone had been working since ten that morning. William, Andy, and Francis were upstairs playing the PS4, while Alex sat with Roy in the kitchen drinking lemonade Nathan had made and enjoying the opportunity to relax.

Roy looked up when the doorbell chimed, suddenly fearful. "That's not your social worker, is it?"

"No. She's coming tomorrow."

Nathan was cleaning up the garage, so Roy rose to answer the door. Alex wheeled along behind him. Roy nearly gasped when he opened the door and saw who stood on his doorstep. It was Saul, the kid who'd always bullied him and his friends at school.

"What're you doing here, Saul?" Roy couldn't disguise the contempt in his voice. This guy had mocked Alex once too often.

Saul looked so different that Roy lost his anger. He glanced at Alex, who'd also clearly noticed the change. The boy they'd known used to strut around Mark Twain High like he owned the place. This Saul looked hangdog, with slumped shoulders and both hands in his pockets.

"I heard you guys were back."

"How?" Alex asked.

Saul shrugged. "It's all over the neighborhood. Anyway, I, um, I just wanna tell you guys I'm sorry for messing with you all the time. Especially you, Alex, cause of, well, the wheelchair and all."

Alex looked up at him, squinting against the afternoon sun, and nodded.

Saul squirmed, shifting his position and forcing eye contact with Roy. "Can I talk to you, Roy? Like, in private?"

Roy met Alex's gaze for a moment. Alex nodded, signaling that Saul's change of heart was real.

"Sure."

He stepped out on the porch and closed the door, leaving Alex inside.

"So, what's up?" Roy didn't feel comfortable with this guy after all the crap he'd dished out. Saul was proof that gorgeous looks can harbor an evil soul. And yet, the Saul standing before him, fumbling with his words, really did feel like a different kid.

"Look, Roy, I know you got no reason to believe me, but, well, when I almost died, it was like my entire life as an asshole flashed before my eyes. When I woke up and found out I was gonna live, I wanted to change. I don't got the same jerk friends anymore. Most of 'em think I'm the jerk for ditching 'em, but I don't care."

When Saul stopped to catch his breath, Roy tilted his head and studied the other boy's handsome face for any sign of duplicity. He didn't see any. "Why're you telling me this stuff?"

Saul shrugged his wide shoulders. "I just think you're okay, the kind of guy I *should* hang out with, and I was wondering if you wanna chill sometime? We could meet at the mall or something and just talk."

Roy felt like a truck had hit him and he was momentarily speechless. Saul must've taken his silence as rejection because he said, "Never mind. Dumb idea."

He started to turn away, but stopped when Roy asked, "You wanna hang out with me? A loser?"

Saul turned back, eyes wide with shock. "You're no loser. Anyway, here's my number. If you change your mind, text me." He handed over a small slip of paper torn from a notebook and Roy took it. Scrawled in black ink was a phone number. "Later, Roy."

Saul turned and hurried down the walkway to the sidewalk, never once looking back.

Roy gazed at the number again and then shoved the paper into his jeans pocket before opening his door and entering the house.

"What was that about?" Alex asked.

Roy shrugged. "Dunno. It was weird. I think he's really changed, says it's because he almost died. He gave me his cell number."

"You think maybe he's gay, but just been hiding it at school?"

"I don't know. He says he wants to hang out with me. And how would he know I'm gay, anyway?"

Alex shrugged. "You gonna do it? He has changed inside. I could see that."

Roy considered for a few moments. Had Saul been hitting on him? Or did he just need a friend to talk to who wouldn't judge him? "I'll think about it."

***

The big event the next day was the visit from Alex's social worker at four o'clock. Colonel Walker and Mr. Davalos were present, and Mr. Davalos had brought in a cleaning crew who made the place look brand new. Roy was stunned at the absence of dust anywhere. All the carpets had been vacuumed, and the bathrooms scrubbed and polished.

"First impressions are everything," Mr. Davalos told the boys with a wink.

Alex was a little nervous, but not too much. His social worker, Ms. Quigley, had always been cool and had even gotten him his stunt wheelchair that had been destroyed in that ghost town in Nevada. He didn't think she'd object to the other boys all living in the house, especially the way the bedrooms were arranged now. But he did know Nathan had to do lots of paperwork and stuff to have them all living with him.

Nathan made sure all the boys looked clean and well-dressed and had them sitting in the living room when the doorbell rang promptly at four. Colonel Walker and Mr. Davalos stood off in one corner of the room like they didn't plan to say much. Nathan returned with Ms. Quigley, who wore a nice, rose-colored dress and had her brown hair tied back. She carried a briefcase that Alex knew housed all her paperwork. Even with Jane, there had always been paperwork. She broke into an enormous smile upon seeing Alex.

"Alex, I'm so happy to see you. We were all so worried when you disappeared. Especially when we found Jane—" She stopped herself there, looking sheepish.

Alex flinched. He'd completely forgotten about Jane and how she'd died, but he also remembered that he shouldn't know she was dead. "Something happen to Jane?"

Her face clouded, and she glanced around at the other boys, who were listening with interest. "Well, yes. She was found…dead, in her bedroom."

Alex gasped, acting as shocked as he could.

"The police think she surprised a burglar who killed her."

Alex tried to look sad, but it was hard since he'd hated Jane so much.

"That was the same day we found you and the other boys had gone missing. Poor Juan and Carlos." She studied Alex for a long moment. "I always felt something was off with Jane, but could never prove it, though it was obvious you boys didn't fancy her. Am I far off the mark?"

Alex met her gaze. "No, ma'am, you're not."

She nodded and looked over the other boys, almost gasping when she studied Andy's face. "It's astonishing how much he looks like you, Alex. Andy, I'm Ms. Quigley."

She offered her hand, and Andy shook it. "Nice to meet you."

She stared even harder, and Alex knew she was fixated on his brother's long, silky hair. Then she focused on William and Francis. "Which one of you is William?"

William stood up and offered his hand. "That's me, ma'am. Nice to meet you. I'm Alex's cousin." He made sure not to smile because his family was supposed to have just died on Purge night.

"I'm so sorry for your loss, William." She shook his hand and he reseated himself on the couch. "And yours, as well, Francis," she added, looking with deep sympathy at the young, dark-haired boy. "I can't imagine what it must be like for you both, going through something like this."

Francis, looking appropriately glum, nodded, and looked down at his sneakers.

Ms. Quigley eyed Roy, seated in his dad's favorite chair. "Of course, I know Roy. You and Alex have been inseparable."

Roy smiled. "Nice to see you again, Ms. Quigley."

Mr. Davalos stepped forward and offered his hand. "I'm Mark Davalos."

She shook his hand and smiled. "Yes, Mr. Davalos. Thank you so much for filling me in on what Alex and the others went through."

"If I can be of any further assistance, please let me know." Mr. Davalos nodded and returned to the colonel's side.

Nathan stepped forward. "What would you like to do first, Ms. Quigley, talk with the boys or see the house?"

She looked around the spotless living room, clearly impressed. "I think I'll inspect the house first."

"Sure," Nathan replied, waving Roy over from his place on the couch. "Roy will be happy to show you around."

"That would be wonderful. Thank you, Roy."

Roy offered her a smile and said, "I'll show you the downstairs first."

He led her from the room and Nathan let out a hearty breath of air, waving one hand in front of his face.

Alex placed a hand on Nathan's arm. "I told ya she was cool."

Nathan nodded.

"So far, so good," Colonel Walker said. "Hopefully, she won't have too many issues with the house. Mark, you might suggest to her, or maybe it might be better for you, Nathan, to suggest that she be the social worker for all the boys. That way you cover everything with the same person and not four different individuals."

"That's a good idea, Colonel," Mr. Davalos said, turning to Nathan. "I agree you should ask that, Nathan. It would certainly make your life a whole lot easier."

"Yes, it would." Nathan looked calmer now. Alex had spun some of his anxiety away but would never embarrass his adoptive father by telling him.

William leaned into Francis and whispered, "Do you remember your part?"

Francis nodded.

Alex eyed Andy, stoic as always. "You okay, bro?"

"Yes."

They waited in silence for twenty minutes before Roy reentered the living room with Ms. Quigley. He was smiling, so Alex figured the tour must've gone well. Ms. Quigley set down her briefcase on the coffee table and said, "Mr. Phillips, I'm impressed with your home. It's almost spotless and the bedrooms look quite suitable. Who sleeps in which room?" She pulled out a notebook and flipped it open, awaiting Nathan's answer.

"Uh, well, I'm keeping them by family, I guess you'd say. Downstairs is Alex, Andy, and William and upstairs is Roy and Francis. And I got the other room, of course."

She wrote in the notebook and said, "Very sensible arrangement. I don't know who will be assigned to the other boys, but they should not have an objection."

Davalos nodded to Nathan, who cleared his throat. "Well, Ms. Quigley, I was kinda hoping you might be able to handle all of 'em. They's good boys, I can tell you that. I mean, it seems easier if not so many people has to come checkin' on the same things for each boy, right?"

She considered his words a moment. "You make a good point, Mr. Phillips. I'll take it up with my supervisor. Now, if I may have a place to interview each boy separately?"

Nathan strode forward. "Oh, yeah, the kitchen's good. Boys are always eating anyway."

She laughed and turned to Alex. "Might as well start with you, Alex."

"Okay."

He smiled at Nathan and wheeled himself from the living room. Ms. Quigley followed.

Later, after she'd talked with all the boys, Alex was pretty sure she would approve the placements. She reminded them that her supervisor had the final say, but she was very impressed with how well-organized Nathan had everything. After she left, the boys sat in the living room with the adults and shared their stories. Francis assured them that he remembered everything about his "parents" who had been killed, and William had wowed her with his memory for details. He'd apparently added even more than Mr. Davalos had given him.

Andy said, "She asked me a lot about the people who kept me prisoner, but I answered them all just as we rehearsed. I think maybe I could be one of those people you showed me on TV, Big Brother. You know, an actor." Alex was stunned, but then Andy's stoic face broke into a beautiful smile, and he pinched Alex on the arm. "Gotcha, Big Bro."

Everyone was hungry by that time, so the adults slipped away into the kitchen to prepare dinner, leaving the boys to watch a movie on the fifty-inch flatscreen. Playing off Andy's joke, every time a new character appeared on screen, male or female, someone would say, "There's a part for you, Andy." At first, he didn't understand, but after they kept doing it, he joined in the laughter.

"Just you wait, all you funny guys," he finally announced. "I just might become an actor. You'll see."

It seemed like the day couldn't be any more perfect. But then Martin showed up unexpectedly, and everything changed.

CHAPTER TWENTY-SEVEN

HOW OLD IS THIS KID?

ALEX WAS HAPPY TO SEE Martin, as was Andy, who bounded out of the living room the moment he heard Martin's voice in the entry hall. The other boys followed to find Andy staring at Martin with a kind of hero worship.

Martin greeted Andy and then turned to Alex. "Hi, Alex. How are you?"

Alex extended his arms at the house and the people, including Nathan, standing around him. "Great, Martin. I'm home."

"Yes, well, that's partly what I came to talk with you about. You too, Nathan, since it concerns you and all the boys."

Nathan's smile slipped into a look of confusion. "What's up, Martin?"

At that moment, Mr. Davalos and Colonel Walker entered from the back hallway and strode forward, extending their hands.

"Good to see you, Martin," Mr. Davalos said, giving Martin's hand a vigorous shake.

The colonel also shook Martin's hand. "You look tired, Martin."

Martin nodded and, now that the colonel had mentioned it, Alex noticed that he did look tired, not full of his usual energy.

"You wanna stay for dinner?" Nathan asked. "Dane'll be over soon, and I know he'd like to see you."

Martin shook his head. "Maybe some other time. Lots to do back at ShawTech. But I do need to talk to Alex before tomorrow. It's rather urgent, and I want you all to hear what I have to say. May we go into the living room, Nathan?"

"Course." Nathan ushered him toward the living room and Martin crossed the entry hall to enter it. Alex caught Roy's eye and his best friend just shrugged.

Once everyone was seated around the room, Martin stood facing Alex, whose chair rested in the center of the room next to the couch. "Alex, I have some news for you that's going to change your life."

Alex froze. "My life?" He didn't like the sound of that. Was Ms. G back? Had she survived somehow?

"Before I tell you, I need to show you this." He held up a small flash drive. "Do you have a DVR or Blu-ray player I can plug this into, Nathan?"

Nathan pointed to the entertainment center beneath the television. Underneath were double glass doors housing a Blu-ray player.

Martin strode to the console and popped open the glass doors. While he fiddled with the player and inserted his flash drive, Alex glanced at Nathan, who bore a worried expression. Alex wanted to smile, but he was too anxious.

Martin turned to face them all, remote in hand. "Russell Shaw recorded this message for you, Alex, while he was still on the base, before the big battle. He had a premonition, he told me, which is like a feeling of doom, that something might happen to him and, well, I'll let him tell you."

Alex's mouth felt dry as dust and he really wanted some water. What could Mr. Shaw have wanted to tell him?

Martin pressed a button on the remote and the TV sprang back to life. Only this time there was no movie. Mr. Shaw's face filled the screen and the back wall looked like one of the rooms on the Air Force base, maybe Sergeant Stern's where he'd been staying. Shaw looked calm, like always.

"Alex, if you're watching this video, it means I'm dead."

Alex gasped.

"I hope I died in a heroic fashion during the battle and didn't just slip and fall off a cliff." He smiled, something he seldom did. "Alex, from the moment I met you and you agreed to help Allison without making any demands in return, I knew you were special. The more time I spent around you, the more you confirmed that impression. I've come to think of you as the son I never had, and Allison is very fond of you, maybe more than fond. I believe you have the power to change the world, and the assets of ShawTech will go a long way toward making that happen. Therefore, I've revised my will and left everything to you and Allison, fifty-fifty, except for specific amounts to key people like Martin Briceño. I've spent a lot of my life making money just to make it, Alex, but money without purpose isn't worth much. I know you'll help make ShawTech into a company that will dedicate itself toward helping others—because that's who you are. Some of the company board of directors may complain, but let Martin handle them. He will be in charge until you and Allison turn twenty-one, and Martin will remain with the company for as long as he chooses thereafter. I wish I could watch you change the world, Alex. Who knows, maybe I'll find a way to peek in now and again. Best success to you and Allison. You'll make a great team."

The screen went blank.

Alex stared at the blank TV, dumbfounded. He looked at Martin, eyes wide with uncertainty. Mr. Davalos and Colonel Walker clearly understood, though, and looked stunned.

"Does this mean, Martin," Colonel Walker said, his voice a bit unsteady, "that Alex has inherited ShawTech?"

Martin nodded. "Yes, Colonel, that's what it means."

Nathan cleared his throat. "Martin, I don't understand, and I can see Alex doesn't either."

Martin squatted down to face Alex eye to eye, something few adults ever did. "Alex, tomorrow, Mr. Shaw's bequest—what he's given you—will be made public. With Allison gone, everything goes to you."

"Whadda ya mean, everything?" Alex felt cold and afraid.

"Just what I said. You now own ShawTech and all of Mr. Shaw's other companies. You own his homes, his cars, his private plane, and all his cash assets." He placed both hands gently on Alex's quivering shoulders. "Alex, you're a billionaire."

"The hell?" Roy stared at Alex like he'd never seen him before.

"The media will be swarming around here like those roaches in the desert, wanting your picture, trying to talk to you," Martin went on, ignoring Roy's outburst. "It will be insane. This is like those young boys who, in the past, became kings in European countries when the monarch died, only this is bigger because I don't think many kids your age have ever inherited so much."

Alex was speechless, his stomach twisted into knots.

Martin frowned with concern. "Alex, say something."

"Mr. Shaw…I didn't know he liked me that much."

"Russell hid his feelings well, but trust me, he talked about you non-stop. When you were taken from that safe house, he determined to get you back or die trying."

Alex looked around at the silent faces staring at him in awe. They all understood the basics—Alex was now rich. Not just rich, but super rich. He'd never had anything in his life except the measly allowance Jane and other foster parents had been forced to pay him.

Martin stood and faced Nathan. "Nathan since you're planning to adopt Alex, this affects you and your family. The money and assets belong to Alex, but there is a clause stipulating that you will always have money in the bank to raise him and the others." He took in the wide-eyed faces, all of which looked dumbfounded. "Mr. Shaw has a house in Palos Verdes Estates. A big house, easily big enough for all these kids. Each can have his own room and you can still invite guests to visit."

Alex looked up, startled. "Leave this house? But Roy grew up here. He remembers his mom here, right?"

Roy seemed to snap out of his daze and shrugged. "I guess, yeah."

Martin looked at Mr. Davalos and Colonel Walker. "Maybe you guys can help them understand." He faced Alex once more. "Alex, tomorrow at noon when that will is made public, you will be one of the most famous, and recognizable, people in the world. The media will be the least of your problems. It will be worse than winning the lottery. You have no protection here. The house in Palos Verdes has high-tech security, and guards patrolling the grounds. I know you have William, but he can't keep you away from the paparazzi."

Alex screwed up his face. That was a word he'd never heard before.

"People with cameras following you everywhere hoping to get photos and then sell them. Eventually, the attention should die down, but that won't be for a long time."

Roy stepped up to his dad. "Dad, I know how much this house means to you. So much of mom is still here."

Nathan faced his now taller son and placed both hands on his shoulder. "That's true, son. So many good memories. But bad ones too, cause Dane's mother also lived here. The only reason she didn't take the house after the divorce was because she hated it so much. And me." He lowered his arms and faced Martin. "We'll move, Martin. I want my family to be safe."

Martin relaxed for the first time since entering the house. "I'll be over early in the morning with some cars that hopefully won't attract too much attention. Pack up all your stuff tonight and be ready to leave by nine. I want you in the house and secure before noon. I won't feel comfortable until I know you're all safe."

"We'll be ready, Martin," Nathan said. "Sure you can't stay?"

"I'm afraid not. But you'll be seeing me every day at the house. I live there too." He placed a hand on Alex's shoulder. "Gotta teach my boy here how to run a billion-dollar company." Alex's eyes bulged with fear, but Martin only grinned. "Russell couldn't have made a better choice. You'll rock this, Alex."

That brought a smile to Alex's face, though inside he was confused and worried. Martin left after that, and the astounded group silently entered the dining room to eat their dinner. Despite everyone chattering about Martin's news, Alex remained quiet throughout the meal, answering questions, but not engaging even with Roy. He couldn't imagine what a billion dollars looked like, let alone that he now had that much money. And a huge company and houses, even a plane. It didn't feel like him at all, and yet Mr. Shaw had left him everything. This man who had built up one of the biggest companies in the world thought Alex, who knew nothing about such things, could maybe do a better job of running things than he did? It was almost too much for him to handle, so he did his best to put the enormity of his new life out of his mind for now. Step by step. That's how he'd handle it. Step by step.

***

Roy never saw a house so big and fancy except in the movies. Martin had sent cars and vans around for them in the morning, as he'd promised, and several men packed all their stuff into the vans before loading them into two four-door sedans. The Colonel and Mr. Davalos had arrived even ear-lier and followed the two sedans in Davalos's Mercedes.

The drive took maybe forty minutes because there was a lot of traffic on the road. Roy was seated at the back window with Andy in the middle and Alex at the other side. He craned his neck when Martin turned up a short driveway. He almost gasped at the size of the tall wooden gates, painted gray, that swung open as their car approached.

"We're here," Martin announced, though that part was obvious.

They moved along a lengthy driveway past a circular path with an enormous palm tree in the center and then approached the house. Roy quickly learned that "huge" was the magic word with this place. The entire house was painted white and had those curved tile roof shingles he'd seen on some other homes on their drive over. Most of the house looked one or two stories high, but Roy knew one section had a third floor because of the small square windows announcing it. The house seemed to sprawl outward in all directions—and he couldn't even see all of it.

Martin stopped the car and stepped out. Roy exchanged a wide-eyed look of wonder with Alex and Andy, both of whom wore the same amazed expression. He exited the car as Martin pulled Alex's wheelchair from the trunk and wheeled it around. Andy stepped out on Roy's side and stared at the house in awe. Roy glanced around at the spacious grounds. He knew there was a pool and tennis courts, but he couldn't see them from where he stood. Alex wheeled himself over in silence, that look of amaze-ment still plastered to his face.

Martin joined them and extended a hand toward the house. "Wel-come home, boys."

The other cars and vans pulled up and everyone clambered out to gaze at the house in silence, especially Nathan. Roy saw that his dad couldn't imagine living in a place this fancy. And they hadn't even had a look inside yet!

"C'mon," Martin said, "I'll show you around."

He strode toward the front door. Roy nudged Alex, who seemed to be in a trance, and his best friend began wheeling after him. Roy and Andy followed, and the others trailed after them.

Martin pushed open the double front doors, which looked to be made of rich, expensive wood, and led them into an entry hall that made

Roy's place look like a doll's house. The ceiling seemed miles above them with a ginormous chandelier hanging from it. The floor looked like fancy marble he'd seen in private homes his dad had worked on. Marble stairs curved upward to a second floor, and hallways branched off in all directions.

Martin called the house "Hacienda style," but this place had so many rooms and levels Roy thought he'd never figure it out. William and Francis wanted to run around and explore.

Martin turned to Alex. "That okay with you, Alex? It is your home."

Alex seemed to shake himself out of a trance to face Martin and the younger boys. "Well, it's their house too, right? Go for it, guys."

"Out back is the pool, tennis courts, and a small putting green," Martin told the excited William and Francis.

Both boys, clearly not understanding any of that, just shrugged and vanished into the house. The best part of the whole place, in Roy's opinion, was the elevator, which meant Alex could easily go up to the other floors. Martin showed them the small movie theater, the bathrooms—which were larger than Roy's old living room—and the vast upstairs bedrooms, one for each of them. Roy decided he could get used to having all this space.

Alex had not asked anything yet, so once they were all gathered in the massive kitchen after the tour, Roy asked him, "Well, Alex, do you like your house?"

Alex looked up at him, that expression of wonder still on his face, and grinned. "It's wicked, ain't it?"

"You know it."

Nathan seemed a bit overwhelmed by the sheer size of the house, which Martin said was fifteen thousand square feet, had ten bedrooms, nine full bathrooms and six half-baths, a wine cellar, and seven fireplaces.

"A lot to keep clean," Nathan said, looking worried.

"Not to worry, Nathan," Martin said with ease. "There's a full-time staff to keep up the house, including a cook to prepare meals."

Nathan's eyes bulged out and Roy's did the same. People working for Alex. How crazy was that?

William and Francis ran into the kitchen, breathless with excitement.

"There's a big square hole out there filled with water," Francis exclaimed, his bright eyes wide with the thrill of a new discovery.

Alex made eye contact with Roy and they both cracked up.

Each of them had chosen a room—Martin had shown Alex which room he thought should be his, but never said if Mr. Shaw had used it—while the others chose their own based on how they liked the setup. Roy chose one that, like Alex's, had its own fireplace. All their belongings were brought up by several men and women dressed in mostly black who were very polite and asked Roy if he needed help putting his clothes away.

Roy had already explored the walk-in closet and didn't think he'd ever own enough clothes to fill up even a small part of it, but he was still uncomfortable with the idea of people doing things for him. He'd always been independent, so he declined the man's help and said, "Thank you." What was the man's name again? He couldn't remember as the middle-aged man left his room and closed the door.

Martin had told them all to meet in the large family room where there was a seventy-five-inch flatscreen TV (in addition to the movie theater!) at 11:55, so Roy kept checking his phone while he put his underwear and shirts into an elegant bureau made of solid wood, maybe oak, if he'd learned anything from his dad about construction materials. He hung his pants and button-down shirts in the closet, which smelled pleasant and had a door made from sweet-smelling wood. Cedar. He was sure of that. His dad had told him cedar was helpful against moths breeding inside the closet.

Soon enough, it was 11:15 and he realized he was hungry. He'd scarfed only a bowl of cereal that morning before they'd left the house, so he knocked on Alex's door to see if his friend wanted some early lunch. He found Alex sitting before a large window with the drapes pulled back. Roy ambled to his side and gazed out at the grounds below and the Pacific Ocean beyond. They weren't within walking distance of the ocean—he'd noticed on the drive up that these homes were on a cliff high above the water—but the rippling blue of the ocean provided a stunning view.

"I can't believe this is real, Roy," Alex said quietly, his gaze fixed on the distant horizon.

Roy placed a hand on his shoulder. "It's real, bro."

Alex looked up. "Is it time for us to go down?"

"Not yet, but I'm starved. Figured we could raid the kitchen."

Alex frowned. "You think that's okay?"

"Dude, it's your kitchen."

Alex pulled an expression of surprise. "Oh, yeah."

They cracked up again.

***

Alex discovered when he and Roy entered the kitchen that the cook—a middle-aged lady named Donna—had already prepared food on Martin's instructions. Because they needed to be in front of the TV at noon, the plan was for everyone to eat at 11:30. There were two large islands in the center of the kitchen and Donna had laid out platters of meats and cheeses, along with more bread choices than Alex had seen at Subway, not to mention every add-in he could think of, like relish, mustard, ketchup. You name it, she had it.

William and Francis bubbled over with excitement when they entered the kitchen while Alex and Roy were making their sandwiches. Even Andy looked happy, for a change. He'd gone exploring with the younger boys and liked what he'd seen. The grounds were extensive, and he proclaimed, "I feel so free here."

The adults soon joined the boys, but the kitchen didn't feel the least bit cramped. They carried their food into the dining room. It had a table so shiny that Alex was afraid to eat there, but Martin assured him not to worry. The long wooden table could easily seat ten, and Roy pulled one of the chairs away to make room for Alex.

Conversation focused on the magnificence of the house. Even Mr. Davalos, who had been in many wealthy homes, joked to Alex, "So, Alex, when can I move in?"

Alex froze in the act of biting into his sandwich, caught Mr. Davalos's mischievous smile, and grinned. "Any time."

After eating, Roy stood to clear the plates and Alex rolled away from the table to help. Andy and the younger boys also stood to clean up, just as they'd done at Amanda's place.

"You boys don't need to bus your dishes," Martin said. "The staff will do that."

Nathan eyed him a moment and said, "Martin, I want my boys to carry their own weight in life."

Martin smiled. "You're right, Nathan. Go for it, boys."

The boys gathered up dishes and piled some on Alex's lap before heading down the short hallway to the kitchen.

After cleaning their plates—much to the dismay of Donna—they all entered the massive living room which had a magnificent view of the grounds and the ocean beyond. As Alex planted his chair in front of the flatscreen, he realized that he was gripping his wheel handles with great intensity.

Must be more nervous than I thought.

He released his grip and glanced around at his family. Roy sat cross-legged on the thick, luxurious carpet to his left, Andy to his right. William and Francis plopped down in front of his wheelchair, looking content after having eaten their fill. William had finished off five thick sandwiches and Francis four. Alex had barely finished one, though it was delicious.

Martin slid a wooden chair with curved arms and flowery patterns on the cushions over near Alex and sat down. The other adults selected a massive, curved sofa that was a single unit and seemed to wrap around the television, but far enough back so the full screen would be visible.

"Don't be nervous, Alex," Martin offered with a tight smile. "The media will erupt with surprise when you're revealed as the heir, but Russell's attorney is ready."

"How? He never met me."

"That's a good point, but I've told him all about you. George, the attorney, knew Russell better than most and he believes everything Shaw said about you in the video." He glanced at his watch. "It's time."

He raised a remote control that looked bigger than Alex's foot and clicked a button. The screen glowed to life and a logo appeared, CNN. The image changed to a guy sitting at a desk. Behind him, projected in the background, were photos of Mr. Shaw and Allison. In the center was an empty photo frame with a large question mark in the middle.

Alex felt a lump of sadness fill his throat upon seeing Allison and her dad. But then the guy on camera began speaking, and Alex listened as Martin raised the volume.

"—since the tragic death of Russell Shaw and his fifteen-year-old daughter, Allison, after a kidnapping ended in a massive cave-in of Superstition Mountain in Arizona. The government, which oversees that monument, has dug through the rubble to the best of their abilities and recovered the bodies, sadly too disfigured to even hold a funeral service."

Alex jerked his head over at Martin. That was the first he'd heard about bodies.

Martin whispered, "They're fake, but we had to assure the world Russell was dead."

"The big question on everyone's mind has been, who will inherit Russell Shaw's empire?" the news guy went on, his face expressionless. "Today we will find out. Mr. Shaw's chief attorney, George Gladstone, has read the will and will speak to the world today." He turned to the side, and the camera widened out to include another man, older, but not ancient. He had gray sprinkles in his hair and a thick mustache, but his eyes were bright and alert.

"Thank you, Brent, for allowing me this forum to announce Russell Shaw's successor. As you know, we're being simulcast on all networks, cable or otherwise, just so the viewers out there don't think I'm playing favorites."

"Of course," the news guy replied, but said nothing more. The camera cut to a large audience of men and women, some sitting, but most standing with their hands up even though Mr. Gladstone hadn't said anything important yet.

When the camera returned to him, Mr. Gladstone said, "Before I reveal the heir to all of you and provide more details for your various headlines, I brought a video of Mr. Shaw himself explaining why he chose this individual. At the time he made this recording, he never imagined anything would happen to Allison, so she is mentioned too. However, due to her death, there is only one heir. You will see from the video that Mr. Shaw's mind was sharp and coherent, lest any of you question his sanity."

He turned to look behind him, as did the news guy. The images of Shaw and Allison disappeared, and a video began to play. It was Mr. Shaw, with the same nondescript background as in the video he made for Alex.

Alex once more felt that punch to the gut to see the man who'd come to love him so much that he'd given him the world.

"Good day, ladies and gentlemen," Shaw began, his tone even and calm. "If you're watching this video, I am dead. Some of you might be happy I'm dead, but I hope that number is small. I've been thinking of late about the future of ShawTech after I'm gone. Naturally, my daughter Allison was always intended as my sole heir, but someone else has entered the picture to make me rethink that plan. This young man restored my faith in humanity. And trust me, my faith in human beings was at its lowest. Alex Maracle helped me by accomplishing something of the greatest significance, something that I, with all my vast wealth, could not do, and he did so without expecting anything in return. When I pressed him to name a reward, he did, but it was something even I couldn't give him. The more time I spent with Alex, the more he felt like the son I'd never had with my beloved wife, Nancy."

Alex began to tear up, despite his resolution not to. He felt hands gently taking hold of his and glanced down to see Andy holding his left hand and Roy his right. He gave them a squeeze of thanks.

"—and so, I decided to split my bequest between Allison and Alex, because I know that Alex—maybe even more than my daughter who is, naturally, much like me—will steer my company in a better direction than I have. My goal was always to be the biggest, the most powerful, the wealthiest. There's nothing wrong with profit. Without profit, what's the point of manufacturing anything? But Alex will shift the tone of Shaw-Tech. He'll invest in sectors not simply to expand the company, but for what those sectors can do to help mankind. Because Alex may not yet be of age at the time of my death, my dear friend and associate, Martin Briceño, will act as CEO until Allison and Alex turn twenty-one. Even if they are of age, he will show them the ropes. Make no mistake, ladies, and gentlemen. The young people will be making many, if not most, of the significant decisions, but Martin will be signing the contracts as required by law. Martin, I know you're watching this. You have been my trusted friend and associate for many years and I have provided well for you in the hopes that you'll stay on and care for Allison, and guide Alex. So, that's my announcement. Mr. Gladstone will take over now. For those of you who'll miss me, thank you, and for those who won't, oh well."

The video ended, replaced by the same photos as before, including the one with the question mark. The crowd in the studio started shouting questions. With all those reporters yelling and screaming, Alex was happy Martin hadn't let him attend in person.

"What did he mean?"

"Who is this Alex?"

"How old is this kid?"

"You're saying Shaw left everything to a kid?"

Mr. Gladstone said nothing, leaving the main news guy to yell into the microphone to quiet the reporters down. Then he turned to look at the photos. The question mark vanished and was replaced by a photo of Alex. It was a full shot of him in his wheelchair, the one Martin's photographer had taken that morning before they'd left Nathan's house.

Another explosion of voices drew the camera to once more focus on the crowd as men and women shouted questions and screamed comments. The one that hit Alex hardest was, "But he's in a wheelchair!"

Martin offered Alex a look of sympathy. "What a jerk. I'm sorry."

Alex shrugged. "Been getting that all my life. For some reason, people only see the chair."

By now, the main news guy had gotten control of the crowd again and threatened to cut off their mics if they continued shouting.

Mr. Gladstone looked disgusted. "Alex is fifteen years old, and he's watching right now."

"Why isn't he here in person?" It was the same jerk who'd made the crack about the wheelchair.

Gladstone glowered at that guy something fierce. "To spare him from idiots like you, sir, who seem to think because he's in a wheelchair, he's not a whole or competent person." He looked directly into the screen. "I'm sorry, Alex, for that man's ignorance."

The camera cut back to the rude reporter, who seemed to shrink down among the others as though he wanted to disappear. He didn't speak again.

Mr. Gladstone went on to tell a little about Alex, but nothing about him being special ed, for which Alex was grateful. Gladstone assured the media people that, at some point, Alex would meet with them to answer questions.

"But bear in mind, Martin Briceño is running all of Mr. Shaw's assets, so he is the spokesperson. Alex will meet the board later this week and, once he feels more confident in his new role, Martin will arrange another press conference." He glowered down at the rude guy. "You, sir, will not be invited."

The boys around Alex clapped. Andy and Roy released his hands to join in, and Alex felt validated.

Mr. Gladstone answered a few more questions and then left the studio. That's when Martin turned off the TV and faced everyone.

"Now comes the fallout."

"What do you mean?" Alex asked, looking up at the tall man.

"The whole world will weigh in on you inheriting ShawTech. Some of it will be positive, some negative. I don't want any of you watching the news. In fact, I don't want you going back to school." His gaze took in Andy and Roy. "None of you."

"Why not?" Roy asked, though Alex thought he already knew the answer.

"Mark Twain High will be surrounded by the media tomorrow morning hoping to snap photos or get the first interview with the Boy Billionaire, which is what they'll call you, Alex. They don't know you've moved, but it won't take long to find out. Then they'll park themselves outside Peninsula High and all the other high schools near here."

"So, what do I do about school, Martin?" Nathan asked, looking concerned. "His social worker will need to know."

Martin paused a moment in thought, and then he snapped his fingers, his face brightening. "You homeschool them, Nathan."

Nathan pulled a comical face. "I don't know nothing about that."

"I can help you. We'll hire the best teachers to work with the boys here at the house. All of them. That solves the problem of educating William and Francis, which the social worker will want to know about. And I predict, these boys will learn much better here than at most schools."

Alex protested. "But what about Java and Izzy?"

"And Jorge," Roy put in.

"Yeah," Alex went on. "We can't leave them alone over there."

Martin took another moment to think, pacing the room. He stopped, and his face again lit up with an idea. "I can call their parents and make the same offer. They can attend school here with qualified teachers free of charge. Unless the parents are thrilled with that school, and I suspect they're not, they might jump at the chance to see their kids make real progress."

Alex nodded, digesting the idea. He turned to Roy and the other boys. "Whatchu guys think?"

Roy shrugged. "As long as we're all together, I'm down. Always hated MTS anyway."

Alex focused on William and Francis. "How about you guys?"

The younger boys both shrugged, looking much like Roy. "We've never had school," William said, "but as long as we stay with you, we're happy."

"Excellent," Martin said. "Nathan, you and I will get on the phone later today after I round up some teachers. We want the other boys' parents to know we're serious. Oh, and you'll have to disenroll them from Mark Twain."

Colonel Walker gazed at Martin with that twinkle in his eye. "Take good care of Java, my future recruit."

Martin grinned. "You got it." He turned to face Alex again. "Now, we need to prepare you to meet the board of directors."

"What's a board of directors?"

"A group of men and women who, along with Mr. Shaw, ran the company and made the decisions. Many of them will think they are better suited to run the company than you and me. We're going to prove them wrong."

"How?"

"Just be yourself," Martin replied with a smile, "and heal them of their doubts."

Alex furrowed his brows and eyed the boys around him. Andy shrugged, Roy smiled, and William grinned, flexing one arm.

"You got this, Big Brother," William said. "And if they're mean to you, I'll toss 'em around."

Alex laughed.

CHAPTER TWENTY-EIGHT

I'M COUNTING ON IT

ALEX SAW ON THE NEWS the following day how Martin had been right about Mark Twain High being swamped with media people. He felt sorry for Mrs. Davis and the other administrators trying to keep those people off-campus so the students could enter the school. Nathan had called her and explained why Alex and Roy would not be coming back, and Mrs. Davis tried to explain to the men and women with their cameras that Alex wasn't present, but they didn't believe her.

Alex's first brush with the enormity of his new fame was when Martin drove him to a high-end men's clothing store to buy him a suit. He'd explained that Mr. Shaw had his suits tailor-made, which Alex didn't understand, but given that they needed something fast, Martin chose a store he'd done business with before.

The man in charge instantly recognized Alex, as did all the patrons. Fortunately, they arrived just as the place opened and it wasn't crowded. Still, people gawked, even in the parking lot when he exited Martin's SUV to enter the store. The store owner waited on them personally and Alex was soon fitted out with a dark blue suit, light blue shirt, and a paisley tie that he insisted on getting because it was cool. The suit needed some work to fit him perfectly, and the man promised it would be ready and delivered to the Shaw residence the following morning.

Martin corrected him. "It's the Maracle residence now," and indicated Alex, who felt that bug under the microscope feeling he hated. But, he realized, he'd better get used to it.

***

The board meeting had been going on since five, but Martin told them he would bring Alex at six so they could conclude whatever business they had beforehand. It was 5:55 p.m. as Alex rode up in the elevator at Shaw-Tech, fidgeting in the stiff new suit, Martin standing at his side. Martin looked so different in his tan suit and red tie, almost like a different guy.

"You ready?"

Alex looked up at him. "Yeah, I think so. I remember what you told me about the board, and I been practicing what I want to say."

Martin smiled. "Just be you."

Alex fought to stop the butterflies in his stomach. The elevator doors opened with a *ding* and Alex found himself on the very top floor of ShawTech. Just ahead were large, wooden double doors, while hallways branched off on both sides. Martin stepped out of the elevator onto expensive-looking, maroon-colored carpeting and ushered Alex out. Alex wheeled onto the carpet, finding it thicker up here than on the lower floors. When they reached the heavy-looking doors, Martin grasped both doorknobs and pulled them open.

He offered Alex a final wink and stepped inside.

The room was dominated by an enormous wooden table that stretched almost from back to front. Seated around this table in tall, fancy wooden chairs were the fourteen members of the board of directors. Martin had explained about the number fourteen; it was because Mr. Shaw would always be the deciding vote on split decisions. Most of the board members were older, with the youngest members in their thirties. There were nine men and five women, all of whom stared at him with less-than-friendly looks on their faces.

As he wheeled past them, Alex sensed hostility, incredulity, and amazement. But from some he felt sadness and pain. He took a deep breath and expelled it as he stopped beside Martin at the head of the table where the chair for Mr. Shaw had been removed to make room for him.

"Ladies and gentlemen of the board, I present our new owner and CEO, Alex Maracle."

He clapped, but none of the board members joined in. They kept staring, like this was a joke being pulled at their expense. Alex knew he had to be strong and fearless, or he'd never win them over.

"Mr. Shaw was a great man and a good man," he began, his deep voice steady. "I don't know why he left me in charge. I'm just a kid, but

I trusted him, and he had my back, so I'm not gonna disappoint him. I want him to be proud of me, so I wanna learn everything there is to learn, not just from Martin, but from all of you. You're the people who made this company so great and I want to know how you did that. Martin is teaching me, but he's only one part of the deal."

He paused to gauge their reactions. Some of the glowers had faded when he admitted that they had knowledge he lacked, so he pushed on.

"I've seen some of Shawtech before, especially the labs and the doctors doing research. That's an important part for me. Mr. Shaw promised he would have his doctors try to make it so I could walk, which would be cool. But what's even better would be all the other kids who could walk or hear or see if something new was discovered. I hate it when anyone is hurting and I always wanna do what I can to help them. I think a huge company like this can help a lot of people, and I think that's why Mr. Shaw left it to me. I don't know noth—anything about technology, but I can imagine things that can help kids walk or see or hear better, maybe even help special ed kids learn how to read and write better. That's a direction I'd like to see us go, but I need your help and experience."

"Young man," said an older, white-haired guy whose scowl never faded, "the point of manufacturing is to produce products that will sell and earn money for the shareholders. We are not a charity."

Fortunately, Martin had explained about the shareholders, and Alex already knew what a charity was.

"I saw an old movie on TV before," Alex went on, "about these two big stores that wa—were always trying to outdo each other in making money. This old guy comes along and is hired to be Santa Claus for Christmas, but he doesn't wanna try and talk people into buying toys they don't want." Alex could see from their faces that all of them knew this movie. "Anyway, he starts sending parents to the other store so they could get the right toy and it turned out the parents were so happy that both stores made more money than ever."

The old man grunted with disgust. "Young man, a fantasy movie from the last century has nothing to do with business today."

Alex smiled. "Maybe not, but I think people are still the same. They like it when companies try and help their kids and they'll tell all their friends about it. I think ShawTech will be more popular than ever because people will like that we're helping others."

"Did you put him up to this, Martin?" the old man barked, still not convinced.

Martin shook his head. "I taught him some basics about the company and what we do. What he's saying now comes from his heart. I, for one, like his thinking."

"So do I," said a woman who looked around thirty. She had auburn hair hanging around her shoulders and wore a welcoming smile. "People trust big tech less and less these days. Showing ShawTech with a heart can swing many buyers over to us."

Alex beamed, knowing people loved his smile. "Thank you, Ms....?"

"Filbert," the lady replied, her voice smooth and silky. "Andrea Filbert."

"I really want to meet each of you one at a time and get to know you," Alex affirmed, making eye contact with as many of them as possible. "Can we start next week? Martin can make the appointments, right, Martin?"

"Absolutely," Martin replied coolly.

"Oh," Alex added sheepishly. "'Cept they have to be after school." He shrugged.

That seemed to unfreeze the group and laughter broke out, with more smiles appearing on their serious faces.

"I've asked our photographer and videographer here tonight to take photos of you all with Alex," Martin said to the board members, his tone business-like. "It's crucial to appear united behind Alex. Any sign of weakness on our part might frighten our shareholders. Can we count on your solidarity?"

Some of the board members turned to the grumpy guy who always seemed to scowl. He gazed at them and then faced Alex once again. Alex wheeled himself around the table to where the man sat and stuck out his hand.

"What's your name, sir?"

The old man eyed his hand, clearly torn, and grumbled, "Wilbur Erskine." As though making the biggest decision of his life, he reached out a wrinkled hand and shook Alex's.

"I hope you'll give me a chance, Mr. Erskine. I want what you want, to make ShawTech the greatest company on earth."

That drew a nod from Erskine as he retracted his hand into his lap. "I can teach you a lot, sonny."

Alex grinned. "I'm counting on it."

That line drew more laughter, and suddenly all the board members were out of their chairs and surrounding Alex, shaking his hand, and welcoming him to the company. Martin walked to the back and opened the double doors. Two guys entered, one with a large camera and the other with a video camera. Martin got everyone's attention and gathered them at the head of the table. Alex was placed dead center in front, with Martin directly behind him and the board members standing all around them. Mr. Erskine muscled his way forward to take a spot right next to Alex and Martin.

"Age has its privileges," he said, and the group chuckled.

The photographer snapped some photos of everyone looking happy and united, and then the guy with the video camera filmed the board members shaking Alex's hand and asking him how he felt to be a billionaire and other questions about his background, which he answered the best he could. The gathering finally broke up and Martin promised to let everyone know available appointment times to choose from so they could meet with Alex one on one.

Soon, it was just him and Martin in the big empty board room and Alex expelled a huge sigh of relief. Martin clapped him on the back.

"You were fantastic. I don't know what made you think of that old movie, but it worked."

"Thanks," Alex replied, proud of himself, and relieved that it was over. "That old man, Mr. Erskine, he has a lot of pain inside. I felt it when we shook hands. I'll try to spin him when we meet so he won't be so grumpy."

Martin chuckled. "Good plan. He drove Russell crazy with his constant complaining about any idea that didn't come from him."

Alex laughed, then turned serious. "You know how I was talking about doctors helping kids, finding ways to get around handicaps?"

"Yes?"

"I wanna hire someone to run our ShawTech labs."

Martin furrowed his brows. "Who?"

"Dr. Shepherd."

Martin flinched, but Alex plunged on.

"She's super smart and knows all that genetic stuff. And she could see William more often to help with his aging thing. And, well, she'd be close to you."

"I see."

"You know you miss her, Martin. I see it in your face, and I feel it when I'm with you. You do want her around, right?"

Martin looked flustered, something unusual. "'Course I do. But she might not want to leave Davalos."

Alex shook his head, feeling rather pleased with himself. "I already asked Mr. Davalos, and he said he's done with all that genetic stuff. He's gonna take care of his creatures and get 'em ready for missions. That's all. He loved the idea of Dr. Shepherd working for me."

Martin gaped at him a moment, then grinned. "Russell made the right choice, that's for sure. Shall I call her?"

"I can do that. Gotta practice my hiring skills." He grinned.

Martin laughed. "C'mon, Boy Wonder, let's go home."

Alex felt strong and confident as he wheeled himself out into the hall, knowing he was off to a good start.

***

Liz was tooling around in the lab, bored and lonely without Martin. Because of Shaw's death, he'd had to return to California immediately and barely had a moment to kiss her goodbye. Now, with Davalos and the colonel gone, she had no assignments or projects to work on, so she'd spent the past few days struggling to come up with an answer to William's aging problem. In the evenings, she joined Amanda for dinner and wine, which helped alleviate her loneliness.

Of course, she and Amanda had heard about Alex inheriting Shaw-Tech, and she knew that Martin would be busier than ever running the company and teaching Alex the ropes. While thrilled for Alex, she felt sorry for herself.

She'd always been so independent—even with Victor—which undermined that relationship. But now, maybe due to her age, she wanted something more stable and permanent. She wanted Martin and knew he felt strongly for her. They just needed more time together to seal the deal, but with so much distance between them, not to mention wildly different responsibilities, that might prove impossible.

Her tablet beeped with an incoming video call. She strode past her workstation to where the tablet lay on a countertop she'd polished three times already. Flashing in the center of the screen was "Video call from Colonel Walker." Smiling, she tapped the flashing message, and the screen sprang to life.

Bryan's face filled the screen and lit up her day. "Hello, Colonel, this is a welcome surprise. Incredible news about Alex."

"Nice to see you, Liz," he replied. "And yes, everything has changed for Alex, but I must say, he's handling it well." He squinted. "You look… bored."

She laughed. "I am. How's Martin?" It slipped out before she could stop herself.

The colonel smiled. "He's right here, but before he comes on, Alex wants to talk to you." He leaned away from the camera and then his face was replaced by Alex's soft, beautiful features, his usually unkempt blond hair combed and styled and, was that a suit he was wearing?

"Hi Dr, Shepherd," he said, excitement in his voice. "How are you?"

"I'm still working on William's dilemma," she replied. "It frustrates me, but I'll solve it."

"I know you will. That's why I want to hire you to run the ShawTech labs. They got everything, doctor, let me tell you. You'll be close to William, and you can help find cures for diseases and, well, Martin's here." He leaned into the tablet and lowered his voice. "Trust me, he's never gonna be able to teach me how to run ShawTech without you here. He's too distracted." He pulled back from the screen, and she spotted a large hand giving his shoulder a playful nudge.

Her voice caught in her throat, and she was momentarily speechless. "But, well, I work for, you know, Mr. Davalos."

Davalos's face squeezed into the frame beside Alex's. "Not anymore, Doctor. You're a free agent. I suggest you take this boy's offer. He's drunk with power and not to be trifled with."

Alex looked aghast and then laughed. "Don't listen to him, Doctor. But please come work with me. I miss you, and so does William."

Don't cry, Liz, whatever you do, don't cry!

She managed to hold herself together. "I accept your kind offer, Alex. When do I start?"

"As soon as you can get here," Alex answered, his grin infectious.

Still fighting the tears, she brushed some hair off her forehead. "In that case, I'll start packing."

The colonel reappeared as Davalos removed himself from the frame. "I'll arrange transport for you tomorrow, Liz. That give you enough time?"

She nodded, mouthing, "Thank you."

"Don't thank me," he replied, pulling Alex back on camera. "It was all his idea."

Her eyes were beginning to water, and she couldn't stay on much longer. "You're the best, Alex." She paused, unsure if she could handle it. "May I speak with Martin?"

Alex grinned and pulled away. Moments later, his face was replaced by the man who accelerated her heartbeat into overdrive every time she saw him. His smile was infectious, and she hoped he'd use it more.

"Was this your idea?"

Martin shook his head. "All Alex. I only wish I'd thought of it first."

There was an awkward pause, then both said, "I can—" They stopped and laughed.

"You first," she said quickly, wiping her eyes, still on the verge of losing it.

"I've been busy, obviously." He chuckled. "But I never stopped thinking about you. Alex knew that. You know how sensitive he is to people's feelings. That's what gave him the idea."

She smiled. "Then it *was* your idea in the first place."

He grinned. "Yeah, guess so. See you tomorrow."

"Tomorrow."

She couldn't hold it together any longer and ended the call. The dam broke. She'd honestly never been so happy. Being sucked into that Weapon Project by her dad while still in med school had taken charge of her life in an almost suffocating way. Now she was free. Finally free to pursue life and love and what made her happy—pure research that could benefit generations of people. Ready to squeal like a little girl, she practically ran from the lab to tell Amanda the good news.

***

The following day brought about the departure of Colonel Walker and Mr. Davalos, and Roy was sorry to see them go. He'd come to look up to both, but the arrival of Dr. Shepherd made Martin and William very happy. Roy figured Martin and the doctor must've done all their kissing at the airport when he picked her up because they were calm when they got to the house. Roy thought it funny to hear a grown lady like her thanking Alex, a teenager, for hiring her.

Alex was, as always, humble, insisting that she was doing him—and especially William—a huge favor by joining ShawTech. She went straight to William and said, "I think I'm getting close to an answer, William."

The boy smiled and his sweet face lit up the room. Roy could see him being super popular with the girls when he got older, if he got older. He could probably get tons of girls now with his buff body. Roy didn't use social media much, but he always noticed that all a boy needed to do was show off his abs and he got tons of likes and comments, mostly from girls, but sometimes from boys—and grown men, which wasn't cool. Roy didn't have much in the way of abs and showing off wasn't his thing anyway. It wasn't William's either, and he hoped the younger boy would stay that way.

They all gathered in the huge entry hall to say goodbye to Mr. Davalos and the colonel. Colonel Walker assured William and Alex they would have regular video chats and personal visits whenever possible. William looked sad, which touched Roy's heart. The younger boy shook the colonel's hand, but Roy knew he wanted more. Obviously, the colonel did too because he pulled William into a hug.

"Goodbye…Dad," William mumbled into the colonel's uniform coat.

"I'll see you soon, son."

They separated and William wiped a tear from his eye. Roy was astounded by how far that boy had come in just the short time he'd known him. How the government could have ever thought William less than human, Roy would never understand.

Those photos and videos of Alex and the board of directors hit the news big time and seemed to calm fears that, as Martin had explained to them, ShawTech was a ship without a rudder, which Roy didn't completely understand having never been on a ship before. But Alex's face suddenly exploded everywhere in the media. It embarrassed Alex, but pleased Roy. If anyone should be getting attention, it shouldn't be cute boys with abs. It should be Alex, who had already changed the world for the better and would continue to do so.

Dane finally got his stuff moved in late that afternoon. He'd had an early shift at MTS for a change and Roy was excited to see him. Dane looked good—happy, more confident—than he had before all this stuff with Ms. G had started. Nathan gave Dane a huge hug and welcomed him home. Dane, like the rest of them, was amazed by the size of the house, and Roy volunteered to show him around.

***

In the days that followed, the homeschooling classes began, and Alex found he liked it much better than MTS. The teachers were four ladies who were experts in various areas, but had gotten tired of, as they told Martin, "The politics of education." Roy and the other boys also took to the instruction. Alex felt like, for the first time—except with Ms. Ashley—that he was learning and improving. Soon, Java, Izzy, and Jorge joined their "classes," and the former "Losers" were reunited. Cuong's absence was felt by all, especially if the word "Nintendo" was mentioned, but as time went on, his loss grew slightly less painful.

Alex thought it kind of nice that Saul kept texting Roy, saying he missed him at school. At first, Roy wondered where Saul had gotten his number because he'd never contacted him, but Izzy confessed he'd told the other boy while still attending MTS.

"I think he's got a thing for you, Roy. And he ain't the way he used to be."

So, Roy had been texting back and forth with Saul and had finally agreed to hang out after Christmas.

It made Alex happy to think of Roy with a boyfriend. If anyone deserved that, it was Roy. When Francis found out, he told Roy, "If he hurts you, Dane will have my help kicking his ass."

Roy and Alex laughed.

***

Alex was nervous as Christmas approached. The past weeks had been busy, but productive. His reading, writing, and math skills were improving. Besides the homeschool teachers, Martin regularly coached him on how math was used in the running of ShawTech. Suddenly, those numbers that always seemed random and unconnected in school, made more sense when applied to money, sales, expenses, profits, losses. He finally stopped hating learning and began to enjoy it.

Everyone would be at the house for Christmas dinner, and he wanted the day to be just right, perfect, in fact. He hadn't had a family Christmas since his adoptive parents died in that car crash when he was four. And he'd never had much money to buy anyone a present. Now he did, but he wanted to pick the perfect gift for each of his loved ones. He still didn't think of himself as rich, even though he knew, in the back of his mind, that he was beyond rich, and he sure didn't want to embarrass anyone by giving them something crazy like a car. Instead, he thought long and hard about each person in his immediate and extended family and came up with a gift that fit that person.

He still didn't go out to shopping areas or grocery stores much because his face was too new and too popular, and he was mobbed by people wanting to take his photo. William was always with him for protection, but the feeling of so many people pressing in on him was uncomfortable. Then there were the girls suddenly saying he was cute and wanting to hang out and handing him slips of paper with their phone numbers on them. He threw all those papers away because he knew those girls weren't interested in him. It was his money and fame they wanted.

He now knew the meaning of the word "ironic," and how it applied to him. Prior to being rich, girls, and most other people, only saw the wheelchair. Now they saw the money he controlled. Would he ever meet any girl like Tami or Allison who saw him just for himself? He hoped so, but knew in his heart it was a long shot.

He was super excited by the impending arrival of Colonel Walker and

Amanda on Christmas Eve, along with Mr. Davalos, whom he'd come to trust and admire. They would be staying for a few days and, other than video calls, it would be his first time seeing Amanda since he left the base. He, Andy, William, and Francis got together on a gift for their surrogate mother that Alex hoped she would love. He'd done all his ordering online using a debit card Martin had given him, and found that, if he knew what he wanted, it was much easier than going from store to store. The real trick was hiding the presents for his brothers *from* his brothers, but the house staff was a huge help. They were all nice people and Martin suggested they get a bonus for Christmas, which Alex, of course, agreed to.

Martin had set up bank accounts for all the boys and put in spending money so they could buy each other gifts. William and Francis initially had no idea how to use money, but budgeting was part of their home-schooling classes and they caught on fast. Since these were Christmas presents, everyone was secretive in their gift buying to keep everything a surprise. They'd decorated the house and put up an enormous tree in the living room. All the boys had a blast decorating it and the result was bright and colorful and green. Alex almost couldn't believe so much good fortune had befallen him, the loner kid who'd been in eleven foster homes and had lost hope of ever being adopted. Now that process was in motion, he had a family and friends, and an amazing home to live in. It was almost like a movie.

Amanda swept all the boys into a group hug the moment she set foot in the house. Andy almost cried upon seeing her, which touched Alex deeply. His twin had come so far in so short a time, almost like Pinocchio in that old movie where he learned how to be a real boy. Colonel Walker hugged William and the younger boy was happier than he'd been in weeks. Mr. Davalos was wearing a bright, ugly Christmas sweater, and Alex thought he looked more relaxed than ever. Andy volunteered to show Amanda around while the rest of them hung out in the living room. Martin and Dr. Shepherd soon joined them there, and everyone shared stories of what they had been doing since they'd last been together.

The weather had been cold the past few days and cloudy, like it might rain. Living so close to the ocean made the nights colder than they'd been in Hawthorne. Christmas Eve dinner was festive and fun. They'd be having turkey and lots of side dishes the next night, so Christmas Eve was pasta night, because Alex loved pasta and had requested it.

After dinner, Nathan excitedly passed out one gift to each of the boys, including Dane, and kept one for himself, saying, "In our family, we always open one gift on Christmas Eve." He paused and glanced at Roy. "At least, we used to when Roy's mom was alive, so I want to start that again."

The boys ripped open their packages, and each found a set of pajamas.

Dane groaned, "Oh, Pop."

Nathan grinned, holding up his own set of Batman pajamas. All the others were different superheroes. William got Superman, which Alex thought was perfect, and Francis got the Flash. Roy got Aquaman, Dane Green Arrow, and Alex got Green Lantern. They thanked Nathan, even Dane who, despite his tough exterior, was touched by the gesture, and then the other adults insisted all the boys change into them so everyone could gather around the roaring fire.

The boys agreed if Nathan put on his pajamas too. Their dad laughed and said yes, so everyone scattered to change. Alex hadn't worn such comfortable pajamas in years. With the colder weather, these new ones felt snug and cozy. Soon, the living room looked like a Justice League meeting as all the "superheroes" gathered around the fire with Martin and the other adults and played board games until bedtime. For Alex, the night couldn't have been more perfect.

***

The area around the Christmas tree was piled high with colorfully wrapped presents of all shapes and sizes, but Alex and the other kids decided they'd await the arrival of Java, Izzy, and Jorge, who would be dropping by with their parents before heading off to their relatives' homes for Christmas dinner.

By the time the other boys arrived, Alex was itching to have everyone open the gifts he'd selected for them. The adults sat around the spacious living room chatting and drinking eggnog or wine while the kids separated out the gifts into piles according to name tags. This was the first Christmas for William and Francis, and they were as excited as any kids could be, so the older ones let them do most of the sorting. It also helped Francis practice his reading skills, which had greatly improved.

Java, Izzy, and Jorge had all brought gifts for Alex, Andy, Roy, William, and Francis and those were opened first. Izzy had picked out ugly Christmas sweaters for all of them, but Alex's got the most laughs. It had all the Christmas colors and a reindeer on it along with the words, "Merry Christmas, Ya Filthy Animal," which he remembered from one of the *Home Alone* movies.

Java had given them all sports equipment to use outside, since the grounds were so big. Jorge had been working on drawings of each boy for many months and presented them as gifts. Alex and the others were all impressed by how real they looked on the paper, and they congratulated Jorge on his incredible talent.

At that point, they all lit into the piles of gifts in front of them and the room filled with "oohs" and "aahs" and "thank you so muches," and there was much hugging among kids and adults. Java loved the home gym Alex had given him, and his dad looked excited too.

"We'll build it together, son."

"That'd be great, Dad." Java grinned. "Then I'm gonna get you buff like me."

His dad laughed.

To Jorge, Alex presented DVDs of all the "V" movies and shows, which excited the boy, but earned a groan from his mother.

For Izzy, he'd gotten some new video games for his system, ones he knew his friend didn't have.

Andy, William, Roy, and Francis all looked stunned when Martin brought out from the dining room brand new bikes, one for each boy. Andy, William, and Francis stared at the shiny, colorful bicycles in wonder.

"What is it?" Andy asked, running his fingers over his smooth red handlebars.

"It's a bike," Alex said with a laugh. "You seen 'em on TV."

"How do you ride it?" William asked, studying his bright blue eight-speed. "There's no engine like on my motorcycle."

Alex laughed. "You use your legs. Roy can show you, right Roy?"

Roy grinned. "Sure. We'll ride around later."

The adults commenced opening their gifts. Colonel Walker was very moved by William's gift to him. It was a keychain that showed the shadow of a man holding the hand of a boy. On the back, William had had these words written on it: "I love you always, Dad. Your son, William."

Alex honestly thought he saw the colonel crying, or at least coming close, as Walker pulled William into a tight hug that lasted several seconds.

Amanda's scream of joy drew all eyes to her as she gazed at the framed photo in her lap. She made no attempt to stop her tears as Alex, Andy, William, and Francis gathered around her. Alex had used the company photographer to take a portrait shot of the four boys huddled together and smiling into the camera. Then he'd uploaded it to an online place that had enlarged it, and wrote on the image in handwriting script, "We love you, Mom." Under each boy was his name— "Alex, Andy, William, Francis."

"Do you like it?" Alex asked.

For a long moment she couldn't speak. Then, between tears of joy, she said, "I love it."

Andy grinned, offering Alex and William a high five.

"We thought," Andy said eagerly, "that you could put it up in your house and then, you know, brag about us when people visit."

"Yeah, like how cool we are," William added, grinning. "Right, Alex?"

"Right, William," Alex agreed.

Francis nodded vigorously.

She set the framed photo aside and pulled them all into another hug, leaning forward to include Alex. "You're darn right I'll brag about you. Best boys a mom could ever have."

Alex relished that moment, having not had anything close to a mother since he was four, and he knew how important her love was to the others, as well. They hadn't included Roy in this one because he'd had a mom who loved him, and her death was still an open wound for him.

Alex gave the colonel a cool utility knife on which he'd had engraved the words, "To Colonel Walker, with Love and Respect, from Alex," and to Martin he presented a "Best Teacher" trophy engraved with the words "Thanks for being such an awesome teacher and friend. Alex."

Dane was overwhelmed by a gift from Colonel Walker. Alex thought it was just a card, but it was more than that. Dane (who'd been working with the homeschool teachers, also) read it aloud, "Dane, if you're interested, I'd love to have you join the Air Force. I can use a good, solid man like you. Give my business card to any recruiter and have them call me." He held up a business card and looked at the colonel, stunned. "You really think I got what it takes?"

"I wouldn't say so if you didn't," Colonel Walker replied, serious. "Like Java, you're the kind of man I want to work with."

Dane almost shook with excitement, glancing at Nathan shyly. "In high school all I wanted was to join the military with my buddies, but I was too stupid to pass that test they make you take."

"Don't worry about any tests, Dane," Colonel Walker assured him. "I'll make sure you have the chance to show us what you can do. Trust me, if you want in, you're in."

Dane broke into a huge grin, making him look younger and more handsome. "I want in." He stepped forward and shook the colonel's hand.

"Welcome to the Air Force, Dane Phillips." Colonel Walker smiled, and Dane, practically floating, sat back down and stared at the card in his hand like it was made of gold.

For Nathan, the boys had all gotten together and bought him a new table saw and arc welder. He'd set up a workshop in one of the many garages to work on his truck and build projects for fun. He was thrilled beyond belief.

Alex was happy with everything he was given, but he was especially touched by Andy's gift to him. His twin had framed a photo of the two of them that Roy had taken with Alex's new Shawtech phone. It was a good picture, too, with Andy sitting on one wheel of Alex's chair, one arm wrapped around him, long white hair spilling down his front. They were both laughing because Roy had told a bad joke to make them smile. The frame was wood and along the bottom was carved in white letters, "I Love My Brother."

Alex felt choked up. Had Andy ever said he loved him? He didn't think so. "I love you too, bro."

Andy grinned with delight.

Colonel Walker stood up and reached into a large carry bag he'd placed next to Amanda. "I have something here for each of the boys, from the president."

Alex reacted with surprise, as did the others.

The colonel smiled. "Remember, boys, how the president promised to find some way to thank you?"

They nodded.

"Well, here's his gift." He handed small boxes to each boy. The top of the boxes displayed the presidential seal, which they all now recognized. Alex felt his box. It was small enough to hold in one hand, but heavy.

"Open them," the colonel urged, looking excited.

Alex pulled the top off his box while the other boys did the same. There was soft material filling the box and in the center a medal of some kind hanging from a blue and white strap with an eagle on it. The medal was a white star with a blue center and thirteen gold stars. The white star was up against a red background surrounded by gold eagles. He looked up at the colonel in confusion. The other boys, he noticed, seemed just as puzzled.

"That's the presidential medal of freedom," Colonel Walker announced. "It's the highest civilian honor that can be given to American citizens. Normally, the president would award these to you in a ceremony on television, but given the secret nature of your part in saving the world, he sent them with me."

Alex stared in awe at the magnificent medal, glancing at Roy and Andy, who also gaped. William and Francis placed theirs around their necks and looked proud.

"All of you put them on," Colonel Walker said, "so I can take a group photo for the president. I did promise him."

Alex grinned and slipped his over his head. Once all the boys sported their medals, the colonel snapped some photos of them in front of the tree. Alex still didn't quite understand the significance of this medal, but the colonel and Martin beamed with joy, so he figured presidents didn't give these out to just anyone.

Once all the gifts were open, Martin announced that there was one more present for Alex. He left the room and returned moments later pushing a large, wrapped box along the carpet. He stopped in front of Alex and said, "This is for you from Mr. Shaw."

Alex gasped, and everyone in the room reacted with surprise.

"He ordered this for you before…" Martin trailed off, momentarily emotional. "Anyway, it arrived a while back, but I decided to save it for Christmas." He stepped back next to Dr. Shepherd, who slipped her arm through his. "Go ahead, open it."

Alex took in a long breath and let it out. The room was silent, which was good because he needed a moment to process his feelings. He'd somewhat gotten used to the idea that Mr. Shaw was gone, but this moment brought back all those feelings of guilt that the man had died for him. He slowly tore at the wrapping paper, tossing it into a pile that Roy stomped on to make it smaller.

Beneath the paper was a large cardboard box. The colonel handed Alex his new pocketknife and he sliced along the edges. Martin and Roy helped him pull the sides away, and Alex suck in a shocked breath at what he saw—a brand new, shiny, high-tech wheelchair! Then he remembered Mr. Shaw telling him he'd ordered something special back when they were on the base, even though he'd just given Alex his current chair.

This one was similarly styled, but thicker, sturdier, and it had a large box hanging beneath the seat. Alex stared at that part, as well as the larger front and rear wheels, trying to figure out what it meant.

"It's a high-powered chair, Alex," Martin explained, stepping forward and pointing to the box. "It's powered by electricity and can reach speeds up to thirty miles per hour."

Alex's mouth dropped open in awe.

"That's sick," Roy exclaimed, running his fingers over the wheels, and gazing at Alex.

"Mr. Shaw wanted you to have it in case goons who work for angry tech moguls ever chase you again." He grinned.

It took Alex a moment to understand, but then he laughed as he recalled trying to escape from ShawTech and having those guys chase after him.

"Can I try it out?"

"Sure can," Martin agreed. "I made sure it was fully charged before wrapping it."

Nathan wandered over and examined the chair. "Beautiful piece of work." He turned to the other boys. "Why don't you boys try out your bikes while Alex tries the chair. Plenty of roads and paths around this house."

"Hell, yeah!" Roy exclaimed.

Andy eyed him fearfully. "You're gonna teach me how to ride this, right?" He pointed to his new bike.

Roy threw an arm around his shoulder. "Course, I am. You guys too," he added, grinning at William and Francis.

After replacing their medals in their boxes, the boys headed outside with Alex learning the controls on his chair while the others mastered their bikes. William and Francis caught on right away, but not being as athletic, Andy took a bit longer. Roy was super patient and walked around holding on to Andy's arm while he got the hang of peddling. By the time they could all manage on their own, Alex was ready to go. The air was cold, and a sharp breeze had sprung up, blowing their hair in all directions.

"Race you guys to the front gate," Alex challenged, grinning. "I'll even give you a head start."

"You're on," Roy said, returning the grin, his face flushed from the cold. "C'mon guys, we're off!"

The four bikes took off down the drive at various speeds. Java, Izzy, and Jorge, still wearing their presidential medals, cheered them on. William pulled ahead quickly, and Andy lagged a bit behind. Alex put his chair into gear, keeping the speed to ten miles per hour to start, then grabbed the armrests—something new to him—and set off after his brothers.

The whoosh of cold air slapped him in the face, and he laughed with joy as the chair took off like a bullet after the bicycles. He'd always loved speed, which was why he liked being pulled from the back of Roy's truck, but this was different. This was so exhilarating he almost screamed with happiness. He easily passed Andy, tossing him a thumbs up, caught up with Roy and did the same. His best friend laughed as Alex increased his speed to catch the super-powered William who was pedaling that bike like there was no tomorrow. Alex finally passed Francis at twenty miles per hour but had to crank his speed up to full just to pace William. They ended up in a tie, though Alex found slowing the chair more difficult than increasing his speed and nearly crashed into the closed front gate.

He managed to swerve into a sharp turn that would've tipped over his old chair, but this heavier one stayed upright and sent him back up the hill until he slowed. It was the most fun he'd ever had, so naturally they did it again and again, riding all through the grounds until Roy and Andy were too tired to continue.

Java, Izzy, and Jorge had to leave, but dinner with everyone else was wonderful. Father Pat joined them, his duties at the church finally finished, and Alex felt that his family was complete. The food was good, of course, but it was the company, the laughter, the smiles, and good spirits, that made the meal the best one ever. This was his home, and these were his family. Father Pat had said grace before the meal began, but as Alex looked around at all the laughing, joy-filled faces, he added his own, "Thank you, God, for my family. I couldn't do anything without them, and I'll try my best to help as many people as I can."

The storm broke that night just before everyone went to bed, and Alex couldn't sleep. The pounding rain and occasional flashes of lightning reminded him of those storms back in Hawthorne, the ones when the evil cat always showed up. He clambered out of bed in his fancy Green Lantern pajamas and wheeled down the hall to the elevator. Gold inside, it was shiny and sleek and quickly returned him to the first floor. He entered that large living room with the huge bay window and wheeled himself over to sit in front of it.

Outside, the wind howled, rain lashed at the glass, and trees whipped back and forth. There were small lights all around the estate and he could see thick raindrops pelting past each of them. He shivered, thinking back on his life since moving in with Jane. She was horrible, but if he hadn't lived there, he'd never have met Roy and none of this would've happened. It was another lesson about good being thrown in with the bad.

A hand on his shoulder almost made him jump. He turned to find Roy beside him sporting his Aquaman PJs. Alex had been so lost in thought, he hadn't heard him come in.

"Couldn't sleep either?" Roy studied him in the dark.

"Too much on my mind."

"Good or bad?"

"Mostly good. Thinking about you."

"Me?"

"Yeah. How if I'd never met you, none of this would be happening."

Roy looked down and Alex was sure he'd blushed. "You don't know that."

Alex faced him. "Yeah, I do, 'cause you changed my life. Your love and friendship made me better. Before I met you, I didn't want much to do with people, remember? They always treated me bad or used my power like Jane. But you became my friend just because you wanted to and that made all the difference."

"Being your friend is easy."

Alex smiled, and they fell silent for a few minutes. Something moved behind them, and Roy whirled around in fright. A pale face and long white hair appeared, and Roy relaxed.

"Andy," he said, a bit breathless. "You scared me."

Andy settled in on Alex's other side. "Why should you be scared?"

Roy shrugged, looking embarrassed.

Alex said, "It was storms like this that Ms. G used to try and control me."

Andy nodded. "She's gone now."

Alex shivered again. "I hope so."

"Today was the best day of my life, Big Brother," Andy said after a pause. "I didn't think I could ever be this happy."

Alex smiled. "Me either. All I ever wanted after my parents died was a family, and now I have the best one ever."

"Not to mention a ton of money," Roy added with a chuckle.

"Oh, I don't care about that," Alex said, pausing to collect his thoughts. "I think Mr. Shaw knew I wouldn't care about the money, only about helping other people. But if I had to choose between that money and you two as my brothers, that money would go bye-bye."

Roy's eyebrows shot up in surprise. "Really?"

Alex nodded. "Really. I love you guys, and that's for real."

Andy smiled. "I love you too, Big Brother." He glanced shyly at Roy. "And you too, Roy."

Roy blushed again and reached out to hug them both. "Love you guys, too."

They quickly separated, embarrassed by so much emotion, and Alex stared at them in the dark. "I don't know what will happen down the line, but as long as I got you guys with me, I'll be good."

"Same here," Roy announced, while Andy nodded his head.

Another few minutes passed as they gazed out of the window. Alex thought he saw movement in the tree just outside, but when he stared harder, nothing happened.

"Well," he finally said, "maybe we should go back to bed."

He wheeled himself away from the window and started across the living room, eyeing the dark Christmas tree near the hearth. The other two padded after him. Alex suddenly felt a chill envelope him and he halted, spinning around to face the window again.

"What?" Roy said, following Alex's gaze.

"For a second it felt like…"

"Like what?" Andy asked.

"Like someone was watching me," Alex finished, eyeing his brothers' curious faces.

"I don't feel anything," Andy said. "You, Roy?"

"No."

Alex shook the feeling loose. He decided it had been his imagination and continued across the room toward the hall. His brothers followed.

***

Outside the window, two orange-red eyes stared through the glass at the retreating boys until they left the room. Then, with a swoosh of its thick tail, the large gray cat perched atop a thick branch turned and vanished into the night.

THE END

ABOUT THE AUTHOR

Michael J. Bowler is an award-winning author of the five-book urban fantasy series *The Lance Chronicles*, the mystery-thriller *The Film Milieu Series*, the supernatural-sci-fi *The Healer Chronicles*, and several standalone books. He also writes screenplays. His horror screenplay, "Healer," was a Semi-Finalist, and his urban fantasy script, "Like A Hero," was a Finalist in the Shriekfest Film Festival and Screenplay Competition, and his sci-fi screenplay, "The God Machine," was the 2017 Scriptapalozza First Place Winner.

He worked as producer, writer, and/or director on several ultra-low-budget horror films, including "Fatal Images," "Hell Spa," "Club Dead," and "Things II."

He taught high school in Hawthorne, California, both in general education and to students with learning disabilities, in subjects ranging from English and Strength Training to Algebra, Biology, and Yearbook.

He has also been a volunteer Big Brother to eight different boys with the Catholic Big Brothers Big Sisters program and a long-time volunteer within the juvenile justice system in Los Angeles.

He has been honored as Probation Volunteer of the Year, YMCA Volunteer of the Year, California Big Brother of the Year, and 2000 National Big Brother of the Year. The "National" honor allowed him and three of his Little Brothers to visit the White House and meet the president in the Oval Office.

His goal as an author is for teens to experience empowerment and hope; to see themselves in his diverse characters; to read about kids who face real-life challenges; and to see how kids like them can remain decent people in an indecent world. The most prevalent theme in his writing and his work with youth is this: as both a society, and as individuals, we're better off when we do what's right, rather than what's easy.

CONNECT WITH MICHAEL

Website:
http://michaeljbowler.com/

FB:
https://www.facebook.com/michaeljbowlerauthor/

Twitter:
https://twitter.com/MichaelJBowler

Instagram:
https://www.instagram.com/michaeljbowler/

tumblr:
http://michaeljbowler.tumblr.com/

Pinterest:
https://www.pinterest.com/michaelbowler/

Goodreads:
https://www.goodreads.com/author/show/6938109.Michael_J_Bowler

YouTube:
https://www.youtube.com/channel/UC2NXCPry4DDgJZOVDUx-VtMw

THE LANCE CHRONICLES

ONCE UOPN A TIME IN the City of Angels, chaos was king, and carelessness ruled. Street gangs roamed the city. Most politicians bettered their own lives, not those of the people they were elected to serve. Neighborhoods declined to slum-like conditions. The Los Angeles school system stumbled headlong toward total Armageddon. And the most victimized segment of the populace?

The children. The teens. The next generation.

Limited choices and often abusive or neglectful home lives forced hundreds, if not thousands of children, into the streets to join gangs, turn tricks, do drugs, sell drugs, drop out of school, get arrested and sent to prison for life, and in all ways subjugate their goodness in the name of survival.

All hope seemed lost. Until the mysterious "tag" appeared throughout the city, spray-painted on walls and over graffiti, obliterating gang markings without mercy, without favoritism, with impunity.

A "tag" that became the symbol of a revolution.

A small, lean boy appeared at the mouth of an alley and darted quickly into the protective shadows behind a large dumpster. A sheriff's car cruised slowly past the mouth of the alley and then continued on out of sight. The boy stepped from his hiding place and dusted himself off. Lance Sepulveda, a fourteen-year-old orphan, warily glanced around. Between avoiding gang members and cops, he lived a very cautious life.

The gang members liked to beat him up and the cops put him in juvy as a runaway. There was no place in Los Angeles for kids like him who *didn't* commit crimes, so they had to bide their time in juvy to wait for yet *another* group home to take them.

A smart, clever boy with unusually green eyes—which drew derisive comments from other Latinos—Lance preferred the freedom of the streets, living for a time with this friend or that friend, having no ties to anyone. He wore a pair of baggy overalls with the straps hanging down and a gray hoodie flipped up to obscure his face, clothes given to him by one of his friends. He lugged a bulging, ratty-looking backpack in one hand and an old skateboard in the other.

Lance continued warily down the alley. Tonight there were no unusual sounds save the occasional plane practically landing atop Lennox on its approach into LAX. From the shadows around him loomed two large black youths. Lance was grabbed and spun around. The skateboard flew from his grasp and clattered to the concrete.

Broad-shouldered, muscular Justin sneered at the fear flitting over Lance's startled face. "What's the hurry, Pretty Boy? We got business wit' you."

Reaching out one arm, he slapped the hood off Lance's head, allowing the boy's long hair to tumble about his shoulders, and then snatched the old backpack away so hard it tore open with a loud ripping sound, scattering clothes, candy, and junk food onto the ground.

Taller and built more for basketball than boxing, Dwayne sneered at the junk. "Man, what a loser!"

Lance fought down his fear and glared at both boys, ignoring his hated nickname, "Pretty Boy." Justin grabbed him by the front of his shirt and practically lifted him off the ground. Lance fought and struggled, but he was no match for the muscular boy. "Mr. R. says he had a talk with you about workin' these streets for him."

"Yeah, he did, and I told him no. I don't want no part a that! I run myself." "No problemo, Mexicano," Justin sneered, tossing Lance to the ground like a ragdoll. "'Cept Mr. R., he don't like guys who know too much 'bout his business. Especially guys who *won't* work for him."

Lance landed and rolled, leaping to his feet almost at once. His heart thumped wildly, his green eyes blazing with equal parts fury and fear. "I don't know nuthin'!" he spat angrily, visibly shaking with panic. "'Cept you jerks slang that crap for 'im! Who would I tell? What could I say anyway?"

Dwayne flipped open an evil-looking switchblade and pressed the razor-sharp point to Lance's throat before he could even flinch.

"You could just say no—to life, ya little runt!" He began slowly pressing the knife into Lance's throat, a wicked smile creasing his dark, tatted face.

A deep, harsh voice echoed from behind the three boys. "Unhand that lad, or forfeit your lives!"

Dwayne whirled to look over his shoulder.

From the shadows, confidently approaching, rode a man on horseback! The three youths merely gaped in astonishment. None of them had ever even seen a real horse before, much less one in this neighborhood. When the rider emerged from the darkness into a patch of streetlight, they gasped anew. He wore a full suit of knightly armor and carried a massive, gleaming sword that looked capable of slicing all three of them in half at the same time! The boys could not make out any facial features, as they were covered by a helm and mouthpiece.

The three stood frozen to the spot, Dwayne's blade pressed against Lance's throat as the knight halted his horse a few feet away.

Dwayne found his voice first. "Say what?" He couldn't believe what he was seeing! He needed to stop sampling R's stuff, that was a *for sure*.

"I do believe my intent was clear," calmly stated the knight in a strong voice tinged with something like a Southern accent. "Unhand the boy or forfeit your lives."

With speed seemingly impossible underneath all that armor, the knight flicked his sword downward and across, and Dwayne's pants dropped to his feet.

Startled, the boy reached down to retrieve them, and the knight swung the sword again, this time slicing open the hand holding the knife, causing Dwayne to curse and fling the blade to the ground.

Without pause, the knight just as swiftly swung the sword deftly back up, letting the point rest against Justin's throat. The muscular boy whimpered in terror.

"Okay, you win," he muttered fearfully, the tip of the sword already drawing blood. He stepped away from Lance.

The mysterious knight looked down at Lance. "Shall I kill these two for you, lad?"

Lance sucked in a sharp breath. He didn't know what to say.

Justin keened with fear. "Hey, man, ya'll can't kill us cuz my dad's a cop!" Dwayne trembled, but he was too hard-ass to show it. "Shut up, fool!"

The knight ignored them, focusing his attention on Lance, who gawked like a fish out of water. "Well, lad?"

Coming back to his senses, Lance realized that the man wanted an answer. *Would he really kill these guys if I asked him to*? He didn't think he wanted to find out. "Let 'em go."

Without pause, the knight pulled his gleaming sword back from Justin's throat, but still gripped it firmly, ready to strike. He gazed down at the two older youths. "Methinks we shall meet again."

Always the bolder of the two, Dwayne spat viciously on the ground in front of the horse, causing it to neigh in annoyance. "Like hell!"

Then he and Justin turned and bolted, Dwayne struggling to keep his pants from tripping him up. They quickly vanished from the mouth of the alley.

Lance gazed upward at the knight, still speechless, staring at the horse, the sword, and the armor. His breath caught in his throat. He didn't do drugs, so it couldn't be that. So, what the hell was going on?

The knight sheathed his sword as he stared down at the boy, his eyes shimmering slightly within the helm. "Have thou no manners, to not thank me for thy life?"

That helm and those hidden eyes creeped Lance out something fierce. "Oh yeah, sorry," he stammered. "Yeah, uh, thanks." He paused a moment. "Would you, would you really have killed them guys for me?"

"No. Not unless my life or yours be at stake. I wished merely to discern something of your character."

"Huh? You talk weird, mister."

The knight ignored Lance's comment. "What be thy name, lad?"

Lance's hackles instantly rose. "Uh, they call me, well, 'Pretty Boy'. I don't think I am, neither, but I guess it's the hair."

"Thou art a handsome youth, so the name appears to fit thee. Why doth you dislike it?"

"Cause they don't mean it like a compliment," Lance replied sourly. "They just do it to mock me."

"If it displeases you, I shall not use it. Hast thou no Christian name?"

Lance never shared his true name with anyone. On these streets, knowing one's true name could be dangerous. Yet somehow, this man's commanding tone and presence forced his guard down. "Huh? Oh, uh, Lance. Lance Sepulveda." It was practically a whisper. Then he felt his old boldness return. "What's it to you, anyways?"

The knight reacted with surprise. "Thy name be Lance?" "Yeah, so?"

The knight squinted through the helm, studying Lance's shadowed face.

"Of course, that be thy name, lad," he murmured, almost to himself, almost as if Lance wasn't even there. "All is as it should be."

Lance stood warily gazing up at him, a shiver flitting up and down his spine at those mysterious words, as though everything really *was* as it should be. But that didn't make sense. *None* of this made sense.

The man noted Lance's scattered clothes on the ground. "Tell me, young Lance, are these all your worldly belongings?" There was deep sadness in that voice.

Lance bristled. "What about it? I move around a lot." He set about picking up his stuff and shoving everything into the torn backpack.

"I see," the knight observed, his tone unreadable.

Lance retrieved his skateboard and stared at the knight, uncertain what to do next. His breathing had calmed, and he found himself deeply curious about this guy, even though curiosity on these streets could get you killed.

"Have you a place to lay thy head this night?" the knight inquired in a conversational tone.

Lance went rigid, his breath hitching in his throat, his heart pounding anew. "I always got places," he announced, prepared to leap onto his board and jet out of there.

The knight made no threatening gestures, nor did the magnificent white horse even shuffle its feet with impatience.

His body tight with tension, Lance still eyed the animal admiringly. It was the most beautiful thing he'd ever seen.

"Come with me," the knight offered. "I have a bed for thee."

Lance leapt back and whipped a knife out of his pocket. It was small and wouldn't do much damage, but even that short blade gave him a tiny sense of security. Sweat broke out on his face as he gazed upward and gulped. "You queer or somethin'?"

"How odd that after so many centuries, some words still retain their most common meanings."

Lance knew he was a smart kid—teachers had told him that since the first grade. But he didn't have a clue what this guy was talking about. What kind of English was he speaking, anyways?

"Huh?" was all he could muster, his heart still thrumming with fear.

"Be at peace, young one," the knight assured him. "The answer to thy question be nay."

Lance continued to eye him with great uncertainty. "Nay" sounded like "no," and that made him feel more at ease, slowing his heart a bit. "You got food at your place?"

"Yes, lad, all you could possibly eat. Now, if you get up on mine horse, we shalt be away."

Lance's extreme hunger did the deciding for him. Sure, he had the junk food in his pack, but real food was always better. "Okay. But if you try anything, I'll cut your throat."

"Agreed. Up with you now. We have a long journey ahead."

The knight reached down with a gauntleted hand. Lance eyed it for a long moment, then put away his pocketknife and reached up to do something he hadn't done since he was six years old—he grasped the hand of a stranger.

With strength and ease, the knight hefted the boy up and onto the saddle behind him as though Lance weighed no more than a stuffed animal. He was caught off guard by the man's physical power, and shook his head in admiration.

"Man, you're strong!"

The knight glanced back over his shoulder at the wide-eyed boy behind him. "As will you be, Lance Sepulveda."

The knight spurred his horse, and the large animal cantered softly down the alley, rounding the corner and disappearing into the dark streets of Lennox.